I0674144

This is a work of fiction and any resemblance to any person, living or dead, any place, events or occurrences, is purely coincidental. The characters and storylines are created from the author's imagination or are used fictitiously.

Sin & Discipline: Copyright © 2019 by Lily White

lily@lilywhitebooks.com
http://www.facebook.com/authorlilywhite
www.lilywhitebooks.com

SIN & DISCIPLINE

A student/teacher romance by Lily White

LILY WHITE
BESTSELLING AUTHOR

If you are interested in reading additional books by Lily White or would like to know when new books are being released, Lily White can be found on:

Facebook, Instagram **and**

Twitter

Join the Mailing List!

If you are interested in receiving email updates regarding additional books by Lily White or would like to know when new books are announced or being released, join the mailing list via this link.

http://eepurl.com/Onoeb

Join the Facebook Fan Group!

If you are interested in receiving exclusive previews for upcoming novels, or to participate in giveaways, join the fan group for Lily White Books.

FAN GROUP LINK

Follow Lily on BookBub!

https://www.bookbub.com/profile/lily-white

OTHER BOOKS BY LILY WHITE

MASTERS SERIES:

Her Master's Courtesan
(Book 1 of the Masters Series)
(Available on Smashwords and lilywhitebooks.com)

Her Master's Teacher
(Book 2 of the Masters Series)

Her Master's Christmas
(Novella in the Masters Series)

Her Master's Redemption
(Book 3 of the Masters Series)

Her Master's Reckoning
(Book 4 of the Masters Series)

STANDALONE NOVELS:

Target This
Hard Roads
Asylum

Wake to Dream
Four Crows
Crazy Madly Deeply
Rules of Engagement
Wishing Well
The Five
Sin & Discipline

ILLUSIONS DUET

Illusions of Evil
(Book 1 of the Illusions Duet)

Fear the Wicked
(Book 2 of the Illusions Duet)

**DARK EXCLUSIVE - Available only on
LilyWhiteBooks.com:**

The Director

Music Index

Mozart
16th Sonata in C Major K545

Beethoven
Piano Sonata No. 29 'Hammerklavier'
Sonata No.8 in C Minor 'Pathetique'

Chopin
Nocturne op. 9 No. 2

Clementi
Sonatina in C Major op. 26 no. 1

Bach
Prelude in C Major

Debussy
Clair De Lune

Stravinsky
The Firebird (The Infernal Dance)

Scarlatti
Sonata in D Minor K141

Liszt
Sonata in B Minor S.178

Table of Contents

CHAPTER ONE

Please forgive me, Lennon. I know you will find me. I'll stand in the ether watching you struggle to save a lost life, a broken heart, a fractured and doomed soul...

Lennon

I dream of music in the way most people dream of love.

I was born to it, the tones sprinkling down like raindrops to bathe my skin in a melody of harmonious notes. Music lives inside me, breathing, beating, expanding, decorating the walls of my organs with chaotic chords and running through my veins on a frenetic pulse.

The dissonance of dark melodies dominated me long ago. Helpless, I surrendered to it. Wanton, I clambered toward it. Through my life, I've crawled beneath its living skin and became that which I loved.

Music has never been kind to me, yet it hasn't been cruel. It simply stays with me as a whispering passenger, keeping me company in the moments I need it most.

Music was with me now as I climbed from my car to survey the ramshackle landscape of a memory I'd hoped to leave in the past, the crumbling buildings and trash strewn streets of inner Sheldon, one of the worst parts of town just south of St. Petersburg. It played in my head, a dirgeful melody of bitterness and regret.

The abusive Florida sun blinded my eyes before I had a chance to shield them with my hand, the double

1

tinted sunglasses I wore doing nothing to soften the angry blaze hovering just over the horizon.

There's nothing like the sunsets in this state as long as you keep your eyes to the sky and avoid glancing down into the direct path of it.

Blinking away the dark spots in my vision left behind from the onslaught of light, I slammed my car door, hit the button to lock it, and walked toward Jennison's - an out of the way music store owned and operated by one of my oldest friends.

A half balled sheet of paper rolled across my boots as I crossed the uneven, pothole-ridden lot.

Glancing down, I lifted a brow at the hot pink color, the grainy black and white photo of a local garage band feeling big and bad because they'd finally scored a gig in a run down hovel bar. Kicking it away, I covered the remaining distance with a ground-eating stride, guitar strings strumming above my head as soon as I opened the caged, glass front door.

Turning, I cocked a brow at the design of the entry alarm, wondering when Dizzy had replaced the tinkling bell his father had hanging there for over twenty years.

"Lennon, holy shit, man. How long has it been?"

Dizzy ambled toward me on long, thin legs, his jeans doing their best to remain in place over his hips. Stretching out an arm, he slapped his palm against mine before we knocked knuckles, the handshake reminding me that some things never change.

"Eight years, I think. Maybe ten." Running a hand through my dark hair, I cocked a brow. "What happened to the bell?"

2

He laughed, the full sound reminding just how high on life this son of a bitch had always been. It didn't matter that he'd grown up struggling, or that he'd inherited the mess of a store his father had left behind, Dizzy was the type of person who saw vibrant color in the problems most people viewed as black and white.

"Time's change, brother. Life is a river and I'm just rolling along with it, not giving a damn that the rocks are scraping my skin and the sun is burning my eyes."

Peering at him, the corner of my lips twitched. "When did you become such a beatnik?"

Brown eyes scanning me up and down, he shook his head. "When are you going to learn how to properly match clothes? Were the lights out when you got dressed this morning? With your career, I would think you could afford electricity."

To say my style was eccentric would be an understatement. My clothes were always a mishmash of tastes, decades, old fads and new. I never paid attention to what jeans or pants I pulled on with a Henley, button down, or band shirt. The pattern of my suspenders, when I wore them, never mattered, and nine times out of ten, the fedora on my head never quite complemented the scuffed leather of my boots.

I wasn't trying, if that's what some people thought, merely so negligent in giving a damn that I reached blindly into my drawers and closet to put on whatever covered all my parts.

The people who knew me were used to it. And those who wanted to be me attempted to copy it. Yet, they never pulled off the effortless look, simply because they cared.

"How many millions are you worth now and you're still wearing a raggedy old Nirvana shirt with holes in it?" Dizzy laughed, waving a hand to tell me to follow him. "Hate to tell you this, Lennon, but the nineties called and they want their wardrobe back."

Hopping up on a stool, he grabbed two drumsticks, crashing the tips against the snare, bass and cymbal. *Ba Dum Tiss...* The perfect sound effect to highlight his lame joke.

Spinning my direction, he gripped the drumsticks between two hands. "I have to admit I was surprised when you called me this morning. What brings you all the way back to Sheldon?"

"Work. What else?"

I'd never planned to return to this godforsaken place, never wanted to drive past my old house to see it condemned, never wanted to drag my gaze across dirty streets where Dizzy and I had spent a majority of our lives living like we were large even though we never had two dimes between us to rub together.

The only regret I had about not returning here was never seeing Jennison's again. Yet, here I stood within its walls, the smell of wood varnish and musty, forgotten sheet music attacking my nose.

"You playing around here?"

"Something like that. I have a few things going on." I didn't want to talk about me. I was more interested in hearing what he had been up to over the last few years.

It hurt to think that for as close as we'd been growing up, we hadn't kept in touch as much as I would have liked. That didn't mean I wasn't watching out for him though.

Every couple of months, I'd look over his website and buy the most expensive instruments I could find. I had them delivered to schools in the area. He never knew it was me. I'd purchased them through an LLC I'd established as a charitable organization that couldn't be traced back to my name.

The purchases kept the store open and helped contribute to any up and coming musicians who were young and wanted to learn.

Most kids couldn't afford instruments or music lessons in this area. Buying the instruments was my way of giving back to the community, and also my way of returning a favor to the man who'd taught me how to drag my fingers across eighty-eight keys.

"It's all the same. I wake up, kiss my wife and head into the store to open up and watch the few talents we have living here wander in to drool over the stuff they can't afford. I keep myself busy teaching kids. The money isn't great, but it keeps things going."

It killed me that Dizzy hadn't hit the road with me the minute he'd turned eighteen. A true musician, he could play any instrument you put in his hands. He'd grown up in this store and spent his afternoons learning whatever his dad had available. Unlike me, Dizzy had obligations to family, plus a girl that had stolen his heart.

While I attended Hastings, a prestigious performing arts conservatory I wouldn't have been able to afford without a full scholarship, Dizzy had stayed behind to get married and run the shop with his old man.

"How's Renee doing? Have you given her a kid yet?"

His mouth opened on a burst of laughter. "Do you see a rugrat running around here blowing on horns or banging the keys or drums? Not yet. We're still young, but she's starting to get that look in her eye every time we pass someone with a little one. I'm sure in the next year or so she'll be asking."

He had a point. Dizzy wouldn't waste any time before bringing his kids in here to learn the instruments like he had done.

At the front of the store, the guitar strummed to alert us to a customer. Dizzy leaned left to peer around a bookshelf stacked with sheet music. "Be right with you, little brother."

The customer didn't respond, but it was still my cue to get lost and let Dizzy tend to business. "I only popped in for a few minutes to say hello, but I'd like to take you and Renee out for dinner tonight or tomorrow. Will you be available?"

Eyes meeting mine, he blew on his fingernails and polished them on his shirt. "Depends on where you're taking me. I don't put out for just any fast food joint."

Asshole...

Through laughter, he reached out to slap my hand. "Of course, Lennon, you name the place and time and I'll make sure Renee and I are there."

His customer rounded the bookshelf, a young kid that didn't look older than thirteen. Lifting his brown gaze my direction, he paused for a second, searching my face with the haze of recognition.

"Are you-" Pausing to take in my clothes, the kid shook his head, his loose, black beanie sliding over the back of his neck. "You're Lennon Carter, aren't you?"

6

"Yes, he is," Dizzy answered for me. "Lennon and I grew up together."

Surprised that the kid knew me, I shook his hand, noting the threadbare shirt he wore and the jeans that had to be two sizes too big on him. "You know me?"

"Know you?" His lips pulled into a wide smile, pink staining his cafe au lait complexion. "Man, I don't just know you. I idolize you. Well..."

Stepping back he gave me another thorough once over. "Not your clothes, you can keep those, but your music? Hell yes. Those songs you wrote for Hollister were epic, and to think you can just bounce between what you do with bands and playing in the freaking symphony?"

Shaking his head again, the kid stared at me wide eyed. "I want to be you when I grow up."

Dizzy threw an arm over the kid's shoulders. "Lennon, this is one of my students, Kyle Hart. You should hear him on the keys. If he keeps practicing, he might just give you a run for your money later on."

A smile creased my lips, my heart thumping to see so much enthusiasm for music in a kid who was undoubtedly growing up hard. It's difficult to appreciate art when you're wondering where you'll get your next meal. I should know; I'd been there.

"Tell you what, Kyle, I'll be in town for the summer. If it's all right with you, I'll get together with Dizzy and schedule a time to come in and listen to you play. Sound good?"

Kyle practically froze in place, his mouth gaping as if he wanted to speak but the words weren't coming to him. Dizzy gave the kid a good shake, laughing when he didn't move.

"Yeah, Lennon, you should go. I think you just gave my star student a stroke."

One nod of my head before I slapped Dizzy on the shoulder and headed toward the door.

"I'll call you."

The guitar strummed above me as I stepped out into the deepening twilight, the bright warmth of the sun being swallowed by the rise of purple night.

Halfway to my car in what I thought was an empty lot, my head spun right when a kid ran past me, bumping my hip as he passed.

The kid raised a hand in apology, but tucked it back into the pocket of his black jacket, a hood pulled up to conceal his face.

Two things stood out to me immediately: Number one, it was early June, the temperature a balmy ninety degrees, meaning there was no need for a damn jacket. Number two, an empty parking lot wasn't exactly the kind of place where two people could collide as if by mistake.

Hand reaching for my back pocket, I discovered it was empty. The little punk had stolen my fucking wallet.

"Hey!"

The second I called out to him, he took off at a dead run. Not even twenty-four hours back home and already I had to teach some stupid kid a lesson.

Adrenaline flooded me, an unwelcome rush that I hadn't wanted this early on in my visit to Sheldon. A heavy thud against pavement, the beat of my thick soles was faster than the crunch of his tennis shoes. If I didn't catch him around this next corner, he'd be lost to a maze of alleyways, never to be seen again.

It wasn't that I cared much about the wallet. The money wasn't important, the credit cards could be turned off, but there was a note inside there I couldn't live without. Losing the last memory I had of my sister would destroy me. She was everything to me, a bright smile gone that I could never replace.

The thought angered me more and granted me a burst of speed. A few inches closer and I could reach out to grab him.

"Stop, you son of a-"

Lunging for him, my fingertips skimmed the cotton jacket, but he had another burst of speed as well, placing more distance between us. He was small, several inches shorter than me at least, yet he moved with finesse, dodging obstacles easily as we rounded another corner into the alley.

Shadows swallowed us, but I wouldn't let it stop me. I wasn't a small guy, not like this asshole. However, getting jumped by friends waiting in the wings was a distinct possibility in Sheldon. If I didn't stop him through this last narrow path, my wallet and the note inside it were as good as gone.

A few more inches and my hand locked on his jacket. Pulling him back, I knocked him off balance, my wallet still stubbornly clenched in his hand.

The kid fell to the ground, landing on his back with a gust of air bursting from his lips. Straddling him, my knees jammed into his thin thighs. I locked one hand over his throat to keep him from sitting up and grabbed his wrist to bang his hand against the ground until he released what was rightfully mine.

Tenacious, he wouldn't release it at first, but after two hard cracks of his knuckles against the cement, he screamed, "Not the hands."

The wallet dropped to the ground, my head snapping left, not because I'd finally broke the leather free from his hold, but because that voice wasn't male.

With my fingers still locked over the kid's throat, I reached to shove the hood away, a pair of teal eyes glaring up at me, the *girl's* anger not enough to distract me from the fact that she was playing one hell of a dangerous game.

The shadows concealed the true depth of eyes that were framed by thick, dark lashes. Without her hood, long brown hair spilled free, the ends of it splashing over filthy concrete. High cheekbones cast more shadows down her face. Her jaw line elegant. Her lips full.

Damn it...she's beautiful.

It only pissed me off more.

"Are you kidding me right now?"

Everything about her brought out a side of me I tried to keep under lock and key. A part of me I kept hidden from those who weren't invited to my bed.

The women I fucked never complained about my nature, but this girl didn't know me – didn't understand she was playing with fire.

Thrashing beneath me, she was no match for my size and weight. Her hands lifted to mine, trying and failing to release my fingers from her throat. Easing up on my hold just enough to let her speak and breathe, I stared down at her, absolutely pissed that she would put herself in this situation.

"Let go of me." She could barely say the words, her lips parting as she coughed, her head turning as she continued to struggle and thrash.

"Let go of you? You just tried to steal my wallet and now you're making demands of me?"

A harsh laugh burst from my lips, my knees still grinding into her thighs, my hand holding her head against the cement.

"I should turn you over and spank your ass for this. What in the hell do you think you're doing acting like a stupid punk?"

The girl's hips bucked in an attempt to dislodge me, but she was too small, and I was too angry. Teeth bared at my threat, her eyes met mine again.

"Try and I'll-"

"You'll what?"

Leaning over, my chest brushed hers, my mouth so close to her ear, she could feel my breath against her cheek. Her entire body quaked with terror, her wide eyes holding mine, the pupils dilated. Breath poured over her lips in shallow spurts, and I could almost hear the rapid pulse of her heart.

I was scaring the shit out of her.

I didn't care.

She needed to be scared.

My voice had lowered into a deep growl, my need to teach her a lesson taking over. Fortunately for her, it was a rule of mine not to hit women in anger.

Unfortunately for me, I really hated my rule at that moment.

"What exactly will you do right now? I'm a hell of a lot bigger than you, and judging by how your struggling is doing nothing to dislodge me, I'm a hell of a lot stronger. How do you plan on doing anything to me?"

She fought harder and launched her hands at my face, forcing me to release her throat to grab her wrists and protect my eyes. It only took a second to trap both of them with my fingers, pin her arms above her head and lock her throat down with my free hand.

"As I was saying: What are you going to do?"

I wasn't going to hurt her, but she didn't know that. Still, I didn't let up to make this moment any easier on her. The best lesson she could learn right now was that there were men in this world who shouldn't be toyed with.

Tears leaked from the corners of her eyes to trail down her cheeks. "Just let me go."

"No."

Had I been the type of guy that hurts women, she'd be in a world of pain right now, her body violated, her soul shredded.

What made all of this worse was that she was a pretty girl. Not just pretty, but the type of girl that would turn my head if she weren't so aggravatingly young. I was drawn to her even when I knew I shouldn't be.

"How old are you?"

Refusing to answer, she continued to fight, fear shining behind narrowed eyes. It painted her pale cheeks red.

"Answer me, sweetheart, or I'm not letting you go."

"Eighteen."

Our eyes locked, and I forced myself to ignore the fact she was technically legal.

"What is your name?"

Another wild buck of her hips, the movement awakening something inside me she didn't want to mess with. My hand tightened on her wrists, my gaze dropping to the front of her jacket, disappointment flooding me that it didn't give a single hint of the body beneath.

My voice was a calm command. "Tell me your name."

"Melanie. Now get the hell off me."

Leaning down, I kept my stare locked to hers, our noses practically touching as I softly spoke my warning.

"I could have killed you for this, Melanie. Do you understand that? Could have done all sorts of horrible things to your body when I caught you. Lucky for you, I'm not a creep looking to hurt little girls. You might not be so lucky next time."

Her eyes darted right, chest heaving with her refusal to hold my stare. Even terrified, she was a rebellious little beauty that made my palm twitch with the need to adjust her thinking.

"Let me go," she whimpered. "I'm sorry, okay? Just let me go."

"I suggest you stop stealing. Next time you want to lift someone's wallet, you should remember this moment and make a better decision."

More tears. This girl wasn't a hardened criminal; she was an amateur with a death wish.

"Say please."

Shock filled her wide gaze, anger sparking just beneath it. "You're hurting my wrists. Just get off me."

I smirked. "Say please and I will."

Melanie needed a good lesson in manners, but that wasn't the sole reason for my demand. There was something about that word on a woman's lips that rounded my shoulders with satisfaction, the need to assert my desires on a willing partner brought to life by the sound of the word crawling from their throat.

How much more inappropriate could I possibly be in this moment? I should hate the girl, but instead I found myself auditioning her for a role I was certain she didn't want to fill. She needed to say it so I could release her and forget this entire thing happened.

"Say it," I growled.

With her eyes holding mine, her pouty lips parted, a trembling breath pouring out. "Please."

The huskiness of her voice was an arrow hitting its mark dead center. Walking away now was in my best interests before shit took a weird turn.

Still, it was in *her* best interests that I leave her with one last threat. "Do something like this again, and I'll be sure to redden your ass for it."

14

Releasing my grip on her wrists and throat, I snatched my wallet from the cement and pushed to my feet.

She stared up at me like I was a snake coiled and ready to strike, her movement uncoordinated as she crawled back until she was out of arm's reach. Quickly, she climbed to her feet.

The short amount of distance between must have made her feel safe, although I couldn't understand why. I'd already proven I could outrun her.

Canting my head right, I scowled. "Take off before I change my mind about that spanking."

She was fast. I'd give her that. It only took seconds for her to make it to the end of the alley, her eyes meeting mine with one last glance before she turned the corner and was gone.

I shook my head and brushed off my clothes, a heavy sigh blowing over my lips for the welcome home experience she'd given me.

Not even twenty-four fucking hours and already I hated this place again.

CHAPTER TWO

If you want to know a person, look to their hands. Grace is hidden within the movement of their fingers across an instrument. Strength is shown in their grip...

Amelia

When it came to a person's hands, my father had always been a stickler. He judged a person on the line of them, how they spoke with them, how they held their wrists, or in the confidence of their handshake.

It came to him fairly, that criticism, only because he'd spent his entire life striving to be a musician. The hands, to him, were everything.

From early on, he'd struggled through school; math, literature, and science lost to him because it was the music he heard in his head that stole his attention, the daylight hours counting down until he could get home to his antique piano. My father worked hard to become a symphony pianist. His one goal in life that he achieved, but gave up after having children.

Both my parents were amazingly talented on the keys. They'd met while attending Hastings Conservatory; their early years together spent discussing music theory and their favorite sonatas and concertos. Mom and dad both had aspirations for the symphony stage, but mom had given it up when my brother was born, my dad following her example once I came along.

Through teaching, they managed to support the family in a nice suburb outside Sheldon. Unfortunately, our happy family took a turn for the worst when mom fell ill, the floor dropping out from beneath us when she died.

Despite all of that, my father still taught piano, paying special attention to me. He was always commenting on my hands, whether they were touching the keys or not, always reminding me that, like my eyes, they were a window to the soul.

If dad were to see my left hand now, he would shake his head and lecture me, his disappointment plucking at my heart because I'd always wanted to please him.

Water stung my scraped skin as soon as I stuck it under the faucet. Gritting my teeth, I washed the grime away, not looking forward to the antiseptic I'd use next.

That asshole in the alley had done a number on my knuckles. He'd banged them against the ground, not giving much of a damn that he was choking me and crushing my legs at the same time.

Crying the entire way home, I didn't want to admit to myself that I'd been terrified. In all my schemes, nobody had ever caught me before. Being pinned down like that was more than I was willing to endure.

He could have done anything – *anything* – to me, and there wasn't a damn thing I could have done to stop him. He *knew* he terrified me, the entire time grinning down with the knowledge that when it came to who was in charge and who was trapped, I was the mouse held beneath the hungry cat's paw.

18

His eyes held something inside them that both drew me and pushed me away. I couldn't deny he'd stolen my breath when he was close enough for me to memorize the strong features of his face.

But still, despite what he looked like, despite the scent of him that was earthy and seductive, he scared me while smiling to do it.

I should have known better than to pick his pocket, but I knew he had money. The temptation had been too much to resist.

It's rare to see a car worth ten thousand dollars in Sheldon, Florida, but to see an Escalade worth over one hundred thousand dollars was like spotting a unicorn in the fiery depths of hell.

The second I'd noticed it, I knew whoever claimed the wheel would have cash tucked away in their wallet. At least one hundred dollars, but I hoped for more. So rather than passing through Jennison's parking lot as I'd intended, I decided to wait it out and lift the wallet from a person I was sure wouldn't miss it.

To say I was surprised when he strolled out wasn't the half of it.

Wearing a faded and torn Nirvana shirt with tartan plaid pants and a pair of beat up oxblood Doc Martens, the guy didn't strike me as a man of means. If anything, he looked like someone I would loan money to just so he could buy some new clothes from a thrift store.

His dark hair was a stylish mess framing his face, his thick biceps and corded forearms leading the eye down to leather cuffed wrists and hands that looked like they could strangle an elephant. That alone should have deterred me from attempting the lift, but I was hungry and figured I was small enough to outrun him.

He was halfway to his car by the time I stepped out into the fall of twilight to accidentally bump his side. Hauling ass, I thought I'd gotten away with it, but then he called out to me and the chase was on.

I knew I was toast when he caught me, my shock at his speed rendering me mute as he dragged me to the ground to straddle my lap and wrap one of his elephant strangling hands over my throat.

But it wasn't the way his knees pinned my femurs with the threat of snapping bone, or the grip of his punishing fingers blocking my airway that scared me the most; it was the damage he inflicted to my hand.

My only chance at a scholarship to Hastings Conservatory was an eight week summer program that started tomorrow. I needed my hands to prove I was trained and capable of playing the piano for thousands of people on stage. I needed my knuckles and fingers to drill those keys over every note of Mozart's 16th Sonata or Beethoven's 29th.

For years, I'd dedicated myself to learning the fastidious technique and grueling speed needed for a large majority of classical pieces, and I'd be damned to let that jerk ruin it for me.

Looking at the swelling in my knuckles combined with the split skin, it appeared he'd succeeded in not only damaging my hand, but also my chances to advance through the program.

Tears pricked my eyes as I applied antiseptic cream and bandages. Hatred flooded my thoughts to think about how the man had grinned down at me and demanded I say please.

To make matters worse, if not for the fact he was sitting on top of me, choking the shit out of me, and generally being a complete ass, the guy was jaw-dropping gorgeous when I finally took the time to look at him.

It was too dark to see the true color of his eyes, but he had the face of a damn model, chiseled in all the right places, the strength of his jaw dusted with stubble that made me want to reach up and explore the rough feel of it.

Whether angry or smug, he was a man I would gladly give my number, the type that would have me checking my piece of crap phone every thirty seconds to see if he'd texted or called. I wondered while I was fighting to break free of him what he would look like with a genuine smile.

That only served to piss me off more, and now I was hiding in my bathroom, ignoring my father's raised voice as he yelled at his home nurse, wishing I could start the day over to make better choices.

Leaning heavily against the door, I stared at myself in the mirror, wondering how much more I could take in my life.

"Leave me alone, you stupid bitch. Tell me where my wife is..."

Alzheimer's is a horrible condition. Years ago when the warning signs appeared, I thought my father was simply becoming forgetful. It started soon after Mom died, and we all ignored it, believing the stress of losing her was jumbling his thoughts. But as the years rolled on, the memory loss only became worse until eventually Dad was an entirely new person.

Some days were good for him, but today was a bad one. Ever since I'd walked through the door, he hadn't stopped screaming at the top of his lungs.

It made the day a bad one for me, too.

I had to get out of here, had to hide away and gather my thoughts or I was going to be a disaster tomorrow for my first day of class.

Sneaking out of the bathroom, I swallowed down my guilt for leaving the home nurse alone to manage Dad, but I couldn't handle it today, couldn't bite my tongue and not yell back, because it was the condition, not *him*, that made living here so difficult.

It would be easier if I could afford to put him in a good home, but what little money my brother, Ben, and I could scrounge together through less than legal means was barely enough to cover the bills, let alone pay for a nursing facility.

Neither Ben nor I could handle being here too often, so we did what we had to do to pay for the nurses who could. Thankfully, state aid helped pay for home care. Otherwise, we'd be screwed.

Quietly shutting the front door on my way out, I jumped in my beat up hatchback and gunned the engine down the road en route to Julia's house. She was the only friend I had in Sheldon despite being as old as my parents.

Julia was my mother's best friend. She had taken over teaching me piano after mom died and dad forgot how to play. She was also the person who got me a seat in the Hasting's summer program by being one of the two teachers.

A Hasting's graduate in the same class as my parents, she'd made sure I was ready by the time I finished high school and could attend the yearly program.

Pulling into her driveway, I stared out the windshield at her small, yellow house, my bandaged hand throbbing over the wheel. She was used to my showing up unannounced, always ready with tea and cookies, as well as a listening ear.

She must have seen me drive up. I hadn't yet turned off my car and already she was stepping outside to greet me. A groan bled from my lips as I stepped out of my car.

"Do you want to explain what happened to your hand?"

Leave it to Julia to laser in on the damage. Her brown eyes missed nothing. Taking the last few steps up to her porch, I flashed a smile, attempting to pretend that it wouldn't be a problem. "I tripped and scraped it today. No biggie."

Arching a plucked brow, she crossed her arms over her chest. "Let me see how bad it is."

"It's really not-"

"Amelia Harmony Dillon, remove that bandage right this second and let me see what you did."

My full name. Julia meant business.

I pulled the bandage free and winced at the concern in her eyes.

"How are you going to play tomorrow with your hand like that? They won't excuse you for the injury. Not with the other students who will be competing against you."

We walked in her house side by side. After closing the door, I nudged her shoulder. "Hey, it'll be fine. Plus, I have a feeling my teacher will understand since she's known me since the day I was born."

Her expression fell as she led me to the couch and sat down. "I won't be your teacher, Amelia. Lennon Carter will be. Since we're the judges of which students will be allowed to advance forward to audition, we have to be impartial."

The floor dropped out from beneath my feet. This was just one more crappy thing to happen to me today. "Who's Lennon Carter?"

"Another graduate of Hastings. From what I know he's done very well for himself in music. Not only has he secured a seat with the Florida Symphony, but he also works with popular bands in his free time."

With that kind of resume, I highly doubted he'd be easygoing when it came to my injury. I thought it might be possible I could flirt with the guy, maybe buy enough sympathy to weasel my way through the first week.

Unfortunately, I didn't have much experience in that department. My brother made sure I hadn't dated. He was always looking out for me, always worried I'd ruin my chances at a future if I allowed guys to distract me.

I played a big game for the most part, but in truth, I was a fledgling when it came to anything having to do with men.

24

My stomach churned and I felt dizzy. "I'm sure my hand is fine. I can play something now and see how it feels."

Julia shook her head, the dusty red hair framing her face falling over her shoulders with the motion. "I think you should rest it tonight. Thankfully it's your left and not your right. The demands won't be as bad, but I fear for your range of motion. Some of the pieces you'll be required to play demand a full octave stretch."

Leaning against her wall, I pulled the bandage back in place. A heavy sigh blew from my lungs. "Will the first day be that bad?"

She nodded and straightened the skirt of her demure green dress.

"Students are coming from all over to attend the program. This is the first time the program has been held in Tampa, but it's intended for the entire state. I only secured your seat because I had a friend on the board who owed me a favor. The other students have all been recommended by the youth orchestras and high schools they attended."

That information did nothing to make me feel better. I knew the program would be challenging, but I didn't understand the full scope of it. "How many students will there be?"

"One hundred to start with, and it's our job as teachers to whittle that number down to two by the end of the summer."

Maybe I should just give up now. Going up against one hundred other students was bad enough, but to do it with a busted hand? The odds were impossible.

"If it's not broken, then I think it should be okay. I want you to ice it tonight to help the swelling go down. Perhaps it's not as bad as it looks."

The pain in my hand when I clenched my fingers said differently, but I wasn't going to worry her more by telling her.

"It'll be fine," I breathed out, hoping to convince her because I sure as hell wasn't convincing myself.

Casting me a sympathetic grin, Julia patted the couch next to her. "Come sit down. I have a feeling you're here to avoid being at home with your father. Is he having a bad night?"

Pushing away from the wall, I sat down beside her, appreciative of her arm wrapping around my shoulders to tug me into a hug.

"I won't let you down tomorrow, Julia. I hope you know that."

"I know, sweetheart. You've been preparing for this your entire life. I'm sure once you show them all you've accomplished, Mr. Carter won't be able to help but fall in love with you."

Hoping she was right, I closed my eyes in an attempt to keep from crying again.

Tomorrow couldn't be as horrible as today had been.

At least that's what I told myself.

CHAPTER THREE

*I know you'll have questions. So many damn questions; ones I'm not
sure I can answer in a way that will make the world understand...*

Lennon

Two miles outside of Sheldon sat another place I'd
never wanted to see again. Walking along a dirt path
with a dozen roses in hand, I stepped over tree roots
and wound my way through rows of bushes and
headstones. The sky above my head was as grey as my
mood, and the wind whispering through the boughs of
the Live Oaks caused the hanging moss to sway softly.

Hillside Memorial Gardens was the last place I
wanted to be this morning, but nightmares had
plagued me so much over the last few nights that I
knew I wouldn't escape them until I visited Emaline's
grave.

My sister was only older than me by two years, but
she was better than me in every way possible. Smarter,
kinder, more talented on the piano than I had ever
hoped to be, Emaline was born to be a star.

Despite living in poverty, my parents worked two
jobs each to pay for her music lessons. No dime was
spared when it came to her, which meant there was
nothing left for me.

If it hadn't been for Mr. Jennison, I would have
never learned the keys. I didn't hate my sister for it. She
deserved every dollar my parents gave her.

Her headstone wasn't much, and with my living out
of state and both of my parents dead, there was no one

to tend the ground. The grass and plants around her grave had become overgrown. Ripping them away as much as I could, I laid the flowers down and traced my finger over her name.

Memories rushed back to me: the boyfriend that broke her heart, and the day I found her hanging in her room.

"Damn it, Ema, why did you have to throw so much away over a worthless guy?"

I'd turned eighteen three weeks after she killed herself, never looking back once I had the freedom to run. I would have given anything to kill the son of a bitch that broke her heart, but I didn't know his name. In the two years they'd dated, I'd only seen him once or twice. I would recognize him if I saw him again, but I doubted our paths would ever cross.

Spending a little over an hour by her graveside, I arrived back in Tampa as the sun was finally brightening the sky. Class wouldn't start for another forty-five minutes, so I stopped to introduce myself to the second teacher judging in the program.

An older woman turned to me as soon as I stepped in her large classroom. Already she had the sheet music set up on the pianos, a class roster clutched between her fingers.

"You must be Lennon Carter."

Crossing the room toward me, she had kind brown eyes and silver streaked red hair. Taking a moment to study to my clothes, the corner of her lip crooked up as she offered her hand.

"I'm Julia Pickens. It's a pleasure to meet you, although," her lips twitched again, "I'd pictured you differently when I read your resume. I guess it's true what they say about artists being eccentric."

This wouldn't be the first time a person couldn't match the image to the reputation. It wasn't the tenth time, or the fiftieth either. Most people read my stats and presumed I'd walk in decked out in a suit and tie, my clothes carefully tailored to represent my wealth or career.

All those people had been wrong, and they learned to get over it. As for today, I'd attempted to look presentable. I assumed the tan chinos, scuffed navy blue Docs, skull patterned suspenders and white Henley weren't cutting it.

Julia reached to touch the brown leather cuff on my wrist. "This is nice."

A grin stretched my lips, my eyes meeting hers.

"You don't have to try so hard. You're not the first to have been fooled by what you read about me. Should I have worn a jacket?"

It didn't bother me that people looked at me as either a piano virtuoso or a freak who desperately needed to install a light bulb in his closet. I'd happily own either of those reputations, as long as another reputation I'd earned stayed out of public knowledge.

All they knew was that I was a stern disciplinarian behind a piano. They didn't need to know that the discipline didn't stop when I took a woman to my bed.

I winked and her cheeks tinted pink, a soft laugh bursting from her throat. I was nothing if not a brazen flirt.

"Oh, Amelia is going to have fun with you."

"Amelia?" Cocking a brow, I eyed her and leaned a shoulder against the doorframe.

Waving a hand, Julia shook her head. "We're not supposed to discuss students. Forget I said anything."

An early bird student walked past us en route to my classroom. I shook Julia's hand again, told her it was a pleasure to meet her and followed after the young boy. He didn't look a day over fourteen, but I knew he had to be a high school graduate, at least, to have been granted entry into the program.

Skirting past him to open the door, I didn't fail to notice the curious expression on his face. To his credit, he didn't say a word.

He attempted to walk in behind me. I blocked the doorway with my body and asked him to remain in the hall until I set everything up.

With every class I taught (a rare occurrence given my other work) I had a routine to accomplish before allowing the students to shuffle through the door.

Three Steinway pianos were arranged in the room. Why they'd provided so many, I wasn't sure. It would be impossible for all three to be played at the same time, and really, only one was necessary for what I planned to do.

Walking past them, I dragged my finger down the white keys of each one, my head canting slightly to the right as I decided which one's sound resonated the most inside me.

People often think that every piano sounds like the next, but that's where they are so horribly mistaken. The strings used, the quality of the wood body, the construction of the hammers; all of it contributed to the tone of an instrument. It was my job to select the instrument that was just right.

Doing so, I glanced over the sheet music provided for the first week in class, boredom setting in immediately. Bach, Clementi, Debussy, and Chopin. All were meticulous composers, yet none of them spoke to my heart.

The one student who would remain standing in this classroom by the end of the summer would be the one who could seduce, through their music, the darkest parts of my soul. And these composers? Yeah, no. They wouldn't cut it.

For the first week, they would have to do. I set the music aside and glanced over the class roster. Thirty-eight girls. Twelve boys. I didn't like the numbers, but it was typical. Boys are often pushed into sports while girls are sent away to piano lessons.

The same thing would have happened to me if my mother had her way. Thankfully my father didn't pressure me into reaching for her goals. He knew I was learning from Mr. Jennison, and he never made a move to stop me.

Fingertip running the list of names, I paused by Amelia Dillon. What was so special about this girl that Julia had thought to mention her?

A quick scan of her credentials didn't answer the question. She wasn't sponsored by a high school or youth orchestra. I found the lack of information interesting, and made a note to keep an eye on her.

By the time I was finished setting up, it was nine on the dot - time to let the students in to discover who had what it took to move forward and who would be returning home.

I opened the door and turned toward my desk as shoes shuffled in behind me, the squeak of chair legs and quiet murmurs a chorus of excitement mixed with anxious anticipation.

Once I was certain that every student was settled and waiting, I turned toward the hopeful fifty to scan my eyes over their faces. One face in particular caught my attention, my body freezing in place with recognition.

Well, well...

The last time I'd seen those teal eyes and perfect pouting mouth, the girl had been beneath me fighting to break free, her gaze narrowing on me every time I threatened to spank her ass red.

My anger with her vibrated just beneath the surface of my skin, and I was tempted to teach her a lesson right here in front of everybody - a reminder as to why we don't pickpocket strangers who are bigger and badder than ourselves.

Like a deer in headlights, she stared back at me, her bandaged hand slipping from the top of her desk to fall in her lap where she could hide it, her face draining of color.

She knew me, and she was well aware that I knew her. I smiled to see she hadn't forgotten the moment we first met. Terror bled behind her wide eyes, her lips parting just slightly, the movement drawing my attention.

Something inside me awakened to witness her body shrink down into her chair. She wouldn't challenge me.

Not this girl. However, having her in my class was a complication I could have lived without.

Refusing to openly acknowledge my recognition, I continued looking over the rest of the faces before dropping my eyes to the roster. There wasn't a single student in here named Melanie.

Who the hell was she?

Conducting roll call, my voice snapped over every name on the roster, each student straightening in their seat when their name was called, fear saturating their expressions when I didn't react to their hopeful smiles.

"Amelia Dillon."

My mugger raised her right hand, her arm trembling as she averted her eyes, still refusing to meet my stare.

She wanted me to ignore her. I was too much of a bastard to make it that easy for her.

"Not the hands..."

What she'd yelled in that alley was finally making sense. It didn't make me feel sorry for the injury I'd inflicted to extract my wallet.

"Amelia, do me a favor and spell your name."

Every student looked at me with confusion, but there was only one set of eyes I was interested in. The same set that only reluctantly turned my way, meeting my gaze with trepidation.

"What?"

"Spell your name. You've had it your entire life. It should be easy for you to remember how it's spelled."

She wanted to roll her eyes, but caught herself before doing so. "A-M-E-L-I-A."

I scratched my jaw and glanced down at the roster, the short stubble rough against my fingertips.

"Strange. That's what it says here, but-" My eyes lifted to meet hers again. "I just thought that had to be a mistake since it's a weird way to spell Melanie. Don't you agree?"

Her face blanched, and I was positive she was about to be sick.

"I noticed your hand is bandaged. Are you sure you'll be able to play to the best of your ability today?"

Shrinking down further into her seat, she nodded her head. The criminal she'd introduced herself as was suddenly shy and submissive.

It bothered me how much I liked that.

My point had been made, and I moved on to call the names for the rest of the class.

Dropping the roster on my desk once all students were accounted for, I locked my hands together behind my back and took a moment to memorize their faces, careful to avoid staring at one in particular for too long.

I didn't want to notice that rather than the black hoodie, grungy jeans and sneakers she wore yesterday, today Amelia wore a yellow sundress, the thin straps showing off her tan shoulders, the modest neckline giving a small peek of her chest, the skirt falling just below her knees, revealing a set of toned calves that explained how she'd almost outrun me.

Anger burned through me again to think she was on the streets taking chances with her life and body.

"There are fifty of you in this class today because someone believed you should be here and recommended you for a Hasting's scholarship. It's my

34

job to tell you that by the end of tomorrow, only twenty-five of you will remain in this classroom."

Fifty sets of eyes widened in shock to hear the first cuts would be so soon and so dramatic a number. Good. Let them be scared because I wasn't here to handhold or coddle. I was here to determine who in this room was worthy of the ultimate prize.

"My name, as some of you may already know, is Lennon Carter. I graduated Hastings six years ago and have used that degree to secure a seat with the Florida Symphony, as well as maintaining a career in popular music. I've worked with bands such as Hollister, Gregori, Crimson Pawn, and others. You may have heard some of their work."

Nervous chuckles followed that last line. The three bands I'd named were known everywhere, their music so popular that every show they played was sold out, every album they released hitting the top of the charts within hours.

"But I'm not here to talk about me. What I am here to talk about is what I expect of you when it comes to your music, and what you can expect of me as not only your teacher, but also your judge.

"By the end of this summer, I will select one of you to move forward and audition for the scholarship. You will be competing against the student selected by the other teacher in this program, Julia Pickens. I won't go easy on any of you, because when it comes to competition, I hate to lose."

Careful to scan over the top of Amelia's head rather than look at her directly, I slowly paced a narrow path in front of my desk while continuing my opening remarks.

"Every one of you will be judged on your skills, technique and knowledge of the piano. The music selected to move you forward will increase in difficulty with each passing week. However, do not think that hitting each note properly and doing so according to how it's written will earn you the top spot.

"I don't give a damn if your technical skills are top-notch. What matters to me is whether you are living and breathing the music you play. In my opinion, we feel the music first, see it second and hear it last. If your music does not affect me on an emotional level, then you will be asked to leave. If your music puts me to sleep, then I ask that you kindly wake me up on your way out the door. It's as simple as that."

A few students shifted in their seats, their faces turning a sickly shade of green at how strict I would be on them.

"A bathroom is located at the back of the classroom. If you need to puke at any point, I prefer you do so in there."

More nervous laughter, although I was sure a few of them would run in that direction before the end of the day.

"Four pieces have been selected for the first round of cuts. Debussy, Bach, Clementi and Chopin. They are not technically difficult, and all of you should be familiar with them already. I will randomly assign which one each of you will be playing. Be sure to make me feel the music when you do."

My gaze wandered to Amelia to discover she was staring back at me, some unspoken thought obvious behind her eyes. She wasn't happy I would be her teacher, that much was clear, but she would either learn to accept me or she'd walk out my door. I had no intention of going easy on her.

My cock twitched at the thought of disciplining her in the best way I knew how. I hoped her performance would be worthy of what I could teach her.

"To begin, I'll play each of these pieces so you can hear what will be expected of you. Once I'm finished, the first performances will begin. It will take me all of today and most of tomorrow to go through the first round, so you may leave once you've had a chance to play. Any questions?"

The early bird boy raised his shaking hand. Nodding in his direction, I waited for his question.

"May I-" He swallowed hard, his face paler than when I first saw him. "May I be excused to the bathroom?"

If he was sick already, I knew he wouldn't last the first round of cuts.

"Go," I answered and turned to look at the rest of them. "And from now on, don't bother asking me before going to the restroom."

The boy practically launched from his seat, uncoordinated feet stumbling over themselves in a mad rush to reach the back of the classroom.

Shaking my head, I caught Amelia's eyes one last time before heading to the piano to show them what it meant to live and breath the music they played.

CHAPTER FOUR

A person's hands imitate their thoughts. They clench when angry.
Flutter when caught in a dream. They convey emotion as much as the
eyes, the mouth, the heart...

Amelia

The universe was fucking with me.

That's all there was to it.

At some point in my life, I'd pissed off the cosmos and it had chosen the perfect moment for revenge.

Of all the men I'd decided to pickpocket, of course it would be this one.

Lennon Carter. I'd never heard of him before, yet somehow I knew his name, his face, his reputation and voice would stay with me for the rest of my miserable life.

It didn't take a genius to figure out that he would be the man to ruin my lifelong dream.

All because I had a moment of weakness.

All because I'd chosen to do a stupid thing.

When I first walked into the classroom, I was too nervous to check out the instructor. Almost because my piece of shit hatchback wouldn't start, I'd arrived to class with just enough time to run inside at the back of the parade of shuffling students, sweat dripping down my temple and between my breasts because it was ninety degrees and my car lacked air conditioning.

39

My hair was a mess from driving like a maniac with an open window, and my cheeks were stained pink from what I assumed was stroke inducing blood pressure. But still, I'd managed to get here on time and make it appear I was as punctual as the other students.

After taking my seat and arranging my bag, I'd lifted my head to see a man standing at the front of the class wearing an odd jumble of mismatched clothes. It should have clued me in immediately.

But no. I'd been too focused on the way his pants hugged his perfect ass and strong thighs like they were designed to showcase his bottom half. The way his shirt clung to every hard muscle and ridge of his back, stretching over his broad shoulders. The way his sleeves were shoved up to his elbows to reveal corded forearms.

Unable to ignore the odd choice of skull-patterned suspenders he wore, I still hadn't put two and two together until he turned to scan the class with critical eyes, a smirk tugging at his sculpted lips immediately when our gazes met.

I would recognize that smirk anywhere after what happened. I hated that smirk, and feared it. Mostly, I remembered how he'd worn that smirk when forcing me to say please.

As if his backside hadn't been beautiful enough, Mr. Carter had turned around to reveal his ridiculously tempting face. Dark stubble still shadowed his strong jaw. He had observant blue eyes that were gorgeous now that the light could reach them, and a set of lips that pulled into a stern line to match the tension in his square jaw.

I wanted to shrink beneath my desk in response to the look on his face, fear freezing me in place as his dark stare studied me with lazy fascination.

It was entirely possible I'd died in my seat for several seconds, my breath absent, my heart skipping far too many beats, and my thighs squeezing together when his eyes scanned down to check out my legs.

The moment he began calling names, I had a full body reaction to his voice, the smooth, deep tone and cadence reaching me in places it shouldn't have been allowed. Anger straightened my spine to remember how that same voice had sounded when his body was pinning me down.

This situation wasn't just bad, it was cataclysmic. I had no doubt he would show me the door before the end of the day just to get even for my attempt to rob him.

My knuckles throbbed as he went through his opening remarks, my mind disbelieving that someone like him could make a piano sing. But when he sat down on the bench to play through Chopin's Nocturne op. 9 No. 2, I melted in place along with every other girl seated around me.

How was it possible that his elephant strangling hands were able to pull off the soft sounds, the light touch, and evoke the emotion of the piece? The same hands that had gripped my wrists with bruising strength. The same hands that had held me down by my throat while he promised to paint my ass red for attempting to lift his wallet.

41

Dad had been wrong when he'd said you could judge a person by their hands. Lennon Carter's were deceiving in every possible way.

I couldn't pull my eyes away from the flash of his dexterous fingers, the snap of his wrists as he elicited perfect resonance from the piano, touching those keys with just the right pressure to evoke stunning emotion from the notes.

I felt the music just as he'd demanded, every soft note targeting a place between my thighs that left me embarrassed, conflicted, and so out of breath that I feared I would be the next student running to puke. The sensation was far too much.

Perhaps being booted on day one would work out in my favor because spending an entire summer with him would damn near destroy me.

Finishing that piece, he moved on to Clementi's Sonatina in C Major, the melody more jovial, my emotions shifting again to imagine myself in an open field with the sun warming my skin. I became lost to it, stunned that a piece I'd played a thousand times sounded different beneath the stroke of his expert hands.

He moved to Bach's Prelude in C Major after that, the first few measures spilling out smoothly before he slammed his hands down on the keys, the jarring sound causing us all to jump in our seats.

Grabbing the sheet music, he tossed it behind him, the paper angrily fluttering in the air before sliding smoothly across the ground.

"That shit will put me to sleep," he said without turning to look at us. "Nobody's playing that."

A few seconds later, the first hypnotic notes of Debussy's Clair De Lune floated through the room, enchanting me into a mindless stupor.

By the time he finished, the last note left echoing in the room on a whisper, not a single student moved or dared to disturb the tranquility of the moment.

Mr. Carter spun on the bench, his eyes scanning over the stunned faces of his students to land directly on me.

"Now you all know what I expect of you. Be sure to give me nothing less than what I demand."

My heart dropped into my stomach.

Standing from the bench, Mr. Carter crossed the room, plucked the student roster from his desk, sat down in his chair, and turned to face the white board on the opposite wall from the pianos.

"Mark Alexander. You're up first."

He kept his back to the class and the instruments as a gangly, brown haired boy stood from his seat to take his place on the bench. "Play Clementi," Mr. Carter demanded, never facing the student even when the first notes were played.

Instead, he allowed his head to relax back, his eyes closing while the first student moved through the song. I thought he'd fallen asleep, but as soon as the student finished, Mr. Carter opened his eyes, scrawled a few notes on the roster, and called the next student's name.

"Kristen Avery. You'll be playing Chopin."

While Mark returned to his seat to collect his bag and leave, a pretty blond girl rose from her chair to approach the piano. On the first few notes she played, Lennon closed his eyes again.

On and on and on, until it should have been my turn.

I was pushing to my feet when he called out, "Peter Eisner. Play Debussy."

What? The last student was Claire Demarco. I should have been next.

Embarrassment heated my cheeks to have to retake my seat, a blond haired boy pushing to his feet instead. As he crossed the room, I glared at the asshole who'd just blatantly skipped me, my anger pulsing and expanding with each additional student he called. Not once did Mr. Carter bother to turn and look at me.

Five o'clock rolled around quickly, twenty-five of us remaining who had yet to perform. I was a ball of rage by that time, certain that he had skipped me on purpose. Would he cut me without even taking the time to listen to me play?

"The rest of you can go home," he said, spinning in his seat to face us. "We'll finish the first round tomorrow."

Without bothering to meet my eyes, Mr. Carter stacked some papers while the remaining students gathered their bags and shuffled through the door. I remained in my seat, far too angry to move.

When we were alone, he dragged his gaze from his papers to me. "Did you not hear me, Miss Dillon? The class has been excused."

"You skipped me."

With a blank expression, he asked, "Did I?"

Attempting to mug your teacher is a bad idea, but yelling at him on the first day of class would probably

44

only make it worse. Still, I wouldn't let him ruin my chances at Hastings just because he had a bone to pick.

"You can't do this to me because of what happened yesterday. It's not fair and I won't let you. I've worked too hard to be here."

His brows lifted a fraction, the only outward response he had to what I'd said. Meanwhile, a set of lips that were intended for the darkest of pleasure and sin remained a relaxed line, eyes that saw too much boring through me.

I thought the silence would suffocate me before he finally broke it. "Come here."

My butt was glued to my seat, fingers curling into my palms. "No. I want to know why you skipped me."

A spark of challenge rolled behind his stern eyes. "When I tell you to do something, Amelia, I expect you to obey immediately. Now come the fuck here."

The controlled tone of voice did something to me, fear and fury blending together into a toxic poison within my veins. I stood from my seat on shaking legs, hating how he watched me closely as I crossed the room to approach him.

I was in arm's reach when he held out his hand and demanded, "Let me see your injury."

My fingers curled more, pain throbbing over the knuckles. Sheepish, I attempted to maintain control over my actions. "No."

Mr. Carter cocked a brow, his fierce gaze holding mine. "Don't make me tell you again."

Standing this close to him, I could smell the masculine notes of his cologne, could feel the pulse of his energy tingling across my bare skin. He saturated

45

the space around him with calm determination, focused control, and absolute assurance that I would do as he said.

"Say please..."

The memory rolled through me on a shiver, rage tinting my cheeks red.

Tension bled between us, my refusal to acquiesce to his demands clashing against his confidence that I would eventually give in and obey.

This wasn't fair. We weren't on the same level in this classroom. I was the student begging to earn a scholarship while he was the teacher who stood in the way of my dreams.

I extended my left hand, a spark passing between us when our skin touched. He pulled my arm out farther to remove the bandage and explore the damage he'd caused.

His skin was warm, the calluses on his palms rough. My mind reeled against him as my body responded. Muscles weakening, my legs shook and my breasts felt heavy. This man was too much - too talented, too successful, too gorgeous, too *stern*.

His voice was soft when he asked, "Did it ever occur to you that, due to your injury, I was giving you another day to heal before making you play?"

Blue eyes lifted to mine, his fingers clamping down in refusal when I attempted to pull my hand away.

"Answer me."

Shaking my head, I wet my lips, my mouth and throat suddenly dry and sticky.

"No." Pausing, I wasn't thinking when I opened my mouth again to ask, "Doesn't it bother you that you caused this injury?"

Without an ounce of remorse, he answered, "You deserved it."

Silence beat between us before he asked his next question, his voice deeper than before. "Does it hurt?"

"Yes," I breathed, my hand trembling in his.

Nodding, Mr. Carter released my hand and stood from his seat. At his full height, he towered over me, his broad shoulders, strong chest and trim waist unhidden by the white Henley shirt.

Out of instinct, I backed away, my retreat stopped short by a hard wall behind me while a wall of tempting muscle and flesh caged me in from the front.

With one hand braced next to my head, Lennon stared at me, his gaze tracking a slow path down the front of my dress and up again. "Who are you, Amelia Dillon?"

Confusion flooded me. "What?"

It bothered me how my question came out more as a startled squeak than a word.

He grinned, just the corner of his lips curling with lazy satisfaction. Reaching out with his free hand, he trapped my chin between his fingers, holding my gaze to his without concern that I hadn't invited the touch. Electricity sparked where his skin met mine, my head dizzy, my breath as uneven as my heartbeat.

"Who are you?"

Ah, hell. I wondered if he could tell my nipples were hard as rocks and my lungs were struggling to draw in a breath.

As it was, my heart was in my throat beating staccato so hard that I swore I was a few seconds from passing out. "I don't-"

The gentle tone of his voice was at odds with his question. "Are you the shitty little thief hiding in a hoodie and baggy jeans? Or are you a musician who demands respect based on her talent and discipline?"

He was enjoying this moment far too much, the truth of his amusement written in the line of his lips, the sleepy look in his blue eyes. It only frightened me more.

"I'm a musician," I whispered.

Mr. Carter leaned forward and I panicked, my eyes locked to his lips. He shouldn't have been this close to me. There had to be rules against this. He didn't seem to care.

I wasn't a girl to be pushed around or controlled. Yet, in his presence, I stilled in place, unable to find the willpower to fight or move away.

Breath hot against my cheek, he whispered, "I don't think you are. I think a musician would know better than to risk her hands acting like a stupid hoodrat that robs people. I think a musician knows better than to question the man who will be judging her performance. I think-"

My lips parted on a tremulous breath.

"-you didn't believe me when I warned you I would spank your ass red if I ever caught you doing something so stupid again."

There was no question about it; I was three seconds away from passing out.

He knew it and I knew it, his blue eyes locked to mine when he warned, "You should know that threat extends to you questioning me in class as well."

Our eyes remained locked, mine as wide as saucers and his gleaming in the low light between our bodies.

After a few seconds, he released me and pushed away. Relief flooded me.

Tucking his thumbs in his pockets, Mr. Carter smirked, the expression becoming far too familiar.

"Have a nice night, Amelia. I suggest you go straight home and do your best not to mug another person."

He didn't have to tell me twice.

My legs wouldn't cooperate and walk with a smooth gait, my arms putty as I reached my desk and grabbed my bag. I could feel his eyes burning holes in me, observing with perfect clarity the amount of effort it took me not to tear up in response to the storm of volatile emotions rolling through my veins.

I was almost out the door when he said, "I hope you impress me tomorrow, Miss Dillon. It's the only way you'll remain in this class."

Flinching in response to the warning, I ducked my head and hurried from the room, my nerves on edge as hatred exploded in my chest.

Pushing through the outside doors, I bent over and locked my hands to my knees, my body breathless, my mind in a state of shock. Gulping air like a drowning woman who had just broken the surface of water, I willed my heart rate to slow down, the heat of the sun helping to warm my skin and chase away the chills Mr. Carter had forced through me.

He shouldn't have scared me as much as he did, but my entire future was gripped in his cruel hands, his warnings echoing in my head as I straightened my body and walked to my car.

I made the drive home in silence, my thoughts racing through every time our eyes had met across the classroom, over every word he'd spoken. Despite no longer being in the same room as him, I could smell his cologne, could feel the heat of his body encroaching on mine when he'd caged me against the wall.

On the surface, Lennon Carter seemed like your ordinary successful and driven man, but there was something else lingering just beneath his skin, something that drew me in and terrified me at the same time.

It didn't help my state of mind that my father was yelling again by the time I returned home, his nurse glancing up from a magazine she was reading on the couch.

"Bad day?" I asked, the truth of it bellowing through the clapboard house.

She nodded, her brown hair bobbing at the sides of her head. Elaine was a good nurse, usually relentless in calming my father down. Tonight, her dark eyes were exhausted.

"He's been upset since this morning. I wouldn't let him go for a walk by himself and he's been yelling ever since. Your brother is here taking care of him while I take a break."

"Did you try playing music for him? It might help calm him down."

"Honey, I've tried everything. This is just one of those days."

Sadly, *those* days were becoming more common, far outnumbering the good ones. "I'll go back and see if I can help."

The magazine rustled in her hands. "I gave him a mild sedative a few minutes ago. It should take effect soon."

"Thanks, Elaine."

Heading down the hallway, I dropped my bag off in my room before walking to dad's door. He was attempting to get up from the bed despite Ben's efforts to hold him down.

Seeing him like this broke my heart. Dad had always been the picture of calm serenity growing up, like a peaceful Brahm's sonata weaving around me to comfort and soothe. Now my father was like Stravinsky's Firebird - chaotic, atonal and difficult. The story and music fit him perfectly because The Firebird was a Russian ballet about a man lost in a fantasy world with the one hope of saving the woman he loved. Not usually a composition for the piano, I'd fallen in love with the chaos of the music in certain parts, learning and perfecting how to play The Infernal Dance on the piano.

I couldn't look at my father without hearing that song.

Despite how badly I wanted to walk in his room and wrap my arms around him in a warm hug, I couldn't will my feet to move. I stood quietly observing until the sedative kicked in and Ben finally calmed him down.

While dad drifted off to sleep, Ben and I watched with weary eyes, both knowing that the man who'd raised us was gone regardless of whether his body still lived.

It had been six months since he'd had a lucid moment, six months since he'd looked at me and recognized me as his daughter.

Ben stood from the bed and crossed the room toward me. Clutching my arm, he pulled me from the doorway and led me into his room. After closing the door, Ben collapsed over the mattress of his twin bed, his long legs hanging over the end.

"We need money," he said, his hand scrubbing down his face.

"Do something like this again, and I'll be sure to redden your ass for it..."

Mr. Carter's words whispered through my thoughts at my brother's announcement. If we needed money, whatever we would do to get it wouldn't be legal.

"What do you have in mind?"

He sat up, his dark hair hanging down over his forehead. Ben had mom's grey eyes, his facial structure sharp like dad's. Classically handsome, it was a shame he hadn't gone to college to make something of himself. His refusal to go to college was mostly my fault. Ben couldn't leave me alone with dad.

My brother was twelve years older than me, often jumped from job to job, and made better money scamming on the streets or dealing drugs. Most people looked at him like he was a worthless loser, and maybe he was. But still, he helped me support Dad, and he paid the household bills. He'd raised me and protected me during my last years in high school when our father was incapable.

"Same scam. We'll go to a nice nightclub or bar in Tampa. You'll lure out some asshole with more money than God, and Jackson and I will take it from there."

Our eyes locked, his expression apologetic. "I hate asking this of you, Amelia, but after getting fired a few weeks ago, I fell behind on the bills. We need this to catch up."

My stomach clenched, the taste of bile crawling up my throat because I hadn't eaten anything. I was used to the empty feeling. Over the years, I'd learned to survive on one paltry meal a day.

Ben had only asked me to go through with this particular scam four times over the last two years, and only when we were in danger of missing a mortgage payment or the power turning off.

Still, I hated the process of it. Hated what I had to let someone do. Hated the screams that followed.

"I don't like when they touch me, Ben."

His eyes narrowed, not because he was angry at what I said, but because he hated them touching me, too. My brother was overprotective of me, had chased off every potential boyfriend I had. Mostly because the guys in Sheldon were bad news.

"It'll only be for a minute or two. You know that. I'll keep my eyes on you the entire time. Get him out of sight of other people and it'll be over once I step up. I won't let anybody hurt you, Amelia."

Nodding my head, I scuffed the toe of my shoe against the floor, resigned to what I had to do.

"Okay. When do you want to do this?"

"Tomorrow night. Does that work for you?"

Swallowing down my hatred of our situation, I nodded again.

"Yeah, Ben. Tomorrow night works."

CHAPTER FIVE

I spent days in the sun. You should know that. Remember that. Hold on to it when confused and in pain. I was happy once. My heart open to fill every note I played with the beauty I felt in his presence...

Lennon

Touching Amelia had been a mistake, one I couldn't take back or forget. The instant her skin met mine - at the moment she submitted by reaching out with her injured hand - a sense of calm rolled through me, the soothing warmth of satisfaction that I'd made a demand and it had been obeyed.

Of course, the only problem with feeling that calm warmth was that the girl who'd evoked it in me was about as off limits as someone could get.

She was too young for me. Too timid despite her attempts at being bold. Not to mention my student - a girl I had to judge with an impartial ear and mind.

Still, I'd enjoyed the transfer of power between us, the surrender I'd witnessed in her just before her body shook for reasons I wasn't sure she understood. My body reacted to the way she'd trembled, every part of me coming alive with the need for discipline.

Amelia played a good game, but when push came to shove, she wasn't as sharp-edged as she wanted to lead people to believe. She was the type of woman who would give me everything I demanded, the type who would run and fight until the moment she was caught.

I didn't want to think about how submissive she could become when trapped by the hands of a dominant man.

55

Thoughts of her chased me home that night, an image of her dancing in my mind while I tormented the keys of my piano, memories of her wide, sparkling eyes teasing me while I paced the halls of the large house I'd rented while staying in Tampa.

She was trouble in every possible way, the defiance in her bleeding away in the moment she was cornered by a predator.

I wondered if life in Sheldon had forced her to adopt an attitude that went against her nature. And even though it did nothing to help me break free of my fascination with her, I wondered if beneath the hard shell she was as malleable as I preferred my women to be.

Tossing and turning all night, I'd woken the next morning with the hope that Amelia would crash and burn during her performance in class, hoped that she'd give me a valid excuse to cut her loose so I could forget I'd ever known her.

I didn't need her kind of temptation staring at me every day for the next several weeks. I wasn't sure I could resist tasting it.

Now as I stood waiting for the students to file in to class, my eyes zeroed in on a brown haired beauty walking through those doors wearing a fitted, button up shirt that revealed just how generous Mother Nature had been to her, and a pair of black slacks that did nothing to hide the curves of her hips and ass.

For a moment, I regretted that she hadn't worn her baggy jeans and hoodie.

The students took their seats, settling in with a chorus of scraping chairs and anxious whispers. I stood in front of my desk, feet at shoulder width, my hands locked behind my back.

"Good morning."

Every student's eyes were on me, yet none of their lips were moving.

"I said: good morning."

Waking up, they responded, a synchronized and robotic response.

Inclining my head, I went through roll call, careful to avoid looking at Amelia directly when I called her name. The moment her voice snapped out in response to mine, I wanted to bend her over my desk and show her why little girls shouldn't speak to me with disrespect.

That thought alone disturbed me.

I wouldn't let her win this power struggle, wouldn't allow her to see that her attempts at defiance bothered me.

Addressing the class, I explained, "Today will be more of the same as yesterday. Half the students here still need to perform their piece. Unlike yesterday, everybody needs to remain in class because I'll be selecting who stays and who goes by the end of the day."

Glancing up, I grinned, "No pressure, right?"

In fact, it was a lot of pressure, enough to fill the room with a heavy cloud of trepidation, each student eyeing me with fear even though they answered me with hesitant laughter.

"Let's begin. Haley Kline. You're up and you'll be playing Chopin."

A tall, leggy blond stood to her feet. Yesterday, her hair had been pulled up into a knot at her nape, her face free of makeup, and she'd been wearing a black dress of modest length. Today, her hair was loose down her back, the neckline of her tight, red dress inappropriate, and her makeup was what you would expect from a stripper working a stage.

"Thank you, Mr. Carter."

Brown eyes met mine with so much heat behind them she was melting the cheap plastic chairs beneath the other students' asses.

It never failed. On the first day of class, girls showed up expecting a typical boring old guy or a female teacher. They were conservative with their appearance as a result. But by day two, after they'd had a chance to meet me, they morphed into vixens far too young to understand that, to attract, it was better to be subtle.

A quick glance around and I determined there were seven more girls just like her. Amelia, however, wasn't one of them. Rather than large doe eyes, smoldering with youthful adoration, Amelia looked at me with wariness that transitioned into sharp antagonism the minute our eyes met.

It would be fun breaking her of that habit.

Ignoring Haley's attempt at holding my attention, I walked to my seat, turned my back to the piano and kicked my feet up onto the surface of the desk.

When evaluating the music produced by every individual player, it was easier for me not to watch, my eyes closed as I allowed their sound to sink through me.

Most students find the routine hard to accept, not understanding that, despite the appearance of not paying attention, my focus was solely on them.

I was a slave to sensation, sound conjuring in me emotion, the music pulsing inside my head.

With my eyes closed, I could pick up every missed note, every rushed beat, every mistake in technical skill, while also savoring the heart of the player.

As for Haley Kline, there was no heart at all apparently, her skill suitable for the knowledge it took to understand the music, but her soul utterly absent.

Chopin's Nocturne should be played with a gentle hand, the melody rolling through you with sensual grace, lulling a person into willful abandon if it's played right.

Haley's hard plunking of keys did nothing for the piece, not that this particular composition did much for me anyway. It was too simple, too pure. Absent of the discord and dark, pleading notes I preferred.

When her performance was done, I made my notations, called the next student and assigned them their piece. The routine repeated over and over until, in the end, there was just one student left.

"Amelia Dillon. You'll be playing Debussy."

So far, every student had butchered this song, their heavy hands too forceful over a pianissimo piece. The Clair De Lune was a slow mating dance of sorts, at least in the way I saw it; the treble a feminine whisper in answer to the male demand for dominance.

When played correctly, you could see the seduction that came with a woman dancing away from the man who pursues her, only to crawl back when she understood that she belonged to him. Ebbing and flowing. Back and forth. A tease that draws the eye. Temptation too alluring to deny. They meet in the middle, their opposition coming together to create a harmonious and unbreakable bond.

I had no clue if that had been Debussy's intent when writing the music, but still, it was the image painted in my mind's eye to hear it.

When the first notes of the song floated through the room, my eyes opened in surprise to hear Amelia's soul resonating through them.

It took everything I had not to turn and watch her play. If there weren't forty-nine pairs of eyes locked on my reaction, I would have lost the battle to turn and watch.

Jesus Christ, Amelia, why not just open your legs and tease me with all there is to see?

Amelia didn't just feel the music, she made love to it, every muscle in my body tense with the desire to watch her play - to see if she moved her body as beautifully as the sound she produced.

Gone were my hopes to cut her in the first round. Within the first few measures, it was all too apparent she was one of the best students in the class.

This summer, it seemed, was going to test every bit of resolve I had to avoid making the mistake of dragging her to my bed.

The song ended, the room rendered silent as the last notes echoed and bled away.

Taking a moment to collect myself before turning to the anxious students, I made my notations, dropped the roster onto the surface of my desk and cleared my throat before dismissing them for break.

"You all have thirty minutes free time while I make my decisions."

Shuffling past me, the students cleared the room, giving me a moment to sit back and absorb what I'd just heard.

Was Amelia's performance perfect? No. She still had much to learn. But was her soul written into the sound? Yes, and it was as soft and tender as it was disastrous and profound.

There was dissonance inside of her, a dark, dreary, cacophony of longing that called to and caressed all the similar parts in me.

Scrubbing my knuckles down the stubble along my jaw, I circled her name as a student who would stay, even if it would be the worst thing for me. My eyes drifted to the blank space where no high school or your orchestra was listed. Where had Amelia learned to play?

Thirty minutes passed and the students returned, a mixture of anxious and hopeful faces.

I hated this part, the rejection, the heartache, the loss I knew each one experienced when their name wasn't called. Standing from my seat, I rounded my desk to lean against the front, one hand clutching the roster, the other gripping over the edge.

"Before announcing who stays and who goes, I want to take a second and commend you all for having made it this far, for dedicating yourselves to music, for loving the art of sound. For those who are leaving today, please do not take this as a sign that you should quit or give up that love. Keep going. Keep practicing. Keep immersing yourselves in your art. You were all very good and the decisions I made were not easy ones."

Pausing, I fought not to look at Amelia.

"I'll call the names of those who will remain. If your name is not called, do not return tomorrow. Once I'm done, all of you are excused to go home."

It took me five minutes to announce the twenty-five who would go forward, Amelia's name saved for last. Watching her through my peripheral vision, I saw the moment of relief wither her shoulders to learn that she had made the cut.

"All of you can go. Have a good night."

Haley Kline, a student I was all too happy to boot from the program, flashed me a vicious look of contempt as she passed by. The early bird kid who couldn't hold down his breakfast did his best not to cry. Several other students had tears slipping down their cheeks as they gathered their bags and headed to the door.

Behind them, Amelia hitched the strap of her bag up her shoulder, her eyes finding mine between the movement of students.

"Miss Dillon," I called out. "I'd like a word with you."

Stilling in place, Amelia refused to approach. I could understand her reluctance. The last time she came near me, I'd caged her against a wall and threatened to spank her ass.

The threat was becoming a bad habit.

After the remaining students had cleared the room, silence was heavy between us. Tapping my finger against the roster, I lifted my eyes to her and attempted to ignore the desperate need I had to demand she come closer.

"Who taught you to play? The roster fails to list a high school program and youth orchestra, but that-," I pointed to the piano as if the keys she'd mastered were still humming with the notes of her soul, "-that wasn't a performance a person picks up as a hobby."

Ducking her head, her cheeks flamed crimson.

"My, um," toeing the floor, she spoke low, her voice barely loud enough to cross the space between us. "My parents taught me. They both graduated Hastings and had played with the symphony before retiring to take up teaching private lessons."

Recognition flooded me, the name Dillon resonating in my mind as part of a memory I fought hard not to let haunt me.

Stunned, I gripped the edge of the desk with both hands. "Are you Lila and James Dillon's daughter?"

How had I not made the connection before?

Peering up, her eyes flashed with warmth, the first time I'd seen her face come alive to look at me. "You know them?"

Nodding, I couldn't believe how the gods were fucking with me.

"They-"

My throat was clogged, emotions I'd been pushing away for over ten years were a knot blocking my ability to speak. What are the odds that *this* girl would be the one to try and mug me? That *this* girl would be the one to call to me on a carnal level I was desperate to avoid?

63

That *this* girl would be connected to the worst moment of my life merely by existing?

They taught my sister...

I shook my head. Talking about Emaline was too close, too much to add to an already difficult situation.

"I saw them play in the symphony when I was a kid. Grew to love their work when I was at Hastings. I now understand where your talent comes from."

Her eyes rounded and she took one hesitant step toward me. Just the mention of her parents made her appear thirsty for more information.

"My mom taught me, starting at the age of two. I couldn't do more than bang my fingers on single keys, but eventually my hands grew. After she died, my father took over, but then he-"

Voice trailing off, shadows appeared in her eyes, the moment lost to whatever bothered her.

"Well, anyway, yes. That's how I learned."

Yet she hadn't studied in high school, hadn't joined a youth orchestra or similar program. Instead, she was picking the pockets of people in one of the worst areas of town.

Fingers gripping harder over the edge of the desk, I asked, "With talent like that, why in the hell would you risk throwing it away by committing crimes?"

The question shut her down, all sense of warmth gone until the air between us could have iced over with her scorn. "That's none of your business."

"Make it my business."

Our eyes locked, anger swirling behind her gaze, while the need to strip away all her secrets shone

64

darkly behind mine. I wouldn't give up, not when it came to this girl acting in ways that could get her hurt or killed. Not when she risked tossing away her talent like my sister had done.

It destroyed me every day to think that I hadn't been able to help Emaline. But Amelia was still here. Still fighting. Still able to be saved.

"I had you pinned in a back alley where nobody would have cared if they heard you scream. I could have broken your hand. Could have-"

"Spanked my ass," she interrupted, one eyebrow arching above her eye. "Yeah, you've told me." Crossing her arms over her chest, she glared across the room. "Are we done here?"

Not exactly where I was going with that statement, but it pleased me to hear she'd remembered the warning. She had no clue how close I was to lunging at her and making good on my threat. She was in need of an attitude readjustment.

My voice was a chilling croon. "Yes. I think we are."

Gripping her right hand over the strap of her bag, she nodded. "Good night, Mr. Carter. I'll see you tomorrow."

Without waiting for my response, Amelia stormed from the room. I doubted she had any clue about the amount of heartache and conflicting emotions she had left in her path.

This summer wasn't just going to test my patience...it was going to tear down every wall I had with the temptation of Amelia Dillon.

CHAPTER SIX

Avoid those who use their hands to cause harm because they can.
Trust those who have the ability to tear you apart, yet touch you
with tenderness instead...

Amelia

Jerk.

His name was no longer Lennon Carter. I'd renamed him.

Jerk. It was simple. One word.

Like Prince, Madonna, Björk or Beck.

He wanted to be the all powerful music god? Fine. He could have one name just like them.

Jerk.

It suited him.

Why did he have to keep bringing up what I did? Especially when we were finally, I don't know, bonding? Over something that didn't involve my ridiculous attempt to lift his wallet.

For a single second, I actually believed he had a kind, normal bone inside him, and then he drove me right back to hating him more than I'd ever hated any person in my life.

Where is she? Bring me my wife? Where is Lila!

Tears stung my eyes for several reasons:

Number one: The man who was supposed to be my mentor thoroughly enjoyed pissing me off at every opportunity possible;

Number two: My dad was having another bad day which made getting ready to go out unbearable since I kept crying and ruining my makeup;

Number three: I didn't want to go out, not when I knew a stranger would be touching me moments before my brother mugged him.

Everything about this night was wrong. Yet, here I was wearing a skimpy dress that hung way too low over my chest, and rose way too high on my legs. Here I was, wiping away my mascara for the third time just so I could reapply it.

I didn't even look like myself. I looked like the cheap older version of myself, a version I never wanted to know.

Listen to me! I need my wife!

Mr. Dillon, please. You're wife isn't here. I can't bring her to you...

Pressing my forehead against the mirror, I closed my eyes and wiped away my fourth attempt at mascara.

All I wanted to do was walk away, but if I did that, we would lose the house, lose the nurses, lose everything my father had done for us before he'd lost the ability to take care of himself.

The door banged behind me. "Amelia? You ready? We need to get going."

I would be if I didn't have to keep reapplying my makeup. Taking a deep breath, I fixed my face as much as I could, hoping whomever I flirted with didn't notice the puffy eyes and dark circles beneath them.

Ben stood on the other side of the door, his eyes narrowing as they roamed down to look at my dress. Teeth clenched, he said exactly what I felt.

"I hate doing this. Fucking hate it."

Me too, big bro. You have no idea.

"It's fine. Let's just go and get it over with, and hope we never have to do it again."

Ben was wearing the same black hoodie that I'd worn when I'd tried to mug Mr. Carter. It fit him better, that jacket, a disguise we both used when committing crimes like Batman in reverse. Stealing instead of fighting the bad guys in a ploy to make the world better.

Wrapping his arm over my shoulder, Ben planted a kiss on my cheek, both of us studiously ignoring my father's top lung demands.

Where is my wife?

Mom was the only person he remembered, mostly because he often believed he was back in the symphony, two newlyweds who hadn't yet started a family.

"Come on, let's go. We'll make this quick."

We picked up Ben's best friend Jackson on the way to downtown Tampa. I was in the back seat of Ben's '97 Civic (another piece of crap car that he somehow kept running) while the two of them sat up front deciding where to go and who to target.

"I'm telling you, Ben. We could take this another step further if we case the son of a bitch from the parking lot. Wait for some old dog to pull up in a nice car, watch where he goes, and then we can send Amelia in to do her thing. Not only will we get his wallet, phone, watch or whatever, but we can also grab that ride and sell it to be stripped. I know a place that's not far. The entire thing would take one hour tops."

Peering at the side of my brother's face, I could see he didn't like having to do this, especially involving me, but he considered Jackson's idea, the thought of a few thousand extra dollars swirling in his mind.

It would help pay the bills for several months, would catch us up and keep us floating. That's what mattered to him in the long run, and I hated that dad's problems and mine rode heavily on the shoulders of a thirty year old who never had the chance to make something of himself.

Ben was only twenty when Dad started slipping away. Mom had died one year before that (when I was seven and Ben was nineteen) and for a year after, Dad's symptoms weren't so bad that Ben had to fend for all of us.

However, as the years wore on, Dad could no longer teach, and Ben stepped up to take over. He worked odd jobs, paid the bills, made sure I went to school, had a roof over my head, and food on my plate. Things only got worse from there until we became so desperate that we thought up schemes to make money fast.

We only resorted to this one at times when we were facing losing the house.

I didn't hold it against him. If anything, I worried more for my brother than I did for myself. I'd even offered to skip the Hastings program to get a job, but Ben wouldn't hear of it.

He wanted me to fulfill my dreams, told me I could take care of him when I was a famous musician rolling in cash. They were empty words and we both knew it. If I was lucky, I would end up making just enough to support myself.

Turning a hard left, Ben swung the car into the parking lot of Majori's, a trendy upscale bar that catered to the type of people who could stand to lose some money without it destroying their life.

In a way, we'd attempted to justify our actions by believing we weren't really hurting people, that those we targeted could afford the theft.

He pulled into a space around the building and out of sight, the shadows concealing the getaway car. Twisting in his seat, Ben looked at me, nervousness clear in his expression.

"I'll leave the key in the box above the back tire. Since Jackson and I will be taking off in another car, you can take this one home, okay?"

Closing my eyes, I took a deep breath to calm my racing heart. "Yeah, okay."

I guessed that meant he would go along with Jackson's plan.

Nudging his chin in the direction of the door, he said, "Go ahead and go inside. Sit at the bar and we'll come in to let you know who to go after. Remember to take him deep enough in the alley around the building that no one will see you. We'll be waiting."

"Okay." I moved to open the door, but Ben grabbed my arm.

"Hey, don't worry. We won't let the guy touch you too much before stepping in."

Maybe not in the alley, but they couldn't step in while I was still in the bar. Many men didn't care about being in public. They would paw at me without concern for who was watching. "Yeah."

I got my first fake I.D. at sixteen. Actually, Ben had gotten it for me specifically for schemes like this. It wasn't that I looked old enough, the opposite, really, but that was all part of the charm.

Dirty old men rarely gave a damn about age, and my young face and curvy body were the perfect lures.

Heels clicking on the pavement, I wound my way to the front, the bouncer taking one quick glance at my I.D. before grinning and waving me inside. I'd been in Majori's once before, the ambiance alive with swirling color and pounding music.

Tables were arranged throughout the space, a dance floor set off to the right, with a large wood bar dominating the back that sat at least fifty people in gleaming silver stools. The ceilings soared twenty feet above my head, pendant lights hanging down as accents within the industrial-meets-luxury feel of the place.

Ignoring the staring eyes of several men who were already inside, I walked straight to the bar, took a seat, and ordered a Rum and Coke, knowing I would need the liquid courage to go through with this. Scanning my eyes over the crowd, I noticed the typical painted faces of the women, and the soft-spoken conversations between businessmen.

I must have waited for thirty minutes before a hand tapped on my shoulder. I turned to see Jackson standing behind me.

Leaning in, he motioned to a man who looked to be in his late forties winding around tables and heading to the bar. He couldn't have been taller than six foot, his suit well tailored and his dark hair dusted with silver.

Stepping up to the bar, he ordered a drink and I caught the flash of his gold watch beneath his sleeve.

He wasn't a good-looking guy, but he wasn't ugly either. More average. Someone who wouldn't be noticed too much by beautiful women. My gaze drifted down to see he wasn't going hungry. The weight of his big stomach was hanging over his pants.

"That guy right there. He didn't come with anyone, and he's just ugly enough to ditch this place for a fine piece like you."

Jackson walked off after pointing out my target. It was best if we weren't seen together.

There were still a few sips in my drink, the ice clinking in my glass when I swallowed them down and stood up to approach the man. He was waiting for his drink as I walked up to ask if the stool next to him was taken. Immediately, his eyes raked down my body like dirty fingers wanting to explore all my feminine parts.

"No, it's not. Have a seat." Eyes still locked to my cleavage, he smiled. "Do you come here often?"

He was talking to my breasts apparently, as if they had wandered in all on their own.

"This is my first time, actually. I'm new to the area."

The man made some weird sucking sound with his tongue and teeth, his brown eyes finally lifting to mine. "Can I buy you a drink?"

I flashed him a forced smile. "A Rum and Coke would be great."

Crossing one leg over the other, I fought the urge to pull my skirt down so it didn't ride up to reveal my panties. The game was to make him want me so much he would walk out the door with me for a quickie against a wall. Flashing the goods was all part of the act. Still, it left me feeling naked and gross.

He ordered my drink and turned back to me. "I'm Sam. What's your name?"

Laughing, I played off the lie. "Oh, how funny. I'm Sam, too. Well, Samantha, but everybody uses the shortened version."

Sam pushed up to sit in the stool next to me. "I think that means we're meant to be." His eyes dipped again, down to my lap this time, his lips parting a touch to see how high my skirt had cinched up.

"Are you here with friends?" I asked, hoping to drag his gaze away from my crotch. I could feel it exploring between my legs, revulsion shivering through me.

"No, actually. I was just stopping by after work to grab a drink. I had no idea I'd be lucky enough to meet someone like you. Seems like fate wanted this to happen."

He was the perfect mark. It was too bad I would throw up for the rest of the night after letting him touch me. Reminding myself there were bills to pay, I leaned forward enough to give him a good money shot of my breasts. His eyes dragged down to them immediately.

The bartender brought us our drinks as we talked. Sam prattled on about his job in finance and how much money he made while I nursed my drink and watched him order one after the other.

It drove me insane listening to people brag about their income. Isn't there something more important in life? A special talent or an interesting hobby that means more than how many zeros were on their paychecks? It made me sad for them that the only claim to fame they had was wealth.

By Sam's third scotch, he felt confident enough to touch me. Not that I'd invited it, but I didn't push him away either. His lumbering hand slid up my thigh, thumb sweeping down to brush the crease where my legs crossed. Continuing his path, he stopped inches away from my panties, his chest moving with heavier breath, his head leaning in so he could kiss me.

I hated this part, and fought the urge to vomit all over him. Playing it off, I opened my lips and allowed his slimy tongue to invade my mouth. He pushed closer, just like I knew he would, not caring that we were in a room full of people.

His right hand swept up the side of my body until his thumb brushed the side of my breast, while his left kept inching higher up my thigh to explore beneath the skirt. Every instinct in me screamed to slap his hands away, but I had to let this happen, had to turn him on enough that the thought of sex short-circuited his rational thinking.

Sam was practically fingering me as his right hand cupped my breast and gave it a squeeze.

Breaking our kiss, I played coy, pressed my palm against his chest and locked my eyes with his. He looked drunk, both from the booze and how easy I'd made myself for him.

With a flirtatious grin, I whispered, "You want me, don't you?"

"More than you know," he answered, his eyes staring at my cleavage as he continued teasing me between the legs.

It took effort to remain calm. All I wanted to do was push him away and run.

"Maybe we should find somewhere private to take this a little further? What do you think?"

"Like a hotel room?"

I laughed. *Not a chance, buddy.* "I was thinking against a wall outside. I'm not sure I can wait."

Many men would scoff at the idea, demand the hotel room, or wonder about the type of girl who would so easily drop her panties in public. But men like this, the ones willing to paw at me while surrounded by strangers, they had no issue with the thought of a quick screw in an alley, which made them the perfect target.

Sam made that weird sucking sound with his mouth again, and I bit my tongue to keep from telling him how gross it was.

"Yeah, let me settle the tab, and then we'll go have some fun."

It wasn't going to be fun for either of us, but I kept that thought to myself. Ben and Jackson wouldn't wait too long once I got the guy back in the shadows. I would only have to endure a few seconds of his pawing hands before I could run off, jump in the car and head home. After that I would take a steaming hot shower to scald Sam's touch off my skin.

While he paid, I scanned the room. Nobody was paying us any attention from what I could see, which was a good thing.

I'd only been inside for a little over two hours, so I'd be home in time to get enough sleep for class tomorrow. As far as schemes went, this one was moving along as smoothly as I could hope.

76

Sam grabbed my arm, a bruising hold as he tucked his wallet in his back pocket and practically dragged me from the stool. Calling him eager would be an understatement. One glance at his pants and I could see he was already ready and raring to go.

As we slipped through the crowd, he pressed his chest to my back to whisper in my ear.

"I'm going to fuck your pussy hard. You have no idea what I can do for you. I'll have to cover your mouth to keep you from screaming my name so loud everybody inside hears us."

I highly doubted that, but I smiled and played along despite how sick I felt. Five more minutes tops and I would be running away from him.

Hand still gripping my arm, he shoved the entry doors open and directed me outside. We turned right, my heels clicking quickly over the pavement en route to the alley. Scanning the bushes, I couldn't see Ben or Jackson, but I knew they were hidden somewhere.

My breath was a shallow beat, my heart pulsing in my throat as Sam and I turned into the alley and kept walking until we were drenched in shadow.

He didn't waste a second to spin me and shove me face first against the wall, one hand lifting my skirt while the other reached around to palm my breast. A little too eager, he didn't seem to care about working up to fucking with a little foreplay. He also didn't seem to care that my face was being scraped against the bricks.

Sam flicked aside my panties, running a thick finger up my slit, not caring that I was asking him to go slower.

"Hey, don't you think we should -"

"Shut up. You know you want this."

Several times, I tried to move my hips away, not wanting him to shove that finger inside. I might act like a slut, but really I was just a tease. I'd never had a real boyfriend, had never slept with anybody, and didn't want my first time to be with some strange guy in a dirty alley.

Pressing my forehead to the wall, tears ran down my cheeks just before the sound of running feet came toward us.

One punch and Sam was knocked off me. I didn't bother to look back. With tears still streaming, I ignored the fight occurring behind me as I pulled my skirt into place to run off.

CHAPTER SEVEN

I'm not sure if you've ever known love, but I hope you will. Then you might understand what I've done. I'm empty inside. Cold. Quiet. A hush of wind replacing the melody that sang me to sleep each night...

Lennon

"This place is so beautiful. It must be nice living large, Lennon. You'll have to come down and see us more often so we can live large with you."

Renee nudged my shoulder with her own, her dark eyes twinkling with humor as she lifted her wine glass from the bar top to follow Dizzy and me to a back table. She hadn't changed in the ten years since I'd seen her last. Still tiny, she wore her hair in the same sleek style, her face still bright as ever despite the passage of years. Dizzy and her were made for each other, their love story beginning in junior year when they met.

Sliding into the round booth corner table, I took in the environment. Majori's was one of those places most people preferred, but to me, it was just another overpriced establishment that tried too hard to appear eclectic, the trendiness wearing on me until I wanted to run screaming to a hole in the wall bar to peer through thick smoke at whatever jazz or blues band was playing that night.

If it were up to me, I'd be tucked away elsewhere with a cold beer in hand, lost to shadows while enjoying a place that wasn't pretending to be something it wasn't. But Renee had wanted the glitz and glamour - a break from her life in Sheldon. I was all to happy to oblige whatever she wanted.

"So, you took off so quick back at the store that you didn't tell me why you're in town."

Dizzy watched me, his long fingers spinning his drink over the surface of the table as he spoke.

Flashing him a tight smile, I continued scanning my eyes over the crowd, taking in the men in their flashy suits and the women who clung on their arms. "Hastings hosted its summer program in Tampa this year. I'm one of the two teachers who will be selecting the scholarship student."

Sinatra crooned from the speakers above our heads, lights dancing over the crowd as I turned to look at him and Renee. "Hastings asked that I teach this particular class since I'm originally from the area."

My best friend knew me too well. "You didn't want to come back, did you?"

I tapped my thumb against the side of my glass, the condensation cool against my skin. "You know how it is. Memories suck. But," I sighed relaxing back in my seat, "I can't run from them forever."

Nodding, Dizzy's eyes met mine, understanding softening the rims. He turned to Renee, bumped her shoulder with his. "Did I ever tell you how this ugly son of a bitch and I became friends?"

Renee's lip curled into a smile, her eyes rolling. "Only about a thousand times. I've heard it so much, I could tell it like I was there."

In fourth grade, Dizzy and I had bonded over our unfortunate names. Charles Jennison loved Jazz, and had stolen the name of one of his favorite musicians to hand it over to his son. My father was a Beatles fan, stealing away a last name for my moniker.

80

The teacher had called role that first morning in class and we'd looked at each other and laughed. We were inseparable from that moment on, spending the majority of our days running the streets or tucked away in the music store learning all there was to know about the instruments. My focus had always been on piano, but that didn't mean I couldn't play brass or strum a guitar. We made short work of whatever we could get our hands on.

Sliding my glass across the table, I clinked it against Dizzy's. "Did you know I was almost mugged in your parking lot the other day?"

His eyes snapped to mine, concern tightening his lips. "Are you fucking with me?"

Laughter crawled up my throat. "No. I got my wallet back, so don't worry, but the girl who attempted to lift it ended up being a student in my class."

"What?" Dizzy shook his head. "Did you boot her on day one?"

Taking a sip of my drink, I grinned. "I would have loved to. The only problem is she's one of the best students in my class." A fucking knockout as well, but I kept the thought to myself. "Her parents are James and Lila Dillon."

Dizzy's brows knit together, recognition setting in. "Ah, hell. They taught your sister, didn't they?"

"They did."

"Then what was their daughter doing in Sheldon? I remember them living in that gated community, Tropical Isle, or whatever it was called."

The same question had floated across my thoughts as soon as Amelia admitted where she'd learned to play. The Dillons were well off when Emaline learned the piano, my parents making the forty minute drive twice a week for her lessons.

"I have no idea. Amelia's not perfect, in her music or her behavior. She needs a good teacher and a lot of discipline, but I think she has the potential to become a star."

Dizzy sat back. "Well, if anybody can teach her, it's you. I know you can be a hard ass when it comes to music."

I could be a hard ass in many ways, but not all of them could apply to a young girl who was ten years younger than me. Her age alone should have been a deterrent, but she was also a student. In every way, she was dangerous.

Still, it bothered me that I couldn't get Amelia off my mind. So much so that when I glanced out through the crowd, I refused to believe I saw her coming through the front doors and heading to the bar. She was too young to drink, and the dress the woman wore should have been illegal.

It had to be my imagination, exhaustion wearing on me from being back near my hometown. I blinked my eyes to clear the image of her from my head, but when I looked at her again, I recognized her timid, teal eyes scanning quickly over the crowded bar.

What the hell?

My head had to be playing tricks on me, a symptom of obsessive thoughts about a girl who I couldn't touch. Yet, there she sat, her legs crossed, her tits practically falling out of the dress. The bartender slid a drink her direction and she smiled before picking it up.

Obviously nervous, she took a sip and kept her head down, the length of her dark hair shielding her face.

Renee and Dizzy were talking about something, their laughter mingling with the din of conversation and music blasting from the speakers.

Had Amelia come here to drink alone? I hadn't pegged her for the type, but what did I know? The only conversations I had with her were antagonistic and short. What I did know is that I wanted to rip the eyes out of every man who looked at her like a piece of meat, while also joining those same men in appreciating her curves in a dress that was no more than a tiny scrap of cloth.

Her body was built for sin despite the way she played the piano like a damn angel. I was about five seconds away from storming across the room toward her so I could wrap my jacket across her shoulders and shield her from view.

"Lennon. Hey, did we lose you?"

Tearing my eyes from her, I glanced back at Dizzy. "Sorry, I thought I saw someone I knew."

While Dizzy launched into a story about the students he taught, my eyes kept sneaking back to Amelia. She remained in her seat for twenty minutes with nobody to talk to. Nursing her drink, she kept tossing hesitant peeks across the room, her eyes almost spotting me before I turned my head to hide my face.

Nodding at what Dizzy said, I barely heard a single word, my focus fixated on a girl who had no business being here. Looking back, I stilled to see a tall guy whispering into her ear.

Dressed head to toe in black, he made a quick comment before Amelia's eyes drifted right at another man approaching the bar. Standing from her seat, she moved closer to the second man while the first took off to leave the bar.

Granted, I hadn't known her long enough to guess the type of guy she usually went for, but I hoped she would be more interested in a man like me than a pudgy businessman who looked old enough to be her father. To each their own, but something about this was rubbing me the wrong way.

"Lennon-"

Returning my attention to Dizzy, I couldn't ignore the need to watch her, my eyes continuously drifting right while I struggled to listen to what my friend had to say. Losing the battle, my focus was on Amelia again, my gaze arrowing directly to where the man ran his grubby hand up her naked thigh.

Bristling to see him touch her, my hand clenched around my drink. There was no way in hell she was enjoying it. A quick check of her tight expression only proved I was right. Normally when a woman wanted sex, her eyes become soft, her shoulders relax and her mouth is an easy, sultry smile. Yet to look at Amelia, you'd believe she was in a dentist's chair or being led to the executioner.

Tension bled from her with painful rigidity, her eyes clenching every time the man's hand inched higher up her thigh. Color draining from her face, she allowed him to reach up and caress the side of her breast, casually leaning away from him rather than pressing forward into the touch.

Rage flooded me when I finally understood what I was seeing. It wasn't hard to pick up on the subtle nuances, the inconsistencies that painted the picture of a young girl being used, her pimp pointing out her next customer. What the fuck was going on that she would have to resort to this for money?

From what I knew her parents were well off, but I knew her mother had died. Eleven years ago, if I wasn't mistaken, her father taking over my sister's lessons once Lila could no longer teach.

The second the man's lips touched hers, my jaw ticked and I fought not to jump from my seat. How many times has she done this? Was she even doing it willingly? Who the fuck was that asshole who'd pointed her in the other guy's direction?

The man paid for their drinks and they stood up, his hand gripping her arm like she was a possession to be used more than a young woman. There was no way in hell I could let him leave with her.

Tapping my hand on the table, I excused myself. "I'm going to hit the bathroom real quick. I'll be right back."

Shooting me a funny look, Dizzy grinned. "We'll be here."

I was out of my seat before he could finish speaking. Working my way through the crowd, I felt like a stalker prowling after Amelia, but I had to see where she was going, had to know if she was selling her body.

Slipping out the front doors, I ignored the wave of humid heat that assaulted me, my eyes scanning the dark parking lot until I noticed movement to my right.

My head snapped in their direction just as they turned to walk down a side alley. It only pissed me off more to think she would *service* that guy right next to the dumpsters.

I wasn't just going to redden her ass, I was going to make sure that she couldn't sit down for a week without thinking of me and my demand she stop doing stupid crap.

Boots thudding against the pavement, I marched in the direction of the alley, my hands fisted at my sides and the muscle in my jaw leaping with the clench of my teeth. I turned just in time to watch Mr. Pudgy shove Amelia against a brick wall to lift her skirt. It disgusted me to see her treated so poorly, to see her allowing anyone to shove her around like she wasn't worth an ounce of respect.

Taking one step into the alley with the intent to teach the son of a bitch manners, I was beaten to the punch by two thugs in black hoodies. Literally. Both of them jumped the guy while Amelia dodged right to pull her skirt over her ass and head in my direction. So busy looking back at the man being mugged, she didn't notice I was standing in her path until she was right up on me.

My fingers locked over the back of her neck, a startled squeak volleying from her throat as she struggled to break free of my hold. Our eyes met, mine swimming with a maelstrom of conflicting emotions, while hers widened with shock, understanding sinking in quickly that I'd just caught her involved in yet another crime.

"Mr. Carter, I-"

The excuse fizzled like a deflating balloon, the truth of what she was doing clearly evident from the ongoing beat down still occurring at the other end of the alley. Leaning down to growl against her ear, I ordered, "Walk back to the front of the bar and wait for me. If you are not there when I return, you can forget about returning to class tomorrow. Understand me?"

Her voice was a terrified whisper. "What are you going to do?"

It took effort to unlock my fingers from her neck so she could go. "Do as I say. Now."

Stalking off, she cast me a worried look over her shoulder, her heels clicking over the ground in her retreat.

It wasn't that I felt sorry for the guy who'd thought he could use Amelia for sex. Maybe he deserved the beating he was getting. Still, I couldn't leave him there to get killed. "Hey!"

My voice caused both of his attackers to turn toward me, the hood having fallen from the head of one, his face knocking me back into a past I was still running from. A punch to the chest, that face, the features ones I swore to never forget should our paths cross again. A renewed wave of rage tore through me.

I hadn't seen him since before my sister died, but every detail of his face was still clear in my mind. The promise of revenge rolled through me, the day finally coming when I could get even with the asshole who had broken Emaline's heart.

"Come here."

Not that they would listen. Instead they took off running in the opposite direction, my legs pounding beneath me as I chased them into an open parking lot, dodging cars to catch up.

Unlike Amelia, they both were faster than me, their agility making it easy for them to lose me within seconds. I was left spinning in circles, my eyes narrowed on shadows, the blood rushing from my fingers from the strength of my fists.

"Fuck!"

The one word echoed over the empty lot, my booted steps heavy as I returned to the man now lying in the alley with blood pouring from his nose and multiple cuts in his face.

Crouching beside him, I shook him by the shoulder. "You okay?"

"Those fuckers took everything. My phone, my wallet, my keys."

He looked like he was going to cry. I didn't feel sorry for him. It served him right since he thought he could treat a woman like she was nothing but a piece of meat.

"I'll have the bar call the cops for you, as well as an ambulance. Do you need help getting up?"

Shaking his head, he sat up and leaned back against the wall. I didn't want to add insult to injury given that the guy would be hurting for a few weeks to come, but it had to be said.

"Remember this the next time you want to take a young girl into an alley for an easy fuck. You wouldn't be here right now if you'd kept your hands to yourself."

Struggling to open his swelling eyes, he attempted to glare at me.

I pushed to my feet and walked away to find Amelia waiting where I told her to be. Her arms were crossed over her chest, mascara dripping down her cheeks with each fat tear. Ignoring her long enough to tell the bouncer to call the cops about the man mugged in the alley, I wrapped my hand over the back of her neck to lead her to my car.

"Where are we going?"

"Away from here."

"That doesn't answer my question."

Grinning, I did give much of a fuck to answer anything. "You're not exactly in a position to be demand information at the moment."

No. If anybody was going to do that, it was me. But only in the privacy of my car. Where we would go from here? I hadn't gotten that far in my thinking, but I knew it would be someplace where I would be the one demanding answers.

Unlocking my door, I stepped aside and motioned for her to climb in. "Get in the car, Amelia."

Eyes narrowed on my face, she scowled and stepped back as if to run.

"I wouldn't try it. As we already know, I'm faster than you, and you won't get very far in your stripper heels. Don't try me right now. Just get in the fucking car."

"Where are you taking me?"

The truth was I had no idea. "Get in."

With another huff, she finally did as I said and climbed into the Escalade. I tried to ignore the way her ass cheeks peeked out from beneath her skirt, had to grab the leg of my pants to keep from reaching forward to tug the dress down the backs of her thighs. Or, hell, shove it up higher.

Slamming the door, I managed to do neither, my stride quick as I rounded the back en route to the driver's seat.

Once we were both seated inside, I bit the inside of my cheek to keep from yelling at her.

The engine roared to life, the wheels giving a little squeak over the pavement when backing out. Tool blasted through the speakers - a wall of music preventing me from immediately interrogating her.

It wasn't until we were on the road that I remembered Dizzy and Renee. Thankfully they'd driven their car and weren't stranded because of a stupid little girl who was in serious need of an attitude readjustment.

Waiting until we reached a light, I tapped out a quick text to Dizzy telling him something came up and I had to dip. I didn't wait for a response before shoving my phone in my pocket and turning to glare at my hostage.

Amelia sat hunched over in her seat, arms crossed over her chest and her skirt riding up her lap a little too far to be comfortable. It was an unwelcome distraction, one I forced myself to ignore so I could drive.

I was caught between wanting to take her over my lap and teach her why pretty girls shouldn't be committing back alley crimes, and pulling the damn car over to lock my hand over her throat while demanding the name of the two punks she was working with.

One of them had led to my sister's death. One of them was the nameless face I'd been hoping to see again for ten long years.

Taking a deep breath, I regained control of myself with the intention of keeping her with me until all my questions were answered.

I turned down the music and waited for her to look at me, her timid eyes slowly sliding my direction as she sat shivering in her seat.

Grinning to have her full attention, I asked, "Do you want to tell me what happened back there? Or would you prefer I take an educated guess?"

CHAPTER EIGHT

The hands can punish and they can soothe. They can create and destroy. They can take and give. Our actions define us. And because we act through our hands, they too define a person...

Amelia

Kissing Sam had made me sick. I didn't know if it was the scrape of his fingers up my legs that caused my stomach to roll, or the bucketfuls slobber he dumped in my mouth as if he were bailing out a sinking ship.

It could have been the suffocating scent of his cologne, or maybe just my nerves for what I knew would happen to him. By the time we'd walked out of the bar and into the shadow of the alley, bile crawled up my throat, an acidic taste that choked me while my forehead was scraped against the rough brick wall.

In the moment when my skirt was lifted up above my ass and Sam's scrambling, greedy fingers dug between my legs like a desperate miner looking for that last nugget of gold, I had actually believed nothing that happened tonight could be much worse.

The relief had been so sudden when Ben and Jackson stepped in, I was able to take a full breath and swallow down the knot of revulsion. Guilt stepped in to dance with that relief because Sam hadn't done anything I hadn't invited him to do; still, I felt it. It was like coming up for air to walk away, like finally kicking my feet hard enough to reach the surface of turbulent water only to discover I'd breached in the eye wall of a hurricane.

My heart jumped into my throat at the moment my eyes locked with Mr. Carter's. It stayed there for a split second. The fight faded away behind me. The world's rotation stopped. And my heart pulsed one last frantic beat before dropping into place inside my chest, beaten and bruised, to flat-line the instant he wrapped his hand over the back of my neck.

One moment, I'd believed my night couldn't get much worse, and in the next I learned why it was foolish to tempt that fat bastard called fate.

"I asked you a question, Amelia. I highly recommend you start talking. Otherwise, I'm going to continue believing that I just watched you set a man up to be mugged."

His voice was calm. Too calm. And he wasn't wrong. That's exactly what I'd done.

That calm voice became a dark croon, the gentle tone somehow violent. "But you wouldn't do that, right? Not after what happened between us in an alley? Certainly not while knowing that if anything went wrong, you were risking losing your spot in the program."

Damn red lights. They kept happening at the most inconvenient times. Now Mr. Carter wasn't just talking to me, he was burning holes in the side of my head with murderous eyes.

Maybe not murderous. More seething. A stare that promised expulsion from the scholarship program as well as who knows what else.

"Where are we going?"

"To a place where I can ask you a bunch of questions."

I was barely whispering, my voice shaking as thoroughly as my body. "You can ask me questions here."

He grinned, but I was too scared to look at him fully. Instead, I watched him in my peripheral vision.

"Here won't work. I'll run out of gas before I'm done."

I glanced at his gauges. "The tank is full."

"Exactly."

The light turned green and the SUV lurched forward, silence settling in between us. I'd preferred the loud music from earlier to the deafening lack of sound now.

At first I thought he was driving around aimlessly and without a specific destination in mind, and maybe he was. The turns didn't make sense, more like large circles around the city.

Eventually, Mr. Carter blew out a heavy sigh, glanced at me and back to the road. His hand clutched over the wheel as he made a hard left, and hit the gas with enough force that my body rocked against the seat, the tension between us suffocating.

"Where are we going?"

"To my house."

"What? No. I need to go back to the bar. My car is there." Ben would be worried and pissed if I didn't get back to the house.

"I'll take you to your car when we're done."

"Done what? I need to get home and go to sleep. I have class tomorrow morning."

"Do you?" He turned his head to look at me, eyes dancing with emotions I didn't know and couldn't understand.

Shifting in my seat to stare back at him, I was practically begging him not to expel me. "I deserve to be in that program. You can't force me out over this."

Eyes back to the road, a river of light and shadow flowed over his skin from the passing streetlamps. "Actually, I can. The students who continue forward are entirely up to me, and I'm not sure I want to recommend a criminal for the scholarship."

Terrified that he would make good on his threat, my eyes watered with stinging tears. Blinking didn't help stop them, the hot, wet traitors rolling down my cheeks, slow rivulets revealing my loss of control.

"Please don't do this." I'd been reduced to begging, every emotion inside me welling up until I was drowning.

He was silent as we pulled into the driveway of a large house, the tires bouncing over unleveled ground. Pulling to a stop, Mr. Carter didn't move to get out of the car, didn't bother to look at me.

"Please," I said again, "I need that scholarship. I deserve it."

It was too thick, the silence, too abrasive and cold. My skin crawled as it stretched and solidified, darkness swallowing the space between us while the blaze of headlights illuminated a garage door.

Fingers drumming slowly on the steering wheel, Mr. Carter bowed his head, his eyes closing as his fingers slowed to a stop and gripped the wheel as if to strangle it.

On a bare whisper, he spoke without looking at me, his eyes shut, his jaw tight with indecision. "You have no idea how much I like that word on your lips. No fucking clue."

A shiver twined around my spine at the admission, whether in fear or surprise I wasn't sure. I was uncertain and confused, a thousand competing thoughts racing through me with such force that it held me in place. What word?

Say please...

Like a ghost, the memory was there and gone, a word he'd demanded when we first met, a word I was shamelessly tossing at him now.

Without speaking again, he opened his door, exited the SUV, and slammed the door before knocking on the window, motioning for me to follow. I watched his back as he walked a stone path that led around the side of the house and out of sight.

I had no choice but to follow. What was I going to do? Sit in the truck all night? I thought about it, considered it, rolled it around as a viable option until Lennon appeared at the bend in the path, his face masked in shadow, his shoulders high and tight.

He didn't to make the threat for me to know he would drag me from my seat if I didn't willfully follow.

One click, and the seatbelt unlocked, a soft whir as it rolled up at my side, the interior of the SUV bathed in light as I opened the door and climbed down from my seat. The night was muggy and damp and yet I was shivering in my barely there dress, the feeling of exposure consuming me.

97

Perhaps Mr. Carter felt the same. As soon as I stepped up to him, he stripped the patterned jacket from his shoulders and handed it to me. I didn't argue, quietly slipping it on as we walked along the path, the scent of his cologne hugging me in its tight embrace. It was unfair how much the scent affected me, a tangle of earthy, masculine notes that were seductive and subtle.

When he led me inside, I froze in place to see a kitchen that was three times the size of my living room. The appliances gleamed beneath low recessed lighting, a center island of white carved cabinets with a black stone top dominating the space. Pendant lights hung down from the ceiling, the glass shades an Art Deco design in red, black and white that cast an eerie glow..

We crossed over black marble floors that transitioned to a deep cherry wood, the click of my heels the only sound breaking the silence. Led into a living room with vaulted ceilings and a stone fireplace that I could have easily camped inside, I was directed to sit on a leather couch while he took a seat on the bench of a gorgeous Steinway grand piano in black.

It was intimidating to be in his private space. In the classroom, I took comfort in the students that acted as a buffer. In a way, they blocked him from consuming the space around me, from siphoning my power away merely by looking at me.

Here, I had no such buffer, the quiet calm between us pregnant with possibility.

With legs spread slightly, Mr. Carter rested his elbows on his knees, his shoulders hunched and head lifting to look at me. "Start talking."

I fingered the fabric of his jacket, my nerves on edge. "About?"

"About what I witnessed back at the bar."

Too gorgeous for words, he locked his blue eyes with mine, his dark hair a disheveled mess around his head, the sleeves of his white button down shirt rolled up to his elbows. My gaze traced the muscle in his forearms, the bones of his strong hands. It still surprised me that he could elicit such tempting music with the softest touch.

"I was out for a drink and met someone." A lie, bold faced and unconvincing, but it was all I would give him. Admitting the truth would only implicate my brother and me, would threaten the tenuous hold we had on our house and our ability to care for our dad.

A single brow arched above his eyes. "Not only are you a terrible thief, you're a horrible liar. Let's try this again. Who were the two men who were with you?"

My hand fisted the jacket. "No clue. They just came out of nowhere. I was worried they would -"

"You have one more chance," he interrupted, "before I bend you over my knee and make good on my earlier threats."

Pulse fluttering, I shook my head. "You can't do that."

"That's your choice. Either tell me what I want to know, or choose the punishment. I'm not playing with you, Amelia. I want to know what happened tonight. Who were the two guys with you?"

Dizziness assaulted me, the room wavering out of focus, my stomach rolling left, then right. Mr. Carter wouldn't actually -

Swallowing hard, I thought he might.

Still, I couldn't say a word. He would turn us in, expel me from the program, and then everything would fall apart. "You wouldn't do that."

"Try me." Pausing, he flexed his hand where it hung between his knees. "Who are they?"

In the distance, a grandfather clocked played through its haunting melody, the hours counted down by the slam of hammers against the chimes. By the time the tenth hour was counted, a hollow echo of sound was left floating in the room. I shook my head, refusing to answer.

"Come here."

"Mr. Carter, this is ridiculous. I'm not-"

"I said come here. Don't make me say it again."

I felt tugged forward by his controlled tone, my body reacting while my mind still fought that this was happening. I wasn't a child. Spankings weren't something done to women my age.

On trembling legs, I stood and crossed the room slowly, his eyes refusing to release mine. He waited until I was within arm's reach to crane his neck and repeat my options.

"I told you it was your choice." Straightening is posture, he said, "Tell me who they were or lay your body over my lap to be disciplined."

"This is insane." My voice was barely a whisper.

"You don't know the half of it. Now choose."

I could leave. It wasn't like he could hold me captive. What would he do if I just turned around and walked out?

He'd expel me from the program, and with the information he already had on me, with what he'd already seen me do, any rules I could turn to about interactions between student and teacher would be tossed out a window. Sure, he'd be replaced by someone else, but it wasn't like he needed the job.

The only person who needed to stay there was me.

Stepping forward, I held my breath and lined my body up at the side of his lap. Lennon's eyes watched me closely, his mouth a tight line. With a huff of indignant breath, I lowered myself down to lie across his lap, my breasts hanging over the right leg as my ass hung over the left.

A twitch of the muscle in his thigh was his only response for several seconds, a heavy breath expelled above me before his fingertips ran up the back of my thigh to lift my skirt above my hips.

Blood rushed to my head, my body trembling with fear of the pain, embarrassment for the exposure, and anticipation of his touch.

"Say please."

I swallowed, tears already welling in my eyes. "Please."

The first strike was a sharp clap of sound tearing through the room, my body, jolting forward as fire spread across my skin. I bit my lip, tears dripping down to the floor beneath me, a heavy exhalation of breath bursting from my chest. Disbelief raced through me to dance with the pain his hand had inflicted.

"Will you tell me who they were now?" His voice was gritty and dark, so controlled that it forced shivers up my spine.

101

Shaking my head, I clenched my eyes shut and refused.

As I struggled to remember how to breathe again, he rubbed his palm over the sore skin, pulling it away before repeating, "Say please."

My body quaked, everything inside me refusing what was happening, a tidal wave rushing with such speed that I couldn't see straight, couldn't think. Despite it all, the word slipped free. "Please."

Another strike on the opposite cheek and my mouth opened on a silent cry, the sound trapped in my throat, my eyes wide.

Endorphins flooded my veins, the room spinning. This wasn't happening. This couldn't be happening. Except, it was, and as my tears continued to pour down my face, a surge of emotions coursed through me, like a floodgate had been opened and all the stress and heartache I carried came pouring out.

"Will you tell me now?"

I shook my head, refusing.

His warm palm rubbed the spot he'd struck. "Say please."

The tears wouldn't stop. "Please."

A strike against the crease where my ass met my thigh and suddenly my head was too heavy, my body melting over his lap.

Warmth bloomed through me, expanding until I swore my skin blushed pink. I released a tremulous breath.

"Last chance before I give you three more strikes, Amelia. Tell me who they were."

My hands splayed over the floor beneath my head. "I can't."

He didn't make me say please again, his palm delivering three more strikes, each one harder than the other, a crescendo of sensation firing across every nerve ending until I was left helpless and shaking.

I couldn't have shoved away if I'd wanted. Every muscle was weak, my thoughts chaotic.

Several seconds passed, the beat of time a slow crawl while my mind caught up to understand what had just happened.

It was like I was floating in some weightless place, my body trembling while a need surged through me that was foreign and unrecognizable. Warmth spread through my muscles, my lungs erratic in their attempt to draw in enough air.

For some reason, I didn't want him to stop.

Mr. Carter's voice was soft when he said, "Sit up."

My arms and legs wouldn't cooperate, but somehow Mr. Carter was able to help me up, turning me to cradle my shivering body over his lap and against his chest. Fingers gripping the material of his shirt, I submitted to the intensity of emotions ravaging me, my breath coming out on a tremulous shudder.

It was so cold except for the heat of his strong body, the silence between us soothing me until my eyes closed in need of sleep. With a gentle stroke, he rubbed my back, the beat of his heart a rhythmic thump against my ear.

Cheek pressed to the top of my head, he spoke, the words disembodied as if I were dreaming. "You have no idea how dangerous you are for me."

Lips against my forehead, his breath was warm against my skin as he brushed the hair from my face.

"Did you like it?"

Unsure if he'd actually asked the question, I nodded my head, the admission surprising me.

I felt weightless, the experience an odd release, all my problems, the hell that was my life, gone while he held me.

"Damn it," he whispered, his arms tightening over my body as he stood from the bench and carried me to the couch. Lying down beside me, he kept me cradled to him, his scent, his heat, his quiet strength surrounding me.

Without thinking, I ran my fingertips up the broad plane of his chest, indulging in the hard ridge of his collar bone, the warmth against my palm as my fingers slid through his hair to wrap around the back of his neck.

Arms tugging me close, Lennon breathed deeply, his shoulders becoming rigid when I tilted my head to kiss the line of his jaw, a teasing brush of my lips over the rough stubble of his skin. I didn't know what possessed me to do it, didn't know why I pressed closer to him and trembled to feel the hard length of his erection against my leg.

This wasn't right.

"Amelia."

A gritty warning, his fingertips trailing down my spine.

"We can't-"

The sentence hug open-ended, his head turning until our mouths were a tempting inch apart. What was I doing? This was my teacher, my mentor, the man who could change his mind tomorrow and shove me away, destroying my dream of becoming a musician in the process.

It was stupid of me to tempt fate.

Still, I wanted to know what it was like to kiss him, wanted to experience his hands play over me with the same tender touch he used when stroking the keys.

It was the first time in my life that I'd ever wanted a man to touch me.

"Dangerous," he whispered.

Lennon's mouth brushed across mine, our breath mingling, the tease of a kiss hovering on my lips until he pressed down again and flicked his tongue against mine.

"Please," I whispered against his lips, not understanding what I was asking for...or even *why* I was asking.

CHAPTER NINE

I don't know what happened. He was there and then gone. Hot and then cold. He woke me up to know what it meant to hear another person's song, so that it could bleed from my fingers onto the keys...

Lennon

Middle C.

An innocuous note when played; however its importance is tantamount to the dance between the treble and bass clefs.

It's the first note we're taught when learning the keys, the dividing line between what our left hand is doing as opposed to our right.

Standing in the absolute center, it is the precise point between what I view as male and female, the median that separates the harmonious or discordant steps of the dance. It is the precipice I always shuffle back to when the music inside me stops. It is a rest giving me a single moment to gather my breath, to decide whether to give up or move on.

Amelia had pinned me at Middle C, the prelude coming to a halt, the music silent with the question of whether I would venture forward into a flurry of decadent and obscene notes, or pull back and rip my hands from the keys.

She'd learned the one word that could undo my tenuous hold on control, and the only person who could be blamed for teaching it to her was me.

107

Our mouths hovered an inch apart, our lips brushing softly as my fingers curled against her back. Closing my eyes, I fought to remember that she was off limits, a student, a young girl, a thief.

Already, I'd lost ground.

Yes, I'd made it a bad habit to threaten to spank her ass. But to do it? That had crossed dangerous lines, pushing me too many steps forward into a mess of a situation.

I'd lost control, my anger causing me to act in ways that went against rational thought.

Who were those guys with her tonight? And why would she take being spanked over telling me their names? Just the thought of it caused my blood to rush to my head, my pulse to pound like rolling thunder.

I had to know. *Had* to, if for no other reason than to know the identity of a man who had played a part in my sister's death.

That thought alone sobered me before I could take this moment further, driving me to a point where I wasn't sure I wouldn't take it out on Amelia's body.

Middle C.

What the fuck was I doing?

"No."

Pushing away from her, I shoved to my feet, backing away as if the distance would set everything to right, as if it could stop me from giving in to what my body demanded of the girl staring up at me with confusion in her eyes.

"I need to take you home."

Pacing away, I stabbed my hand through my hair, trying to make sense of what I'd done. None of it made sense. This couldn't happen. Not again. Not when her future was hanging on the line.

The one thing I was bitching that she needed to protect and here I was threatening it just as much, if not more so, than her back alley schemes.

When I spun back, she was pushing herself up into a sitting position, a wince tightening her features when the skin of her ass met the couch.

Good. I hoped she felt that because it was becoming clear as fucking day that her parents had missed a few opportunities to tan her ass red. If anything, she wouldn't forget me for the next day, at least. Not with my handprint painted all over her taut skin.

"Did I do something wrong?" A faint whisper, her voice wavering with shame.

"You've done a lot of shit wrong, but what just occurred on that couch wasn't part of it. Everything that's happened since we entered this house is on me."

"Fuck." The word hissed over my lips. "I should never have brought you here."

How stupid could I be? How reckless and blindly arrogant? If Hastings found out about any of this, her chance at the scholarship would be stripped away. It didn't matter that they would fire me immediately; I had a career to fall back on. But Amelia? She would be escorted out of there without another word.

Grabbing my keys from the piano, I stalked toward the kitchen. "Get up. We're leaving before this goes any further."

I hadn't forgotten that she had more questions to answer, but I'd painted myself into a corner by spanking her ass.

It would take time to get the information out of her. For now, I needed to get her home, to her car, *wherever*, just so the threat that I might turn around and make good on my desire to fuck her would be a fantasy in my head rather than a blatant mistake I'd have to answer for later.

Amelia was too much of a temptation, only making it worse by admitting she liked what I had done.

"Let's go."

"Lennon-"

"It's Mr. Carter." I spun on my heel to face her. "Get up. We're leaving."

Doused in confusion, Amelia peeled her body off the couch, following me with the *click click click* of a set of heels that captured my attention.

The drive back to Majori's was absent the indecision, aimless turns and meandering roads I'd taken to get to my house. A straight shot, I managed to keep my eye on the brake lights and traffic signals in front of me rather than give in to the allure of Amelia's too-short skirt.

Beside me, she was silent, her head bowed and her hands gripping the sides of my jacket to hold it closed. A better man would have consoled her, would have explained the sudden shift in mood, the distance placed.

After roughly twenty minutes of sticky, tense silence, we pulled into the parking lot. Majori's was still open, the interior flooded with light and people, music filtering out when a man opened the door to walk inside.

"Where's your car?"

"Around the corner." She lifted her hand to indicate a shadowed slot, so far out of the way that it only served to aggravate me further.

"You know, it's not safe for a woman to park where a person can hide in wait of her."

Then again, the most dangerous people who'd been here tonight were apparently her friends.

Pulling up beside the beat down, black Civic, I threw the SUV into park but kept the engine idling. "Are you going to tell me who your friends were?"

Amelia fidgeted in her seat and turned her head toward the passenger window so I could only see the line of her jaw. "Wasn't planning on it."

Clipped and tight, her tone gave away exactly what she was feeling.

"You're upset."

She didn't answer, her fingers playing over the fabric of my jacket.

I leaned my head against the seat. "Where are your keys?"

"In a magnetic box above the back tire."

For fuck's sake...

"So anybody could be in your car right now? Hiding out in the back seat just waiting for a stupid little girl to climb inside to be subdued?"

Head snapping my direction, she scowled. "Why do you care? If anybody was trying to subdue me, it seems to me that's already happened. Or do you not remember laying me over your lap to spank me?"

I remembered it. In excruciating detail. The curve of her ass, the pale flesh that highlighted every mark I'd made on her, the sharp clap of skin on skin echoing across the room. *Please*, a harmonic note rolling over her lips, driving me closer to a dangerous edge each time she said it.

Opening my door, I rounded the SUV to approach her car. The magnetic box was above the rear tire just as she said, plucking at my last nerve. A quick glance and I knew the back seat was empty. Still, I unlocked her car and checked every shadowed corner to make sure nobody was hiding in wait.

"What are you doing?"

"Checking to make sure nobody besides me realized you're the easiest prey known to man."

I turned to her, tossed the key her direction, and stepped aside so she could climb down from her seat and into her car. "Drive carefully."

Those damn heels clicked against the concrete, her neck craning as we stood facing each other in the deep shadow of the parking lot. Neither of us spoke, moved, hell, breathed in the still silence of our parting.

Amelia was the first to move. Shrugging off my jacket, she handed it to me.

I shook my head, refusing it. "You should keep it. At least until you get home and find some actual clothes to wear."

So heavy, the look in her eyes. "I can't. If I take it home-"

Her voice quieted, the words she hadn't spoken driving a hot spear of rage down my spine.

Familiar, that fury, a face from the past resurfacing, trapping me beneath the weight of what I'd lost because of him. Just the thought that he had his hands on Amelia, too, locked the muscles in my jaw. Was it the man in the alley that she would to rush home to?

"Tell me you're not dating that guy from the alley. The one who's name you refuse to give me."

A slight uptick at the corner of her lips. "No. He's not-" Sighing, she shoved the jacket against my chest. "Just take this so I can go."

Careful not to brush her hand, I accepted the jacket and folded it over my arm. Just turn and go, I told myself. Leave before she can draw you back in. She was an event horizon like no other.

A point of no return.

The breeze that blew past us rustled her hair, dark silk blowing over her shoulder. My hand moved as if separate of my thoughts, my fingers trapping her chin to lift her face up to mine.

Amelia stilled in place, lips slightly parted, teal eyes wide with apprehension.

"What happened between us tonight goes no further. Tomorrow, when you return to class, I'm nothing more than your teacher and you my student. Do you understand that?"

Her breath was warm against my palm, her gaze narrowing just enough to tell me everything she was thinking.

With effort I pulled my hand away, stepped back and waited for her to climb into her car. When she was safely inside, I turned to round my SUV, her voice catching my attention.

"Penguins."

Confusion knit my brows as I turned back to her. "I'm sorry?"

A tilt of her chin. "Your jacket. From a distance it looks like tiny black dots, but up close, they're little penguins."

To be honest, I'd never really noticed. Glancing down at the fabric folded over my arm, I studied the pattern. "You're right."

"Where do you buy your clothes, Mr. Carter? Your wardrobe looks like what happens when a thrift store eats something bad and throws up."

My lips kicked up at the corners. "I've never been one to care much."

"It works on you. Your style."

Lifting my gaze to hers, I inclined my head. "Drive safely, Amelia."

A moment of hesitation before Amelia straightened in the seat and shut her door. I stepped away. Gave her room to back out. Leaned against the back of my SUV waiting to ensure she made it out of the parking lot without any problems. The taillights of her car were tiny points of light in the distance by the time I climbed into my vehicle as well.

My hand slammed down on the steering wheel, a tiny bleep of the horn echoing across the dark night.

If she were any other woman, I wouldn't have regretted what I'd done. But Amelia was forbidden fruit; a student, an aggravation, a woman so fucking reckless I wanted to spank her ass again every time I thought of what I'd seen her do in that dark alley.

Head falling back against the seat, I scrubbed my hand down my face, aggravated to have seen that face from the past, to not know his name even when I'd found a person who could tell me.

This wasn't done.

It couldn't be done.

Not until Amelia broke down and admitted to me the name that went with the face.

CHAPTER TEN

A person's hands can be patient or they can hurry through every action. You'll know their thoughts by how quickly they play, or if they can keep a slow, steady beat even when they want to rush to the end...

Amelia

Every second. Every minute. Every hour.

Time is a set of beats, a metronome ticking down the days, perpetual, ceaseless, unrelenting as it drives you forward regardless of whether exhaustion weighs heavy or whether your mind is screaming for just one paused second in order to catch up.

A never-ending beat ticking, a count to which no person alive has always been able to keep. Every musician will stumble over the notes of a racing melody, just like every soul will stumble on the days when time moves too fast and reality stops making sense.

I was that musician. I was that soul. And while I waited for Lennon to arrive to class and open the doors, I drummed my fingers over my bent knees, counting the beats, begging the universe to rest long enough for me to learn how to breathe easily again.

"Admit it, Jess, he's hot. And rich. I looked him up the night after our first class and he knows *everybody* in the music industry."

To my left, a group of girls sat against the wall, their heads angled toward each other, their quiet voices floating down the long hall where other students stood waiting patiently.

"If Mr. Carter wanted to keep me after or class for some private tutoring, I'd happily bend over his desk and -"

"Morning everyone. Sorry I'm late. Something kept me up last night."

My head snapped left, gaze lifting to *Mr. Carter's* face. It felt stupid to call him that after what we'd done.

He approached with a bag slung over his shoulder, his scuffed olive green Docs a heavy beat against the linoleum floor.

Perhaps it was a phantom pain, or a trick of the mind that made my ass tingle with the sting he'd left last night. Even this morning, my pale flesh was tinged a faint pink, a handprint clearly outlined on the right cheek. Thankfully, it wouldn't bruise, but the visual reminder has sent a collision of contradictory emotions storming through me.

Anger.

Shame.

Embarrassment.

Want...

Lennon nodded at some students, smiled down at the girls who were giggling and twirling their hair like a bunch of mean girl middle schoolers.

Yet his eyes scanned right over me. No acknowledgment whatsoever. Not a simple passing glance or second thought. I didn't want to admit to myself that being looked over hurt, that for a moment I'd held my breath wondering if it would be possible to meet his eyes and not see the glaring truth of what we'd done.

Guess it didn't matter much to him. What's worse was that I wondered what exactly it had been that kept him so occupied he'd not slept. Where had he gone, or who had he done, after parting ways with me?

Why did I even care?

Pushing myself up from the floor, I filed in behind the other students, making a point not to glance in his direction, fighting every damn instinct I had to turn and look at a man who had the uncanny ability to piss me off and turn me on all at the same time.

As if taking my weight were a chore, the legs of my chair screeched across the floor loud enough to draw attention when I sat down. Immediately to my right, Jillian Bates turned her head, sneering at me as if I weren't good enough to scrape the mud from the bottoms of her name brand shoes. She could kiss my ass for all I cared. Just a few minutes ago, she'd been the one fantasizing about bending over Lennon's desk while I was the one with his handprints painting my skin.

I wasn't sure what that said about me, but if it gave me a leg up in this class, I would take it.

Like a curtain, my hair hung down around my face, a tiny slit open through which I could watch Lennon arranging the papers on his desk. He looked good today, despite having been *kept up*.

Ripped jeans hung loose over his narrow hips, a blue band shirt tight to his sculpted body. I couldn't see which band, just the tour cities and dates running a list in small print down his back. His suspenders hung loose against the sides of his legs. Why wear them if they weren't snug over the shoulders? For that matter, why did he wear them at all?

He turned to the class and I averted my eyes, trying to convince myself that it was because I didn't care, and not because I couldn't handle the rejection again if he couldn't be bothered to notice me.

Maybe I was just one of many.

Maybe the first time I'd let a man touch me in an intimate way was nothing more than another game Lennon could expertly play. Maybe he'd used me just like every other asshole I'd lured to the shadows for another one of my brother's schemes.

Shoulders shaking with silent laughter, I imagined letting Ben beat Lennon's ass just for thinking he had the right to touch me.

Not that I'd said no, but still, my mind has a habit of getting vengeful when my heart twists with confusion and hurt.

"Twenty-five of you remain in this class." He paused, but not before the deep resonance of his voice could carry across the room to stroke me in all the forbidden places. "By the end of this week, only ten will stay."

A chorus of squeaking chairs, heavy sighs and concerned murmurs filled the room, Lennon's observant eyes studying the class from his standard perch against the front of his desk.

Say please...

Damn it. The memory of what he'd done to me wouldn't stop playing in my head, my heart gripping again when his blue eyes scanned over me. It was as if I no longer existed in his world.

"Although it's understandable that you all are worried, and a kinder teacher would tell you the worry is for nothing, I won't lie. I have no intent to coddle you. You *should* be worried. The first round of performances proved to me you deserve to be heard, but none of you were perfect. Not one of you have the discipline, the drive, the talent, to put me in my place and show me what it means to make music."

He was an asshole. I was sure most of the class would agree with me. All except his fan girls, of course, but even they were a little pink in the cheeks. How dare he belittle us?

"That being said, what I intend to do is make you all better." He pulled his hands from his pockets and gripped them over the edge of the desk.

Silence, all eyes on him, all minds focused with rapt attention.

Say please...

My gaze dropped to his hands. The same hands that had played my body as effortlessly and as masterfully as they could a piano. The same hands that had threatened to cut off my air when wrapped around my throat.

"But first I need to work with each of you individually to determine if you're worth the effort."

He pushed away from his desk, his movement fluid and sure as he grabbed a single sheet of paper from his desk, crossed the room to the whiteboard and clipped it in place. Turning to the class, he tipped his head just slightly to the paper.

"This is the schedule of private instruction..."

My shoulders tensed at the thought of being alone with him, shivers like tiny skittering fingers running down my spine. A psychosomatic response, the cheeks of my ass burning to remember his hands on my bare skin. Heat burned my face to remember the way my body had responded.

Did you like it...

Crossing my arms over my stomach, I leaned forward and pressed my forehead against the cool wood of the desk.

"...each student will be given forty-five minutes to prove they can handle criticism and follow directions. I won't tolerate hurt feelings or disobedience."

Ha! Thankfully I didn't laugh out loud. Not that what he'd said was funny. It was a little too truthful, yet nobody in this classroom knew it besides me.

"Miss Dillon."

Sitting up so quickly that it wrenched the muscles in my neck and back, I met his eyes for the first time since last night, a stern warning glimmering in the deep blue.

Lennon's eyes were a churning ocean, violent and chaotic, tiny specks of light reflecting like whitecaps breaking in the distance.

"Am I boring you?"

A few students giggled, namely his fan club of slutty girls who couldn't be bothered with wearing anything appropriate to class.

"No, Sir."

Slowly, his eyes blinked, a muscle jumping in his jaw. Arrogant male pride flashing behind his gaze to hear me call him Sir.

"By the looks of it, we might be keeping you awake. Do you want to be here today, or did you have something better to do?"

Like rob a bank or set up some poor idiot to be mugged, he didn't say. Not that he needed to. The man could speak with his eyes. Right there in the depths of that storm ravaged sea, he managed to drown me in the censure of his thoughts.

"No, Mr. Carter. I'm just-"

Exhausted? Embarrassed? Hurt? Turned on?

Hell, he could take his pick and it wouldn't be wrong. I was all of those, confused mostly, conflicted and desperate to be understood.

Mostly, I was being shredded at the edges by the desire to know this man who had haunted my every thought for the last ten hours. I was torn by my refusal to give in to him, not in life, in body or in music. Who was he to critique what I had done when he couldn't keep his hands to himself?

Who was he to judge when he had a slight obsession with punishment in a blatantly sexual manner?

I would have given anything to join Julia's class. To step away from a man who had tastes that went beyond the ordinary. And to think I'd only touched on the surface of all that was Lennon Carter.

"I'm just tired."

A silent pause, his eyes searching my face before his mouth ticked up at the corners. That damn smirk. I would gladly smack it from his handsome face.

"I'm sure you are."

Eyes narrowing on him, I curled my fingers against my palms. His gaze tracked down to my desk, noticed the loose fists, the smirk deepening before he lifted that tempest storm stare back to my face.

"You might want to listen more closely while I explain to the class what is expected of you. It would be a shame for you to lose your place in the program because you couldn't be bothered with appropriate behavior."

I fought not to roll my eyes. Who knows what form of punishment he'd come up with for that?

Unaffected, he clasped his hands together behind his back, his strong legs solid beneath his houndstooth patterned pants, feet set at shoulder width apart. If I didn't know his backstory, I would have believed this man had been in the military for the way he moved with such confidence, for the way he stood still as if he could run you down without warning.

I already knew he was fast. For three years in high school, I'd run track. I was the fastest, my endurance superior, yet Lennon had caught me that day in the alley without barely breaking a sweat.

"We have three days to get through all twenty-five of you. During these sessions, my focus won't be on the skill and technique you've already developed, but more on your ability to take instruction, to learn, and to improve. The ten who remain following these three days are expected to know how to alter their thinking, to receive a critique and conform to what is being demanded of them."

Another flick of his eyes toward me. "To prove they can be as disciplined as me."

A full body shiver coursed through me at the thought of just how *disciplined* he wanted me to be. Had wanted, actually. Past tense. After spanking my ass he'd practically sprinted to take me back to my car.

Still, my mind couldn't stop drifting to the image of Lennon with Jillian bent over his lap, jealousy stepping in to mingle and dance with the other caustic blend of emotions I was already battling.

"The list has times for each of you to be here. If it's not your forty-five minutes, you're free to do whatever you like. Go shopping. Go home. Or, in Miss Dillon's case, take a nap."

The class laughed softly around me.

Refusing to react, I stayed in place while the other students pushed from their chairs to walk over and scan the schedule. Lennon moved out of their way, dropped his weight into the leather seat behind his desk and lifted his feet to desk.

I studied him through the curtain of my hair, watching as he flipped a pen through his fingers, uncaring that I hadn't moved a muscle, hadn't jumped up to see when we'd be alone again.

After the other students noted their time slot, they returned to their desks, grabbed their bags and shuffled out of the room, a slow crawl of bodies until there were only a few left. Sitting here wasn't doing me any good. It's not like my show of defiance had drawn his attention.

Or maybe it had.

"Miss Dillon, your time is not until late this afternoon. As such, I suggest you go home and catch up on the sleep you obviously need. It might put you in a better mood."

He didn't bother lifting his eyes to me, didn't turn his head, just leaned back in his seat flipping that damn pen between his fingers with his eyes closed.

If anybody needed a nap, it was him. What had kept him up so late? Again, why did I even care?

I pushed to my feet, slung my bag over my shoulder and marched toward the door.

"Don't you want to check what time, Miss Dillon?"

Stilling in place, my skin bristled, anger crawling like fire beneath my skin. Every instinct in me demanded I disobey him, that I keep walking forward without concern for whatever time he'd selected for me. But then, I'd be the one out of luck. The scholarship as good as gone. My future relegated to back alley schemes with Ben.

Lennon dangled that over my head without giving a damn what he was doing.

Over to the schedule I went like the obedient student I was, my eyes searching the bottom to discover I was the last student to meet with him that afternoon.

Time noted, I moved toward the door to leave, but not before he could lob one last reminder at my back.

"Drive safely, Amelia."

My eyes closed, a breath leaking out of me as I was returned to the night before, as I remembered in all too vivid detail the moment we'd almost kissed.

126

I knew he'd used those words on purpose. A not so gentle prodding to remind me that when it came to who held the power between us and who was to remain obedient, I was the weak link, a girl who needed him a hell of a lot more than he needed me.

Stepping through the door, I made my way down the hall toward the parking lot, wondering if he was getting even with me for not telling him that the men with me last night had been my brother and his friend.

Lennon wouldn't get the information out of me no matter what he did. Losing Ben would be the end of my family. It would tear us apart and leave us homeless.

With six hours to kill before it was my turn to be locked in a room with that asshole, I climbed in my car to notice I was low on gas. Driving home and back wasn't possible, so I sat in the Florida heat with my windows opened, the screech of cicadas rising and falling across the parking lot, the low murmur of voices whispering when other students passed by.

Maybe I was tired after all. Eventually my eyes closed, sweat beading on my brow and between my breasts while the gentle hum of Florida wildlife lulled me to sleep.

I woke to a loud bang on the top of my car. Eyes flicking open, my head jerked left to see a pair of blue, stormy eyes staring down at me.

"When I told you to get some sleep, I meant in a bed where you were safe from strangers watching you as they passed by."

Anger was the stern line of Lennon's lips. I was beginning to believe there was nothing I could do to

127

please the man. Perhaps I'd been born with the sole purpose of pissing him off.

"Do you know what time it is, Amelia?"

I didn't, but judging by the setting sun behind him, I assumed it was a lot later than my allotted time slot. Shit.

"I'm-" My voice was groggy from sleep.

"You're an annoyance riding my last nerve, is what you are. Follow me inside so we can complete your evaluation."

He spun on his heel and stalked off, his bag slung over a shoulder. Lennon must have been leaving when he found me sleeping in my car.

Stumbling from the car, I walked like a drunk woman, my legs uncoordinated, the thick fog of sleep still wrapping around me. A gust of cold air slammed into me when I let myself into the building, my shirt stuck to my chest and back from sweat. The only noise was my feet hurrying down the empty hallway, the shuffle of Lennon rifling through papers when I turned to enter the room.

Blue eyes peered up at my face, tracked down to my sweat soak shirt over my breasts and up again before narrowing. "It's like you want someone to take advantage of you. Why not just skip all the stupid antics and tape a sign to your forehead that says 'rape me'?"

Startled by the vehemence of his comment, I stood frozen, unsure what to do with my hands as he stared at me.

My nipples were hard in response to the cold air against my wet shirt, the material molded to me like a

128

second skin. Lennon didn't appear to miss that fact as his gaze dragged down me, his eyes closing for a brief second before he threw an arm out to his right

"Piano. Now."

It was instinctual to respond immediately to his voice, the sharp tone and intolerant demand forcing my feet in the direction he'd pointed, my brain not quite catching up until I was seated on the bench with my fingers lightly caressing the keys.

This was my happy place, a respite from the world, a safe harbor where it was just the music and me. Nothing mattered. Nothing hurt. Nothing could touch me while the notes wrapped around me in a thick, soft blanket of sound that blocked the rest of the world from view.

"You'll be playing Scarlatti's Sonata in D Minor, no.141-"

I scoffed, the sound hissing over my lips before I had time to think about what was I doing. I'd mastered that particular piece when I was still in middle school.

"Is there a problem?" he asked, his words clipped, tone dark.

Answering quickly, I breathed out, "No. Sorry. I didn't mean to-"

He was closer now, sneaking up on me with such silence it was frightening. "Obviously, there is. Why don't you enlighten me as to your thoughts."

"No, it's-"

"That wasn't a request, Amelia." Closer now. "Tell me what you're thinking."

Teeth clamped over the inside of my cheek, I closed my eyes, imagined where he stood in the room. How he stood. The expression on his face.

"Although the piece is pretty, Scarlatti isn't exactly difficult music, at least not the Sonata in D Minor."

My fingers pressed down on the keys, enough to nudge them while preventing the hammers from striking the first notes. Preferring to rebel and refuse to be Lennon's trained monkey, I understood that to impress him, I needed to throw him off balance. Steal his control. Show him that I was worth more than the back alley girl he chose to see rather than the musician I knew I would become.

He hadn't moved another step, but then, he didn't need to. I'd memorized that particular piece a long time ago.

My fingers moved over the driving tempo without him asking me to start, the sheet music in my mind's eye, a rush of notes as my wrists snapped, my fingers nimble, a crescendo driving up the keys and back down again, my left hand jumping back and forth over my right like a child playing hopscotch, the melody chaotic, so delicate yet demanding.

Sweat beaded at my temples again, although for an entirely different reason. I was lost, the scaling notes pushing me high before crashing down again like rolling thunder. Fortissimo to pianissimo, hard to soft, loud to quiet. Over and over, until there was no aggravating man standing behind me, until my mother wasn't dead and my father hadn't forgotten me, until I no longer lived in a town where the midnight hours were a monster threatening to swallow me.

I was just a woman and a song, notes dancing delicately across the air, blowing within the frenetic winds of a warm, spring day.

Just me.

Removed and forgotten.

A soul having left its body to discover what lies on the other side.

The piece didn't particularly call to me. It wasn't dark enough, demanding enough. But still, it poured out through my hands, the resonance of the last notes carrying through the quiet room before my fingers could lift from the keys.

Music, to me, wasn't just a series of notes, it was poetry without words, a story without pages, life beyond the confines of a stark reality.

"Was that good enough?" I finally asked, the high of playing wearing off to reveal the distrust I felt to have Lennon standing behind me.

The silence was deafening. Chills, like ants crawling over every inch of my skin.

Had I angered him yet again?

Only when I thought the silence would suffocate me did he speak.

"That was-" He paused, his voice just above my head. His close proximity startling.

"Proficient," Lennon finally said, voice deep, the heat of his body against my back, causing my breath to catch and my thighs to clamp together.

Unable to bear having him so near, I rounded my shoulders, took a breath. "You're in my space," I whispered.

"I'm owning your space," he answered without concern for what he was doing to me.

Strong hands slammed down on the piano keys on either side of me, the noise jarring, his body leaning over mine until his mouth was against my ear. On a whisper, "And you might as well get used to it."

The knot in my throat was a choking hazard, my pulse racing out of beat. Lips parting, I attempted to drag in a breath, to gain control. But that, he'd apparently stolen as well.

Hypnotic, his scent, masculine and earthy. It trapped me in a memory, my body buzzing with the sensation of having lost the will to fight.

"Mr. Carter-"

It was a bare whisper, so low I doubted he'd heard me speak.

If he had, he didn't react to it, his head beside mine, his mouth so close to my shoulder I could feel the heat of his breath wash over my skin.

The metronome of time kept ticking, a steady beat that paused for no person, no moment, no seduction or sin.

Only, in this, it was Lennon's beat I followed.

Helpless.

Hesitant.

And afraid.

CHAPTER ELEVEN

My heart knows only sorrow now. How could I have been so stupid?
How was I so deaf and blind that I didn't see this coming?

Lennon

Amelia was an enigma.

That's all that could be said about a young woman with so piss poor an attitude, but yet had the ability to produce near perfection of sound when she played.

Perplexing.

Puzzling.

Incongruent in attitude versus talent.

She wasn't a girl who should be pickpocketing men or running scams in back alleys. She was a woman who should be sitting before an audience daring them not to react to the music bleeding from her fingers.

All day, I'd listened to the other students stumble through the Sonata, their fingers uncoordinated, their brows furrowed as they fought the piece tooth and nail, some proving their ability to learn, others practically crying when the music proved to be the better opponent. My criticisms had fallen on deaf ears. My demands had proven to be too much.

I didn't begrudge them the failure. This particular Sonata is a difficult piece, but not the most difficult by any stretch of the imagination. In truth, although the Sonata was complicated, it was still too simple to my ear. A jumble of scales that made sense, treble dancing against bass, the notes in accord.

It didn't cause my pulse to surge, didn't catch me off guard, didn't freeze me in place as my body absorbed it and my mind fought to make sense of the dichotomy of notes assaulting me all at once.

Until it was produced by Amelia's hands, at least.

But not because she'd changed the piece. Only because she shared her soul while playing it.

Her dark soul.

Her beautiful, dissonant soul.

A soul that called into the shadows in answer of mine.

Now I understood why I couldn't get her out of my head, why after a day of fighting to keep her at a distance, I was now so close I could hear the rasp of her breath, could see the flutter of her pulse, could feel the heat of her body reach out to tangle with my own.

In music, we were the same.

In life, we couldn't be further apart.

In this class, we were forbidden from touching each other in the ways I was desperate to touch her now.

"Mr. Carter..."

A soft voice dragged me further into a moment where my self control wavered. Our bodies an inch apart. Mine hard as a fucking rock simply from listening to her play.

Lifting my hands from the keys, I traced the shape of her arms, barely touching, listening to the music still pouring through her with each soft breath, every pulse of her heart, the creak of the wooden bench beneath her body when Amelia stilled in place.

"You're impossible," I murmured, voice low, fear of shattering the slow adagio between us, the beat of my heart the first ominous notes of Liszt's B Minor Sonata. Deep, dangerous, a Sotto Voce pulse, a whisper, a *warning*.

"Lennon-"

My fingertips brushed over her shoulders, left hand hovering, right hand breaking every rule I'd made for this woman by wrapping softly over her throat.

She swallowed, the movement harsh against my palm before I clasped the point just beneath her jaw and tilted her face up to mine.

A question fell from my lips before I could think to stop it. "What are you doing to me?"

Leaning over, my lips hovered a teasing inch above hers.

"Oh, there you two are. I saw your cars in the parking lot and-"

At the sound of another voice, I pulled my hands from Amelia's body and turned, pulse racing, my gaze meeting Julia Pickens' where she stood in the doorway.

"Julia," I answered, clearing my throat of the grit, praying to all that was holy she wouldn't look down and notice the half-mast tent in my pants.

Behind me, Amelia stood from the bench, pink dusting her cheeks. "Hi, Julia. You're here late."

"As are the two of you." Glancing between us, an odd glimmer in her eye betrayed her curiosity. "I was actually leaving, but then I saw Amelia's car in the parking lot."

135

Her gaze pinned me in place, accusation written into the arch of her eyebrow. "I was worried it had broken down and I came to make sure she was okay."

"She's fine," I assured her. "We were just discussing her performance of Scarlatti's Sonata."

Julia's face brightened, pride in Amelia shining through to replace the concern that had been there just seconds before.

"Oh, isn't she amazing on that piece? She knew it before beginning her studies under me." Turning to Amelia, she asked, "It was your dad who taught you that one, wasn't it?"

From where I stood, I could feel the nervous energy of Amelia's body, waves crashing against me as if I were the jagged rocks of a battered shore. "Yes. He wouldn't let me stop until I'd memorized the entire piece."

Back to me, Julia asked, "Has she told you who her parents are?"

My fingers curled against my palms.

Not anger.

Frustration.

"She has. As the daughter of two symphony performers, she represents her family line well. I'm not surprised to hear her accomplished style and technique."

Go the fuck away... Repetitive, that thought, my desire to chase this woman from the room overbearing.

Shifting her posture, Julia smiled. "She does. It's a shame her brother didn't follow in the family's musical footsteps as well."

Amelia tensed beside me at the mention of her brother. I found the reaction interesting, suddenly wanting to continue this conversation.

A brother. I never knew she had one.

Turning to study the woman at my right, I grinned. "I didn't know you have a brother."

Her throat worked again, a slow ripple as she refused to meet my stare.

"Oh, yes. Ben is twelve years older than Amelia, and their mother just didn't know what to do with him. But you know how it is. Some people have music inside them while others have other talents. From what I remember Lila telling me, Ben was more into sports. Isn't that right, Amelia?"

Twelve years older...meaning this mysterious Ben was the same age as my sister. Son of Lila and James. A boy who would have been in the house while Emaline was there for her lessons. A man who now had access to Amelia.

"Yes," Amelia finally answered, her voice a touch too soft. "Ben was on the track team in high school, much like me."

Remembering how fast the son of a bitch had run from me in that alley, the pieces were falling together quite nicely.

Ben. Perhaps this was the name Amelia had refused to give me last night.

"Yes, our Amelia is quite talented in many areas." Julia paused, her eyes bouncing between us. "Shouldn't class have ended an hour ago?"

"I was late," Amelia admitted, the quick response drawing Julia's attention. "Lenn- Mr. Carter was doing

137

private evaluations today and I was supposed to be here at 4:15, but I fell asleep waiting in the parking lot."

"Ah, well, that explains it." Her laugh was forced, her expression disbelieving. "I'll let you get back to it then."

Shrewd eyes hard on me, Julia said, "I hope you've now learned how valuable Amelia would be to Hastings. Try not to ruin her."

Whatever the hell that meant.

"You two have a good night."

With that, she turned to walk from the room, her low heels against the floor echoing in her wake as she disappeared down the hall. Amelia and I stood motionless, so many unspoken thoughts running through each of our minds.

She was the first to dare disturb the silence. "Will you?"

Two words. Simple. Yet loaded with a million possibilities.

"Will I what?"

"Ruin me?"

Exhaling slowly, I closed my eyes, my hands fisting tighter. Would I? Despite it all, I thought I might.

Nothing good could come of acting on what I wanted, yet my willpower to remain distant was slowly shredding apart.

"I will."

Amelia's body winced next to mine, our bodies so close, yet not touching.

"How can I improve my performance?"

The question caught me off guard, my head turning to see she still looked forward, her eyes locked on the doorway where Julia had stood.

Shaking my head, I was reminded of my role. I had to clear my throat to answer. "You hit every note, however the tone was lost in parts where you played too fast, punched the keys too hard."

"Show me."

My gaze tracked across the floor, over my shoes. Could I listen to her play again without losing the ability to stay away?

"Sit down on the bench. Run through the first twenty measures."

Amelia did as she was told without question, her hands moving to the keys, fingers quick, wrists agile.

"Stop."

I wasn't sure why I needed her to quit playing that particular song. There was nothing wrong with it, the composition precise for a player of her skill, but it was rubbing against me in the wrong way.

My curiosity got the best of me.

"Forget Scarlatti. Play the piece that speaks to you the most."

She paused, fingers stroking the keys softly, unsure. Behind her, I stood motionless, our heat mingling, the fabric of my pants brushing softly against the back of her shirt.

The first notes clapped through the room with the violence of a lightning storm. Chaos vibrating from the strings. The hammers pounding wildly in response to Amelia's rage on the keys.

I recognized the piece. Stravinsky's Firebird, a composition of notes, scales, and chords that made no sense from one measure to the next, but somehow fit together perfectly.

This wasn't romance that pulsed through a room built for sound; it was pain, pure and undisguised. It was violence weaved within moments of ecstasy. It was a song I would have chosen myself.

A lonely soul screaming at the sky, a whisper responding with the promise that the heart will heal once you discover another person who has also been destroyed.

Amelia knew destruction, her soul screaming, and I was the whisper that welcomed her home.

"Stop."

Her hands stilled, the last chords resonating over both of us, the room refusing to relinquish the sound of discord and fury that had opened her up to reveal the scars on her soul.

"Stand up."

I had to know, had to see, had to toss aside every internal warning and find out if she could be taught to obey.

The legs of the wooden bench scraped against the floor when she did as she was told. My heart beat a strong, steady pulse. My thoughts erratic.

I should have walked away. Should have shut this down. Should have thought before acting. But still, her song played inside me, chaos erupting, a pain so enchanting that it mirrored my own.

Sometimes you don't need to know the cause of what decimates another person to understand, to taste, to experience and recognize that the same destruction exists within yourself.

"Turn around."

Silently, she spun to face me, her cheeks flushed, her lips parted with the rasp of her breath.

Only the bench prevented us from being chest to chest. A small piece of furniture that was my last reminder that what was happening between us should go no further.

I shoved it out of the way, stepped close, her ass pressing against the keys of the piano when she stepped back out of instinct.

Her eyes widened in the instant she knew she was cornered.

On a rasp of breath, "Mr. Carter-"

Rolling my neck over my tense shoulders, I met her eyes and begged, "Tell me to stop."

Not that it would matter. Not that anything she could say would bring me to heel.

Eyes flicking over my shoulder, she answered, "The door is wide open."

That didn't fucking matter. Nobody was in the building, the distance so damn quiet I would have heard a pin drop. That also wasn't Amelia telling me no. If anything, it was a hint that she wanted what she knew I would do to her.

Stepping closer, I watched her breasts lift with every labored breath, the tips softly brushing my chest.

Our eyes met again. "That wasn't you saying stop."

Air shuddered over her lips, her eyes holding mine like the prey she was. Cornered, trembling, terrified.

Ripe for the taking.

Her voice was a bare whisper, a lure, a fucking tease. "I don't want you to stop. I don't know why, but I -" Her voice trailed off. She stared up at me with a defeated expression, confusion swirling behind her teal eyes.

We were risking everything. Out in the open. Exposed so that if anyone were to walk by, her future at Hastings would be out of reach. All because of me. All because I couldn't tell myself no.

There was nobody in the building.

Fuck, I hoped that was true.

Leaning forward, I smiled to feel her body shake, the quick shiver to feel my breath against her neck, to feel my hips press against hers.

"If this happens, nobody can know. It will ruin you. I will ruin you. Do you know that?"

It didn't matter, her answer. Amelia could never understand just how thoroughly I intended to destroy her in every way I knew how.

In her music, I heard violence, the notes plucking a string inside me that resonated with a fevered pitch.

Without moving, she inhaled sharply, the air hissing over her lips before she said, "Maybe I'm ruined already."

Not in the way I plan to do it.

Amelia and her damn secrets. Her music. Her aggravating disregard for safety. There was so much to correct in her, to pull from her, to develop if she'd ever be ready for Hastings.

Convincing myself that I was doing this scared young girl a favor, I lifted my hand to her hip, reveled in the tremor of her body, closed my eyes to listen to her breath pour across her lips.

"There are rules you must follow." Turning my head, I was speaking against her cheek. "Break them and this ends. Everything. The program. Your music. Me."

"I know how to keep a secret. You should know that by now."

Her words were a taunt that only made me want her more.

My fingers clasped her hip tighter, my cock a hard line against her leg, my lips pulling into a hard grin. "Fine; then rule number two: You'll stop committing crimes while learning under me..."

Learning music. Learning to fuck. Learning to obey every god damned command I gave her without complaint or hesitation.

Amelia's head turned just enough that the corners of our mouths were an inch apart. "What else?"

"Rule number three: Whatever I tell you to do, you do. Immediately."

Our heads turned toward each other more, our mouths lingering, breath crashing together. "Anything else?"

"No secrets," I whispered, hand lifting from her hip to grip her chin. I would find out more about her brother, but now was not the time. For now, all that mattered was learning what it would be like to brush my lips across hers, to know what it would feel like for our tongues to dance in the beat that I set for her.

"Is that all?" she asked, so low, I could barely hear her.

My eyes closed and opened again to meet the sparkling depth of glimmering teal. "I own you from this moment on. Every day. Every second." My grip tightened on her jaw. "Every fucking thought. Every action is mine. Can you live with that?"

Without giving her a chance to decline, my mouth slanted against hers, more jarring notes from the keys as her body was shoved back, her tongue shyly skating over mine. A passing flicker of the soft tip, almost as if she didn't know what to do with it.

I liked that she was shy. Scared. Timid. It's more fun to peel a woman open than to have her offer herself up like a present. And maybe that makes me an asshole, but I've never pretended to be sweet.

The face I show the world is of a talented musician who dominates the keys. But the face hidden behind shadows is a man who likes to destroy pretty little things. Who likes to grasp a heart of innocence, break it down, strip it bear and demand it spreads its legs.

Not stupid enough to believe that Amelia wanted all that I could give her, I knew she was curious, testing the waters, enamored by the excitement of a forbidden relationship. What she didn't know was that I would take so much advantage that she *would* be ruined when I was done, a girl sent away to find her dreams while I returned to my life.

Every note she played for the rest of her life would be mine. Every man she fucked would be drowned beneath my shadow.

I knew the truth.

144

I knew to stop this from happening.

I just simply stopped giving a fuck.

Breaking the kiss, I captured her bottom lip between my teeth, her legs parting to wrap around my waist, my hand claiming what was between them with such possession, she startled and squeaked.

"From now on, you'll wear skirts to class to give me free access."

Her body tensed beneath mine, eyes wide with apprehension.

Driving my hand up her shirt, I palmed her breast, my fingertips scraping her skin when I pulled the cup down to reveal the taut nipple and skin. She trembled as I traced my thumb in a circle around the beaded tip, my mouth aching to taste it.

"Disobey me and you'll be punished. Fuck up your music and I'll spank you over the damn keys. And if I find you playing games again with shitty thugs out on the streets, you better fucking believe it will be the last time you'll ever see me."

My cock was painfully hard, aching for relief and she'd pissed me off by wearing jeans that denied me access. Reaching behind me, I unwrapped her legs from my waist, stepped back and decided to see just how much she still wanted me now that she'd broken the surface of who I could become.

"Since you've already broken so many of the rules, I think it's only fair you show me what that petulant little mouth of yours can do."

The pink staining her cheeks deepened to crimson, her eyes darting down to my pants and back up again. Indecision was so obvious in her expression that I wondered for a split second if she would change her mind.

"What do you want me to do?"

Only a bastard would lie. "I'd like to fuck your mouth."

A flicker of fear and surprise raced behind her eyes.

This was up to her.

I wouldn't push.

Wouldn't make demands.

Wouldn't take that final step over the boundary until she told me she wanted what I could give her.

Mouth swollen from the kiss and eyes demure, Amelia licked her lips and met my gaze to say the one thing I hadn't expected from her.

"I don't know how."

My head angled to the side. "What do you mean?"

Fidgeting over the piano, she winced at the sound of the hammers hitting strings.

"I know you think I'm...well...I know what you saw last night at Majori's. But," a heavy breath poured over her lips, filled with something I couldn't quite name.

"What are you trying to tell me, Amelia?"

Her gaze dropped to the floor at her feet, her body stilling as she made the confession.

"I'm a virgin. I've never actually been with a man."

Son of a fucking bitch.

That changed everything.

CHAPTER TWELVE

There is energy in our hands, an extension of ourselves, a means with which we reach out to touch the world and leave a part of our souls behind when we're gone...

Amelia

You know, it's funny. All my life I'd assumed men were always chasing virgins, as if there were some badge they received on their man card for having busted that hymen, deflowered that woman, or popped the holy grail of cherries. Those badges were like priceless trading cards they could display in clear plastic containers, a prideful moment proving they had been there first.

Not Lennon.

No, he stood stock still in front of me, eyes searching my face, skin turning a sickly shade as the shock of what I'd said tore through him.

I went from feeling somewhat good about the tease of it being my first time to wondering if I should have said anything at all.

From sure of myself to embarrassed.

From ready to give it all up, to feeling naked and exposed.

"Tell me you're kidding," he said, further making me believe that my inexperience was a bad thing.

I didn't know what to say. Folding my arms over my stomach I stared back at him, slightly hurt for the reaction. "I would, but you said no secrets."

Driving his hand through his hair, he turned, the suspenders at his sides swinging out with the movement. He stalked away, slammed his palms down on his desk, his head hanging down.

Okay. So, what was I supposed to do now? Understanding that my news wasn't something he'd wanted to hear, I adjusted my clothes back into place before quietly pulling my ass from the keyboard of the piano. Thankfully the hammers didn't strike, didn't make a single noise to draw his attention back to me.

Maybe I should go.

Or stay.

I wasn't sure.

His voice was a deep growl, more a vibration from his chest than anything his throat had produced. "How is it possible you're a virgin? I mean, for fucks sake, I met you while you were picking my fucking pocket. I caught you taking a guy to an alley-"

"Just because I've done some messed up stuff doesn't mean I spread my legs for every man that looks my direction. Plus my br-"

Cutting myself off before mentioning Ben, I bit my tongue, my lips slamming together before we broached that topic. Julia had already said too much and I was scared Lennon would put the pieces together to figure out who had been with me at Majori's.

I had to say something to fill in the blank. "My family is super protective of me. Up until recently, at least."

He laughed, the sound harsh. Lifting his head, he looked at me. "Just in time for me to waltz in and screw up the one good thing they did for you."

Slightly taken aback by his comment, I bristled, anger swelling up in me that he'd once again led me right to that edge of being with him, only to shove me aside and walk away. "I'm an adult. What I do with my body is no longer their concern."

"I'm the worst thing for you, Amelia. Especially now that I know-" He cursed under his breath, pushing away from the desk to round the edge and stuff papers into his bag. "This can't happen."

Like hell it couldn't...

"No wonder you're so damn clueless about the types of things that can be done to you." He glanced up, his gaze seething.

"You throw yourself into the most dangerous situations because you have absolutely no idea how many ways a man could tear you apart."

Now he was just pissing me off. "That's not true."

"Yes, it fucking is. Just the fact that you're looking at me now like I'm some kind of a loss tells me you are too naive to understand what I almost did to you. What I still want to do to you regardless of the consequences. But it's not love I feel, Amelia. Not even a passing crush."

The words stung, the truth of them staring be blatantly in the face. "Are you saying all you care about is sex?"

His expression softened, the anger bleeding away to be replaced with sympathy and regret. "A more experienced woman would have known that. I didn't even bother to close the door."

Unsure what that had to do with anything, I rolled back my shoulders, my chin tipping higher even though the last thing I was feeling in that moment was pride.

His bag fell heavy onto the desk, his eyes lifting to mine again. "You deserve better than me for your first time. Someone who actually cares for you and doesn't just want to fuck you until you're begging for it to stop."

Eyes rounding at the admission, I hugged my body tighter. Did I care that sex was all he wanted? I wasn't sure.

"You need someone who will be gentle, and I can promise you, Amelia, that man is not me. Do you want pain for your first time? Because that's all I have to offer you."

The body reacts in strange ways, I've come to learn. At the mention of pain, my thighs clenched together, air shuddering through my chest. "I'm okay with that."

Lennon's jaw ticked, his hands curling into fists over his bag. "You think you're okay with that."

"I liked the spanking."

Heat rolled behind his angry blue eyes, storm clouds surging in with the promise of violent, unrelenting rain.

Lips stretching at the corners, Lennon flashed me a feral grin. Why was he so angry about this? It wasn't like I'd lied to him.

"You did like that, didn't you?"

Nodding, I shuffled my feet over the floor, my muscles tensing when he rounded the desk and marched toward me, his long legs eating the distance as his hands worked to pull the suspenders from his pants.

Reaching me, he didn't give me a chance to run, to cry out, to lift my hands in a defensive move before he gripped a hand over one of my wrists, tied one end of the suspenders over it, and gripped the other to do the same. Bending me backwards over the front of the piano, he used the third end to tie me in place, my spine protesting the awkward position, my chest arched forward and my legs struggling to remain balanced.

"Don't move," he growled against my ear, not that I could with the way he'd bound me to the music stand of the piano.

Yanking my shirt up to expose my bra, he reached behind me to unclasp it with one hand, the elastic popping loose as he lifted the cups from my breasts, his teeth locking down on one of my nipples so hard that a cry of pain burst from my mouth.

"Ow!"

But then...*then*...his teeth released me to be replaced by his lips, his tongue laving over the pain as he sucked it into his mouth, his left hand palming my other breast, molding it to his palm.

It didn't matter that my back muscles were screaming for relief, didn't matter that my legs had gone weak and my mind was about to shatter, the feel of his mouth on such an intimate part of me was all that I wanted in that moment.

His hand released me as his mouth moved to the other breast, teeth then tongue, sucking then biting, back and forth until his hands dropped at my sides and from the strings behind me rose the most beautiful music I'd ever heard.

He was playing while working my breasts with his mouth, not even bothering to look at the keys, his skilled hands driving a melody that was hard and then soft, fast and then so full of longing my body responded in kind.

How in the hell was he able to do that?

Soon, it was just his right hand racing over the keys, his left yanking at the button of my pants open, slipping down over my panties to...oh my god.

My back screamed as my body arched more, my legs like gelatin, held in place by the position in which I was bound, his thumb rolling over my clit as his fingers traced down over the soaked cotton.

And still, above my head, music like I'd never heard before. A dark melody bursting through me as his hand played me as expertly as the keys. Lennon's mouth continued moving from breast to breast, the nipples sore from the constant sensation, pleasure being forced through me without him giving a damn what he was doing to me.

My body responded in ways I'd never experienced before. Warmth bloomed through my core, every muscle tense and shaking as my insides clenched and relaxed, over and over again until I couldn't catch my breath, couldn't think, couldn't process that he was driving me to a precipice of such intense pleasure, my heart would feel like it could rip from my chest and my mind would become mush in my head.

Still, the pleasure exploded through me, a bomb I hadn't expected, a moan crawling up my throat to escape my lips. My hands pulled at the suspenders binding me in place, my legs shook so much that I thought I would collapse if not for the bindings.

I came, my eyes clenching shut as my insides rippled in need of more, my legs losing strength, the music Lennon played coming to a slow and soft end as I was left quivering in place.

The entire time, he'd watched me with fascination. Not that I could meet his gaze. I just somehow could feel the way he studied every reaction in my body.

After I was done, Lennon stepped away and said nothing for what felt like hours.

Fuck! My back hurt so bad as tears rolled from the corners of my eyes down my cheeks, my body desperate to stand up or sit down or shatter apart entirely.

"I won't fuck you here. Not like that. Not when you don't understand how much I love to see the tears dripping from your face."

He didn't so much as slip a finger inside and he made me come. How in the hell would I survive letting him toy with me in other ways?

"I could leave you here, just like that. The janitors would find you. The students pouring in the next day. How long do you think you could stay like that before your body is writhing in pain?"

"You wouldn't," I breathed out.

"I might. I'm just that type of man. Is this still something you want?"

No. He wouldn't. Not a man who kept screaming at me to protect myself. Lennon was trying to scare me. I wasn't stupid enough to let him.

"Yes."

"Fuck, you're asking for it." The words hissed over his lips before he moved toward me and untied the suspenders, one arm wrapping around my back to help me up.

Fire burned the muscles down my spine, my mouth opening in a silent cry of pain, my legs almost giving out beneath me when he lifted me up to cradle me against his chest.

It was like I weighed nothing. Lennon carried me across the room, sat me down in the chair behind his desk and caged me in with his hands on the armrests.

"One crime. One complaint. One act of disobedience and this ends. Do you understand me?"

I nodded, my voice trapped in my throat.

"And don't for a second think that because this is happening, you'll be the student I select to compete for the scholarship. If that's why you're doing this, you might as well stop right now. To win this, you will work you ass off. Practice until your fingers feel like they'll fall off. Listen to every damn thing I say. Cut open a vein and fucking bleed on those keys if that's what it takes to impress me. Do you understand that as well?"

Another nod, my throat fighting to swallow.

Leaning forward, his lips met mine with such a tender kiss, it stole my breath. Speaking against my mouth, he said, "You're going to be the death of me, Amelia."

Lennon shoved away from the chair and finished packing his bag. "Fix your clothes and let's get going. If we're here much longer the cleaning staff will wonder what the fuck we're doing."

He was angry. At me. At himself. At the situation. For what reason, I didn't know, but his normally fluid movements were stunted, his voice clipped, his jaw tight.

Shouldn't he be happy? Excited? Hell, turned on? I was, but to look at him you would think someone just ran over his puppy. Twice. With big loud screeching tires and maniacal laughter pouring out the driver's side window.

"Let's go."

Without bothering to look at me, he stood at the door waiting for me to grab my things, the soft squish of my sneakers against the linoleum a counterpoint to the heavy beat of his boots. I could barely keep up, a wave of warm wet heat assaulting me as soon we were outside, the cicadas buzzing, frogs singing despite the lack of a body of water nearby. It was the usual Florida chorus that began when the sun set and the day transitioned to night.

Walking me to my car, Lennon didn't say a word. I turned to him, dared to meet his eyes. "Are the rules still in place?"

A clipped nod, his eyes averted.

"Okay," I whispered, still not understanding why he was so mad.

"Drive safely," he said, stepping back to watch me climb into my car.

With the door open, I asked, "Who was the composer?"

A storm-blue gaze met mine. "What?"

155

"The music you played. When we were- When we were together. Who wrote it?"

Silence beat steady, the metronome ticking, time refusing to stop for even this split second. I would always remain a prisoner to his beat. His pace. His rhythm. I just didn't know what that would mean for me in the long run.

"I did."

Surprise flooded me. Admiration. Jealousy that music like that could flow so easily out of him. It spoke to me, the song, and not because of what he was doing. I heard the story. Saw the images. Felt everything the music had been written to convey.

"It was beautiful."

It was raw pain, that melody.

Lennon nodded his head, took another step back. "Have a good night, Amelia."

Dismissed, I shut my door and started the car. Slowly, I backed out of the space, my eyes meeting Lennon's one more time before I turned the car to leave. I watched him in my rear view mirror, noting that he watched me leave until I was pulling out onto the road.

Only then did he turn to walk to his car.

Lennon was lost to shadows as I focused on the street ahead of me, my mind racing with a million conflicting thoughts.

CHAPTER THIRTEEN

I gave him everything I had. My purity. My grace. My love and my music. Looking back, I know he didn't understand what those gifts meant...

Lennon

A virgin.

Of all the things she could tell me, of all the damn truths she could reveal to me in that moment, it had to be one that stopped me in my fucking tracks.

A woman being timid and shy is one thing. Innocence another. But to be untouched? It was an entirely different arena than anything I wanted in my life.

She deserved someone who would love her the first time, someone who would hurt if the relationship didn't work out and he had to walk away. Someone who wasn't planning to leave before anything could even get started.

And to think it was only the tip of the iceberg with Amelia. To think that her brother could be the one person I've hated for my entire adult life.

My bag slammed down on the desk in the classroom, the students not expected to pour in for another hour, a full day and a half having passed since the last time I saw Amelia. Still, it hadn't been enough time to make a decision as to what I planned to do with her.

Dropping my weight in the seat behind my desk, I kicked up my feet to the surface and leaned back, my hands scrubbing down my face as frustration poured out of me.

I'd returned home that night after touching her with an erection that wouldn't fucking stop, had jerked off with barely any relief, had gone to my piano to work out the music that was surging inside me with so much agony and chaos, it wouldn't subside.

For hours, I'd played despite having to get up early the next morning, a glass of whiskey in one hand, a cigar in the other.

It wasn't often that I smoked the damn things, but I needed the distraction, needed the focus on anything besides a woman who was driving me fucking mad.

As the night wore on, the music changed, a soft melody revealing itself with such innocent sound. My fingers were light over the keys, note after note running higher until my left hand beat on bass chords in answer, chasing it...chasing her. Threatening her serenity, warning her that, despite the smile I could evoke, pain and heartache were just around the corner.

Eventually even that frustrated me to no end and I managed a few hours of sleep before returning to class the next day. Over and over and fucking *over* again, I'd listened to students fumble through Scarlatti, my mind only paying them half the attention it should.

Still, I was happy for the break, happy that Amelia wouldn't return again until the following day. I'd thought, maybe, it would be enough time for me to come to my senses and call this thing done between us.

But who the fuck was I kidding? I wanted her just as much then as I do now.

With a few more evaluations to perform, I had a few hours, at least, to make a decision.

Already, she'd proven herself the best in my class. Kicking her out wasn't going to happen, but what did that mean for us?

I wasn't sure I could show her tenderness, wasn't positive I could give a damn she'd never had sex before.

Would her first time be bent over a desk with the sound of floor cleaners humming in the distance as the cleaning crew began their nightly routine?

As far as romance went, that was ... well ... shitty.

Eventually, Tony Salisburg waltzed through the door, fresh faced, eager to perform and I had to abandon my thoughts of Amelia to lead him to the piano. Another fumbling-fingered butchery of the Sonata for me to enjoy.

While I should have been critiquing him, carefully noting every error, every area where he could improve, I was standing behind him with my thoughts locked to one particular student I couldn't quite forget.

My eyes scanned over the Steinway, a vision of her bent backwards and bound coming to mind, the heavy weight of her breasts exposed, her nipples tight and swollen from what my mouth had done to them.

Fuck. She was beautiful.

The music stopped, Tony turning to look at me with anticipation in his expression. I'd only half listened.

"That was fairly good," I finally said, forcing myself to stop seeing Amelia helpless where she'd been bound, to stop feeling her body tremble and wet heat rush over my fingers when she'd come.

159

"Run through the last few measures for me again. Hit the notes harder in the areas marked fortissimo. I'm sure Scarlatti meant it when he wrote it."

The music started and all I could imagine was Amelia kneeling at my feet, her defiant gaze peeking up at me before I demanded she suck my cock.

I didn't know what it was about her smart mouth that made me want to punish it. I would, though, before all was said and done. Shutting her up with my dick was a temptation impossible to resist.

After Tony, another student. Another. And another.

Eventually the day rolled forward long enough for me to have gone over my notes and selected the ten students who would remain, Amelia's name circled twice because I knew she would be my biggest challenge.

Would she follow the rules? Or was she smart enough to have decided moving forward with me wasn't in her best interests?

Fifteen minutes passed before I knew that answer, my cock coming to life when Amelia walked through the door wearing a skirt that flowed down from her hips, the hem dancing around her knees.

Careful to keep my eyes from locking on her to reveal all the dirty things I wanted to do to that body, I flipped a pen between my fingers and kept my gaze down on the roster of students on my lap.

In my peripheral vision, I watched her take a hesitant peek at me as she passed, her hair falling down her back just begging to be fisted by my hands.

Once all twenty-five bright-eyed hopefuls had taken their seats with a chorus of scraping chair legs and the heavy thump of backpacks hitting the floor, I tapped my pen against the roster and said, "Good afternoon."

They answered, fifteen of them not yet knowing it would be the last time they stepped foot in this classroom.

Pulling my feet from the desk, I stood from my seat with roster in hand, rounded the desk and sat against the front edge. My eyes scanned over the students, briefly meeting Amelia's teal stare before moving on again.

I'd expected some form of reaction from her, some hint in her expression that would give away what we had done together. But she played the role of average student wonderfully. Keeping the secret wouldn't be difficult.

"Rather than wasting everybody's time, I should just get this over with. I'm going to call the names of the ten students who will continue forward. This, in no way, is a rejection of the talent of the fifteen who are leaving. My decisions are becoming more difficult as we move on and every one of you should be proud of the accomplishments you've made. If you are leaving today, I ask that you not let being cut discourage you from music. You have what it takes, but weren't yet ready for this particular competition. That being said..."

Running down the list, I announced the ten who would stay, quieting when those whose names hadn't been called gathered their things and shuffled out of the door.

Once they were gone, I dropped the roster on the desk and crossed my arms over my chest.

"Congratulations, all of you."

Beaming smiles. Bright eyes. Excitement and an undercurrent of smugness ran through them. All, except Amelia.

Her eyes were soft, thoughts distracted, legs held together so primly at the knees that I imagined pushing them open so I could taste her every reaction.

I wouldn't fuck her yet. Not today. Not here. But soon. And in a place where I had her all to myself without the threat of being disturbed.

"Next week, we'll begin going over the music selected to be performed for the competition. There are still seven weeks of the program left and in that time I will work with all of you as a group and individually. Ten are here today and I have to cut another five by the end of next week."

That got their attention, the smugness wiped away with the reminder that only one would remain by the end of the summer.

It drove me nuts that I still hadn't been able to dismiss Jillian and Krista, two girls whose clothes continued getting more revealing with each passing day, whose tongues had a tendency to peek out when I looked their direction. Unfortunately, they were excellent musicians and I would continue to endure their whispers and stares, the open invitation of their bodies, whenever my eyes met theirs.

I hadn't failed to notice the contempt they showed to Amelia, either. Another factor that made me want to strangle the life out of them.

"All right, it's late and we all want to get home and have a good weekend." Grabbing a stack of music from my bag, I walked down the rows to give each student a copy to practice and study, my leg brushing Amelia's elbow as I passed.

That one simple touch was enough to awaken the beast inside me.

Returning to my desk, I dropped the remaining copies on the surface and said, "Be ready Monday morning. I won't go easy on you if you're not proficient in the music you just received. Have a good weekend."

Everybody stood and made their way to the door, Amelia strolling out behind them.

She wasn't getting away that easily. "Miss Dillon. A word."

Stilling in place, the corner of her mouth tilted with a barely there smile. She knew, as well as I, that I wanted more than a word with her.

Speaking softly, I tempted fate. Broke rules. Tossed aside all reason because my desires had taken over my rational mind. "Shut the door, Amelia."

The room fell into silence following the quiet click of the door, Amelia turning to stare at me, her teal eyes uncertain.

"You're wearing a skirt."

A nod of her head, lips stretching just a fraction wider. "I hear it's a rule I should follow."

A better man would tell her to have a nice day and watch her walk her beautiful ass out of here.

I wasn't a better man.

"Go stand on the other side of my desk, bend over and wait for me."

I wouldn't fuck her. But that didn't mean I couldn't enjoy playing around.

She set her bag on a chair near the door, her eyes meeting mine as she walked past me to do as I'd instructed. For the love of all that was holy, I wanted to tear her pussy up with my cock, make her beg and plead for me to stop while also begging that I keep going.

This was a lesson in patience. A cosmic fucking joke by the universe.

Thankfully, my control kept me in line enough not to hurt her out here in the open and smile to do it. Julia would most likely wonder about the muffled screams and come running just to see how thoroughly I could ruin her star student.

"What did you do yesterday with your day off?"

From behind me, "Slept in. Practiced the piano. Watched television."

My mouth quirked at the corner. "Sounds boring."

"Well, it was on my calendar to rob a bank, but I had to cancel seeing as how a certain teacher of mine forbid it."

Oh, I had plans for that smart little mouth of hers. Amelia's inexperience in that area didn't matter. I was happy to teach her.

Pushing up from the desk, I rounded the end, my steps slow and steady, my eyes tracing the line of Amelia's body where she stood waiting for what I would do. Glancing up, she met my stare.

"Eyes down, Miss Dillon."

A spark of apprehension, but she obeyed, her torso balanced on her forearms, ass pushed out in wait. She was nervous. Scared.

I enjoyed it a little too much.

The leather of my chair groaned when I sat down, a muscle in her thigh jumping. She tensed knowing I was behind her, my eyes roaming greedily over the perfect heart shape of her ass.

I took my time, eventually reaching out to run my hands up the back of her legs, noting every flinch of her body as I lifted her skirt to reveal blue cotton panties, nothing frilly or sexy for a girl who hadn't yet learned what it meant to be tortured in sensual ways.

Leaning forward I pressed a kiss to each cheek of her ass, my thumbs curling beneath the sides of her panties to drag them down over her hips and allow them to fall down her legs to her ankles.

Fucking hell...

Her pussy was pink and swollen, the skin glistening with how turned on she already was.

"Watch the door," I said, my voice gritty with want.

Her voice shook in response. "What should I do if somebody walks in?"

With my fingertip, I traced the center slit slowly, my attention stolen by a part of her body no other man had enjoyed. "If somebody walks in," Ah, hell. "We're screwed."

Pushing the tip of my finger inside her, I ignored the hard line of my erection, my ear picking up the burst of breath falling over her lips.

"When you say you're a virgin: Does that mean you've never-"

"I've kissed two other guys besides you. But that's it."

Oh, Jesus Christ...

Utterly pure, this feast for my eyes. I should have pushed away, told her to pull up her panties and march out that door to escape a man who looked at her pussy like it was a toy to be broken.

Instead, I slid my finger down to circle it over her clit. She jumped in place, but my other hand clamped down on her thigh to hold her still. "Don't move."

The heat of my breath washed over her skin, her thigh trembling beneath my palm.

Just the tip of my tongue at first, a tiny taste, dragging up the slit as Amelia stilled, her body unsure how to react to so soft a sensation.

"Mr. Carter-"

"Shhhh. No talking, Miss Dillon. I don't appreciate being interrupted while teaching."

Another taste, my tongue dipping inside her as my finger continued playing over that small bundle of nerves that I'd used to make her come once before.

She whimpered, her body trembling as I took my time teasing her, toying with her, slowly building my pressure and speed. The musky scent of her was driving me absolutely fucking crazy, the desire to grab her hips and pull her body down on my lap damn near impossible to ignore.

"Lenn-"

I grinned against her. "We're in class, Miss Dillon. Using my first name is highly inappropriate."

Silence, and then, "I'm sorry, Mr. Carter."

166

Oh, you're going to be. But not here. Not now. Not until I can get you alone to show you exactly why you should have run when I first gave you the chance.

My right hand continued playing with her clit as I thrust my tongue inside her. In and out before licking up and down, nipping at the skin, causing her to jump with each threat of a bite. Releasing her thigh, I swept my left hand up and traced my thumb down the crease of her ass, brushing the hole and smiling to hear a squeak burst from her mouth.

"Mr. Carter -"

"No complaints," I reminded her, my mouth moving against her wet little hole.

All three sensations were driving her over an edge, heavy breaths and shocked sounds falling over her lips before I pulled my mouth away, to trace my right hand up and thrust a finger fully inside her.

"Oh!"

"Does that hurt?"

Fucking virgins. Having to go slow was driving me crazy.

"No," she whispered in response.

I drove a second finger in and watched with utter fascination as my hand explored a part of her that had never felt what I was doing before. She was a student in every conceivable way.

Slowly thrusting in and out, I asked her, "What are your plans for tonight?"

Amelia could barely answer, her body responding to the way I toyed with it. "Nothing."

"You're coming to my house."

"Okay."

I was done playing around. Using one hand to pinch her clit, rolling it between my fingertips, the swollen bud so sensitive from what I'd already done, I used my other hand to continuing thrusting two fingers inside her, small moans escaping her mouth as I drove her to an orgasm I could watch.

When her body finally shattered in front of me, I stared with intense fascination at the muscles clenching over my fingers, the glistening wet evidence of the moment she came.

Had she been more experienced, I would have turned her around in that same second, forced her to her knees and made her thank me for what I'd just done for her.

Instead, I sucked the sweet taste of her body from my fingers, lifted her panties into place and pulled her skirt down to let it fall just above her knees once again.

Pushing back in my chair to put distance between us, I scanned my eyes down her trembling legs. There was no two ways about it, I needed to get this first time over with so I could stop playing games.

"Turn around."

Slowly, she did so, her eyes hooded and soft, her lips slightly parted.

"Do you remember where I live?"

A nod of her head, her pulse fluttering in her throat.

"Meet me there at eight. This is your last warning though, Amelia. I'm not one to be soft and tender."

"That's okay."

She had no idea what she was saying.

"Go. We'll continue this later."

Nodding her head, Amelia walked away from the desk, my gaze tracking her every move as she grabbed her bag and left the classroom.

With the scent of her still on my lips, I folded my hands behind my head and leaned back in my chair wondering just how much control it would take to keep from making her first time a nightmare.

CHAPTER FOURTEEN

The hands are a blessing and a curse. Always pay attention to how you use them. Always be careful of who you let touch your body, heart and soul...

Amelia

A knock at my open door drew my attention. Glancing over my shoulder, I found Ben staring at me, his shoulder against the doorframe, grey eyes meeting mine with exhaustion staining them.

"Are you going out?"

In the background, I could hear the home nurse tending to my dad. Today was actually a good day, no violent episodes, no screaming filling the house. "Yeah."

Don't ask where....please, don't ask...

"Where?"

My shoulders tensed. I hated lying to him, but he would kill me if he knew the truth.

"A piano lesson." Flicking a glance his way, I smiled. "For the program. I'm one of the last ten students left."

"Of course you are. You're amazing." Gaze tracking to my window and the sun that was beginning to set, Ben arched a brow. "Bit late to be meeting with Julia, isn't it?"

Fuck. "Um, no, I'm not practicing with her. I'm meeting my teacher-"

"She's not your teacher? I thought she was the one who got you into the program?"

"She was, but because we have a personal relationship, she couldn't be my judge."

Finished tying my shoe, I straightened on the side of my bed, internally begging him to let it go.

"Who's your teacher?"

Damn it. "Lennon Carter."

Ben's brows knit together, shadows behind his eyes. "Isn't he around my age, maybe a little younger?"

I shrugged despite knowing Lennon was precisely two years younger than Ben. "I guess so. Why?"

"The name is familiar. I think-" He stopped, his eyes blinking closed and open again. "I think your teacher is Emaline's brother."

Emaline...

God, I hadn't thought of her in years. A student of my parents, she'd dated Ben for over a year. He was madly in love with her, his heart broken when she'd died suddenly. Suicide, we'd heard, why she'd take her life was beyond me.

I remembered meeting her several times when she was attending lessons with my parents. I was so much younger than her, but she reminded me of a princess. Long wavy brown hair, vibrant green eyes and a smile that lit the room. She was always so sweet to me.

Needless to say, her death had damn near destroyed my brother. It was around that time that he stopped caring about sports or school, had turned to drugs and partying as a way to get over her.

Emaline's name was another dark shadow over this house, but I didn't think she was Lennon's sister. From what I remembered, she'd been so poor, my parents had adjusted their usual rates just to teach her.

"I don't think so. Lennon is insanely wealthy. I highly doubt he grew up around here."

Ben stared outside, his hand lifting to rub at his jaw. "The name is so familiar."

Oh, well, that was understandable, given Lennon's reputation. "He's worked with a lot of popular bands. He also plays in the Florida Symphony. I kind of lucked out to be assigned to his class. He's an amazing musician. A hard ass, but still. If he can teach me to play like him, I'll be lucky."

"Yeah," Ben answered, his thoughts somewhere else. "Maybe." Finally looking at me, he asked, "Isn't it a bit late on a Friday night, though?"

Shrugging again, I made up something that wasn't exactly a lie. "Music is demanding. To be the best, you have to keep a busy schedule."

"So, you're meeting him at the school?"

"Yeah."

I couldn't look at him while telling the lie. He would know. Instead, I busied myself with packing music into my bag.

"Okay. What time are you getting home?"

Ugh! I needed him to stop asking so many damn questions. "Not sure."

Not a lie. But still, not entirely the truth.

"I have to go to work in a few hours, so I'll see you tomorrow."

"See you then."

Ben walked away and I glanced at the clock to see it was seven. I didn't want to be late getting to Lennon's and risk pissing him off. I remembered the general area where his house was, but knew I should leave early in case I got lost. What would I do if I couldn't find it? It wasn't like I had a way to contact him.

Stilling in place, I racked my brain over the idea that he might be Emaline's brother. Was it possible? Was Ben right?

No. It couldn't be. Lennon wasn't the type to live in the ghetto, he hated everything about it, his expression darkening every time he mentioned the crimes and tricks infamous in such a bad area of town.

Hiking the strap of my bag onto my shoulder, I left the house, jumped in my car and drove into a wealthy area of Tampa, weaving my way down streets I remembered from the other night, my mind recalling the spanking I'd received from Lennon for catching me running a scam.

I hated ripping people off, a fact I didn't think he knew, but given our situation at home and with Dad, I'd never thought I had much of a choice.

Eventually, I found his neighborhood, the belt of my car squealing just enough to be annoying. Desperately needing a new car, I tapped my hand on the steering wheel as to comfort its pain.

Lennon's house came into view, but I wasn't entirely sure it was his until I heard the faint sound of a piano whispering through the warm, night air, a melody I didn't recognize, but one that caused my breath to catch in my lungs.

Pulling into the driveway, I turned off my car, my engine wheezing and pinging in chorus to the music that kept pouring out of a window that must have been cracked open in the house.

Staring at the windows. I wouldn't have been sure he was home if not for the music. The windows were dark for the most part, a faint glow behind them that looked more like nightlights then anything.

Sweat made my palms sticky against the steering wheel, nervous anticipation rolling through me in waves.

I wanted this man. There was no question about how I felt, but I wasn't sure I could handle what he'd offered me.

When it came to Lennon, I saw heartbreak on the horizon, his promise of pain making me want to rethink what I'd agreed to do.

He would deliver. I knew that. The spanking he'd given me just a taste of what I assumed were his tastes when it came to sex.

Yet, here I was, inexperienced and terrified, still opening my door ready to deliver myself to the devil if it meant I could pretend for just a little while that he felt something for me.

As I walked up the path, the music grew louder. A crescendo of sound followed by the soft answer of a sad melody. Not recognizing it, I wondered if it was something else he'd written, the tone of it more contemporary than classic, the feel of it dark and intimidating.

It called to me, regardless, as if he'd plucked some small part of me out from where I kept all my thoughts hidden, and had turned it into a song I would carry with me for eternity.

Reaching the door, I knocked, but the music kept playing, absolute chaos in the notes, so hard and desperate that I doubted he'd heard my knuckles against the wood.

I must have stood there for several minutes, the music never stopping, never ceasing, drawing me closer with each strong chord followed by the sweeping answer of the melody.

Not knowing what else to do, I tried the knob, the door slowly opening to reveal a dark foyer, a small crystal chandelier above my head shimmering with the faint glow of lit candle sconces on the walls.

The floors were black marble. The walls, from what I could tell a pale grey. A large black-framed mirror hung just to the right of me and I caught sight of my rounded eyes in the reflection.

Such a beautiful house. I couldn't believe he didn't have it fully lit just to show off the leather furniture and gleaming silver and crystal vases on the tables.

Legs shaking, I wound my way through the house, inching closer to the room where I knew his piano stood, the music fully swallowing me the closer I got.

Candles were everywhere, all different shapes and sizes, their light dancing across my skin, over the walls, barely illuminating the space.

I turned a corner and froze in place, my gaze locked to Lennon's body where he sat playing the piano, his nimble hands practically tearing apart the keys.

Shirtless, every muscle was defined beneath his skin, the gleam of sweat caught in the flicker of candlelight at his back.

Still wearing the plaid pants he'd worn in class, he moved with every angry punch of a chord, swayed with every sweep of the melody. The looped ends of his suspenders were lying on the bench on either side of his hips, just the sight of them reminding me how he'd already used them against me.

I was captivated, to say the least, unable to look away or clear my throat to let him know I was standing there. I stepped farther in to take a closer look at a man who was drawing me in to some tangled web with promises of discipline for my defiance, and reward for my obedience.

Would I ever play like that?

Could the music pour out of me just the same?

Perhaps with Lennon teaching me how to set it free, I could hope to one day be as talented as him.

A few minutes later, the music stopped, his head bowed over the keys, my breath caught in my lungs.

"Do you always let yourself into other people's houses?"

His voice was gritty, dark, and exhausted, the deep tenor brushing against my senses with stern warning. I froze in place, swallowed, unsure if I should answer him or turn around to run like hell.

"I knocked, but you didn't hear me over the music."

How did he even know I was standing here? I hadn't made a sound, my body so still because I'd been entranced by what he was playing.

He spun on the bench to look at me, his eyes shadowed, his chest gleaming with sweat. It was the first time I'd seen him without his shirt, and dear God, he was sculpted. Every hard ridge and shallow dip was perfectly defined, candlelight highlighting his skin because it, too, couldn't help but reach out and touch him.

I wanted to run my tongue over the definition of his chest, wanted to feel the strength of his thick biceps wrap around me, wanted to experience what it felt like to have him move over me while making me sing as beautifully as his piano.

Breath heavy, Lennon reached up to run his fingers through his hair, his eyes locked on my face. "I'm giving you one gentle time, Amelia. One. And only because I don't want to tear you apart when you don't know what it is like to have a man move inside you."

Pausing, he raked his gaze down my body, his mouth a sensual line when he said, "But after that, all tenderness goes out the window."

"Okay." The response was more a squeak than my normal voice.

"Last chance," he warned.

I was beginning to think a smarter girl would turn and get the hell out of there.

"I'm still here," I whispered.

Lennon grinned, shook his head, and crooked a finger for me to walk to him. "Come here, little girl. Let me show you why you should have run."

My legs shook when I tried to take the first step. I knew he could see my unsteady gait even though his eyes refused to release mine, his expression hard and intense. I could feel that gaze distinctly, fingertips against my skin exploring all the places I'd never allowed another man to touch.

By the time I reached him, I was out of breath, my hair a curtain at the sides of my face that blocked the light reflecting across his high cheekbones.

Here we were, in the first place where he had touched me, his body positioned on the bench much like the night he'd laid me over his lap. I didn't know what to expect. Fear raced through me to find out.

"Put your hands on my shoulders, Amelia."

"Why?"

Neck craning back to glance up at me, Lennon shook his head. "Because you look like you're about to fall over."

Embarrassment tinged my cheeks red, my shaking hands reaching forward to touch the heat of his skin, to feel the steel of muscle beneath his sweat slickened skin.

It was suddenly far too hot in this room, as if the heat of the candles were as warm as a wall of fire.

"Relax," he breathed out, his fingers moving to the buttons of my blouse, slowly opening them one by one, working from the top down.

Unfastening the last one, he pulled the sides apart and left them hanging over my arms, his hands gripping my waist.

Lennon leaned forward and softy kissed a trail from the arch of my rib cage down past my belly button, my fingers gripping tighter over his shoulders, my breath coming out in tiny, raspy bursts.

"Are you scared?" he asked, his lips moving against my stomach.

"Yes."

I expected him to try to comfort me, but instead he replied, "Good. You should be."

His deep voice rolled through me like a crashing wave, the reality of what I was doing finally setting in, my entire body quaking with nervous expectation.

Fingers moving to the button of my skirt, he made quick work of it, a sharp yank of the zipper and the material fell to my ankles.

"You can go ahead and kick that away, as well as your shoes. You won't be needing them for a while."

I did as he said, my ankles slamming back together when his hands gripped my ass and he pulled my hips toward him to stick his nose between my legs and breathe me in.

Pure heat bloomed over my cheeks, my eyes closing when he said, "You smell scared. I like that."

Oh my god...

Yeah, no. I was in way too fucking deep with this man. I should have started with a different person for my first time, a fluffy puppy dog instead of a hungry wolf.

His teeth locked over the front waistband of my panties, his thumbs hooking on the sides. Slowly, he dragged them down my hips, letting them fall to my ankles silently.

Stormy blue eyes lifted to meet mine, the smirk that always drove me so fucking crazy tilting the corner of his lips. "Take off your bra."

The instant I released his shoulders, I wavered on gelatin legs, his strong hands gripping my thighs to keep me balanced. I shouldn't have been this damn nervous, but with his face eye level to my stomach, giving him an up close and personal view of my tits and pussy, I was way more exposed than I thought I ever would be for my first time.

In most of the movies I've seen, the couple are doing it beneath sheets, or sometimes in the shower. But still, the guy didn't have his face between her legs breathing her in like she was a perfume tester sheet or a fine wine.

Then again...I'd never watched porn and everything about Lennon was apparently pornographic.

It took me three attempts to unclasp my bra, my fingers fumbling and uncoordinated, breath shuddering from my lungs as Lennon's face tilted up to watch me. His fingers scratched softly down the sides of my ass with warning.

Finally pulling the damn thing free, I held the cups in place, a serious case of shyness overtaking me as the straps slid down my arms over the shirt that still hung open. Lennon's smirk deepened. The jerk was enjoying every second of my timid behavior.

"I said off, and that includes the shirt."

"You're doing this on purpose."

His eyes blazed with heat. "You better fucking believe it. Why do you think I kept giving you chances to change your mind?"

Closing my eyes, I let the bra and shirt fall from my arms, my hands returning to his shoulders when a wave of ungodly apprehension rolled through me.

I was so turned on, yet terrified. So shy, that I wished he would just speed this process up and get it over with. Maybe he was right. Maybe I needed the hearts and flowers, maybe-

He slid a finger between my clenched legs, curled the tip and moved it slowly in and out of me, the entire time staring up at me past my breasts, watching my every reaction.

"Play with your tits, Amelia."

My eyes rounded, knees almost buckling. I could barely think past the threat of his finger, the warning in his eyes, and he was demanding I touch myself in front of him?

"Lennon-"

"No complaints." His finger slipped inside me fully with the gentle reminder.

Releasing his shoulders, I brought my hands to my breasts, molding them and pushing them up and together.

"Squeeze the nipples. Let me know you like it."

Asshole...

Fuck! As soon as I did as he said, it was like an electric current shooting down between what my fingers were doing and what his were doing. Eyes wide, I watched Lennon pull his finger from my legs, open his mouth and suck my taste off from knuckle to tip.

My head fell back in that instant, his arm pushing between my legs until I was practically straddling his bicep. Bending his elbow, he grabbed my long hair in his fist, pulling it to keep my head in place.

When his free hand grabbed one of mine to direct it back to his shoulder, he whispered one more demand, "Grind your pussy over my arm, beautiful, while playing with your clit with your fingers. Let me feel what you can do."

His teeth took hold of my nipple, his fist still secure in my hair. When I didn't immediately move like he'd said, he slapped the cheek of my ass with his other hand causing my hips to buck so I shifted forward over his arm.

What in the hell was going on? I was grinding against Lennon's bicep while he sucked and nipped my breast, a collision of sensations driving through me until I found it difficult to breathe.

I couldn't look down to see if he was watching me, didn't want to know what he was thinking about a girl who would masturbate so close to his face.

"Jesus, Amelia, you're practically dripping on my skin."

Heat bloomed in my cheeks again because I knew he wasn't lying. I could feel lithe slickness every time I moved my hips, my finger working my clit without any sort of precision. My mouth opened on a silent moan as Lennon's thumb pressed against it to deepen the circles and set an intoxicating rhythm.

It was happening again. Just like in the classroom. Just like when I'd been bound to that piano without any way of defending myself against the pleasure Lennon could force through me.

I understood what was coming, an orgasm, a release so violent that I would lose the ability to breathe, to think, to speak anything but his name over and over again.

The only thing holding me in place was his arm between my legs. When I came, I feared falling backwards, my entire body trembling with waves of pleasure as he let my hair go to catch me.

I looked down at him to watch as he lowered his head to breathe me in again, his lips pulling apart with a devilish grin. "There, now you don't smell so scared anymore."

Son of a bitch, I was going to die right then and there and Lennon would be the murderer.

In one deft move, he pulled his arm free, stood from the bench and lifted me up to throw me over his shoulder, one arm wrapped over the backs of my legs while the other hand clapped down on my ass cheek so hard I flinched as he carried me from the room.

What had I gotten myself into?

It was like I weighed nothing to him, his legs spry beneath us, my body bouncing over his shoulder as he ran up the stairs, turned down a hallway, burst through a door and flipped me down on my back over a mattress.

This was him being gentle for my first time?

I didn't have time to process what was happening before he gripped my legs beneath the knees and dragged me down. Pressing his palms against the insides of my thighs, he spread my legs wide, his breath hot between my legs before his mouth covered my pussy, his tongue licking along the slit before thrusting inside me.

My hips bucked toward his face, my chest arching as my eyes closed and my hands fisted the sheets beneath me.

Fuck! He was owning me in this moment. Tasting me. His mouth moving over every part of my swollen skin, his tongue teasing my clit before moving down again to dip inside me and show me just how thoroughly he could force me to surrender.

Another climax surged before I had time to know it was coming, my legs struggling against the way he held them open, my body writhing beneath the pleasure he forced through me, wave after gloriously excruciating wave.

I didn't think I could endure its violence, and yet I never wanted it to end.

Still holding my legs apart with his hands locked over the insides of my thighs, Lennon looked up at me, his eyes shadowed and dark, that damn smirk of his telling me he didn't give a damn that he was driving me to madness over and over again.

"Do you have any idea how delicious you are?"

I shook my head, so confused by this point, I didn't know if the question had been real or rhetorical.

It only made him grin more, like a wolf staring at me licking his chops in anticipation of his next meal.

"Let me show you."

He pushed forward, his chest barely touching mine as his mouth claimed my lips, the taste of my body filling my mouth as his tongue swept in to tangle with mine.

I could feel how hard he was, his hips pressed to me, his hands still locking my legs in place as his erection just barely brushed against my swollen pussy.

He kissed me until my body had come down from the last climax, and left me in a puddle of desperation for more over his bed as he released my legs to push away from me, his height towering over the bed.

Standing in front of me with feet set shoulder width apart, he hooked his thumbs in the waistband of his pants and stared down at me with an expression that promised every sinful, dirty act known to man.

Lennon's chest glistened beneath the low light of the room, his strong shoulders moving with every breath.

"Turn over."

When I didn't do as he said immediately, he canted his head and cocked a brow. "Don't tell me you're getting shy again. I'll be sure to break you of that bad habit."

Threat spoken and received, I shook while turning over. Lennon grabbed my hips and lifted me up onto my knees, his hand flat against my back to keep my upper body pressed against the bed. With his knee, he pushed my legs apart and I buried my face in the sheets absolutely mortified that he had a front row view of all my intimate parts.

A fingertip rubbed softly down the center slit. "So beautiful, this pussy."

I felt the mattress dip beneath me just seconds before his tongue licked the track his finger had just taken, the tip of his nose a hard point as he dipped his tongue inside me. "So wet."

Behind me, I could hear him stripping out of his pants, and God how I wanted to see him fully naked, but in the position he'd left me, I couldn't see a damn thing.

The rip of a condom wrapper grabbed my attention just before the thick tip of his cock began rubbing up and down my slit slowly as if testing each individual part before finding the hole.

"This may hurt, Amelia. I'm not going to lie to you."

Notching the head of his cock at my opening, he gripped a hip with one hand while using his other to play with my clit. When he penetrated me with the tip, my entire body tensed up, my fear overwhelming.

Rather than driving himself inside with one hard, full thrust, he slowly pushed in, pulled out and then went deeper again with his next slow thrust. The fullness was awkward. Unexpected. I wasn't sure what to do.

But then he pushed all the way in and my body tensed around him, the discomfort noticeable, but not so much that I cried like I thought I would.

"Fuck, you're tight."

Lennon didn't move immediately, the pause giving my body time to adjust to him, to relax and mold to his length and girth. He filled me up entirely, his hands gripping my hips as he finally lost the ability to remain still and his body began to move.

While his cock moved inside me, he released one of my hips to roll a finger over my clit again, his deep voice seducing me as he said, "This is the only time I'll control myself with you." A curse word hissed over his lips in chorus with the slap of skin between our bodies.

Slowly a pressure began to build in me like nothing I'd ever felt before. It was a tidal wave rushing forward with the distinct warning it would carry me away with its violence.

I moaned into the sheets, my body quivering as he continued relentlessly, his pace picking up as his cock seemed to grow even more.

Unable to fight it, I let go to an orgasm that made me scream, my fingers clamping into the sheets as Lennon fucked me harder, his hips slapping the cheeks of my ass just before a groan rolled over his lips and he pushed deeper and stilled in place.

After a few seconds he pulled out, and I collapsed on the bed, the only sound in the room was the heavy thud of his feet on the floor as he walked away. I heard a door close and knew he'd gone into the bathroom to toss the condom away.

When he returned, he crawled onto the mattress facing me, his fingers trapping my chin as he tilted my head to look at him. Bleary eyes blinking open, I almost orgasmed again just to see the lazy look of satisfaction in his normally stormy eyes, to remember just how fucking beautiful this man was.

"Don't expect it to be so simple again," he said with his signature smirk. "You have no idea how much restraint I just showed you."

I almost laughed that he considered what we did simple, but then he kissed me and every thought I had dispersed on a tempest wind.

CHAPTER FIFTEEN

I felt like I used him in a way. I didn't know. Couldn't have known.
But there had been clues and I ignored every one of them...

Lennon

"I can't sleep here tonight."

Amelia's fingers trailed lazily down my chest, her body curled over mine where I lay on my back with my head resting against my arm. Never had I been a cuddler, but given this was her first time, I gave in to her need to stay near me.

My eyes were half closed, exhaustion overtaking me, not so much from fucking, but from the hours I'd spent working on the music that had been a constant inside my head since I'd returned to Sheldon.

However, her statement came out of nowhere and forced me back to full consciousness. Not because it bothered me she wouldn't sleep over, but more because she'd phrased it that she *couldn't*.

Where in the hell did she have to be that she couldn't shut her eyes and fall asleep beside me? Instantly my thoughts went to all the times I'd caught her doing something fucked up.

"Why not? Tomorrow's Saturday. You don't have school."

"I have to practice the music you gave us."

A lie.

"My piano is downstairs. You're free to use it."

She grew still, her fingers stopping their relaxing movement. Quietly, she admitted, "My family will wonder where I am."

It made sense, but what possessed her to lie about that fact initially? What was she trying to hide?

A thought came to me, the name Julia had given me without realizing she was providing the link I needed to finally identify the asshole who'd driven Emaline to her grave.

"You never told me you have a brother."

Silence, and then, "Do you have a sister, by chance?"

I flinched in response to the question. So many emotions I couldn't handle whenever Emaline was brought up. Although, at that moment, I was more curious as to how she knew that. "Why do you ask?"

"Your last name."

She was hiding something. I could tell by her hesitation to answer, the pitch in her voice when she finally did.

"I remember a girl with the last name Carter who used to come to lessons with my parents."

It's a common last name, nothing that should have given away the connection. She knew something, but didn't want to admit it. My hand fisted beneath my head, yet I refrained from acting on the anger inside me.

"I *had* a sister," I confessed on a heavy breath. "Her name was Emaline."

Amelia's breath caught, the reaction telling me the name meant something to her.

The puzzle pieces, by that point, weren't difficult to put together. Ben was the son of a bitch that drove my sister to killing herself. He was also the asshole who had Amelia luring men to a dark alley to be mugged without giving a damn that his *virgin* sister was being molested by a stranger in the process.

My jaw locked at the thought that Amelia would return to her home tonight, most likely because her *brother* had an issue with her staying out.

I was going to kill the fucker the next time I saw him.

Amelia must not have picked up on the tension in my body. Instead, she allowed her mind to meander back into the past, her lips to part on words that were tearing my heart from my chest.

"She was gorgeous. Emaline was. I was a lot younger, obviously, about seven, maybe eight. But I remember every time I saw her, I thought she was a princess. It was her smile, you know? Like something you'd see in a movie."

Eyes closed, I pictured that smile, darkness crawling out of all the places inside me where the loss of Emaline had been locked away. It lingered just beneath my skin, a pain so thorough that I was crushed beneath the weight of it while Amelia kept talking.

"I'm sorry about what happened to her. We were upset to learn what she did."

Hands clenching beneath my head and over my stomach, I fought not to hurt Amelia just to force her to shut up.

Taking a breath while reminding myself none of this was her fault, I spoke behind clenched teeth, fighting back the monster I knew existed inside me. "It's probably best we don't talk about this right now."

"Oh..."

She fidgeted over the bed, her bare breast brushing over my ribs. "I'm sorry."

There were three outlets that would help expel the frustration I was feeling: fighting, music or fucking.

Regardless of the consequences, I chose the one in closest proximity. Amelia needed to learn who she was dealing with regardless. There was no better time than now.

Rolling over, my weight pinned Amelia down to the bed, my hand closing over her throat. She cried out, part shock, part fear, her teal eyes so wide I could see myself in them.

Still, she submitted perfectly.

"Are you sore?" My lips were pressed to her ear, my voice a dark whisper that asked the question while giving away the fact that I didn't give a damn about the answer.

"N-no." So brave, this girl. Or incredibly stupid.

"Good."

The first time had been about her. The second was all about me.

"Do you remember the last time we were like this?"

Her throat worked to swallow against my palm, head nodding before she opened those pretty pink lips. "In the alley. The first time we met."

Not that it had been that long ago. Barely a week and I already had her in my bed. Naked. Pinned. Her tits brushing my chest as I leaned down to kiss her with my hand still locked over her throat. She moaned as our tongues swept together, her legs spreading out of the same instinct that had my cock swelling with need.

Only this time, her sassy mouth wasn't demanding I get off her. Instead it was meeting me on neutral ground, the tip of her tongue still shy, her body learning to surrender.

I hadn't guessed teaching could be so much fun.

"Touch me."

Her eyes met mine when I released her wrists, a growl emanating from my chest when she didn't immediately obey.

So shy, this girl. It both turned me on and annoyed me.

Eventually, she moved her hand down between us, both our gazes following the motion to watch as she brushed her fingers over my cock. Her hand was shaking, her chest beating with raspy breath as she wrapped her hand over it.

Although my dick was demanding immediate relief, I allowed her to explore, to familiarize herself with the male anatomy.

It killed me to let her take it slow. But eventually, my patience ran out.

I was always safe when it came to sex. Nobody wanted little Lennons running around causing havoc, and for that reason, I kissed her one last time before shifting to pull from her hold.

"Stay," I demanded against her lips, pushing away from her to grab a condom.

She shifted when I stood from the bed, just enough to draw my attention, her arms over her chest, shyly covering her breasts. I'd already figured out Amelia was uncomfortable being exposed, a damn habit that wouldn't do. Eyeing my pants, I rounded the end of the bed, grabbed them and pulled the suspenders free.

Glancing over my shoulder, I found that her eyes were wide and locked to my ass. I cocked a brow. "See something you like?"

Her cheeks blazed red, gaze darting to mine so quickly it made me laugh softly. But then those eyes drifted down to what was in my hand and I knew she was thinking about being bound to the piano.

My imagination was running wild with all the possibilities. Displaying her over the piano while I played first and foremost in my thoughts.

I wondered if she was ready to be hog tied, remembered that she'd only had sex once, and closed my eyes to calm down and be patient with all the devious plans I had for her.

A nudge of my chin. "Arms above your head, Amelia."

Her head shook as if to deny me at first, cheeks blushing deeper, but then she lifted shaking arms above her head, her fingers wrapping around the iron bars of the headboard.

Breath expelled from my lungs on a heavy rush, such beauty in a woman who obeyed even when it scared her to do so. I grabbed a condom from a side table drawer as I made my way back to the bed.

Straddling her chest, careful not to crush her, I used the suspenders to bind her wrists and tie her to the

194

headboard, not missing how her gaze studied my cock like it was the first one she'd ever seen up close and personal.

Damn it...it probably was.

I was more than happy to let her get more familiar with it, but not now. Now I wanted to devour her. Wanted to enjoy the shy little girl who was learning how to properly fuck.

Moving down once she was secured, I kneeled between her thighs, the urgency I'd felt earlier settling into a desire to explore, to study her body, to look at a woman who was just as comfortable stealing as she was sharing her soul through the music she played.

The anger had already dissipated inside me, the monster locked away again as my focus dragged over her supple tits, flat stomach and curvy hips.

"You're beautiful," I said, my eyes meeting hers in the low light, the truth of my appraisal clear.

My fingers wrapped over my cock, forearm flexing as I pumped it a few times while looking at her. Amelia tried to hold my stare, but her curiosity got to her, that teal gaze dragging down to watch me work my dick. Lips parting, she blinked, and I had the desire to know what it would feel like between those full lips.

Later...

So many ideas I had for her.

After rolling on a condom, I grabbed her hips and lifted them from the bed, my eyes on hers as she watched me thrust my cock inside her, her stare locked to the point where our bodies connected and her thighs were spread wide.

Innocence lost in that stare, her mouth opening wider on an exhalation of breath as her head rolled back, her chest arched forward and I rolled my hips between her legs, fucking *dying* to go slow and not hurt her.

Amelia would be sore in the morning and I didn't want to leave her walking funny in front of a family that would notice.

"How does it feel to know I own this tight pussy?"

Her eyes flicked up to meet mine.

Without giving a damn that her cheeks were tinting pink at my words, I continued thrusting inside her, my voice a gritty whisper. "I'll do whatever the hell I want with this. With you. You have no idea how many dirty things I plan to do to this body."

Leaning forward, I pumped my hips while tasting her breasts, my teeth grazing the hard nipples before my tongue licked away the pain. Amelia's arms pulled at the suspenders that bound her as an orgasm threatened to break her apart.

"Lennon..." Spoken like a prayer, she lost the battle and gave in to the waves of pleasure rolling through her.

As soon as her pussy clenched, the muscles rippling greedily over my cock, I lost the ability to hold on as well, my climax rough as I pushed deep one last time.

It took several minutes for both of us to catch our breath and before walking into the bathroom to toss the condom, I tugged the suspenders free to release her.

It wasn't until I came out of the bathroom that I understood just how quickly she needed to return home.

"Leaving already?" Leaning a shoulder against the bathroom door, I watched Amelia getting dressed. She must have run downstairs to grab her clothes and run back up.

A curtain of hair fell over her face as she buttoned her shirt. "I would have gotten dressed downstairs but I didn't want you to think I'd run away."

She looked up at me. "But yeah, I need to go. It's getting late and -"

"Your family will worry."

"I told them I was at a piano lesson."

Eyes closing, I bit the inside of my cheek to keep from asking who, exactly, it was in her family that was so protective of her.

Protective, I reminded myself, unless of course it involved sending her out dressed in a barely there dress to lure men into the shadows.

Rather than demanding the information, I convinced myself to let it go...for now.

I grabbed a pair of sweatpants from the closet and emerged to find her fully dressed. "Come on. I'll walk you out."

Something unsaid glimmered in her eyes. For a moment I thought she might reveal her thoughts, but then her jaw locked and she nodded her head.

Silently we made our way to her car. I kissed her goodnight, trying to ignore her rush to leave and get home. Watching her drive off until her taillights disappeared around a turn, I tilted my head up to the night sky and clenched my jaw.

Everything came rushing back.

Emaline.

Ben.

The pain I'd endured for ten years.

And now a girl I somehow knew would be in danger if she weren't freed from her brother's grip.

The music flowed through me again. Except this time, instead of a melody filled with longing, it was a beat driven by intense anger.

CHAPTER SIXTEEN

Did you know the hands can lie? Like a magician who masks his tricks. Don't believe the lies. Look to the results. Pay attention to the acts that led to them...

Amelia

"Jillian Bates."

My eyes lifted to Lennon's face as he called the names of the five remaining students in class. Another week had passed, the roster being whittled down once again. I hated that Jillian was still in the running. She flirted shamelessly in class, flipping her long blond hair and always wearing clothes that showed off her perky breasts and round ass.

The only relief I felt when watching her smile wide at him, giggle at all his jokes, or show off her talent on the keys while giving his small, promising glances, was knowing that it would be me he fucked after class was over, my body teased and taunted over and over until I was begging him to drive inside me.

"Krista Cross."

Ugh. She was another one, although her advances were shyer, less in your face than Jillian. Krista was a pretty redhead with pale skin and a splattering of freckles across her nose. Best friends with Jillian, she went along with the game they played, of both competing to gain Lennon's attention the most.

"Amelia Dillon."

A snort of disgust burst from Jillian when my name was called. She and Krista immediately launched into whispers, their heads angling together before they turned in unison to glance back at me.

Lennon glanced up from his roster, his observant gaze locked on the two girls who looked down on me because I didn't dress as nicely as them and didn't drive a car worth more than the scrap metal that could be gained from it.

"Is there a problem, Ms. Bates?"

I recognized his stern tone of voice, the sound forcing a shiver down my spine. It was the same one he used with me before spanking me for disobedience, mostly on the days I was distracted and wasn't playing to the best of my ability.

Lennon didn't know about my problems at home, and despite agreeing to a rule of no secrets, I kept them regardless. I was too ashamed to tell him how shitty my family situation was.

And Ben, my ever watchful brother, was beginning to question my late night practice sessions more and more.

"No, Mr. Carter. There's no problem."

Sugar sweet, Jillian's voice, her shoulders rolling back as her chest pushed out. Lennon didn't so much as flick a glance down at the view she was blatantly giving him.

One part of me wanted him to launch into her in my defense, while the other knew he needed to let it go in so he wouldn't be accused of favoritism. Jillian would love nothing more than to have a reason to challenge my standing in the competition, and if anybody discovered my relationship with Lennon, I was as good as gone.

He knew that, and after glaring at her for another few seconds, his eyes returned to the roster, his deep voice smooth over the next names. "Jackson Peters and Keith Williams."

The five students who weren't selected made a few groans of complaint, their bodies shifting over their seats to begin gathering their things.

Lennon set the roster down and locked his hands together behind his back. As usual, he was wearing an odd combination of clothes, the loops of his suspenders free at his hips.

I loved every damn thing he did with those suspenders, and I understood wearing them was more a matter of sexual convenience than a fashion statement.

It didn't matter when or where, he always had a tool to use against me when I smart mouthed him or acted in a way he didn't approve.

"To the five who weren't selected, I think it goes without saying that you are quite talented on the piano. Rather than taking this moment as a rejection, I hope you'll see it for what it is. You made it this far, which says a lot about your progress as musicians. Don't give up."

The students who were leaving nodded their heads, disappointment lining their faces. They shuffled out quietly, leaving Lennon and the five of us who remained. Jillian straightened in her seat, front and center like always.

"For those that remain, I would be a liar to tell you it's an easy road from here. By the end of next week, only two will be left. Eventually, I'll scale that down to one. The student who is selected to compete for the scholarship will then work privately with me for the remainder of the summer."

Hell if I'd let that student be Jillian. She was licking her damn lips at the thought of having all that time alone with Lennon.

"Hastings has provided a list of approved music for you to master for this next round. Each piece is the same in regard to technical difficulty. However, as all of you have now learned with me, it's not solely your skill that I'll judge. If I don't feel that piece, it means nothing and you will be let go. I want you to select which one you'd like to play and take the sheet music home with you to practice this weekend. Beginning Monday, I'll work with each of you individually every day to improve your performance. As such, I've created a schedule, which is attached to the white board. Select your music, note your time on the schedule, and I hope you all have a good weekend."

As usual, I took my time packing my bag, hoping like hell that Krista and Jillian would leave so I could stay behind with Lennon. It was getting more difficult to find excuses to be the last one in the classroom. We had to be careful not to be caught, and Lennon was good about always giving me the last slot on his schedule.

"Mr. Carter. I bought tickets to see the symphony performance you'll be soloing in next week."

Jillian's saccharine voice rang through the room, my ear pricking to listen, although I refused to look up and acknowledge I was interested in the conversation.

"I'm so excited to see you on stage. I bet you look stunning in a tux. Maybe I can visit backstage after the performance? It would be good for me to see what happens behind the scenes."

She was so fucking annoying, mostly because I didn't even know Lennon would be soloing. Not that I could afford tickets, but why hadn't he told me? I would love to see him on stage, would give anything to sit in an audience and stare up at a man who seduced me every time I was near him.

Leaning against the front of his desk, Lennon smiled politely at Jillian. "I'm not sure I could get you backstage, but I'm glad you'll see the performance. Every person in here should see what's expected of a professional."

Everybody but me, apparently. He hadn't mentioned the possibility of me being there to see him play.

"Well," she practically sighed, "I guess I'll see you Monday at one. It's exciting to have come this far."

Nodding his head, Lennon dismissed her with his silence. The room emptied except for the two of us, my eyes lifting to meet his. "I didn't know you were performing."

Blue eyes glimmered from across the room, his strong arms crossed over his chest. "I wasn't sure your family would approve of you being out so late."

There was accusation in the statement, although I wasn't sure why. Every time my family was brought up, Lennon's gaze would shadow with anger, the storm inside him rolling to the surface.

"I don't think they'd mind if it was the symphony I was attending."

In truth, I had nothing to wear even if I did go. And without the money to buy something nice, I would only be an embarrassment.

"I can get you a ticket," he finally said, "but I think you already know we can't be seen together. It would raise too many questions."

A spike of jealousy stabbed through me. "Will you be seen with Jillian?"

His shoulders shook with a bark of laughter. "She does nothing but annoy me, Amelia."

Rolling my eyes, "I did nothing but annoy you when we first met."

"You also made my dick hard as a rock, but that could have been a result of how much you pissed me off."

I grinned, my thighs clenching at the thought of all the naughty things he did with that dick.

Lennon's eyes flicked to the door, his voice quiet when he glanced back at me. "Come here."

Obediently, I walked to him, his fingers capturing my chin before he tilted my face up to his. With his other hand, he ran his knuckles over my shirt and between my breasts, heat rolling behind his eyes.

"I'd still like to punish this mouth of yours."

The corner of my lips quirked knowing full well we couldn't do anything at that moment. From the wall behind him, the muted sounds of a piano filtered into the room. Julia's class still hadn't let out for the day.

"We'll get caught."

A devil peeked out at me from behind his eyes. "Only if we're not careful."

His left hand slid down to take hold of my hand and direct it to his cock. Hard as a fucking rock, as usual.

"Walk around to the other side of my desk and wait for me."

Anticipation rolled through me. Nervousness as well. I'd never gone down on a guy before. Would my teeth hurt him? How would I fit him in my mouth to begin with? Lennon wasn't small in the slightest. Not that I had anything to compare him to, but I could barely wrap my hand around him when he was fully erect.

I was in class to learn, wasn't I?

Doing as he said, I moved to the other side of the desk, watching him as he selected sheet music and walked over to place it on my desk. His eyes met mine.

"You'll be playing that piece for me next week."

"I thought it was my choice."

He grinned. "Not with me, it isn't."

Approaching me, he brushed my body with his as he stepped around to take a seat, his legs spread, the thick muscles of his thighs straining the legs of his pants.

"On your knees, Miss Dillon. You've been quite the challenge this week. Constantly mouthing off, which isn't allowed in my class."

Slowly, I lowered down to my knees, the linoleum floor cold against my skin. Not knowing what to do, I looked up to him for direction.

His eyes flicked to the door again. "Crawl under my desk."

Lips pulling into a tight line, I shook my head and did as he instructed. We were so going to get busted one of these days, but the threat didn't stop me. I wanted him too much.

His chair turned once I was under his desk, his hand reaching down to cup my cheek. I leaned into the touch.

"Take my cock out of my pants, Amelia. Explore it. I want you as familiar with it as I am with the pretty pussy of yours."

Reaching up to open his pants, my hands shook as I fumbled with the button and zipper. I pulled down the elastic of his boxer briefs and my breath caught at the sight of his cock, the tip glistening, a thick vein running down the shaft.

It wasn't the first time I'd touched it, but still, it was intimidating. My hand wrapped around him, steel beneath soft skin that was so warm it surprised me.

Lennon peeked down at me, his lips slightly parted, his blue eyes hooded with lust. "Stroke it, beautiful. Don't be shy."

Yet, I was shy. Scared, actually, that he wouldn't like it.

With loose fingers, I stroked up and down, not quite sure what to do. How much pressure to use. If it would hurt him if I squeezed too tight.

His hand closed around mine, forcing my grip tighter, stroking me up and down to a beat he wanted me to follow.

"A good blowjob starts with a good handjob, Miss Dillon. It's not all about the mouth."

Rolling my eyes again, my cheeks heated to have him *teaching* me, like oral sex was part of the Hasting's curriculum.

Fascinated with his cock, I leaned forward to lick the tip. His thighs flinched on either side of my head.

"What the fuck was that?"

"Me being an advanced student."

A masculine growl rolled out of his chest. "Why don't you show me what else that mouth of yours can do besides piss me off?"

Still nervous, I continued pumping him with my hand, his fingers traveling to my head to fist in my hair. It burned along my scalp when he tugged, but I didn't mind. Lennon had a tendency to get rough, and I was learning just how much I liked it.

Taking the tip into my mouth, I pulled my lips down to keep my teeth from scraping his skin and suckled the tip. His fingers tightened in my hair, urging me to take him deeper.

It didn't take me too long to get the hang of it, the salt of his skin a burst of flavor on my tongue, the sounds coming from his throat inspiring me to take him as deep as I could without choking.

"Fuck, Amelia. I knew that mouth of your would be heaven."

Grinning, I kept licking and sucking, stroking and kissing, my rhythm dictated by his hand directing my head by my hair.

I thought he might lose his ability to keep from coming in another few seconds, but then Lennon tensed in his seat just before a knock at the door caught my attention.

Stopping out of fear of being caught, I started again when Lennon tugged on my hair, the fear I felt making the experience all the more sweet.

"Can I help you?"

How he maintained such an even voice while I was sucking his cock was beyond me. Still, I kept going, careful not to make a sound.

"Yeah-"

That stopped me, the deep voice all too fucking familiar.

"I'm looking for my sister. Amelia Dillon? She said she was in your class."

Pure tension ran through Lennon's body, his hand slowly releasing my hair. "My students have left for the day. And you are?"

"Ben Dillon. I mean, I see that your class is empty, but Amelia's car is still in the parking lot. Is she staying late to *practice* again?"

While I was practically dying right there beneath his desk, Lennon remained calm. However, I picked up a note of anger in his voice when he spoke again, a deep tenor of warning.

"She's not here at the moment, Ben. But she is scheduled for more *practice* tonight. If I see her, I can tell her you came by."

Silence flowed between them, my legs going numb beneath me.

"I just find it odd that her car is still here."

"Maybe she left with some friends from class? Is there something you need from her?"

What the fuck was going on? Both of them sounded pissed, their tones clipped, accusation rolling through every word they tossed back and forth.

"No. Just a family emergency. If you see her, let her know I came by."

Lennon's hand fisted over his lap, the skin blanching from how tight he curled his fingers. "I'll be sure to let her know. *If* I happen to see her."

Family emergency.

Oh, god. Did something happen with dad?

The sound of retreating steps helped me relax, but I knew Ben well enough to know that wasn't the last of him. He'd keep searching until he found me.

"Lennon, I have to go."

He didn't move immediately, although his dick was now soft as he stuffed it into his pants.

"You want to tell me what that could have been about?"

"I don't know, but he wouldn't have come looking for me if it wasn't important. Please, Lennon, let me up."

A moment's hesitation before he pushed his chair away from the desk, his eyes tracking me as I climbed to my feet and practically ran to pack the music into my bag and hike the strap up my shoulder.

"Are you coming over tonight?"

My eyes closed, indecision pouring through me. I worried that something was wrong with my father. "I don't know."

"When will you know?"

Shrugging a shoulder, I looked at him with as much apology as I could. "I have no way of calling you, so if everything is fine, I'll be over there tonight. If not, then I'll tell you what happened on Monday."

Expression tight, he inclined his head. "Take care of yourself, Amelia."

I didn't like the way he said those words, but I couldn't get into it with him. "Bye, Lennon. I mean, Mr. Carter."

Hauling ass down the hallway, I burst through the front doors, a hand locking over my shoulder as soon as sunlight met my face.

"Where the fuck were you?"

Spinning, my eyes widened to see the rage written in Ben's face. "I was in the bathroom."

His mouth quirked at the corner. "Funny, because your teacher said you'd left class, but your backpack was on one of the desks."

It took everything I had not to react. Ben could tell when I was lying. "Yeah, because my stomach was upset and Mr. Carter must have thought I left. As soon as I walked in to grab it, he told me you'd come by."

He was suspicious still, but the excuse must have appeased him enough.

"Is dad okay? Mr. Carter said there was a family emergency."

Ben nodded, "Yeah, Dad's fine. But we might not be. My job screwed me over on my paycheck and we need cash fast."

"But we just-"

"I need you to help me tonight, Amelia. For the house and for dad."

My heart dropped so deep in my stomach I could feel it pulsing in my gut. Not only would I miss

210

spending time with Lennon, but also I'd be breaking his biggest rule.

Still, if we were about to lose everything, it was a risk I'd have to take.

"Okay. I'll meet you at the house and we'll figure it out."

Ben tapped my cheek. "You know I wouldn't ask this of you unless it was important."

"I know," I said, hating that just when life was starting to feel good, it dropped back into the shithole it had always been.

CHAPTER SEVENTEEN

In a way, he lied to me. Used me. Led me to believe that his music was the same as mine. But it wasn't my song he was singing. It wasn't my music he wanted in the stillness of dark night...

Lennon

Amelia failed to show up Friday night, which left me raging for the entirety of the weekend. Several times I'd thought to swing by the address listed on my student roster to check on her, but I wasn't sure I could see her brother without beating the shit out of him right there in her house.

Immediately, my mind went to the schemes I knew her brother made her take part in, anger rolling through me every time I wondered if she would be stupid enough to break one of my rules.

What made it worse was that I had a performance coming up in a week, and with class during the weekdays, I was only left with the weekend and evenings to practice.

It was impossible to focus with Amelia on my mind and every time my fingers stumbled over the keys, I slammed my hands down and grit my teeth, furious that I didn't have a way to contact her.

When Monday rolled around, I was a caged tiger prowling through each session I had with the individual students. Amelia wasn't scheduled until the end of the day and instead of taking my time correcting the performance of the other four, I was snapping at

213

them with enough bite to make even Jillian stop her bullshit flirting.

Already in a piss poor mood, it only became worse when Amelia strolled in ten minutes late, her head hanging down and her dark hair a curtain over her face.

"You know I don't appreciate tardiness in my students, Miss Dillon."

"Sorry," she answered, rushing past where I sat at the front of my desk waiting for her. "My car wouldn't start at first and it made me late."

Dropping her bag on a desk, she pulled out her music and went to the piano.

I cocked a brow at her odd behavior. Remaining at my desk with my arms crossed over my chest, I sat impatiently, eyeing her with every ounce of suspicion, I felt.

A minute must have passed before she finally twisted right to look at me. "Are we doing this, or what?"

My eyes narrowed. "What's going on with you?"

"Nothing. Just pissed off about my car."

I was getting seriously fucking tired of her lies.

Pushing away from my desk, I walked toward her, noting how she turned back to the keys, her hands shaking as she opened the sheet music in preparation to play.

The instant I stepped up behind her, I knew she could feel the heat of my body against her back. There was no space that Amelia occupied that I wouldn't claim as my own, no secret that I wouldn't eventually rip out of her.

Her entire body sat trembling on the bench, hands in her lap while waiting for me to give the instruction for her to begin.

It didn't matter how long it took, I would stand silently until she turned to look up at me, until those teal eyes met mine so I could see all her thoughts written behind them.

Eventually her hands crawled to the keys, and I understood she planned to start without being told to do so, a decision she knew damn well would lead to punishment.

"I wouldn't." The warning rolled off my lips like distant thunder. If she pushed me, the crack of my hand against her ass would be the lightning.

Voice demure, "I just thought you would want me to start quickly since I was late."

Bullshit.

"Stand up, Amelia."

She shook her head, thoroughly testing my patience.

Leaning down, my mouth was near her ear as I spoke past the curtain of her hair. "Are you going to make me say it twice?"

"Please, Lennon..."

That was it. Her behavior was one fucking thing, but the pleading in her voice told me something was seriously wrong. "Stand up."

The legs of the bench scraped the floor as she pushed to her feet. Despite having technically obeyed me, she continued facing the piano. I rolled my eyes.

"Turn around and look at me."

Slowly, she spun to face me, hair hiding her face and her gaze locked on my chest. Capturing her chin, I didn't miss the way her body shook as I tilted her head and used my free hand to brush the hair from her face.

A wave of fire roared through me, every muscle tight across my bones as my teeth ground together. "Who the fuck hit you?"

Black and blue, the bruise blossomed out around the shell of her left eye, the skin below it mottled red. It looked as if Amelia had attempted to cover it with makeup, but the effort was pathetic at best.

A tear rolled from her eye, her lips quivering when she didn't answer me immediately.

My fingers tightened on her chin. "I won't ask you again."

No. I'd just find a torment cruel enough that she would happily toss the information at me just to make it stop. My jaw ticked to think I'd have to get creative to find something that wouldn't further damage her body in the process.

The first thought in my head was that her bastard brother had done this.

"My dad."

Family should never be the nightmare that hides in the shadow. I knew that growing up, pined for normal when I watched the other children doing their best to make their parents proud. And maybe for Emaline, our family had been normal. For me, it had been absent. Morose. So empty of parental love that I'd clung to Emaline for comfort.

In a way, my sister had raised me, which is why her death had destroyed me right along with her.

But if I'd ever been made to choose an absent parent over an abusive one, I would have happily chosen the life I'd lived.

At one time in my life, I'd felt jealousy for all the happy, normal families, ones very much like the Dillons. Now, however, the curtain was slowly being pulled aside to reveal the truth of what had become of them.

I'd had the absent parent.

Amelia's were apparently abusive.

No wonder her brother was so fucked up. Her father was just another name to add to my ever expanding shit list.

She must have seen it in my expression, the rage, a fury so cold that I knew the space between us would have been coated in ice if it flowed out of me.

Slowly, her eyes widened, her hand reaching up to grab my wrist. When she tried to pull her face from my grasp, she whimpered to feel my fingers clamp down refusing to let go.

"It's not what you think," she whispered, the movement of her jaw making the bruise bounce and dance like it was taunting me to do something about it.

With as much control as I had over the tone of my voice, I said, "Then tell me what it is."

Gaze averted, her lip trembled more, shoulders withering. Seeing her like this was pissing me off. Not my Amelia, not a girl who carried music inside her. If anything, what bled from her now was a dirge, dark discordant notes leading mourners beneath a grey, bleak sky.

"My father has Alzheimer's," she confessed on gust of breath. "Lately he's become difficult. Yelling all the time and violent. I was trying to help him, but he lashed out and accidentally struck me."

Her eyes were pleading when they met mine again. "He wouldn't have done this on purpose. Not my dad. Not who he used to be."

So many answers to my question in that explanation of her life. I knew her mother had died when she was young. Lila had been Emaline's teacher originally, but when she passed, her husband took over. Emaline was crushed for months after it happened.

If Amelia's father was sick, it explained why the family was now living in Sheldon.

Releasing her chin, I asked. "When did your dad first start having problems?"

"About a year after my mom died. We thought it was just grief, but as the conditioned worsened and he deteriorated before our eyes, we learned it was much worse than heartbreak."

"Take a seat."

She was shaking so badly that forcing her to remain standing was cruel on my part. Still, energy thrummed through me that needed an outlet. Questions echoed in my thoughts that needed answers.

Clasping my hands behind my back, I stared down at her after she'd dropped her weight on the bench. "Who pays the bills at your house?"

"Ben. He dropped everything after my dad died and took care of me while I was still a minor. Even now, he works to pay the mortgage and utilities while also paying for the home care nurses for my dad."

A pause, the weight of the world forced out with a heavily expelled breath. "We can't afford to put him in a care facility. It's just too much money. So we make due with what we can."

Damn it. I wanted to hate her brother with everything I had inside me, but I had to respect him for taking care of his family. That respect, however, ended at the point where he convinced his sister to take part in criminal behavior.

Another puzzle piece snapped in place. "So, Ben is the one who gets upset when you stay out at night."

Not a question, a guess, one that was apparently accurate, judging by the helpless look on her face.

"Ben has always chased off every guy that comes near me. He doesn't want me to be used or have my heart broken. He thinks my musical talent is too precious a gift to be destroyed by boys."

Damn it, he was right. Not until this moment had I ever wanted to pat a person on the back and shake their hand while at the same time have the intense desire to shove a knife into their chest.

Regardless of what he'd done to care for Amelia growing up, he still had to answer for what he did to Emaline.

"You need a phone."

"What?" Teal eyes locked to mine, confusion swirling behind them.

"So you can contact me when you need help. I'll buy it for you and pay for the plan."

"Lennon-"

Stalking away from her, I barked out a command. "Grab your stuff. We're leaving."

"Where are we going?"

"No complaints, Miss Dillon. No questions."

Her sneakers scrunched over the linoleum floors behind me, a rustle of papers as she packed the music into her bag and raced after me, three quick steps to my one. "You never said no questions. It's not one of the rules."

"It is now," I answered, leading her down the hall, out the door and to my SUV.

"But I thought students were supposed to ask questions of their teachers."

That smart mouth was going to get her in real trouble one of these days. "Not in my classroom," I growled, hitting the key fob to unlock the car and open her door for her to climb in.

Amelia hesitated at the door like a scared rabbit. I stood glowering at her with the unspoken threat that if she didn't climb in the seat, I had no problem tying her cute little ass up and tossing her in.

Needless to say, the stare down didn't last long. Amelia huffed out a breath and hopped up into the SUV, her hair concealing her face as she stared directly ahead and I slammed the door shut.

It was fine that she was mad. I liked her mad. Mad meant she wasn't letting her brother talk her into helping him mug people, and she wasn't sitting around crying about her dad. She could take out all the aggression she felt on the keys while I fucked her from behind for all I cared, just as long as I knew where the hell she was and what she was doing.

The days of being out of constant contact were over. It didn't matter whether she liked it or not.

Peeling out of the parking lot, I made a hard right onto the street, silence lingering between us as I merged onto the highway heading downtown to the nearest cellular store. I was half tempted to hit a pet store next to see if they could install one of those nifty tracking devices just under the skin, one with an app I could use to keep an eye on her whereabouts at all times.

I glanced at her to see she was still refusing to look my direction.

Fuck it, I'd get her a collar too. One with a bell attachment that tinkled every time she moved.

"You never told me where we're going."

My lips kicked up into a smirk. "I don't answer to anybody. Get used to it."

That made her head snap my direction. In my peripheral vision, I could see pink dusting her cheeks, her eyes narrowing on me with enough vehemence the eye daggers were stabbing me in a million different places.

I'd seen this side of her before, the bratty little girl thrashing beneath me in the alley. I was happy to see she was still in there buried beneath all the sorrow and weight of her fucked up family life. What she didn't know was I intended to keep that girl just beneath the surface. Always there staring out and remembering that she belonged to a man who wouldn't allow her to shrink into her shell.

If I had to poke her in the forehead with my damn finger every time she forgot it, I would, not giving much of a damn if she called me every name in the book.

Amelia would be submissive to no other person but me.

Taking an exit into Downtown Tampa, I relaxed against my seat, my fingers tapping against the steering wheel as if it were a keyboard, music flowing out of me without an outlet. Still it was there in my head, the notes crisp and loud, a driving beat that promised pain and pleasure, sin and discipline.

"I'm adding new rules."

It wasn't necessary to see her eyes to know she'd rolled them. "You can't add new rules to an already established agreement."

"I can do whatever the fuck I want."

Another huff, her hair blowing out at the sides of her face. "Fine. What are the new rules? I *might* accept them."

There she was, the tough girl that wouldn't put up with shit from anybody. I'd been looking for her since the day we first met, wondering just how far I had to push her for the brat to come to the surface. Brat and I would play together as soon as I had a chance to get her alone. My cock was looking forward to it.

"I haven't thought of them yet, but you should damn well know I will."

Swinging into a parking lot dotted with palm tree islands and lined with flashy store front windows, I parked in front of a cellular store with all the fancy gadgets I could want to track Amelia wherever the hell she went.

This wasn't for my benefit, but for hers. At least that was what I kept telling myself.

"Lennon, you can't buy me a phone."

"I can buy you whatever the hell I want. That's the fun part of being wealthy. If I want it, it's mine."

"You don't need to rub it in."

My hand gripped down on the door handle, irritation rubbing me in all the wrong places.

Taking a breath, I attempted to calm down the raging desire I had in me to change every aspect of her life, regardless of whether she was okay with it, just so I could put her in a safe little bubble where she could focus on her music like a songbird.

"You're right. I'm just so fucking frustrated that I want to strangle you right now."

"Because my dad is sick? That's not my fault." Her voice was sharp, each word increasing in volume as her anger swam closer to the surface.

"No," I roared. "Because you didn't tell me you were having so many problems. I could have helped you, Amelia, but instead of admitting to me you were living in such hellish conditions, you kept it from me. Breaking, I might add, my rule about no secrets."

Arms crossing over her chest, she tipped up her chin, eyes seething with so much fury it was making me fucking hard as hell. My cock was practically dancing in my lap like an overeager pup wanting to play with the new, shiny squeaky toy sitting next to me.

Fuck, it irritated me how, no matter what Amelia was doing, she turned me on.

Amelia needed to be put on restriction for her own damn good. And although it would go against the independence I knew she was clamoring to hang onto, I had every intention to snatch it away, dangle it in front of her and tell her she could have it back with good behavior.

No. It wasn't her fault her dad was sick and she was hurt by taking care of him. But it was her fault for not telling me the truth of her situation. Not when I would have done in everything in my power to help her.

And sure, we'd only known each other for two weeks, but she'd still had the opportunity to fess up that night at my house. Amelia had admitted her protective family needed her home. What she hadn't said was that all her family problems were practically suffocating her. Endangering her. Threatening her future by weighing her down in crime, illness and poverty.

I couldn't solve all of Amelia's problems, but I could make them easier to bear so she didn't show up in my classroom with bruises on her face, or end up in back alleys with grown ass, horny men groping her like she was available for an easy fuck.

She wasn't.

Not Amelia.

Not when I wanted all those easy fucks to be reserved for only me.

And damn if that thought didn't freeze me in place and piss me off even more.

CHAPTER EIGHTEEN

Not every punishment the hands deliver is bad. Sometimes, to teach,
one must strike out at another. Only accept the strike when it's fair...

Amelia

There are so many horrible conditions and emotions the human body can endure.

Pain. Anger. Sorrow. Loss. Depression. Grief. Betrayal. Humiliation. Embarrassment. Regret.

The list is endless, really. Eternal. Grab a thesaurus and you can discover all the synonyms that will walk you up and down the scale of misery that is part of our everyday existence.

Nobody is safe from them. Nobody is born into a life devoid of suffering. And while some of us blindly stumble into pitfalls that leave us buried beneath those stomach churning, heartbreaking and soul crushing situations, other people, like me, step into it willingly and deliberately, all while knowing they would suffer what I considered one of the worst emotions of all: Guilt.

Those other emotions had nothing on what I was feeling now, because with them, I could pretend it wasn't my fault.

But guilt is heavy bastard that sits on your shoulders reminding you every day that the consequences you are suffering are all your fault.

It sat on my shoulders now, whispering that I'd lied to a good and caring person.

Lennon could tell me all day long that what was happening between us was just sex and nothing more, but his behavior spoke differently. *Actions speak louder than words* my father had always said after lecturing me about judging a person by their hands. I'd never given it much thought, not until I'd met Lennon.

He was generous with me despite his reservations. Always watching out for me even when the last thing I wanted were his opinions or involvement in my less than stellar situations.

Yet, regardless that he was in a league so far outside of mine, he kept an eye on me, reaching out with his annoying advice and bullheaded intimidations.

I was drowning beneath the churning ocean of my lies, the guilt eating at me while Lennon dragged me from his SUV into a large store displaying a myriad of ridiculously overpriced gadgets and toys. And the entire time he walked me around looking at the flashy phones and shiny tablets, I was breaking one of his most important rules by lying to him.

My father hadn't struck out and bruised my face. It had been Ben's fist that left this mark, although the punch hadn't been intentional.

After Ben had come to my school, we'd gone home and waited until later that night to get dressed and go out. As usual, Jackson was in tow as we drove to another upscale bar to run the same scheme as usual. But after luring the man out, his grimy fingers gripping my arm with punishing strength, I'd cried. Not because of what the man was doing, but because I was betraying Lennon.

226

It must have been my tears that set Ben off. He came out of the shadows like a charging bull, and I hadn't moved fast enough to avoid get caught up in the first few punches thrown.

As soon as I fell, Ben turned his attention to me, his concern distracting him enough that the man eventually got away when Jackson couldn't stop him on his own. We left there with nothing to show for it but my black eye.

Not only was my family now about to lose our home, but I was lying to the one person who only had my best interests in mind. All while he was dropping enough money to pay our mortgage for three months on a phone I didn't want or deserve.

Purchase made, Lennon led me from the store back to his SUV, packed me in and dropped the phone in my lap as he pulled out of the parking lot and turned the opposite direction from the highway that would take us back to school.

"Where are we going now?"

"Another store," he answered, his tone curt and unyielding.

"Why?"

"What do you plan to wear to my performance Saturday night?"

Blue eyes darting to my lap before returning to the road, he added, "Not that I mind the plaid skirt schoolgirl look, but it's not exactly appropriate for a night at the symphony."

"Lennon," I shook my head, my mind caught between maintaining the lie so I wouldn't lose a man who was expertly weaving a sticky web around my heart, and fessing up to relieve myself of the guilt that was gnawing at my bones.

Either option resulted in Lennon calling off what we had, a consequence that would tear me apart and scatter the bits and pieces on the wind.

"I can't go, so there is no point in buying anything to wear."

His fingers drummed on the steering wheel. "Why can't you go?"

"I have a shitty, unreliable car, for one." Thinking better on that statement, I quickly tossed out, "and don't you dare swing by a dealership to buy me a new one. I won't accept it."

The corner of his lips curled into a cocky grin. "Even if it's red and has all the fancy features and toys?"

A roll of my eyes. "I hate red cars."

"Black it is."

"Lennon. No. This is too much. I don't deserve this phone. I don't deserve a dress for the symphony, and I sure as hell don't deserve a new car."

We swerved right into another parking lot, the cement and steel facade of Neiman Marcus rising up in the distance. "I can't afford this place."

"Then it's a damn good thing I'm paying. Otherwise, we'd be heading to Hot Topic or Target."

My lips quirked at the thought. Still, I shook my head, refusing his offer. "I have no way of getting to the symphony on Saturday and you can't take me, seeing as how we'd be spotted together."

Lennon opened his door, glancing back at me before stepping out. "You can ride with Dizzy and Renee. I already bought you a ticket for a seat next to theirs. Problem solved."

He slammed the door shut while I was in the middle of asking, "Who are Dizzy and Renee?"

The door opened on my side and Lennon took my hand to pull me from my seat before I could refuse to follow him. Practically marching me toward the store, he was blatantly ignoring the flurry of questions rolling off my tongue.

"Who are Dizzy and Renee? Why are we doing this? What if someone sees us? Is this about the bruise?"

I finally locked my feet to the ground just outside the glass doors of the store. "Lennon, this won't fix anything for me. Why are you wasting your money?"

Stormy blue eyes met mine. "Because I want to waste my money. I know this won't fix your life, but until you reveal all your secrets to me so I can take care of those problems for you as well, I'll handle the problems I already know about. Namely, your lack of a way to contact me when you need help, and your inability to buy a dress for the performance. You'll need it regardless, or did you not read in the Hastings program materials that the final competition requires formal attire?"

Like a fish out of water, my mouth opened and closed, a response locked in the deep recesses of my throat because I hadn't actually read the program materials. Julia told me where to be and when, and there I was fresh faced and horrified to learn the man I'd attempted to mug was also my insanely hot, arrogant as all hell, and ridiculously talented teacher.

Now I was fucking said teacher, and lying to him, unable to accept the gifts he was hell-bent on giving me.

"You didn't read them." Lennon flashed me his signature cocky smirk. "I should have known that."

One tug of my arm and he unglued my feet from the cement to drag me inside. A cool wave of air conditioning was a wall against my body, freezing me instantly to the bone where all my horrible little lies were hiding.

I had to tell him.

I didn't want to tell him.

The confession rolled off my tongue regardless.

"I didn't get this bruise from my dad."

Like a screeching record, everything stopped, even the constant tick of the metronome pausing in response to Lennon's cold fury. I watched as his head canted to the side, his eyes still straight ahead instead of turning to me, as if he was taking a moment to absorb the truth I'd told him.

Breath leaked from my lungs like a deflating balloon, my fingers tugging away from his so I could wrap my arms over my body to cover up the shame of being a con artist forced into schemes to hurt people and a liar who didn't deserve the person standing in front of me.

The truth was out, however, so I was sure we would be spinning on our heels to leave any minute now.

"Your father doesn't have Alzheimer's?"

Lennon's voice was so remote and controlled that it scared me. Yelling, I could handle, but not a deep tenor vibrating with the type of rage I knew could bring this building down around us. "He has Alzheimer's. I didn't lie about that."

His jaw ticked, every sculpted muscle in his beautiful body tense beneath the navy blue Henley he wore. "Who gave you the bruise?"

Around us, the world continued along happily unaware of the bomb about to go off. Women milled about, their fingers testing the material of beautiful clothes displayed on mannequins and hanging from gleaming metallic racks. Airy classical music floated from speakers above our heads as the blended, light scent of perfumes wafted beneath my nose, most likely drifting from the pretty customers and neatly arranged makeup counters.

There I stood with an information grenade held firmly in my hand, the pin pulled in wait for me to release the trigger.

"Ben did it by accident when he was fighting a guy off me in an alley."

Another tick of his strong jaw. "You ran the scheme again."

There wasn't exactly a question mark attached to that response, but I answered like there had been. "Yes."

"Why?"

"Because we're going to lose our house if we don't come up with money fast." My eyes widened to realize what I'd just said. "And no, I won't let you pay for that either."

The guilt dissipated just slightly, now more a hazy fog floating around my head than a stone gargoyle perched on my shoulder. It was only a little better.

Fear had traipsed in with wildly swinging arms to take its place, my unblinking gaze locked on Lennon, terrified about what he would say or do next.

Whatever it was, I deserved it.

Rather than exploding as I'd assumed he would do, Lennon nodded his head as if agreeing with himself on some unspoken thought he had no intention of sharing with me.

Dragged along behind him after his hand sought and locked over mine, my feet tripped over themselves to keep up, my gaze darting to the quick reach of his arm as he pulled a thick leather belt from one of the display racks.

Panic was now dancing with my fear, their bodies spinning, jumping and flipping to the lively beat of swing music, not giving much of a damn what it was doing to my empty stomach.

The belt slapped down on a checkout counter, a saleswoman's lovely green eyes tilting up, the thin line of her lips curving into a generous smile the second she saw the man in front of her. "Cash or charge?"

"Charge," Lennon answered, "and I'd also like to know how much cash it would take for you to lead my friend and I to a back room where we won't be disturbed for the next hour."

What?

No.

He couldn't do that.

"I'll see what I can arrange," she said with a gamine grin.

Apparently, he could.

Belt purchased and bribe money exchanged, we were led back to a conference room at the rear of the store, the smiling saleswoman winking at me before she closed the door behind us and sealed my fate.

"Bend over the table."

"Can we talk about this?"

"You don't want to talk to me about this right now, Amelia." Ripping the plastic tag from the belt buckle, he looped the leather in his hand with such force that the muscles in his forearms jumped. "Bend over the table."

Judging by the tension in his jaw and the fury rolling behind his eyes, I wasn't going to be able to sit down for a week after this. "Lennon-"

"Now."

Panic and fear had stopped dancing by that point and were now leading a marching band straight up my spine.

"Okay," I whispered, unable to find any strength to speak louder.

On shaking legs, I approached the long wooden table, the comfortable chairs tucked away neatly like a small audience to witness this spanking. Bending over, I flattened my palms against the cool surface of the wood, my forehead falling down over it as well.

"Flip your skirt above your waist and drop your panties."

Eyes flicking open at the instruction, I knew better than to complain. As I did what I was told, I wondered if there were cameras in the room that would catch what Lennon was doing. I also wondered if he gave a damn.

With my skirt flipped and my panties pooling around my ankles, I returned my hands to the table, silence stretching out sinuously until Lennon's deep voice broke the tension to fill it. "Say please."

One tear slipped from my eye, the ridiculous drop of salty water an early reaction to the pain I knew that belt would cause.

I deserved the pain. "Please."

A lightning crack of leather against skin split the silence in the room, my body bucking forward as fire bloomed across the skin of my right ass cheek. Mouth open on a silent scream, I clenched my eyes shut, unable to hold back the stream of tears bursting from the rims.

The warmth of Lennon's palm rubbing over the welt was only a minimal comfort. This was his punishment, much like the last time he'd caught me in that alley.

"Say please."

Ohgodohgodohgodohgod....

"Please."

The second strike stole my breath entirely, the belt landing on the opposite cheek, both blows far from the center crease. Tears now dotted the table beneath me, a pool of regret pooling from the steady stream dripping from my face. Again, Lennon's hand swept over the welt, soothing the skin just enough to make the pain bearable.

So low that his voice was rolling thunder in answer of the slap of leather against skin, he demanded, "Say please."

I sniffled, my thoughts racing and my heart pulsing in my throat. But I deserved this for breaking his rule,

234

for giving in to my brother's demands and risking my future for enough money to get by for another month.

I deserved it.

"Please."

The third strike hit the backs of my thighs and across my pussy, my body sinking heavily across the table, my knees buckling from the shock of sensation.

Despite the pain, and despite the horror of being punished in so public an environment, I understood how wet I was, anticipation for Lennon's touch surging through me.

He must have noticed as well because when his hand moved over my skin to soothe the hurt, his fingers dipped inside me, pumping deep and hard as a moan crawled up my throat.

Behind me, a rustle of clothes caught my attention, the rip of condom wrapper following. Strong hands were on my hips, the head of his cock notching in place. I thought he would thrust inside with one hard push, but instead his voice was a deep growl above my head. "Say please."

This time, I meant it. Fuck, how I meant it.

"Please."

Lennon's cock stretched me in all the right places, my body so full of him that my forehead pressed harder against the table, my feet pushing up on to the toes to match the height of his hips.

This wasn't a gentle fucking. He'd kept that promise from the first night we were together, each new experience more primal and rough, carnal and dirty - each time forcing me to struggle over Lennon's demand that I let go of every reservation I had about

235

displaying my body for his satisfied perusal. One week. Just one. And already I was happy to spread my legs or suck his cock in any public place he demanded.

My hips knocked against the table edge with each hard thrust of his body. With strong, steady hands, Lennon pulled my torso up from the table to take possessive hold of my breast with one hand and lock the other one over my throat.

His mouth moved next to my ear, hot heavy breath flowing down my neck. "You're staying at my house tonight."

When I attempted to shake my head in refusal, his fingers gripped tighter, just beneath my jaw, preventing me from moving.

"Accept it, Amelia, and don't argue. You owe me this after breaking my fucking rules and lying to me about it."

He released me, my body falling forward, my arms reaching to brace the fall as his hands returned to my hips and his thrusts increased their speed, so fucking rough that he was forcing me to that edge, my body primed and ready for the orgasm that he refused to give me.

With a deep snarl he finished, pulling away so suddenly that my mouth fell open on a complaint that I wasn't done.

"Get dressed."

Glancing over my shoulder, I watched him remove the condom, tie off the end and toss it in a trash can, his jaw a hard line and his eyes refusing to look back at me as he pulled his pants up his legs.

"I wasn't finished."

"And you won't be for the rest of the night. Not until I think you deserve to get off again."

Lennon's hand landed on the doorknob, his narrowed gaze finally turning my direction. "I suggest you fix your clothes, Miss Dillon, unless you want to walk through the store with your panties around your ankles."

CHAPTER NINETEEN

*He told me he loved me. He promised me he cherished me. Now I know
I was only a fantasy brought to life, the splendor dying away when
he saw me for who I really am...*

Lennon

The expression on Amelia's face was priceless. I would have taken my phone out of my pocket and snapped a picture if I weren't so angry I couldn't see straight.

Amelia glared at me before pulling her clothes back into place, and I answered that glare with one of my own, a look that conveyed every desire I had to continue tanning her ass red for being so stupid.

That fucking bruise on her face was mocking me, daring me to drop her off at my house and hunt down the son of a bitch who put it there.

Before, when Amelia had attempted to paint her brother in a better light, I - for one teensy, tiny, itty bitty single second - had thought I could let everything he'd done in his life go, that I could allow his concern for his sister to ease the hatred I harbored for him inside me.

Now? Now that hatred was a hammer banging at my skull, a thrumming, bloodthirsty pulse just beneath my skin demanding retribution for all the ways he'd wronged me.

Amelia wasn't returning home again except to collect her things and move to my house for the time being. At least until I could figure out a way to help her before she left to attend Hastings.

I wouldn't give Ben another opportunity to destroy her chances at a future in music.

Silently, she followed behind me, the belt abandoned in the conference room because I had no need of it beyond a convenient tool to punish her when my irritation was at its peak.

Back at my place, I had other ways to remedy her disastrous decisions and poor choices in behavior, most of which would paint red across her cheeks for just how imaginative I could be would pushed to my limit.

But for now, she needed a dress, and I wasn't leaving this place without one.

Leading Amelia to what I assumed was the gown department, I approached a brunette saleswoman, plastered on my best smile, and ignored the quick, concerned glances the woman took at the bruise marring Amelia's face.

"I'm hoping you can help me. My -"

Well, damn. What was she exactly? It had never been my intention to be exclusive, especially while knowing we'd part ways as soon as the summer ended. And for some irritating reason, that eventuality drove spikes down my spine, my fingers curling into my palms because the thought of saying goodbye to Amelia was an aggravation I didn't want or need.

"-friend needs some assistance selecting a dress to wear to the symphony."

"Of course," the saleswoman answered, shrewd brown eyes flicking between the two of us, errant strands of her prim hairstyle fluttering at the sides of her head.

Dressed in a stylish, dark skirt suit with a pink blouse and pearl embellishments, she frowned to take a better look at the bruise, deep lines webbing around her mouth when accusation toward me rolled behind her eyes.

I cocked a brow, daring her to attempt to place the blame on me. Sure, I liked to spank women with the intent of fucking them after doing so, but never had I lifted a hand to one in anger.

Besides, if she thought the bruise was bad, I was curious what her reaction would be when she saw the red stripes across Amelia's ass that I'd just put there with a belt.

Assuming they'd have a lot of fun in the dressing room dancing around that particular conversation, I found a small waiting area reserved for bleary-eyed husbands hugging their wives' purses to their chests while silently pleading with the gods to end their shopping nightmare.

A half hour passed before I heard Amelia screech from the interior of the dressing room. *"Three thousand dollars?"*

Three husbands glanced my direction, empathy written across their furrowed brows and shadowed expressions. Shaking my head, I pushed up from my seat, marched past hanger racks and leaned a shoulder against the doorframe of the dressing room.

The instant I caught sight of Amelia in a champagne colored evening gown, the neckline dipping down to reveal her generous cleavage while the barely there sleeves sat just off the shoulders, I thought three thousand was a fair price to ask.

Amelia, with her perfect curves highlighted in shimmering silk, was flawless (except for that damn bruise) and stunning.

I had to clear my throat to talk. "Problem?"

She spun my direction, her lips a firm line of refusal. "You're not spending three thousand dollars on this dress. I won't let you."

She was cute when she assumed she could tell me what to do.

"I'm not under the impression that you can stop me. So rather than giving this lovely saleswoman a hard time about the price, shouldn't you be thanking her instead for finding the dress that apparently was made with you in mind?"

At my words, the sour-expressioned saleswoman was suddenly on Team Lennon, her earlier accusatory eyes now widening with approval. With a succinct nod of her head, she reached to straighten the waterfall of material over Amelia's hips.

"He's right, you know? This dress was meant for you."

"Lennon, the price-"

Wasn't her problem. It was mine.

"Go ahead and give the nice lady the dress, Amelia, and I'll meet you at the checkout counter."

By the time Amelia reached the register, she was practically vibrating with anger. Good. I hoped she was learning what it felt like to have a person do whatever

242

the hell they wanted without concern for how it affects her.

We were now cruising along in the same damn boat, the only difference being my actions were meant for her benefit while she was running as fast as she could toward a jail cell without giving a damn what it would do to me.

The last purchase for the day was made quickly, the plastic cover for the dress fluttering over my shoulder as I led Amelia back to the car, stowed both her and the dress away, and climbed in to take her home to gather her things.

"Where are we off to now? I wasn't kidding when I said no car, Lennon."

My lips twitched at the corners. "You say that as if you could stop me."

"Lennon-"

"I'm not taking you to buy a car," I barked, cutting off whatever annoying complaint she wanted to toss at me. "I'm taking you home to grab as many clothes and other things you'll need to make it to the end of the summer."

"What? No. Why?"

Teeth clenched, I swung a left onto the highway and merged into rush hour traffic. Cars were lined up bumper to bumper, further aggravating me. "I've already told you why. Think back to when I last had my cock shoved in your body and you might remember."

"I can't stay with you."

We weren't moving anytime soon, so I had all the time in the world to turn and stare at her like the spoiled brat that she was. "You can. And you will."

"But Ben-"

"Don't," I warned, my voice a low growl of disapproval. "Don't even mention your brother's name around me. You have a fucking shiner at the moment that pisses me off every time I fucking look at it, and I flat out refuse to allow him one more chance to fuck things up for you with Hastings."

Tears shimmered down Amelia's cheeks. "I can't leave my dad."

"I'll take you to see him every day after class."

"We'll get caught and the Hastings scholarship will be gone anyway."

"No, Amelia, we won't. It's safer for us to work one on one at my house because I can't seem to keep my dick from making an appearance whenever we're alone in the classroom. We might as well be somewhere we don't have to worry about Julia, your brother, or a janitor walking in to catch us."

Traffic inched forward, a constant stop and go that had my fingers blanching white over the wheel. "Tell me where you live."

Amelia was quiet for several minutes and I allowed her that time to adjust to the simple truth that from now on, she was on lockdown until that scholarship was in her pretty little hand.

Shoulders withering with defeat, she said, "You can't come inside with me."

I scoffed. "Why? Because Ben might try to talk me into leading some clueless fuck into an alley for him? I

244

hope he realizes I don't have the tits and ass to make that happen."

A shake of her head. "No. Ben's at work." Exhaling a deep breath, she admitted, "I don't want you seeing my father. He has more bad days than good lately and...it's embarrassing."

Her confession calmed me down, but not by much. "He can't help the way he behaves, Amelia. There's no reason to be embarrassed."

I didn't know much about Alzheimer's, but from what I'd heard, the late stages could be so severe, placement in a facility was the best thing for patients and their families.

"You've taken on too much," I told her, my voice soft despite the fury still pumping through my veins.

"Oh, yeah?" She laughed, the sound anything but funny. "Well, what the hell else am I supposed to do?"

"You could ask for help."

Silence was all she gave me in return. Forty-five minutes of it to be exact, the tension building in the car so thick I could feel it pressing against my skin, suffocating me beneath its unbearable weight.

Finally reaching our exit, I asked, "Where do you live?"

"Fifth Street," she admitted on a whisper.

My stomach turned to drive into the heart of rundown Sheldon again. In silence, we drove past houses in desperate need of repair and yards that hadn't seen a mower in weeks. Fifth Street was just around the corner from where my childhood home stood condemned, bright orange warning signs taped to the windows and front doors.

"This next house on your right."

Pulling into the driveway of a small, white clapboard house, I threw the car in park, killed the engine and opened my door. Her hand locked over my wrist immediately.

"What are you doing?"

"Going inside with you."

"But I already told you-"

Leaning across the center console, I gripped her jaw in my hand and shut her up with a deep kiss. At first, she fought to pull away, but eventually her tongue gave in to dance along mine, her body relaxing as the fight bled out of her.

Our mouths pulled apart, but not so far that I couldn't feel her breath against my face. "I want to see for myself how bad it is."

Weakly, she nodded, her expression twisted with shame she shouldn't have felt for her situation. I hated that she thought it necessary to hide the truth of her life from me. I'd been here once myself, had grown up in it without the excuse that one of my parents was dead and the other one sick.

Stepping from the car, I rounded the front end to open her door, understanding that the next time we had an opportunity to talk, I needed to admit to her that, although I stood in a privileged place in life now, my foundation had been built of crumbling cement and afternoons where I wondered when I'd next eat a full meal.

It wasn't something I liked to discuss. I considered my childhood to be a *before story* that had nothing to do with what came after the dividing line that led to my present. But, for her, I would endure the return to the sinking sand of memories while hoping not to get dragged down beneath the surface.

Amelia led the way up two cement steps and over a small porch. The house wasn't much. It was in need of a good paint job and new roofing, the front door pushing open into a living room that surprised me.

You don't expect to walk into a shack and find fairly expensive furniture, what I assumed was a bygone of the comfortable life she'd lived before her father deteriorated. Yet, here it was. Nice leather couches, polished oak tables, an upright piano against a far wall that drew my attention because I assumed my sister, for years, had learned to play on it.

That reminder would have been enough to floor me if a deep, male voice hadn't boomed from another room, shaking the walls with its violence.

Bring me my wife!

Amelia shrank at the sound of it, her shoulders rolling forward as she hurried me down a low lit hall.

Bring her to me!

Lila!

Where's my wife!

Tears streamed down Amelia's cheeks, her eyes averted as she refused to look at me. I stood behind her unable to accept that this was what she returned home to every night, that *this* is the hand she'd been dealt.

Running toward us from a back room, a woman tossed her hands up, her hair a mess and expression utterly exhausted. "Oh thank God you're home, Amelia. I don't know what to do with him. He's

247

reached his limit of sedatives and still, he's carrying on."

Wrapping her arms over her stomach, Amelia froze in place, the home nurse's eyes finally darting over Amelia's shoulder to see me standing behind her. Surprise widened those tired brown eyes. After giving me a cursory once over, she returned her attention to Amelia. "What do you want to do?"

Mr. Dillon continued yelling from the back room, the house consumed by chaos.

"Have you tried music?"

A thought came to me. "He'll calm down for music?"

The nurse shook her head. "I've tried playing a few CDs, but it's the piano he loves the most."

Amelia appeared shut down and immobile, unable to make a decision, most likely horrified that I was there to witness this.

Without asking, I turned to walk to the living room, pulled the bench from the piano, lifted the lid from over the keys and began a piece that had been Emaline's favorite, one Lila had taught my sister to play before she died.

The yelling stopped immediately.

After a few moments, three sets of footsteps sounded behind me, a male voice softly whispering his late wife's name, his fractured mind not understanding that the woman he loved was gone.

Engrossed in the piece, and doing my best not to allow it to shred my heart to hear again after all these years, I continued playing through every repeated measure, the house falling into a comfortable silence that I wondered if they'd had in years.

I could feel Amelia watching me, her shame, her frustration, her anger at the loss of a normal, well to do life, crashing against me in sorrowful waves.

The song continued on, and with no consideration for what the melody would do to me, I played it a second time and a third, if only to give Amelia a few moments of peace.

This would be the last night Amelia would endure the life she'd been living for years, the last night she would listen to the screaming while wondering how to keep a roof over her head.

Her father would go to a facility tomorrow.

I would be the person paying for it.

And from this moment on, Amelia's only focus from day to day would be the scholarship I'd make damn sure she received, as well as learning how to please her teacher.

CHAPTER TWENTY

We all make mistakes. I've made mine. My hands have caused pain.
But have also created such beauty that I wonder what should
carry the most weight...

Amelia

Beethoven's Sonata Pathétique.

I recognized the piece from my childhood. My mother's favorite, a melody that was so familiar it sang to me of happier days and blended into the darkest months when Mom fought her illness.

Tears slipped from my eyes to see my father slowly make his way down the hallway, his face bright, eyes focused, a memory calling to him as sweetly as it called to me.

But how did Lennon know? Why this music rather than a million other choices he could have played?

It was as if he'd somehow reached into the heart of my family and brought to life the sunshine that had loved us in our younger days, as if he'd pulled back a curtain to remind me that, before the storm clouds had covered my sky, there had been laughter in my heart and smiles on our faces.

I stood dumbfounded at the doorway to the living room, watching as my father sat down on the couch, his gaze fixated on the piano, a smile tugging at his lips, ghosts of memories softening the lines of his face.

As the music flowed around me, I was weightless, the tension in my shoulders easing, a flow of heartache,

251

misery and pain pouring off me to sink down into the floor at my feet.

"My goodness, Amelia, I don't know who your friend is, but perhaps you should hire him to look after your dad. I haven't seen Mr. Dillon that calm in months."

Pamela, the night nurse, stood next to me, her body gently swaying, her arms crossed over her stomach. "And damn if he isn't pretty to look at. Who is he, anyway?"

Shaking away the spell Lennon had so easily wrapped around me, I answered, "Lennon Carter. He's my piano instructor in the program." *A man I'm foolishly falling in love with,* I didn't say.

The song came to an end, my gaze drifting to my father to see joy and peace written into his expression. Slowly, Lennon spun on the bench toward me, his eyes searching my face, unsure what to say or do next.

Thankfully, Pamela was the first to break the silence. "That was beautiful, Mr. Carter. You are welcome to come by and play for us whenever the mood hits you. As for tonight, I think it's time I put Mr. Dillon to bed."

While she helped my father up from the couch and led him away on shuffling feet, Lennon and I were motionless, our eyes locked, so many unspoken thoughts passing between us. He didn't stand from the bench until Pamela and Dad were out of sight, his steps slow as he approached me.

"I'm sorry for just jumping in like that, but I thought, maybe-"

Pushing to my tiptoes, I cupped his cheeks and brushed my mouth against his. A shy invitation for him to deepen the kiss. His fingers wrapped into my hair, our mouths opening and our tongues speaking everything we were feeling without uttering a single word. This man was my hero, whether he knew it or not.

Only when it was necessary to breathe did I pull away, my eyes opening to find he was watching me intently.

"How did you know?"

"Know what?"

It couldn't have been a coincidence. Not that song. "That was my mother's favorite."

Storm clouds rolled behind his eyes, his expression darkening. Clearing his throat he admitted, "Emaline used to play it all the time. She taught me to play it before she-"

He stepped away, his shoulders rounding as the distance between us grew both physically and metaphorically. Lennon always shut down when Emaline was mentioned.

"You should gather your things. We need to go."

Without complaint, I did as he said, relenting to his plan to get me away from my brother for the time being. I didn't know what was going on with Ben, but Lennon was right. I couldn't risk my future because my brother was bad with money.

Once we'd packed my things into the car and were pulling down the street, the tender moment we'd shared in my house dissipated as Lennon returned to his usual bossy self.

"I hope you know that you didn't weasel your way out of practice today. I expect two hours, at least, at my piano."

Laughter shook my shoulders. If practice was his form of punishment, then I'd take it. "Is this your idea of teaching me a lesson for lying?"

His lips curled with mischief, my heart fluttering like a trapped bird in response to the expression.

"No, actually. Your practice session is simply a requirement of the program. As your instructor, it's my job to ensure you're properly taught." He paused, the silence only momentary but still driving me crazy.

"So what's my punishment?"

"That will happen when it's time for me to practice for my performance on Saturday."

"And that is?"

"A surprise."

. . .

The wood was cool beneath my cheek, every note a vibration across my skin, my bare breasts crushed beneath me, cool air sweeping in to chase away the heat between my legs.

I hoped my muscles wouldn't cramp in this awkward position, although Lennon had done well not to make it too difficult. Breathing out a sigh, I closed my eyes and allowed the music to rise up and consume me.

Feeling the music.

Almost laughing, I didn't know that he had meant it so literally.

A finger tapped against my knee for the third time while bass chords pounded against my flesh.

"Open."

My thigh squeaked over the wood as I pushed my legs apart, skin sticking to the veneer. Fully open again, I closed my eyes hoping the salt of my body wasn't ruining the finish of what had to be an eighty-five thousand dollar piano.

"There she is. So beautiful."

Higher notes blended with the lower chords, a piece I'd never heard before, but one I was going to demand Lennon teach me.

Every so often he would stop, replay a measure, the tempo just a little slower or faster, sixteenth notes becomes eighths, and start again. He was such a perfectionist that it made me a little sick. But even then, he managed to introduce his unique voice into whatever it was he played.

I could feel him as easily as I felt the vibration of strings beneath me, the hard hit of the hammers, the press of fingertips against black and white keys.

With the front of my body pressed firmly against the wood, my arms were pulled behind my back, tied in place and secured to my legs that were bent at the knees. Hog tied on top of a piano while he practiced, my most intimate parts displayed to him while he played.

As far as punishments went, this wasn't so bad. Sure, I was exposed, a little cold, turned on without instant relief. But he hadn't walked away from me.

Hadn't booted me from the program for letting Ben convince me to commit another crime. Hadn't followed through on any of the threats that would have destroyed me.

Still, I wasn't dumb enough to break his rules again. I had a feeling Lennon would only put up with so much before he'd had enough.

The music stopped, the room falling into absolute silence. I swear I could feel his eyes exploring me.

"That was beautiful," I said as best I could with my cheek squished against the wood.

A silent beat and then, "Who said you're allowed to speak?"

My mouth twitched at the corner.

"You're beautiful." Two words only, but to hear those words spoken in his deep tenor voice did things to me.

He must have stood from the bench, his bare feet a rhythmic beat against the floor, a sound I could barely pick up. Then his hands were on me and I was being repositioned, my skin sticky against the wood. We really should have used a blanket. I couldn't imagine the damage we were causing.

Fingertips brushed between my thighs, sweeping up and down, teasing touches that made me pull at my bindings.

A light slap on my ass. "Quit moving."

"But this is torture," I answered.

"It's supposed to be."

More sweeping touches, stopping just below the apex between my thighs and stroking down again. A whimper crawled up my throat because I always wanted to rush to the best parts while Lennon, with his ridiculous control and aggravating patience, would take his time when he wanted.

"I should leave you like this all night. Teach you a lesson you won't forget."

Even with the low spoken threat, he continued toying with me, his fingers rushing between my legs, light upward strokes of the tips, the soft downward scrape of his short fingernails. That scrape turned me on more than anything. I loved it when he was rough and lost control.

"Please don't."

I didn't have to look at him to see his smile. "You and that word. It's like a drug."

A finger slid inside me and my lips parted on a soft moan. I was so ready for him and all I'd done was lie there exposed and open to his observant eyes.

Slowly, his fingers pumped inside me, a curl to the tips that teased the inner walls. My breath became shallow as my breasts felt heavier beneath me. I was a bundle of nerves in that moment, a toy for his amusement, every inch of me sensitive and needy.

Lennon pulled his hand away, ignoring my groan of complaint, his hands moving to the bindings to untie my legs. Stretching them out, he massaged the muscles that were sore for holding the position for so long.

Sliding me off the lid of the piano, he caught me and cradled me to his chest, stepping quickly to carry me to the couch and lay me down, my hands still bound, my body ready.

I couldn't have moved my legs if I wanted to. Basically a rag doll, I didn't move, waiting for him to do whatever he wanted.

A thumb rubbed over a sore spot on my skin. "My marks are still here, red ribbons from the belt."

Most likely they'd be there for another day. Sitting in class the next day would be awkward.

That thought was gone as soon as his fingers explored me again, rough, possessive strokes, his teeth biting the flesh of my ass just hard enough to make me jump.

"Oh..." Breath hissed across my lips, shivers erupting over my entire body, bone deep, those small earthquakes of pleasure.

Dragging his finger up, he nestled it over another hole, my eyes rounding. "I think, sometime soon, I'll claim this as well."

What?

"But not tonight." His finger pulled away and my breath poured from my lungs, my body shaking over the cool leather of the sofa.

Behind me, I heard him drop his pants and the tear of a condom wrapper. But rather than mounting behind me, Lennon directed me to my feet. I could barely stand, my legs like gelatin, but as soon as he took a seat, he directed me onto his lap with my back to him and my arms bound between us.

Two strong hands gripped my hips and I was lifted up just enough for him to position the head of his cock at my entrance and pull me down, slowly filling me, stretching me so full that I shuddered above him, my head falling back against his shoulder after he was fully seated inside me. His hand traveled up from my hip, over my rib cage, to squeeze the weight of my breast in his palm.

Without moving his hips, he ran his lips down the line of my neck, his fingers tight on my nipple, my inner muscles undulating over the thick length of his cock.

Son of a bitch. Lennon was going to be the death of me.

I wiggled my hips to urge him on, but he clamped his hand down on my hip to hold me still, his teeth biting at the junction between my shoulder and neck. It forced my insides to squeeze tighter around him.

"You're being punished," he said against my skin, the tip of his tongue licking across the sting where he had bitten me. "So I get to have my fun without you complaining about it."

The knuckles of my bound hands rubbed against the washboard ridges of his abs. All I wanted to do was explore his body as openly as he explored mine.

His other hand brushed up so that he palmed both my breasts while his mouth ran hot kisses down the back of my neck, his cock so full inside me.

I groaned, and he chuckled. "Patience grasshopper."

"I'm going to murder you one of these days," I breathed out, barely able to hold still while he had his fun.

"You're killing me now, Amelia. You just don't know it."

Releasing my breasts, his hands moved back to my hips, my body falling forward just enough that the hard line of his cock stroked along my core as he finally...fucking *finally*...directed my body up and down. So strong, those hands, lifting me and dropping me again, my breasts bouncing with every thrust.

With my hands bound behind my back, I was helpless but to enjoy the ride, my body a slave to his pleasure.

His breath washed over my back, down the spine, over the tight muscles. "I hope you understand that I now own this. You. Every inch of skin. Your thoughts. Your music."

My eyes closed as my body moved over his. He could own everything if he just kept making me feel this way.

"And I won't go easy on you."

Pushing me up until I was hovering at the tip of his cock, he slammed me back down, over and over, until his name was falling over my lips.

Spreading my cheeks apart, I knew he was watching what he did to me, enjoying every second of controlling how my body moved. But I didn't mind. I was so close to an orgasm that I wanted him to watch, wanted him to witness how he affected me.

Like a tidal wave, my climax roared through me, every muscle tightening as wave after wave of surging heat and consuming pleasure took hold. Mouth opening on a deep moan, I trembled beneath the force of it, became lost, felt like I was floating above a man who chased his own release.

"Fuck-"

He drove inside me one last time and I knew he'd joined me, his hands clamping down as he lost the battle to his own orgasm.

Afterward, he tugged at the binding around my wrists, guided my arms to my sides slowly, and rubbed his thumbs down the tight muscles on either side of my spine.

I melted in place, barely able to keep my eyes open when he pulled my back against his chest and wrapped his strong arms around me.

A minute or two passed before I found the energy to speak. "I think I should get in trouble more often."

The words were so slurred I sounded drunk.

He pinched my breast in response, his mouth smiling against my neck.

"Do it again, Amelia, and I'll deny you orgasms for a damn week."

Laughter shook my shoulders, my fingers tangling with his.

This was how I wanted my nights to be. This right here. Alone with him.

It broke my heart to think that at the end of the summer, I'd be leaving for Hastings while Lennon would return to his life and his career.

CHAPTER TWENTY-ONE

I can't go on like this, little brother. I can't continue playing when all the music has come to an end...

Lennon

It aggravated me to no end that I couldn't cut Jillian from the running. All week, I'd worked with the remaining five students, Amelia privately, of course, and when it came down to the other four, Jillian proved to be the most talented.

Unfortunately, the young woman scraped against my last nerves with her shameless flirting. It seemed like when her hands weren't tapping the keys over the music, she was endlessly flipping her hair over her shoulder and back again, tangling the ends between her fingers while staring at me like I was something to be conquered.

Today, I would announce the final two in the running, Amelia and Jillian, which meant next week, my days would be split between the two. The time I spent with Amelia was well worth it, but four hours a day with Jillian would drive me to a point of insanity.

The girl had no shame, her clothes far too revealing, her smiles so sickly sweet that my teeth hurt just looking at them.

What made it worse was the way she treated Amelia whenever they were in the same room, a fucking viper coiled and ready to strike, and I had to be careful not to bring the hammer down on the bitch in defense of my girl.

Nobody could know about us, and we were pushing limits by sleeping in the same house. Thankfully, her car had been an easy fix, so we didn't drive in together. Nobody would know what was going on as long as they didn't figure out where I lived.

Knuckles rapped against the door to the classroom. "Knock knock."

Lifting my eyes from the notes I'd kept on each student, I locked stares with Julia Pickens.

"Do you have a minute?"

Class wasn't due to start for another half hour, so I waved her in, cocking a brow when she closed the door and walked to sit back against a student desk.

"How are things going with the final decisions?"

"Good," I said, dropping my notes down on the surface of my desk before folding my hands behind my head.

My feet were kicked up, my chair leaning back as far as it would go. In truth, I was exhausted from practicing for my performance and keeping Amelia up at night devouring her body like a starving man.

"I've whittled the choices down to two, although it hasn't been easy. You'll be happy to know Amelia made the cut."

Julia nodded, flashing me a tight smile that wasn't friendly. Lips pulling into a thin line, she stared at me for several seconds before saying, "Actually, Amelia is why I wanted to talk to you. I know we're not supposed to discuss our students, but I'm worried about her."

This couldn't be good. "Is there a problem?"

Calm and aloof. If I showed any interest beyond that, Julia would latch on to the interest, would see through me to know that Amelia and I were a lot closer than I wanted to admit.

"Her brother came to my house looking for her last night. He says she hasn't been home in several days and most of her clothes are gone."

Ben. I was going to fucking kill him one of these days. What thirty year old man kept such a tight leash on his sister? I understood Amelia believed he was merely concerned for her welfare, but given the things he made her do, I wasn't convinced.

"What does that have to do with me?"

Her eyes searched my face, trying and failing to discover any small hint that I knew more than I was letting on.

"I just wondered if she was behaving oddly during your practice sessions. I'm not sure if you know, but her father isn't the easiest person to live with-"

Actually, her father was being moved to a care facility this afternoon, but I refrained from telling her that.

"-and I'm concerned she may have left home because she could no longer handle being around him in his condition."

Shifting in my seat, I met Julia's eyes without a hint of reservation. "Why are you telling me this?"

Her gaze narrowed just slightly, suspicion lining her brow. "I wanted to know if her focus or behavior has changed in class that you've noticed? Or perhaps, she's told you something about her current whereabouts or situation?"

A slow blink of my eyes and my lips curled at one corner. "Amelia is a dedicated student-"

More dedicated than Julia realized.

"-and a talented musician, which is why she's made it to the top two in my class. As to her personal life, I'm not sure that's any of my business."

"Well, of course, it isn't," she snapped.

Arching a brow, I silently called her out on getting snippy with me.

Julia straightened the cuffs of her sleeves and regained control of herself. "I'm sorry, I didn't mean to imply you had personal knowledge of Amelia, it's just that the family is worried, especially her brother. He's worked so hard to take care of her after what happened with their parents. I hate to see him upset."

Glancing at the clock, I said, "The students should be here soon. If you'd like to speak with Amelia, be my guest-"

We'd already worked out a cover story that she was staying with a student who had already been dismissed from the program.

"-otherwise, I'm not sure that I can help you. As far as my observations of her, nothing appears changed from when she first walked into my class."

I was actually glad that Julia decided to come see me. If anything, she gave the warning that Ben was sniffing around. I didn't trust the son of a bitch as far as I could throw him, so it was fortunate notice that Amelia had to be careful around the school and while heading back to my house.

Julia stilled in place, her eyes seeking mine in some sort of camaraderie. "You know, when I first met you, I thought Amelia would get along with you quite well. She's...eccentric...like you in a way, a true musician. I'd hoped she would open up to you, not so much as a friend, but as a teacher. I wouldn't be upset to learn you took her under your wing."

I almost laughed. It was a nice change in direction, but it still wouldn't convince me to spill the beans.

Plus, I'm wasn't sure Julia would be happy to learn I'd taken Amelia under me in a myriad of different ways. She was a fascinating student, so eager to learn.

"As an instructor, I'm more than willing to guide her talent. If she turns out to be my finalist, I will."

Nodding, she pushed away from the desk and walked toward the door. "That's all I can ask, I guess. Have a good day, Mr. Carter."

As soon as she was out of sight, I scrubbed my hand down my face and groaned. Amelia would be my finalist, a fact I'd already decided. But to keep appearances on the up and up, my semi-finalist had to be a challenge. Jillian filled that role well. In more ways than she knew.

Pulling my feet from the desk, I made my final notations, not bothering to glance up at the sound of students entering the room. Three would go home heartbroken today and this part of my job was the worst.

Thankfully, I had an appointment this afternoon that would make me feel better. I hadn't yet told Amelia she was coming with me, but I could save that surprise for later.

"Morning, everyone."

A chorus of hopeful voices called back to me, Jillian's front and center as usual. I hadn't bothered to look up yet. It was always a fight not to seek out Amelia's face first thing.

"I hope all of you are doing well." Finally lifting my head to count five student faces staring back at me, I almost scowled to see Jillian's come fuck me smile, and almost laughed to see Amelia's indifferent expression. She was damn good at playing the disinterested student.

"Today won't be a good day for three of you, which I think you already know. Again," I said, pushing up to my feet and rounding the desk to lean against the front, "you all know what I'm going to say here. These last cuts are the hardest and if I could keep you all, I would."

All but Jillian. Unfortunately she was staying.

"So, I'll just jump to it. The two students who will move on to next week are Jillian Bates and Amelia Dillon."

Three faces shifted from hopeful to rejected, something I hated that any young musician would feel. However, this was the business. There wasn't an artist out there, no matter their medium, that wasn't turned away many times over before finding their audience. Having thick skin was necessary if you had any hope of success.

I waited while the three whose names weren't called gathered their things, said their goodbyes and walked out the door.

It was down to two. One I couldn't wait to get beneath me, and another I wanted to swat away like an annoying fly.

"Congratulations, ladies. You earned this. But don't let it go to your heads. My demands only become more difficult from here."

My gaze flicked to Amelia and I almost grinned to know she'd be up to any challenge I gave her.

"Starting next week, I'll be working with you for four-hour blocks. Jillian, you'll have mornings and Amelia, you'll have afternoons-"

Jillian raised her hand. "Mr. Carter, I was hoping I could have the later time slot."

Glancing over her shoulder at Amelia like she was something she wanted to scrape off the bottom of her shoe, Jillian argued, "Amelia always gets the last hour of the day and I don't think it's fair."

My eyes slanted her direction. "Why not?"

She hesitated to be put on the spot. Either that or the fuck off glare I was giving her was coming through loud and clear. "Well, just because I thought, maybe-" Her voice trailed off, the lusty glimmer in her eyes dying a slow death. "Never mind."

"Excellent, now that that's settled, you two are free to go for the rest of the day. I hope you have a good weekend."

"Oh," Jillian spoke up again, her saccharine sweet voice like nails across a chalkboard. "I guess I'll see you tomorrow night at the performance. I'm so excited to see you on stage."

Crossing my arms over my chest, I smiled politely. "I'm sure I'll be too preoccupied to see anyone, but I'm happy you'll attend the performance."

Now get the fuck out...I didn't add.

From behind her, Amelia smirked. She could hear the words I wasn't saying.

Jillian eventually moved along while Amelia was standing at her desk packing her things. Finally alone with her, I stared in wonder at a woman who was slowly consuming my every thought.

"She has it bad for you. I hope you know that."

I laughed. A person would have to be blind not to know it. "She's a non-issue. I happen to have someone else on my mind."

The corner of her lips quirked. "I can understand that. I've been thinking a lot about this really bossy man." Eyes flicking up to me. "You'd hate him. He's such a pervert."

Returning her smile, I scratched my jaw. "Sounds like a decent guy to me."

Amelia laughed and I had to resist the urge to close the distance between us. "I have two things I'd like to talk to you about."

Her shoulders tensed, and I hated how she was always expecting bad news. Amelia deserved better.

"Your brother is looking for you."

Head snapping my direction, she asked, "He came here?"

"No. Julia told me this morning. Apparently he went by her house. I just wanted you to know so you'll be careful in the parking lot and driving away from school."

Nodding her head, Amelia hitched the strap of her back up her shoulder. "What's the second thing?"

"I have someplace I need to go this afternoon and I'd like for you to come with me."

Stepping toward me, she teased, "I don't know if I have time. The bank is only open until three and if I want to rob it, I need to get there before they close."

She would pay dearly for that statement.

"Wait while I gather my stuff. We'll take my car since it's close."

Packing my notes and roster into my bag, I second guessed the idea. There was no telling when or where Ben might show up, and I preferred Amelia's car be out of sight.

"Actually, drive to my house. We'll drop your car off and ride together from there."

"You're worried about Ben, aren't you? It's not like he can drag me off kicking and screaming."

Yeah, but that wouldn't stop me from beating the crap out of him, and with my performance set for tomorrow night, I couldn't take the chance of damaging my hands.

"Just do what I say, Amelia." Tipping my head up to look at her, I grinned. "No complaints and no questions, remember?"

Walking to the door, she shook her head, glanced back at me and flipped her skirt above her waist to show me her ass.

271

"Don't tempt me," I murmured with every intention of putting my mark there again.

Laughter retreated down the hallway. I was still packing when footsteps sounded behind me, the classroom door closing.

I turned to find Jillian leaning against it. "Hey," she said, as if there was some goddamned reason for her to be blocking my path out of here.

"Did you forget something?"

A miniscule shake of her head preceded her mouth turning up into a smile filled with all the promises I didn't want from her.

"I've been thinking," she breathed out, her voice husky. "You and I, we get along really well, and we're both obviously into each other."

My brows knit together. Her lips parted seductively as she took her invitation a step further by pulling at the buttons of her shirt.

Oh, for fuck's sake.

One button.

One step toward me.

A full-bodied hip strut that Amelia wouldn't have done in a million years until I'd stripped her of her modesty.

Yet, here Jillian was, attempting to taste for herself what the forbidden teacher-student relationship would be like.

It was too bad for her I wasn't interested.

"You should stop while you're ahead, Jillian." Crossing my arms over my chest, I flashed a look of boredom. Contempt written into the line of my mouth.

Hands sliding down her chest, she walked toward me, her intent to fuck me right here on my desk painfully clear.

"Please, Mr. Carter. I like you and I get the hint you like me, too."

I'd give it to her, she was a forward little thing. Not shy in the least, her hands continued working the buttons of her shirt, bra now exposed, only the bottom half still fastened together.

"You're mistaken and you should leave now before you piss me off."

Had she been waiting for Amelia to leave? Hopefully she wasn't in earshot. Hopefully she hadn't seen Amelia lift her skirt as a tease.

Another step. Another button.

"Jillian, stop what you're doing and-"

The door opened behind her, Julia's shrewd eyes widening with surprise, and then narrowing with anger to see Jillian's half buttoned shirt, her lips transitioning from a friendly smile to a line of rage.

Son of a –

Things were getting worse as Julia darted a glance between the two of us, fury lighting her gaze.

"I was just telling Miss Bates to stop what she was doing and leave."

This was an added complication I didn't need, but not one I was willing to make worse by jumping up and acting like I was guilty.

Instead, I remained calm, maintained my position and allowed Jillian to come to the quick understanding that propositioning your teacher in class didn't always end in a quick fuck on a desk.

Julia's face was sheened red, her usually friendly eyes narrowing more. Clearing her throat, she waited for Jillian to button her shirt and scamper from the room.

"I came to speak with Amelia," Julia said, her tone clipped, eyes narrowed on me like I was Satan himself.

Grabbing my bag, I stepped toward her, refusing to give ground or offer an explanation for what she believed she saw.

"Amelia left fifteen minutes ago when I dismissed class."

She shifted when I moved to brush past her. Voice low, she warned, "Inappropriate relationships with students is highly-"

"Let me stop you right there, Ms. Pickens. I have never, and never will, have inappropriate anything with that young girl you just saw in my classroom. She was coming on to me, and I wasn't responding. Rather than physically forcing her from the room, which also would have been inappropriate, I was telling her to stop and leave. Is there anything else, you'd like to say to me before I go?"

"No, Mr. Carter."

I almost called her a good girl before fully moving past her to walk down the hall and exit the building.

Thankfully, Ben didn't appear and further complicate my already fucked up afternoon.

Amelia was waiting outside the house when I arrived. She jumped in my SUV as soon as I pulled up, her skirt riding so high on her thighs I was half tempted to march her ass in the house and demand she change. Teenage boys couldn't be trusted to keep their attention on music with Amelia around.

"Where are we going?"

I battled whether to tell her about what Jillian had done. Hoping it was the last time I'd have to deal with the unwanted advances, I decided Amelia didn't need to know. It would only upset her.

"To the place we met."

Her eyes shifted my direction. "Why?

"I thought we could reenact our first encounter, except this time, I'll lift that skirt of yours in the shadows of the alley and teach you why not to steal a man's wallet."

Her mouth quirked, teal eyes glimmering with anticipation. She was always so ready for whatever I wanted.

Shaking my head, I admitted, "Actually, we're going to my friend, Dizzy's, store, the same one I was leaving the night you tried to mug me. He has a student who looks up to me, and I promised to meet with the kid and listen to what he could do with a piano."

Nodding, she kept her eyes on the road ahead of us, her skirt inching higher every time she shifted in her seat just slightly. A dangerous fucking sight for a man who should have had his eyes on the road.

Eventually that skirt crept high enough for the crotch of her pink panties to peek into view, a treat I hadn't yet tasted today hidden beneath a thin layer of cotton.

"Touch yourself," I demanded on a gritty whisper.

Amelia's head turned my direction, surprise widening her teal doe eyes. "Right now?"

I arched a brow. "What have I said about complaints and questions, Miss Dillon?"

Her cheeks flushed, that shy modesty of hers still fighting to make an appearance even as I stripped it away from her day after day. When she brought her hand between her legs to stroke a long pretty finger over the fabric of her panties, I shook my head.

"Pull them out of the way. I want skin against skin."

I was going to regret the raging hard on when we waltzed into Dizzy's place, but I wanted to see this, wanted her to obey without question.

Doing as she was told, Amelia slid the panties aside, her pussy coming into view now that her skirt had hiked up even more to pool around her hips.

This was dangerous in a moving vehicle, but I would be careful. So fucking careful while sneaking peeks at her fingers buried deep inside her body. "Use your thumb to play with your clit while slowly driving two fingers inside."

Already, we were taking the exit into Sheldon, which meant there wasn't enough time for Amelia to push herself to a climax. But still, I wanted to see her finger fuck that pretty pussy of hers, wanted to hear the soft moans that rolled off her lips.

Her fingers glistened as she pumped them between her legs, head falling back as her chest arched forward, her thighs spreading wider while her thumb drove hard circles over her clit. My cock was painfully hard.

This was a bad idea, yet here we were, both primed for a good fuck with no place to go to follow through with it.

Or maybe there was...

Pulling into Dizzy's parking lot, I threw the SUV into park, killed the engine and watched with fascination as her hand moved between her legs, fingers so wet I wanted to taste them. I wasn't even sure she knew we'd stopped, her eyes closed and her lips parted on shallow, panting breaths.

Oh, for the love of God...

I grabbed her wrist and pulled her hand from between her legs to bring it to my mouth. Lips closing over her fingers to taste my girl, I grinned when her eyes opened, the lids hooded with want.

Sucking her fingers clean, I gave one warning after flicking my eyes toward the alley. "You might want to run."

Her eyes rounded with understanding.

Amelia jumped out of the SUV and took off in the direction of the alley. I was right behind her within seconds, our pounding steps reminding me of the first time I'd chased her through these shadows.

I'd been yelling at her since the day I met her about dangerous, dirty men hiding around dark, dank corners, and yet here I was becoming one of them, my mouth watering at the thrill of fucking her against a brick wall.

Two turns and I caught her in almost the exact same place I'd first dropped her to the ground three weeks ago. Out of breath, her chest rose and fell as she struggled against me, her body tight as I turned her around and shoved her chest against a wall.

Palms splayed over the brick, she pretended to fight me, little protests rolling over her lips that I knew she didn't mean.

Pulling her hips toward me, I flipped her skirt and found she hadn't replaced her panties to cover her wet hole, my hand working quickly to free my cock from my pants when an annoying as fuck thought came to me.

"I don't have a condom," I admitted.

"I don't care," she answered, her voice breathless and husky. "Please, Mr. Carter, I need this."

Amelia and that fucking word would be my undoing.

I seriously hoped Dizzy's student didn't take a shortcut through the alley.

Oh, don't mind me, Kyle. Just getting a quick, dirty fuck in before seeing how well you handle the keys. You'll understand when you're a little older.

Pushing that thought from my mind, I thrust inside Amelia balls deep and almost came just at the sound of her deep, full throat moan, my hips moving with enough force to shove her forward and lift her up to her toes with each hard thrust.

Feeling her, skin to skin, was driving me harder, pushing me faster toward a climax that would tear me apart.

Her voice was carrying down the alley, forcing me to wrap my hand over her mouth to muffle the sound. Lips next to her ear, I growled, "Such a dirty little slut taking it out in the open like this."

278

Like I'd pulled a trigger, those words had her pussy clamping tight around me, milking me as I found the tight puckered hole of her ass and pushed the tip of my thumb inside.

She damn near collapsed with the orgasm that surged through her body, her hot, shallow breaths wet against my palm as I allowed myself to let go to the quickie and pulled out just in time to climax over the ground at my feet.

I had no way of cleaning us both up and should have thought this through before jumping to it.

We'd both be rushing to the bathroom as soon as we walked inside that store, but before letting her go to tug her clothes into place, I spun her around to face me, slipped my fingers between her legs and kissed her with enough force to steal her quick gasps of breath.

Son of a bitch.

I hoped Dizzy and his student wouldn't be able to smell the sex on us the second we stepped foot into the music store.

CHAPTER TWENTY-TWO

*When you fall in love, find a person who can lift you up. Stay away
from those who would use their strength to hold you down...*

Amelia

Dad was right. You can tell a lot about a person by their hands. What they do with them. How they move them. The art they produce. Whether they use them to hurt other people or to lift up the souls lucky enough to know them.

Watching Lennon with Kyle was eye opening. There sat a man who didn't have to give his time to a struggling musician. Lennon had achieved his fame and success; he'd made it while the kids in Sheldon were fighting to get by. He could have ignored all of us and it wouldn't have affected his career. Yet, there he sat for several hours lifting Kyle up and teaching him that it's not the life circumstances that makes a person, it's the soul.

If you want it bad enough - if you're willing to fight tooth and nail against all those who would hold you down - you deserve the success, the attention, the *win* that finally comes to you once the fight is done.

I had no doubt that Kyle walked away from that lesson with his chin tipped higher. And in truth, mine was tipped higher as well because I was that same kid, struggling and scrabbling, holding myself by the fingernails to keep my head above water.

Although, you wouldn't know that by looking at me now.

Now, I was an image of luxury in a dress that cost more than my car, my hair swept up in a French twist, loose strands fluttering on either side of my face. Jewelry wasn't needed with this dress. The silk alone glimmered enough that to add anything else would be overkill.

Not that I had any jewelry, but still.

Thankfully, Lennon had remembered shoes this morning and we'd made a mad dash to find some. Otherwise, I'd be wearing sneakers.

I wasn't even going to allow myself to think too much on the cost of the shoes.

With only ten minutes before we had to leave, I was glad Lennon thought to introduce me to Dizzy before today. I didn't feel as nervous rushing down to answer the door when the bell rang. Opening it, I smiled to see Lennon's oldest friend and his wife on the other side, as friendly as could be.

"Wow, you look amazing. No wonder Lennon is so taken with you." Offering her hand, Renee flashed me a beaming smile. "I'm Renee, and you've met this old man beside me, so I'll just shove him aside to escort you to our car myself."

Already, I liked her, my nerves easing as we made our way to the car and climbed in. The conversation was light-hearted during the drive, the shadowed interior lighting up when we pulled into the massive parking lot of the performing arts center. To say I was stunned would be an understatement.

Everywhere you looked, glamorous people walked toward the front doors, the height of fashion marching by in a large parade, thousands of lights illuminating the space and sparkling against the beautiful gowns and jewel accents.

I didn't know how Lennon performed in a place so big without pissing himself before walking on that stage. I was nervous for him, my throat clogged with a knot of apprehension, my legs shaking as we joined the parade toward the front doors.

Once inside, my nerves didn't get much better, especially not after seeing the stage set up, grand piano front and center, with chairs arranged for the accompanying symphony.

We made our way to our seats, the view spectacular, the large room filled with a heavy din of conversation while everybody waited for the performance to begin.

A hush fell across the room when the lights above our heads lowered, the audience lost to shadow, the stage lights becoming brighter as the symphony walked out to take their seats. The conductor stood on his platform facing the audience.

It wasn't long before the opening introduction was made, a crash of applause as Lennon strolled on stage in his tux, stealing the show with how absolutely beautiful he was. His jaw was a hard line, his eyes stern as he approached the piano and took his place. His gaze lifted to the conductor before the first notes played.

I was instantly transported back to being hog tied on top of the Steinway at his home, the heavy bass chords vibrating against my naked body while the melody fluttered against my skin. It was a little embarrassing that my body was responding to the music in ways it shouldn't, but he had that affect on me regardless of where we were.

His performance was flawless, the intermission coming far too soon. Even after he walked off stage, I sat breathless.

Giving in to the demands of my full bladder, I parted with Dizzy and Renee in the lobby and waited in the ridiculously long line for the women's bathroom. While I stood quietly, minding my own damn business, a familiar voice caught my attention, the saccharine sweet screech forcing me to turn my head in its direction.

"We has sex in the classroom yesterday afternoon. I mean he's hot in a tux, but you should see him without his clothes. I happily bent over Lennon's desk while he-"

Fingers curling into my palms, I watched the lying bitch brag to her friend about Lennon. It only made things worse when the dozens of women standing within her vicinity could also hear the lie, their mouths curling with polite smiles, their ears feasting on the juicy tidbits Jillian made up about her teacher.

Lennon wasn't fucking anybody yesterday afternoon. Well, me in an alley, but still, he had been busy teaching a kid from a poor area of town to play better, had been lifting someone up while this bitch did her best to drag Lennon down.

I was two seconds away from dragging her by her fucking hair out of the building, but to do so would only clue her in that I was fiercely protective of him - and that would only lead to questions.

Regardless, he needed to know she was spreading lies, if for no other reason than to call her out on it and replace her in the program.

Thankfully, the line moved along and I was able to use the restroom and walk away, my cheeks blazing red with anger when I found Dizzy and Renee.

"Damn girl," Dizzy teased, "who pissed you off, and when are we planning on killing them?"

I couldn't help my grin. His comment helped ease some of my rage. "I just saw the other remaining student in Lennon's class. She was telling anybody who would listen that they were having sex in the classroom yesterday afternoon."

Dizzy shook his head and scratched his jaw. "Lennon must have a hell of a long cock because that's quite the reach from my music store."

Slapping her husband on the shoulder, Renee laughed and turned to me. "Is there anything you can do about it?"

"Not me. But I'll let him know so he can take care of the problem. I don't want her ruining his reputation."

"Because Lennon would never get together with a student," Dizzy mumbled under his breath with a wink.

Laughter shook my shoulders. "Yeah, well, he's smart enough to choose one who won't go around bragging about it, I guess."

. . .

I met Lennon back at the house later that evening. Walking inside, I found him in the kitchen drinking a bottle of water, his tux jacket already stripped off, his tie loose over the back of his neck and his shirt sleeves rolled up.

I wanted to run up to him and wrap my arms around his waist, but something stopped me. The expression on his face, maybe. The darkness rolling behind his eyes.

Whatever it was, this person wasn't the man I'd kissed before he left that afternoon. After such a stunning performance, I'd assumed he'd want to celebrate.

It was my intention to tell him what I'd overheard while waiting for the bathrooms. Now, there was no way in hell I'd add to whatever was bothering him.

"Everything okay?"

He set the water bottle down on the counter beside him with such force that drops burst up from the top to splash the granite. Worry etched my bones that something happened at the symphony tonight, that he'd messed up and I hadn't caught it, that perhaps the rumors Jillian were spreading had reached him.

Or worse.

The rumor couldn't be true.

She couldn't be -

I thought back to Friday afternoon, remembered waiting outside for over a half hour for him to pull up at the curb to pick me up. Thinking about it now, he should have been right behind me.

Oh god...

"I have somewhere I need to be tomorrow. I'll be gone for most of the morning."

Not bothering to look at me as he said those words, Lennon tapped his fingers on the counter where his arms were stretched to his sides.

"I can't go with you?"

I didn't know what was happening to me. Never once had I not trusted him. Never once had I questioned what we were doing. But now, this new version of myself was crawling out from beneath my skin, a girl with matted hair and torn clothes, dirt staining her paper thin skin, a monster with green eyes and a broken soul. Jealousy sharpening her fingernail claws. Rage staining her eyes red.

"Can I go with you?" I asked again, my voice sharp, tone clipped.

Lennon glanced my direction, the storm in his eyes brewing with such violence that I took a step back as if to run the opposite direction.

"Come here."

It wasn't a request, not with the unwavering strength in his voice, the sharp depth of tone rolling the words out as a command. Even if my thoughts continued to race over every possibility of what he could have done, my body responded. Wanting. Needing. Practically begging for my fears and worries to be untrue.

My mind wanted to ask questions and demand answers. Yet, my feet stepped forward, stopping just before I was in range for him to reach out and grab me.

A nudge of his chin toward me. "Take off the dress."

Stilling in place, my brows knit together, confusion blending with the spikes of jealousy that continued bursting every time I wondered if what Jillian said was possible.

Yet, even with that toxic mix of emotions, I pulled the sleeves from my arms, found the hidden zipper and tugged it down. The dress fell from my body to pool at my ankles, a puddle of shimmering silk.

I hadn't worn a bra, so all that covered me was a scrap of barely there lace panties.

The storm in his eyes shifted, clouds rolling, sharp streaks of lust and lightning crackling in the distance. Lennon closed the distance between us without a word, his hands locking on my hips to lift me up to the counter. I tried to lock my knees together, but he was stronger, faster.

Pushing my legs far apart, he leaned down to breathe me in, my eyes closing as my cheeks pinked with modesty. While his hand tore the lace from between my legs like the nothing scrap of cloth it was, his tongue and teeth worked a path down one thigh and up the other.

I was a sinful buffet, there to cure his every hunger, my body trembling to feel his dark eyes roam over my skin like a wolf staring down its next meal.

Opened wide and split apart, I felt his palms against the inside of my thighs, his thumbs running down the center of my slit, opening me even wider. It was impossible to swallow the cry of pleasure bursting from my throat the instant his tongue explored the swollen, sensitive skin. Thick and hot, tasting me without shame for how exposed I was.

My inner thigh muscles burned from how wide Lennon had splayed my legs, but it was nothing compared to the feel of his tongue pushing inside me, thrusting in and out as a greedy thick tip, his thumb rubbing circles over a bundle of nerves that were swollen and desperate for attention.

I came easily, quickly, my chest arching above the cold, hard granite surface. But he didn't give me time to gather myself together before tugging me forward, dropping his pants and shoving his cock deep inside.

This wasn't a casual fucking, it was a moment of desperation, a feat of flexibility as he lifted my legs to hook them over his shoulders and his hips drove forward with demanding strength.

With my arms stretched down the length of my body, I held onto the edge of the counter, holding myself in place, his thrusts so forceful, my fingers cramped to keep me from sliding back.

Lennon's hand slid up the centerline of my body, between my breasts, over my throat, the hold a threat that he would cut off my air.

I felt owned in that moment. Used. But damn if I didn't enjoy the feeling, the lust, the filthy violence that leaked out of him with every demanding thrust.

At no time did he speak or acknowledge what had made him angry.

Lennon simply took what he needed.

Drove his body against mine.

Brought us both to a shattering climax while I tried to understand his silence while giving him everything I had to offer.

CHAPTER TWENTY-THREE

I wanted him, but he never wanted me. Not me. Never me. Still, I took advantage and opened to him like a song desperate to be heard. A melody desperate to caress the forbidden...

Lennon

July 13th.

It happened eleven years ago today, at some awful time when I hadn't been paying attention.

Eleven years. It's odd to think that an eternity can pass in so low a number, that an entire lifetime can set into velvet midnight, only for the sun to rise again over a world you never knew existed.

Who the hell knows where I was at the moment her chair tipped that day. Rope tight. Body fighting against what was coming.

I could have lifted her up had I been there. I was strong enough. Tall enough. I cared enough to try.

But I was somewhere else. Out with Dizzy most likely, running the streets or laughing like idiots in his father's music store.

I was somewhere else when the only place I needed to be was home. When she'd reached the breaking point and couldn't take the pain for a second longer.

All because of a boy, so stupid a reason it was almost comical.

Eleven years. Her simple gravestone showed the passage of time.

Emaline P. Carter. A name I'd once thought forgotten by everyone but me.

It wasn't until after my performance that I remembered what the next day would bring. A benchmark. An anniversary of the worst kind. A day I'd spent regretting my choices, my absence, every year when it passed by.

This was the first year I'd visited her grave on the same date that she'd died. The first year I'd spent this anniversary crouching by what was left of her, this chiseled stone slab standing within a quiet graveyard and only the birdsong to keep it company.

My weight fell heavy on the ground where I sat staring, my fingers idly pulling at bits of weeds and grass.

Next to her tombstone lay the wilted flowers I'd brought to her several weeks ago. Beside them a new dozen that was a pop of color against the remnants of the past.

It was still early in the morning when I'd arrived here, the sun not yet fully breaching the horizon, a thick, heavy mist hovering over the ground to blanket the grass and grave markers.

When I left the house, Amelia had been sleeping, her body limp over the mattress, exhausted from a night spent surrendering her will to me.

I'd used her as an escape, and she'd allowed it, giving everything without question, intuiting that what I'd needed in those late hours were necessary for me to breathe fully, for my heart to stop its slow fracturing.

Not one question.

Her surrender so selfless that it stole my breath to think about it now.

Like any day, time marched forward this morning, the sun creeping higher as I sat quietly, the trees above me coming to life with the birds. A frog croaked in the distance, the low hum of a lawn mower from a neighborhood that bordered the cemetery.

Behind me, the heavy fall of footsteps sounded over the twigs along the path, a rustle of plastic that forced me to spin in place to acknowledge I was no longer alone.

I wasn't sure if it was instant rage or shock that froze me in place. A flurry of thoughts raced through my head, my fingers curling against my palms with the need for violence. But even as my muscles tensed painfully at the sight of Amelia's brother, I paused, my eyes scanning to his hand where he held a dozen white roses and back to his eyes where I saw the same pain as mine.

"What are you doing here?"

Ben was smart to keep his distance. I wasn't sure I could hold back from the need for vengeance tearing through me.

Gaze narrowing on me with the same hatred I felt for him, he flicked a glance to Emaline's gravestone, his expression softening just a touch. "I come here every year on this day."

"Why?"

Surprise at his confession swept in like a brisk wind kicking up the pristine surface of a calm lake, the image I had of him scattered, a seed of question planted where it had no right to be.

293

"Because I loved Emaline. I was destroyed when she-"

Ben winced, unable to finish the sentence. I knew the reaction well, knew how difficult it was to say aloud the truth of what my sister had done. Even so, how fucking dare he pretend that he hadn't been the cause of it?

Pushing to my feet, I marched toward him, my hands fisted, my face twisted with the hatred bleeding out of me.

It occurred to me that a graveyard was a place of rest and serenity, but I couldn't contain the anger, the red hot rage, the violence demanding blood for all the ways this son of a bitch had wronged me.

For Emaline.

For Amelia.

He didn't deserve one ounce of my patience or forgiveness.

Ben wasn't stupid. When I pushed to my feet and stormed toward him he attempted to back away rather than stand his ground. But I was too fast, too furious, the monster inside finally roaring to the surface when my hand locked around his throat and I backed him into the thick trunk of a Live Oak.

Above us Spanish moss swayed in the branches, a few startled birds taking flight, while at our feet his bullshit roses fell to the ground.

Ben's head snapped back against the trunk, his jaw tight as my fist smashed into his nose, blood bursting with the sharp crack.

"Fuck!" Hands lifting, Ben attempted to break the second punch and the third, but I was a man possessed, my rage at every shitty thing this asshole had done taking over.

"Stop! What the fuck?"

Punches four and five cracked with quick succession before I dropped him, my eyes wide and wild as I stepped back to watch him spit blood onto the ground.

Chest rising and falling with my breath, I was seeing red, the vengeance I'd wanted with this son of a bitch not yet sated because he refused to fight back.

Ben spit again, his neck craning up, one eye already swelling when he glared at me.

"I should give you that shit right back for whatever the hell it is you're doing with Amelia. The only difference is I'm not willing to beat the shit out of Emaline's brother right over her goddamn grave."

I laughed, the bark of sound cutting straight to the bone. "What I'm doing? I'm not the one using Amelia like a damn slut to lure men into alleys. I'm not the one asking her to let strangers grope her so I can get a little bit of cash. Look in a fucking mirror before you question what I'm doing."

He didn't respond immediately, so I filled in the silence for him. "And why do you give two shits about what happens over Emaline's grave? You're the one that put her there."

His eyes rounded, dark saucers reflecting my rage back at me. Surging to his feet, he closed the distance and locked his arms around my body, both of us crashing to the ground with a heavy thud.

Pain shot along my spine, but it didn't shake me free of the need to hurt this man as much as he'd hurt

Emaline, as much as he'd hurt Amelia...as much as he'd hurt me.

His fist slammed into the side of my head, but I was already tipping his balance, rolling him right so my weight would pin him down as I rained blow after blow against his jaw.

Ben had more practice fighting, most likely a result of those back alley muggings, and gained the upper hand again, throwing me off him and jumping forward to jam a knee into my thigh, his fist crashing down into the center of my chest.

"Where the fuck is my sister?"

Another punch impacted my stomach, but he couldn't move fast enough to dodge a blow to the face that knocked him onto his back.

Winded, I pushed to my feet and glared down at the bloody mess of his face. "Why do you care? Do you need money? Because that's the only use you seem to have for her."

This was not how I'd intended to spend my morning, but now that the son of a bitch was here, I thanked the universe for delivering him.

Kicking him in the ribs, I backed off when he spit out more blood, my chest heaving as pain crawled like fire beneath my skin.

"Is she staying with you?" he asked, spitting again before pushing up on his arms to turn and look at me. "Are you fucking my sister?"

He lunged forward to grab my ankle and pull me down. I backed away and kicked dirt into his face. It was a cheap move, but at that point, I didn't care.

My voice was a harsh growl. "Get the fuck out of here and never show your piece of shit face around Emaline's grave again."

"Why?" He yelled, his booming voice chasing a few more birds from the trees. "What did I do to Emaline?"

"You killed her, you son of a bitch. Fucking played her like she wasn't worth your time or respect."

Ben's eyes rounded as much as they could beneath the swelling. "What are you talking about? I treated her like gold. I was in love with that woman. Where in the hell would you get the idea that I did anything to hurt her?"

If I didn't know better, if I didn't have Emaline's note tucked away in my wallet where it had stayed since the moment I found her body hanging in her room, I would have believed him. Ben was genuinely shocked by the accusation, anger vibrating across his shoulders, blood pouring from the split in his lip.

"From her note," I answered, my voice far too calm.

"What note? There was no note. I asked your parents after you moved away."

Stilling in place, I thought back to whether mom or dad had mentioned a visit from Ben. Neither of them lived longer than two years after Emaline died. I didn't speak with them too often before their deaths, but it wasn't like we were completely out of touch. Not once had they mentioned any person coming by to ask about Emaline.

Even if he was being truthful and had spoken to my parents, they wouldn't have known the truth about why Emaline took her life. I pocketed the note as soon as I found her. It was addressed to me, and for that reason, I didn't see the need for any other person to know why my sister felt she couldn't go on living her life.

Pushing himself up off the ground, Ben dropped his weight into a seated position, dirt dusting up around his sides. He stared at me silently, his face smeared with blood, dirt and sweat.

"She left a note when she died," I explained. "One that detailed what you did to her in your relationship. I would have hunted you down that day if I knew who you were. All I knew about you was what you looked like, but I didn't know your name. Not until I saw you again with Amelia. Seeing as how you didn't care to introduce yourself to any of Emaline's family or friends, it makes sense that you would use her and toss her aside. That is why she did what she did. I have it written in black and white."

Shaking his head, he held my stare, ignoring the sweat that dripped down into his eyes. "I dated Emaline. I'll admit that, but I didn't do anything to her. And the only reason we weren't open about the relationship was because she knew your parents would break us apart. They were too focused on her becoming a musician and didn't want her to have distractions. But I wanted people to know we were together. I wanted us to have a future together. Why would I treat her like crap when I wanted that?"

"Emaline said it was you-"

"Did she write my name specifically in that letter? Did she say Ben Dillon broke her heart?"

Obviously not, or I would have known who to hunt down and kill back then. "No."

Shaking his head again, he spit more blood onto the ground beside him. "Do you still have the note? Because I didn't do anything to her. I may be a bastard for some of the things I do now, but I treated your sister like gold. If someone broke her heart to the point where she would kill herself over it, I can promise you it wasn't me."

A bark of laughter burst from my chest. "I'm not sure it even matters anymore."

"Oh, no. Actually, it matters to me. If her heart was broken over a guy back then, that means she was seeing someone else at the same time she was dating me. And I'd sure as hell like to know who that son of a bitch was."

I didn't want to believe him. After all this time and for as much as I wanted to continue hating Ben, the last thing I wanted to believe was that I'd been wrong about who had pushed Emaline to committing suicide. But I couldn't deny he was as upset as me to learn there had been another person who broke her, that there had been another man who used her and tossed her aside.

"Do you still have the note?" he asked again.

"Why?"

His grin was feral. "Because if there is someone out there walking around Sheldon that did something to hurt Emaline, I don't give a shit how much time has passed. I have a bone to pick with that motherfucker."

Everything inside me was screaming to disagree with him. When would Emaline have had the time to see someone else? Ben was right about one thing. Mom and Dad were strict on her when it came to her schedule.

If she wasn't at school or piano lessons, she was home practicing or doing her homework. The fact that she'd somehow snuck a relationship in with Ben was surprising. But for there to be a second guy? It was impossible.

The note was in my pocket. It would be so easy to tell him I didn't have it and go on living my life believing he was the asshole who'd hurt her. But if there was somebody else, if there was the slightest possibility I'd been wrong, I needed to know the truth.

Pulling my wallet from my pocket, I removed the note that was worn thin and had faded over time. I didn't want this asshole touching it, yet I couldn't bring myself to read it aloud either. Not here. Not today. Not while facing a man I still blamed despite his claim that he had nothing to do with Emaline's death.

Staggering over a decision, I battled myself as to whether I should tuck the note back in the wallet where it was safe, or if I should let Ben read it.

If there was someone else...

If it was possible...

"Crawl over here," I finally said, unfolding the note and holding it out where he could read it.

"I'll let you look at it, but keep your damn hands to yourself. This is the last part of her I have, and if you so much as flinch in my direction like you plan to touch it, I'll kick in you in the face so hard you'll need a full set of dentures to replace your teeth."

Ben glared my direction, but finally moved his ass to look at the letter I held out. His eyes scanned the words, disbelief twisting his expression. I saw pain in his gaze as he absorbed Emaline's final thoughts, but I didn't want to believe what I saw.

Shaking his head, Ben pushed to his feet and ran his hand through his hair, dirt and leaves falling to the ground.

"She wasn't talking about me." His jaw was tense, the pain I believed I saw earlier transitioning into anger. "I'll find out who it was. I don't know how, but somehow I'll find out."

I didn't want to believe him. Folding the note and tucking it back into my wallet, I stepped away from Ben, not trusting he wouldn't attempt to start the fight again.

"You need to leave."

A beat of silence and then, "You need to tell me where the hell Amelia is staying."

I laughed. "As far away from you as possible."

I met his stare. "You're lucky I haven't killed you for what you've done to her. How many times have you risked her safety so you could make some quick cash? How many fucking times have you involved her in a crime for money? Grow up, Ben. And while you're doing that, you can stop worrying about where she is. If you're so fucking concerned, you should be happy she's away from the one person who keeps threatening her future."

Turning away from him, I took a few steps to leave the cemetery before he called out to me in response.

"You're the one paying for my dad to be in a group home, aren't you?"

Stilling in place, tension ran across my shoulders. "Yeah, do you have a problem with that, too?"

301

Without looking back at him, I waited for his response.

"I wanted to thank you for it, actually."

Casting him a glance over my shoulder, I shook my head.

"I didn't do it for you. I did it for Amelia. If you want to thank me, get your shit together so she has a brother that makes her proud, instead of a piece of shit that drags her down every fucking chance he gets."

With that I left him standing in the cemetery, the roses he'd brought Emaline crushed and scattered over the dirt.

It wasn't easy putting one foot in front of the other. Everything inside me told me to turn back and finish what I'd started. But where would that leave me?

Amelia's future in music depended on me to get her through the program. Killing Ben would only hurt her. Going to jail would only hurt her.

I refused to be the person that destroyed her chances, and for that reason, I walked silently to my car and drove away, my thoughts scattered and tossed over the possibility that what Ben said about another man involved with my sister had been true.

CHAPTER TWENTY-FOUR

The hands are capable of creating the most beautiful music. But, in turn, they are capable of destroying the world. Destroying the soul. Destroying every life they touch...

Amelia

I stayed up most of the night with Lennon. Not knowing what had driven him into such a dark place. I didn't whine or complain from exhaustion, didn't shy away from every escape he sought in using my body. In a way, the passion between us was in perfect harmony despite the discordant notes that existed inside him.

Feeling every bit of his anger and pain, I endured, not that being with him was a chore, but it hurt to know something lingered within him that he wouldn't reveal.

He left early in the morning, and even though I was physically drained from a night spent meeting his every sexual desire, I couldn't sleep once my head hit the pillow, couldn't get my mind to stop racing through thoughts of what could have caused him to become distant.

A few hours had passed since he'd left, and still my mind raced. I gave up on sleep after a while, found myself wandering his large house in search of my own escape. Eventually, I found myself at his piano, my fingers lightly brushing over the keys in wait of the music inside me to come out.

The melody that finally poured from me was somber and heartbreaking, a song that I couldn't remember learning, yet it somehow was there inside. The house filled with the music, a crescendo of bitterness and regret, the notes driving down until just a whisper resonated through the empty rooms.

Tears welled in my eyes as I became lost to the melancholy, my mind recalling the pain of losing my mother, the pain of my father's disease, the fear I'd lived in since the moment we were forced to give up our comfortable lives and move into the heart of Sheldon.

Despite everything Lennon had done for me, I was still afraid that the bottom would drop out. It wasn't easy for me to trust that the next day wouldn't bring heartache.

What if the rumors were true?

What if he was playing me while playing Jillian as well?

What if I wasn't the only student he was breaking the rules for while telling us both that we had a chance at a future in music?

Why did he disappear this morning without an explanation as to where he was going?

It was stupid of me to be jealous about Jillian. It wasn't like Lennon and I had said we were in a committed relationship. But, even without saying it, why would he bring me to live at his house? Why would he pay for my father to be in a home? If those weren't signs of a man committing to a woman, I wasn't sure what would be.

Then again, how could I even ask for a commitment when in a few shorts weeks, I hoped to be leaving for Hastings, while he returned to his usual life?

My fingers stopped moving over the keys and I laughed. The truth was I didn't even know where he lived when he wasn't in town teaching.

"That was beautiful," a deep voice said from behind me, my body jumping in place to learn that Lennon had been standing in the doorway for who knew how long.

Spinning over the bench, my eyes widened immediately, my body pushing to my feet to rush across the room and gently touch his hands, his face, the injuries that hadn't been there this morning when he left.

"What happened? Are you okay?"

Focusing on the injuries to his hands, I gasped. "Lennon-"

"They're fine," he promised, reaching to grasp my chin and tilt my face up to his. "A little swollen and sore, but nothing is broken."

"Are you going to tell me how this happened?"

He grimaced, but still his beautiful eyes held mine. "You're not going to like it."

The answer came to me without him having to say another word. "Ben. Oh my God, was he waiting for you somewhere? Did he-"

"Hey," he said, snapping me out of the flurry of panicked questions. "We had a run-in at the cemetery. Today is the anniversary of Emaline's death."

That explained his mood last night and this morning.

"I could have warned you that Ben goes to her grave every year. If you had reminded me, I could have told you he would show up there eventually."

Hating to ask the question when I knew how much Lennon disliked my brother, I still couldn't stay silent. For as much of an asshole Ben could be, I loved him.

"Is Ben okay?"

"A little bloody and knocked around, but he'll live."

Focusing on his hands, I studied the broken skin over his knuckles, worried when I noticed the swelling that would prevent him from being able to play. I knew the pain of that swelling, remembered it from when Lennon had slammed my hand against the ground when we first met.

Thankful that this happened after his performance, I still needed to take care of him in some way, needed to wash away the evidence that there was a dividing line between Lennon and my family, a part of me fracturing over the choice of loyalty.

Ben had given up so much and practically raised me to ensure I wouldn't fall victim to the misfortune of our parents.

But Lennon, a man who had no ties to me beyond the fact I was his student, was doing everything in his power to push me along into a wonderful career. He was doing everything he could to make sure I would find a life in music.

Choosing one over the other was impossible.

While one had been the man to watch over me in my past, the other was raising me up to step proudly into the future.

There was no possible way I could make a choice, and yet I feared that if I didn't, I would lose them both.

"You need to get into a shower. Then we need to ice your hand. You won't be able to play if we don't tend to these injuries."

His stormy eyes danced with unspoken thoughts, the lines of his face harsh, sharper due to the pain that was obviously drowning him. "It's not me who needs to play, Amelia."

He wasn't wrong, but it didn't matter. Lennon had done so much to help me – to take care of me – that I needed to take care of him in return.

"Come on. We're cleaning off the blood and dirt."

Allowing me to drag him along, Lennon followed me upstairs and into his room. I practically shoved him into the bathroom before reaching to help him strip off his clothes. Bruises bloomed over his chest and ribs, my heart aching each time I discovered a new injury.

"Who looks worse?" I asked.

His lips tipped up at the corners, a feral glimmer in his eye that answered the question before he spoke a word. "Your brother. But that's probably because I attacked him first."

Sighing, I bit back the immediate reaction I had, the need to defend Ben at all costs. "Why?"

Our eyes locked and Lennon reached up to brush a finger down my cheek. "Because I thought he was the reason my sister killed herself."

The admission surprised me.

Emaline's death had destroyed Ben. He disappeared for a few days after we'd heard the news, his life spiraling down for a full year after it happened. I wasn't sure he ever recovered.

A confession rolled over Lennon's lips that tore my heart from my chest.

"She was everything to me. Emaline practically raised me when my parents were so focused on her they forgot I existed. Every dime my parents made went to her musical training. She was their hope for a future. Their first born. A girl they sheltered while I was left to run the streets. And even though I should have hated her for being the star child in our house, I loved Emaline for her refusal to forget about me right along with my parents. She was meant to be what I eventually became. But she threw it all away. I couldn't protect her as fiercely as she protected me."

Muscles rigid over his shoulders, Lennon closed his eyes, the tension in his jaw making mine hurt in sympathy. The memory of Emaline had shattered this man as thoroughly as it shattered my brother, and I was caught in the middle, trapped in Emaline's shadow.

"I'm sorry," I whispered, my palms lightly cupping his cheeks, the muscle in his jaw jumping against my touch.

He blew out a breath. "You have nothing to be sorry for." His eyes flicked open. "And according to what your brother had to say, neither does he."

Anger rolled behind his eyes that frightened me. My voice was barely a whisper. "Is that a bad thing?"

His lips kicked up into a caustic grin. "Yes. If I don't have him to blame and hate, I'm left to hate my sister for what she did, or myself for my failure to save her."

Shaking my head, I fought the tears that pricked my eyes. So much pain was pouring out of Lennon that it washed over me to sink beneath my skin. "You can't blame yourself."

A huff blew out from his lips. "I've blamed myself for ten years, Amelia. There's no stopping me now."

Such a weight this man carried. I knew then that the storm I'd always seen behind his eyes was a remnant of his heartbreaking past.

"You should get in the shower."

Not knowing what else to say, I stepped around Lennon while he kicked off his shoes and his pants. Turning on the shower, I gathered my thoughts and focused on the water and steam pouring out of the multiple heads. Everything in this house was far too fancy for a girl like me, but it fit Lennon perfectly.

I moved aside. "All right, get in. I want all the dirt and blood gone."

Rather than doing as I asked and walking into the glass enclosure, Lennon backed me against a wall, his large body caging me in place with his arms braced on either side of my head.

"Aren't you going to join me?"

I was still exhausted from the previous night in his bed, but there was something about his deep, dark voice that called to me. It was then that I understood I would never be able to resist this man. Losing him at the end of the summer was going to break me into so many pieces I wasn't sure I'd know how to put myself back together.

All I had on was one of his tshirts and a pair of sleep shorts, so it didn't take much to strip away my clothes, his eyes roaming hungrily over my body as I did so. A shiver coursed up my spine to be openly admired.

Lennon was determined to break me of my modesty and shyness, but I didn't think there would ever come a day where I didn't tremble to know he had me locked in his observant gaze.

Despite the blood and dirt, Lennon was still sexy as hell. I had to admit the dark stains on his skin fit him somehow, revealed the feral nature that I knew lingered inside him. He made me breathless without even trying, just his presence enough to still me in place - to make me want to behave.

I thought he would kiss me without bothering to wash those stains away, but instead he pushed away from the wall, took my hand and pulled me into the heat and steam of the large shower. Multiple heads sprayed down on both of us, and I reached up to help clean the dirt from his skin, my eyes fascinated to watch it trail down his face and body until gone.

He didn't move to stop me, a storm in his eyes brewing as I examined his wounds, my fingers moving over every bruise and cut, my heart hurting for every injury.

Neither Lennon nor Ben deserved the beating, a truth I'm not sure that Lennon knew.

While wiping away a smudge of muck from Lennon's cheek, I admitted on a whisper, "He loved her, you know. More than I think you understand."

That storm inside him rolled and darkened, the ocean of his eyes breaking with violent whitecaps. I knew the mention of his sister would drive him to a place where I wasn't sure I could ever reach him, but he needed to know the truth.

Careful to keep my voice soft, I locked my eyes with his despite how much I wanted to look away.

"When we found out what she did, Ben left for a few days. He came back and he wasn't the same person. He was angry – so angry that I worried he would break beneath the pressure of it. The brother I knew wasn't there anymore, and although the years have helped smooth some of the sharp edges, he's like you when her name is mentioned. He breaks inside and anybody who looks at him knows it. Just like when I look at you after Emaline is brought up, I see that you're fracturing apart."

I wasn't sure what I expected him to say in response, or if he would respond at all. Knowing I was risking myself to discuss the subject, I struggled to breathe, my hair plastered to my back from the water, my hands shaking to continue touching him with the hope of maintaining the connection we had.

Lennon's lips parted just slightly, his eyes locked to mine as water ran in rivulets down his skin. The silence between us was killing me. When he finally moved, I flinched in surprise.

He wasn't interested in talking.

Instead, he spun me around and pressed me up against the cool tiles of the shower wall, his body like a furnace behind me. His hand brushed my hair aside as his lips found my neck and trailed down as if to chase the water that poured over my skin.

The hard length of his erection pushed against my ass, his chest like steel against my back. I trembled as his hands softly grazed up the sides of my body, his fingers exploring my skin as he reached to take a possessive hold of my breasts.

Lennon's teeth locked down at the juncture of my neck and shoulder. I stilled in place, my breath beating heavy, liquid heat pooling between my thighs in response to the threat of his dark mood.

I knew in that moment not to question him or complain. He needed me. Needed my submission. Needed my obedience. Needed my silent permission for him to take everything I could give.

It didn't matter how dangerous his mood was, I would trust him to take care of me while he took what he wanted.

It was odd to think that, in so short a time, this man had become everything I needed in my life.

He was my heart.

He owned my soul.

He was a dark melody that was in perfect harmony with mine. Each note intended to sing together. Each chord a matched beat in our pulse.

Lennon was the music that whispered within the chaos of my thoughts, a melody that shone as the brightest of lights, directing me and welcoming me home.

Curling his fist into my hair, he pulled my head back, his teeth nipping a trail up my neck, his other hand sliding down to lock over my hip and pull it toward him.

His palm curved over the cheek of my ass, his thumb brushing down the crease to push between and hover over the tight hole, taunting me, taming me, owning me.

I would give him anything he wanted.

I would take his pain.

I would become the comfort he needed to move past the monsters inside him.

Lennon must have somehow known my thoughts, a low growl vibrating in his chest when I didn't complain or move away from the position of his thumb.

Mouth against my ear, he whispered, "You'll let me do anything I want, won't you? Even if it hurts you. Even if you're scared. I'm not sure what that says about you, Amelia."

His teeth nipped my ear, the tip of his thumb entering my ass as a tease. "I can feel you trembling."

Hell, just the sound of his voice was making me tremble more. I didn't know where Lennon's mind was at that moment, but I liked what I heard, *craved* him to take me over without giving a damn whether I was terrified of what he could do.

"Do you want this, Amelia?"

My lips parted on an answer that never came, the breath in my lungs caught, my heart beating so erratically I thought I would pass out and slump to the shower floor. Maybe it was the steam, or maybe it was the dizzying heat of the man who had me trapped.

Whatever it was, I was addicted to it, unable to think straight, uncaring what he did as long as he kept doing it.

Lennon pulled his hand away from my ass and turned me around, his storm blue eyes capturing mine and pinning me in place.

His lips kicked up at the corners, a devilish grin that promised every imaginable sin known to man.

Pressing his forehead against mine, he kissed the tip of my nose and whispered, "I think I want to taste you first."

Dropping to his knees, Lennon wrapped his arms behind my legs and lifted me up. I cried out in surprise, my knees hooking over his shoulders as he stood up, my back braced against the shower wall.

He gave me no warning except to say, "Reach up and hold on to the shower head."

Holy shit…

My arms shook as I reached above my head to do as he'd told me, my fingers wrapping over the bar of the head at the same time his mouth covered my pussy, his tongue flicking in an out of my body, tasting me and driving me to an orgasm that I feared would send us both tumbling down onto the ground. Sucking my clit between his lips, his swirled his tongue over the sensitive nub, tormenting it without concern that I was begging him to stop.

I couldn't take the intensity of his mouth, my body shuddering, my fingers wrapping tighter over the bar of the showerhead for fear I would knock Lennon off balance and he'd drop me onto my ass.

I should have known better, his strength so much more than mine.

When the first wave of pleasure tore through me, my legs clamped down on his shoulders as he licked and sucked, the sensual torture driving the orgasm so hard that I feared it would never stop.

My arms strained so much that I worried I would pull the damn showerhead out of the wall, but then the climax eased, his mouth moving slower before he lowered me down, my legs like putty as Lennon caged me against the wall again, a smirk tugging at his lips to see how he affected me.

"You scared me," I said on a breathless laugh, "I thought for sure you would drop me."

His eyes flashed with heat, his erection so thick and hard against my stomach that there was no forgetting he still hadn't taken everything.

Leaning down, he teased my mouth with his. "And if I did drop you?"

Another nervous chuckle floated over my lips. "Then it would have been worth it."

Lennon grinned, but then lifted me again before I knew what he was doing. Directing my legs around his waist, he braced my back against the shower wall and thrust inside me without worry that we weren't using a condom.

Normally so careful, he must have been lost in the passionate heat not to worry about that small detail, but then again, I wasn't worried either.

Feeling him move inside me had short-circuited my ability to think. But then again, he always had the effect on me.

I didn't know who this person was that locked his eyes with mine while driving into me over and over, but if I had the choice of loving both his sides, light and dark, or never knowing him at all, I would happily brave the shadows if it was his music I was following.

His voice was a dark caress against my ear, his words forcing heat through every inch of my body. "Do you have any idea what you do to me, little girl? Your body hugs my cock like it never wants to let go. I can feel every inch of you, can barely keep from hurting you with how hard I want to fuck you until you beg me to stop."

Lennon's hips slammed between my legs, his cock filling me, driving so deep that I was helpless but to grip my hands on his shoulders and enjoy the ride. My back slid against the stone wall, my eyes clenching shut as he continued taunting me with such dirty words that I was blushing to hear them.

"You like being fucked, don't you? Such a smart-mouthed tease in the classroom and such an irresistible slut when I get you alone."

Another orgasm took me over at the deep growl of his voice. Never would I have ever believed hearing someone call me a slut would have turned me on, but something about the words on his lips made me wild inside. My inner muscles gripped him, undulating as waves of pleasure rolled through my body one after another. He chuckled against my ear, the sound dark and dirty because he knew I was losing control.

"That's right, Amelia. Let it out, beautiful girl."

And I did, my entire body caught within the storm of pleasure, stars bursting behind my eyelids for how tightly they were clenched shut.

"Fuck," he breathed out, his hands gripping my hips as he slammed into me one last time. "I can't control myself when I'm inside you."

He moved away once my body had stopped trembling beneath every wave of excruciating pleasure, a smile tilting his lips when he balanced me on my feet but then directed me down to my knees.

Gripping my chin with his thumb and finger, he tilted my face up, his expression as hard as the stone shower walls, his eyes blazing with heat.

"Open up. You fucked my face. It's time for me to return the favor."

I did as he said. No questions. No complaints. Masculine satisfaction filtered into his dark gaze, his fingers releasing my chin to wrap in my wet hair as his cock drove into my mouth.

The back of my head pressed against the hard shower wall, his hips moving as I fought to keep up, my lips wrapping around his girth as he drove his hard length against the back of my throat. Drool dribbled from the sides of my mouth, washed away by the water sliding between us. I closed my eyes, and his voice boomed above my head.

"Open them. I want you watching the man that fucks you."

It was too almost too much, the movement of his body, the water that dripped down the ridges and valleys of his hard body. He was intoxicating, so demanding and firm.

The second our eyes met again, his rhythm became punishing. But I took it regardless, my tongue sliding over the thick vein of his cock as Lennon lost the ability to keep going.

"Swallow," he growled when his climax hit, his thick, hot come shooting down the back of my throat, giving me no other option than to do what he said.

Pulling free of my mouth, Lennon stared down at me for a few silent seconds as we both found the ability to breathe again. It was just long enough for me to see that the pain I'd witnessed in his eyes for the past twenty four hours was finally gone.

Just long enough to understand that I was owned by this haunted and beautiful man.

CHAPTER TWENTY-FIVE

He was everything. My sun. My universe. My darkness and light.
He was the music inside me. Until the day the notes stopped and I
was trapped in intolerable silence...

Lennon

It was early morning when I slammed the door of my SUV and lifted my gaze to see the sun rising over the horizon. Behind the school, a glow painted the sky in pink and orange ribbons, the sky above still dark where the moon refused to give up its throne.

Amelia had been sleeping peacefully when I left the house, her small body curled around a pillow, the blanket draped over her naked hip tempting me to stay home instead of return to spend four hours with Jillian. I had a job to do, one I wasn't looking forward to, but thankfully it would end in a week when I made the final cut and only Amelia remained in the running.

Clenching my hand, I winced at the pain in my swollen knuckles, my cheek painted yellow where a light bruise had formed from my fight with Ben. Not giving a damn what I looked like, I strolled across the parking lot and into the building, my name called out as soon as I passed Julia's classroom.

"Lennon. May I speak to you for a moment, please?"

My thoughts returned to when I'd last spoken to Julia, to a moment when she'd believed she caught me being inappropriate with a student. Judging by the deep scowl she wore and the fire behind her cheeks, I assumed this conversation wasn't what I needed after a shitty weekend.

I stepped into her classroom and leaned against a wall, my eyes meeting her gaze without concern for what she believed she'd caught.

Straightening the cuffs of her long sleeved blouse, Julia said, "You may want to close the door for this conversation. Just in case any students arrive early."

Grinning, I answered, "I'm fine with it being open. I have nothing to hide."

Eyes scanning the bruise on my cheek, then taking their time to trail down to my exposed and injured knuckles, Julia swallowed. "Apparently, you do. Not only are you carrying on a sexual relationship with a student, but you appear to be getting into fights when you're not teaching."

Her gaze met mine again. "That's not the behavior I would expect from a person with your reputation, Mr. Carter."

My first thought was that the sexual relationship she was referencing was Jillian Bates. But then concern etched the hard lines of my expression. Had Ben run to Julia to tell her what he knew about Amelia and me."

"I fell," I lied, "so you can drop your unfounded accusations that I'm a street fighter in my spare time."

She laughed. "That's funny. The last person to show up with a busted hand tried to tell me the same lie. I didn't believe it then and I certainly don't believe it now."

Frustration scraped down my spine. "Are you going to let me know why I'm here, or are we having a pointless conversation, Ms. Pickens?"

Her jaw tightened, lips pulling into a thin line. "One of the Hastings board members will be arriving this morning for a meeting. I thought I'd let you know ahead of time that I've reported you to the scholarship committee for your inappropriate conduct with the girl I found in your office Friday afternoon."

So this was about Jillian. I was thankful for that small favor because my defense in the matter wouldn't be a lie. Still, if Hastings was concerned enough to send a member of the board to discuss the matter with me, whatever they had to say wouldn't be good.

Anger bristled my spine. I wanted to tear into this woman for assuming she had the right to report me, but I knew that losing control would only make the situation worse.

"What you think you saw couldn't have been further from the truth. I hope you understand that."

She scoffed. "What I saw was a young woman revealing her breasts to you in a closed door classroom. I had high hopes for you when we first met, but now that I understand what it is you're doing, I hope the Board replaces you. And here I was worried that you were carrying on a relationship with Amelia. Now I know you're just stringing her along while setting her up for failure."

The reality was I could stand here and continue arguing my case with Julia, only to do it all over again with the board member, or I could walk away and be left to argue my case once while they both were present. Not one to waste energy uselessly, I chose the second option.

"I'll see you in the meeting, Ms. Pickens."

Turning to walk away, I paused when her voice rang out behind me. "I'm protecting Amelia by doing this.

Not only that, but I'm looking out for the integrity of the program. How dare you threaten the future of another student all because you can't keep your hands to yourself?"

My teeth ground together at the accusation. It would have been better to walk away, to allow her to continue believing she was in the right. I couldn't disagree with her that, had she correctly guessed the student I was involved with, the situation would have been unfair. She was only looking out for Amelia, but in doing so, she was running the risk of hurting the one person she was trying to protect.

Spinning on my heel, I locked my eyes to hers. "You'll regret the assumption you're making, Ms. Pickens. Especially when you discover that the effort you're making to protect Amelia will only do her more harm in the end."

"Is that a threat?" Her cheeks bloomed a deeper red, the color contrasting sharply against her pale skin.

"I don't make threats," I answered, tired of this day already.

Walking away, I let myself into my classroom and dropped my bag on the surface of the desk. A quick glance at the clock told me Jillian would be waltzing through the door within the next ten minutes. I wasn't sure I could look at her without wanting to wrap my hands around her neck. She was causing more problems than I'm sure she knew, all because she believed she could convince me to see her as more than an annoying as fuck student.

When Julia walked in with a well-dressed man by her side before Jillian could arrive, I wasn't sure if it was much better.

Standing from my seat, I offered my hand. "You must be from Hastings."

The man looked at me as if I wasn't worthy of the handshake, his thinning brown hair sideswept to cover his balding head, and his beady dark eyes narrowing on my face as he finally gripped his hand over mine.

"Yes, my names is Henry Thorpe, and you must be Lennon Carter."

Julia shut the door behind him, closing us in to speak privately.

Releasing my hand, the man stepped back and straightened his suit jacket, the buttons of his white shirt struggling against the girth of his stomach.

"I don't see the need to draw this conversation out longer than necessary. I'm here to inform you that an accusation has been made against you by a witness to an unfortunate and inappropriate situation between you and one of your students."

Stepping back, I eyed Henry, my gaze flicking up to Julia where she stood assured in her decision to report me. Henry's voice drew my attention back to him.

"Mr. Carter, in light of the accusations, and due to the limited amount of time we have left in the program, it has been decided that you will be replaced with a new teacher effective immediately."

Arching a single brow, I grinned, just the corner of my mouth lifting as a taunt. "Just like that? Without questioning me regarding the accusation."

Julia spoke up behind him. "I clearly saw what was going on between you and that student, Lennon. And favoritism will not be tolerated. Not when it threatens another student's chance at a future in her chosen career path."

Obviously, she was concerned for Amelia's future, but given that Julia had jumped to the wrong conclusion, she was threatening Amelia without realizing it.

"So, that's it?" I asked, my eyes returning to Henry.

"You should gather your things now and leave. Your class will be cancelled for today and will resume tomorrow when the new teacher arrives from out of state."

Although anger was a current vibrating just beneath my skin, I knew better than to argue. The powers that be had made their decision and there was nothing I could say or do to change it.

Flicking my gaze to Julia one last time, I smirked, the arrogant expression causing her face to blanch in response. She wanted me to be upset, and it was the last thing I would give her.

Turning, I gathered my things, leaving behind the class roster, my notes, the sheet music and other documents necessary for the class.

Henry dodged out of my way before I passed, but Julia touched my arm, my body stilling in place as I turned my head to look at her.

"I'm sorry, Lennon. But I have to look out for Amelia."

Grinning, I didn't bother explaining to her that she may have hurt Amelia more by having me fired.

As I was walking down the hall to leave the building, Jillian walked through the doors, her expression brightening at first to see me, but then twisting with confusion to notice I wasn't staying to undergo her session.

"Mr. Carter? Aren't you staying for my practice session?"

Stopping in place, I clutched my hand over the strap of my bag. "I'm not your teacher anymore," I answered as I brushed past her.

From behind me, she called out, "What do you mean? Why not?"

The corners of my lips tipped up in a grin. Without bothering to look back at her, I answered, "Just try to keep your clothes on with the new instructor, Miss Bates."

With that I let myself outside and tipped my head into the sunlight, wondering how I was going to tell Amelia what happened.

The drive home was uneventful, piano music filtering out as soon as I stepped out of the SUV and walked up the stone path to my house. Letting myself in through the kitchen door, I set my bag on the large center island and wound my way through the halls, my feet coming to a dead halt as soon as I passed through the doorway into the living room.

Leaning a shoulder against the doorframe, I watched with fascination as Amelia played through Beethoven's Sonata No. 8, her body moving as fluidly as her hands, her thoughts lost to the music flowing out of her.

But it wasn't the music that had stilled me in place. It was the sight of her long dark hair flowing down her back in loose waves. It was my fedora she wore on her head. It was the schoolgirl, plaid skirt that sat so high on her thighs that I had to fight not to march to the piano, pick her up and toss her over my shoulder to carry her upstairs.

From what I could see, she wasn't wearing a shirt, and when her wrists snapped over a particularly difficult measure, her hair swayed to the side to reveal that all she wore on her upper half was a pair of my suspenders.

The bad mood that had followed me home lifted immediately, replaced with a dark and dangerous need to do dirty things to a tight little body...to silence a smart mouth while stealing from her a few hours of unspeakable pleasure.

The music came to an end while I continued watching, her head bowed over the keys for a few silent seconds, her shoulders lifting with every breath.

I cleared my throat and she spun to face me, the sight of her causing my dick to jump beneath my pants.

"What do you think you're doing, Miss Dillon?"

A devilish grin split her lips, her eyes shadowed by the rim of the hat. "I was just preparing for my afternoon lesson, Mr. Carter. My teacher," she added with a tilt to her head, "is a very strict disciplinarian. If I mess up just once, he'll make sure I don't sit comfortably again for a full week."

Teacher...

How was I going to tell her I was no longer the person who would hand her that scholarship?

I wasn't sure, but it was a conversation that could be saved for later.

Crossing the room with a predator's stride, my eyes focused on the straps of the suspenders that just barely covered her tight nipples. Grabbing those straps with one hand, I pulled them to the center of her body and used them to lift her from the piano bench. She wavered on her feet, her eyes dipping down to my lips before meeting my eyes once again.

My voice came out on a gritty whisper. "I think I need to teach my student what happens when she plays dress up instead of practicing her scales."

The perfect pout of her mouth parted as breath poured across her lips. Holding her stare, I ran my free hand between her thighs, up beneath the plaid skirt to find she wore no underwear.

A growl rattled my chest, every problem and aggravation of my day forgotten as I turned and directed her backward to the leather sofa.

If anybody could bring me to life, it was this young woman, everything about her drawing me in until I was teetering on the brink of control.

"I'm taking every part of you today, Miss Dillon. A punishment for sitting on my piano bench with your wet, naked pussy."

She trembled, her body pressing against mine as she tilted her chin, her mouth begging for mine. Leaning down, I brushed my lips against hers as a tease, grinning against her mouth, when I whispered, "Sorry, Amelia, but you won't be the one to lead this particular dance."

The monster inside me was roaring to life, demanding I mark every part of her body as mine.

Spinning her around, I pressed my palm against the center of her back, bending her forward so that she had to brace her hands against the couch to keep from tumbling over.

"Stay just like that."

She peeked over her shoulder at me, heat dancing behind her teal eyes. "Are you going to spank my ass red again?"

My grin was feral. "I have another idea for your ass."

Amelia's eyes widened.

"Stay there," I demanded before leaving the room to run upstairs. Digging through the drawers of my bedside table, I found the lube I was looking for and ignored the way my heart pounded.

She was ready for this.

I'd teased and taunted.

I'd whispered my warnings.

And she'd pushed me too far by offering herself to me dressed in my clothing...by showing me her soul with the music she'd played to welcome me home.

Racing downstairs, I strolled into the piano room to find Amelia right where I left her, my cock hard and ready, my heart continuing to pound to the beat she'd set as soon as I'd first walked through the doors.

Leaning a shoulder against the doorframe, I played the tube I was holding through my fingers, my voice a low croon. "About that not sitting comfortably for a week, Miss Dillon."

Her hair fell over her shoulder as she twisted to look at me, her eyes darting between the smirk on my face and the lube in my hand. Her gaze widened, her arms giving out for just a second before she caught herself again.

Our eyes locked when I asked, "Do you trust me?"

I could see a shiver roll through her, but rather than question my intentions, Amelia sucked in a breath and nodded her head.

It was impossible to contain my smile. "Eyes forward, Miss Dillon. This is your final exam."

As I was crossing the room toward her, she laughed. "Gee, I hope I pass."

"Oh, I'm sure you will," I answered, stepping up behind her to flip her skirt above her hips.

I would never get tired of this sight.

Never get tired of a woman who kept me on my toes merely by existing.

I dropped to my knees behind her, my mouth covering her pussy as my tongue swept out to taste the sweet flavor of her arousal. Amelia's back arched and her hips swung out, her pussy pressing against my face demanding more. She moaned and almost lost her balance over the couch, my hands reaching to grip her thighs and hold her steady. Licking a line from her clit up to her opening, I pumped my tongue inside her several times before licking down again to tease her swollen bundle of nerves.

It didn't take long for her body to give in to the sensual kiss, her arms shaking and her voice husky as she came against my face. I smiled to know that she was almost there...almost ready...her body primed for what I had to give.

Pushing back to my feet, I slipped two fingers inside her, pumping them viciously as my body leaned over hers and I reminded her that I would own every single part she had to give.

"I'm taking your ass, Amelia."

She trembled against me, but like the brave little girl I knew her to be, she wiggled her hips, her eyes peeking back at me with luscious desire rolling behind them.

Fingers slick with her arousal, I pulled out and tracked up to circle them over her tight hole. Pushing the tip of one inside, I damn near lost it to hear the moan that rolled over her lips.

This girl was going to destroy me, but not before I learned what it felt like to come inside her, what it felt like to mark her as my own.

Still, I wasn't a complete dick. I wouldn't force her into this if she wasn't ready. "Are you sure you want this?" I asked, my finger sinking deeper inside her.

Amelia nodded, her arms trembling to hold her weight. "I trust you," she answered, "just do me a favor and make sure I like it."

Breath rattled over my lips, my cock jumping beneath my pants at what she'd offered.

Pulling my hand from her, I bent down to grab the lube I'd dropped on the floor earlier and stood up again to unbutton my pants. My cock sprang free, like a damn missile seeking her body.

Gripping her hips, I warmed her up by thrusting inside her pussy, her muscles clenching around me as my name poured over her lips. Our bodies were in perfect sync as I pumped inside her, filling her as far as

I could go, pushing her until I knew another orgasm was just on the horizon.

Reaching around her, I pinched her clit, the sound of our skin slapping together a heady beat that harmonized with the sounds rolling up from her throat.

Unscrewing the tube, I squeezed out a generous amount of lube onto my fingers, circling over her ass as I stretched that tight hole with my fingers.

Amelia came instantly, her body opening up to me as I pulled free of her pussy and notched myself at her ass.

Pinching her clit one more time, I pushed the head of my cock inside her, my voice hoarse when I said, "Just remember, beautiful, that all of you belongs to me."

Careful not to force myself in too fast, I continued working her body as my cock sunk inside. Once I was fully seated, I knew I wouldn't last long.

Amelia was practically purring as I began to move deep within her body, my hands moving to hold her still as I took all that she would give.

Sweat beaded at my temples, a climax rushing through me with such violence that I came as a grunt rolled over my lips, my cum spurting hot and thick as waves of pleasure rolled through me.

My name was a prayer on her lips as we both came down from the orgasms that threatened to drown us beneath turbulent waters. And after pulling myself free, I kissed a trail down her spine, laughing when her voice whispered a question.

"Did I pass my exam?"

Slapping her on the ass, I picked her up and cradled her against my chest

"Oh yes, Miss Dillon. I think you passed with flying colors."

CHAPTER TWENTY-SIX

Sometimes, life doesn't always play out the way we want it. Our eyes water, our hearts break, the stress of our souls shattering is directed to the movement of our wringing hands...

Amelia

"Again."

Sweat dripped down my temples, my back aching and my forearms shaking from the position I'd held for over six hours. Unable to understand why Lennon was so adamant about making me endure this, I huffed out a breath, my eyes closing with exhaustion.

He wouldn't stop, not even for small breaks to allow me to regain my strength. It was as if a demon had crawled beneath his skin to take up residence, one whispering relentlessly that Lennon didn't have to worry about breaking me beneath his demands, that I could keep going without complaint.

"Lennon, please-"

He stood behind me, his hands squeezing down on my shoulders. "Don't argue with me, Amelia. Remember the rules. No questions and no complaints."

I wanted to cry, to beg, to plead. Somehow I knew it wouldn't do me a lick of good, not when he was in this mood.

For the past three weeks, he'd been this way. Ever since the afternoon he came home and found me waiting for him in his hat and suspenders. Ever since that afternoon I let him take the last part of me I had to give.

Three weeks of hell.

Three weeks he has been a demanding monster.

Three weeks that had turned a man, who still had the ability to turn me on with nothing more than a look, into an absolute nightmare.

"You're not giving me everything, Amelia. Do it again."

"I'm tired!" I yelled, my eyes bleary and my heart pounding with the anger I was fighting to contain. "Can we please take a break?"

I'd played Mozart's Piano Sonata No 16 in C Major so many times now that I could hear it in my head as I fell asleep at night. Nothing I could do now would make my performance of it any better. It killed me that he didn't understand that.

His hands released my shoulders to latch onto my hips. Instantly, he lifted me from the piano bench, spun me in place and pushed me back against the keyboard.

The hammers pounded on the strings, a jarring sound that blended with the screech of the bench legs scraping across the stone floor as he kicked it away.

What had gotten into him? The question echoed through my mind as his eyes caught mine, that damn navy blue storm catching me in its sensual violence.

Holding me in place, he stepped between my legs, his head lowering so that his mouth was a teasing inch from mine. The heat of his breath brushed across my cheeks and I shivered beneath the knowledge that he was ten seconds away from spanking my ass for daring to argue with him about this.

Whenever it came to practicing, Lennon wasn't hearing my complaints. Not anymore, at least. Ever since he was fired and replaced by Mrs. Crux, he was driving me to tears day in and day out, demanding I become as disciplined as him.

It was like he was possessed.

Catching my chin between his fingers, he locked my face with his, his gaze holding mine, daring me to look away.

"There is no way in hell, I'm allowing you to fail in this, Amelia. You will win that scholarship, and if I have to tame the brat that keeps surfacing whenever you get tired or frustrated, I will. Your new teacher chooses between you and Jillian this afternoon, and I'll be damned to let that bitch ruin this for you."

Tears welled in my eyes because the brat he was referencing was front and center at that moment. I wanted to yell and scream, kick out my damn legs and toss myself on the ground, anything to make him stop standing over me like a damn monster, his constant critiques crushing my spirit when I fumbled my fingers over the keys from exhaustion.

Glaring back at him, I snapped, my patience pushed to the damn limit because I couldn't make sense of why this was so important to him. Did he want to get rid of me that badly? Was he hoping that the scholarship would force me away so that he could waltz back into his regular life without feeling guilty for leaving me behind?

It didn't feel that way at first, but over these last few weeks, suspicion had crept into my thoughts. Every night we fucked like we'd never get enough of each other. Even if I was exhausted from practicing and could barely move my arms, I still met him move for move in bed, my mind lost to endless orgasms before we both crashed into deep sleep.

Yet, every morning, the distance between us returned. Not on my end, all on his, so obvious that it gripped at my heart and made it difficult to play after we finished breakfast and he rushed me to the piano.

I was done with the back and forth, done with whatever was driving him to treat me this way.

"How the hell am I supposed to play well enough for her to choose me if you're breaking me over the keys right now?"

My voice was a lot louder than necessary, but I couldn't help it. He'd pushed me too far. "My arms hurt. My back is killing me. My ass is sore from the fucking spankings you keep giving me, and I'm starving! I know the piece as well as I'll ever know it, and if it's not good enough to beat Jillian, then I guess this scholarship wasn't meant to be."

Yes, we'd come a long way from the playful Lennon who only threatened to paint my ass red. Not that I was complaining so much about it, especially not after he drove his cock inside me so hard after slapping my ass that I could feel the head impact my cervix.

But still, his attitude had only gotten darker with each passing day, something fraying his last nerve when it came to me that made it impossible to impress him when I played.

His fingers clutched my chin tighter, a grin curling the corner of his lips in response to my outburst.

"Is that how little your future means to you? So little that you'll just shrug and toss it all away? What are you going to do with your life if you don't get into

Hastings? Go back to your brother and the back alley schemes he convinced you to take part in to make fucking pennies?"

Even though his voice was so calm it was sending chills across my body, I could see pure rage behind his eyes. This was the first time I'd truly stuck up for myself against him, and to be completely honest, it was pretty much a given I wasn't winning.

The keys of the piano pressed into my ass, undoubtedly leaving an indentation.

"Please, Lennon. I can't keep going like this. It's killing me. And no I wouldn't go back to doing what Ben wants. I'll find something else."

My words only served to piss him off more. Pushing away from me, he stabbed his hand through his hair, pacing the floor in front of me like a caged tiger.

"You have another two weeks after this, Amelia. Then the final competition and you have to be ready for this. Yes, I'm being hard on you, but you're acting like you can just skate by without putting in the effort it takes."

"All I do is play and fuck!" Weird combination, but it was true.

"That's it. We hardly even talk anymore unless it's you telling me how many times I messed up a measure, or how irritated you are I can't run certain scales as perfectly as you want."

His eyes met mine, his hair a mess around his head that made me want to reach out and run my fingers through it. Even when he was pissed off, he drew me in like a moth to a flame, and it was going to kill me when the day came where we had to say goodbye.

And maybe that's why I didn't care about the scholarship as much as I used to. I'd fallen in love with a man who would eventually walk away.

The scholarship was only an excuse for him to do so without feeling one ounce of remorse for doing it.

Without consideration for what it would do to us, I said what I was thinking, just cast the thought out for him to examine and verify was true. "You only care that I get into Hastings because it gives you a reason to go back to your normal life and forget you ever knew me."

He stilled in place, his head snapping my direction as his blue eyes locked with mine. A single tick of his strong jaw told me I'd hit that nail directly on the head.

So dark, his voice, my spine straightening and my muscles tightening over my bones just to hear it.

"Are you telling me you'd be willing to toss your future away over a man? Just like that? You work your entire life and then spread your legs for somebody and none of it matters anymore?"

Lennon stalked toward me, caging me against the piano, his hands locking down on the sides beside my hips. The edge of the keys pressed deeper into the cheeks of my ass, his chest practically vibrating against mine.

"I already lost one person to the same bullshit you're spouting now. And if you think I'm going to stand back and let it happen again, then you might as well pack your shit and head home. If you're in this house, you're pushing yourself to become what we both know you can. But if you want to give up like Emaline did, then you are not the woman I first thought you were."

Surprise burst through me, my mouth falling open as my eyes searched his.

Emaline was why he was doing this to me. His sister was the reason he wouldn't let up and allow me even a second to breathe.

Before I could respond, he pushed away from me again, his steps a heavy beat over the floors as he crossed the room to leave.

Without bothering to look back at me, he called out, "It's your decision, Amelia. Either you're here to learn how to win that scholarship, or you're headed home because you're stupid enough to believe that a man is worth more than your future."

"Lennon!"

I called out to him, but he didn't stop. Launching from the piano, I chased after him, my eyes watering as I yelled, "I'm not your sister. That's not fair."

But he wasn't listening.

From the kitchen, I heard a door slam and I knew he'd left the house entirely. Turning, I ran through the house just in time to open the front door and watch his SUV speed out of the driveway, the engine loud as he gunned it down the street.

My heart shattered as his taillights retreated into the distance, flashing red only briefly before he turned left and was out of sight.

Sliding down against the open door, my body shook with violent sobs, my mind racing over the answer as to why he'd been so adamant that I win the scholarship.

I wasn't his sister. I wasn't a woman so heartbroken that I would toss away my life. Yes, I'd wanted this

339

scholarship since as far back as I could remember, but that didn't mean it was the only thing in this world I was allowed to want.

Life isn't always portioned out into neat little slices, sometimes our desires intersect and rip us apart. I wanted the scholarship, but I loved a man who couldn't follow me into that life. One I would have to let go so I could cling onto the other. When it came down to what was best for me, I wasn't sure what choice to make.

Not that I was even sure I had a choice.

Not while Lennon was running as fast as he could in the opposite direction, placing distance between us as the summer was coming to an end.

Eventually, I found the strength to push myself back to my feet. I found the strength to go inside and get ready for my performance. And somehow, I managed to make the drive to the school without losing myself to the tears that were constantly threatening my eyes.

I wasn't sure of anything anymore. Not Hastings or Lennon. But what I hoped would happen as soon as I walked into the classroom today to reveal my soul through the music I played was that Mrs. Crux would see my talent as deserving, while ignoring the truth that my soul had just been crushed.

. . .

"Please, ladies, take a seat."

Mrs. Crux motioned with her hand for Jillian and I to sit down as soon as we stepped inside the classroom. Jillian had performed earlier that morning, while I'd finished my performance prior to taking a half hour break. During that break, Mrs. Crux had kept the classroom door closed and I'd gone outside to warm myself in the sun. Too much was weighing on my shoulders, my thoughts racing back to Lennon as soon as my fingers lifted from the piano keys.

Unfortunately, Jillian arrived within minutes of my escape outside and my body had gone cold again from the anger I felt for her.

In a way, her lies had pushed Lennon to a point where he felt the need to run me ragged on the piano - her lies had created a situation that woke a memory in him that he had somehow connected to his present relationship with me.

I wasn't mad at Lennon for the argument we had, but I hated Jillian more than I'd ever hated another person for the role she'd played in what was happening to me.

Taking my seat, I ignored the way Jillian cast me one last condescending glance over her shoulder, her lips tilting up at the corners as if she knew I would be walking out of this classroom today while she moved on to the final competition. I won't lie and say I wasn't intimidated by her expression. In truth, I wondered if Lennon's promotion of me in the class didn't have more to do with our relationship than it did my actual talent.

Clearing her throat, Mrs. Crux stood in front of the teacher's desk, her hands clasped elegantly in front of her while her brown eyes peered out at us from behind black-rimmed glasses. My gaze wandered to the silver streaks in her brown hair, and to the motion of her pearl eyeglass chain swinging at the sides of her face.

"I want to let both of you know that I was impressed with your talent and skill. As I've explained before, due to certain unfortunate circumstances that occurred in this class prior to my arrival, I extended the weeks for both of you so that I could develop a fair assessment of your skills. Having worked with both of you individually, I feel I've made a decision that is informed and unbiased, but please know it wasn't an easy one to make."

My foot was tapping frantically against the ground, my fingers clinging to the sides of my desk. What would happen if Jillian won?

What would that mean for Lennon and me?

"Well, it's best to just rip off the bandage." Mrs. Crux turned to Jillian. "Miss Bates..."

My heart fell into my stomach as soon as Jillian's name was said. My shoulders dropped with the weight of defeat, my stomach churning with the fear that this moment would not only drive a nail into the coffin of my future in music, but also give Lennon the final excuse he needed to walk away and leave me behind to return to his usual life.

"...although you have the talent it takes to do well at Hastings and move on into a career involving music, I have decided that for this particular competition, you will not be moving forward."

Wait.

What?

Jillian's chair legs screeched across the floor as she launched to her feet, her hair swinging over her shoulder as she turned to glare back at me.

Her face was neon red, anger flashing behind her eyes as she snatched her bag without saying a word in response to Mrs. Crux. Jillian stormed out of the classroom, leaving Mrs. Crux staring after her, while I sat in utter and complete shock.

When brown eyes turned my direction, I met them with my own, my body shaking from the adrenaline rush from learning I hadn't been cut from the program, and that, in fact, I would be competing in the final.

"Congratulations, Miss Dillon. We only have two weeks for you to prepare. Have you selected which piece you'll be playing for the final competition?"

I couldn't seem to find my voice to answer her, so instead, I shook my head. She smiled at me and tapped her fingers against her palm. "Well, you have until Monday to figure it out. The choice is yours."

Floating on cloud nine and operating on autopilot, I gathered my things and thanked Mrs. Crux before leaving the classroom. There was an added skip to my step as I walked the hall toward the exit door, my lips pulling into a smile as reality settled into my thoughts that I really had a shot at going to Hastings.

So excited to get home and tell Lennon about what had happened, I ran outside and was halfway to my car when I slammed into a person I hadn't seen standing in the parking lot, a wall of muscle that knocked me back.

"Sorry," I said, still not paying attention when the person's hand landed on my shoulder and stopped me from continuing forward.

"Amelia..."

I froze in place, my eyes squinting against the late afternoon sun to realize my brother had been standing outside waiting for me. His expression was hard, worry obvious in his eyes. It was the same look he always gave me when he couldn't pay the mortgage and needed me to participate in some ridiculous scheme.

No. I wasn't doing this. I wouldn't let him threaten everything when the scholarship was almost in my hands.

"Go away, Ben. I'm not helping you anymore."

I tried to pull away from him, but his hand locked down on my shoulder so hard it made me wince. "I'm not here for that."

Spinning on my heel, I glared at him. "Then why are you here, Ben? What could you possibly want from me?"

His jaw ticked, pain rolling across his features when he realized that I was angry for all the ways he'd used me. "Amelia, listen, I know you're mad-"

"I'm not mad, okay I am, but I'm also hurt. I love you, Ben. You were always there for me and you took care of me when Mom and Dad couldn't, but at the same time you made me do things I wasn't comfortable with and-"

"Amelia, stop. Please. I get that. Okay? But that's not why I'm here."

Gripping the strap of my bag, I pulled my shoulder away from him finally and met his stare. "Then why are you here?"

His expression fell, sorrow obvious behind his grey eyes.

"There's something you need to see, Amelia. I need you to come to the house."

Stepping away from him, I shook my head. "No. There's nothing there for me. You're just trying to trick me into helping you again."

From behind me Ben yelled, "Damn it, Amelia, this isn't about me or the house."

I stilled in place, my teeth clenching together because I couldn't understand what else he could want. My voice was harsh when I asked, "Then what the hell else could it be about?"

Turning I locked my eyes with his, clawed fingers gripping around my heart when he said, "It's about Emaline."

CHAPTER TWENTY-SEVEN

I'm a horrible person, Lennon. Please let this go after you've given yourself time to grieve. Please understand that this was all my fault...

Lennon

Through my life, Jennison's had always been a refuge of sorts for me. It was a place that kept me off the streets while other kids were doing drugs or committing crimes. It was a place where I felt welcomed and included when my parents couldn't give much of a fuck whether I was happy, fed or even alive. It was also a place I could run to when I needed advice, and although the man who had practically raised me was no longer in that store to sit me down and talk to me about my problems, my best friend still could be found within its walls - a man who would drop everything to help me.

It wasn't surprising that following my fight with Amelia, the store was the only place I could think to run. And almost as soon as I stepped between its glass doors with the guitar strings strumming above my head, Dizzy had turned to look at me, immediately guessing that something wasn't right.

Sitting me down, Dizzy was much like his father in the way he gave it to me straight for several hours.

"You know, brother, I hate to say this..." He paused, his dark eyes meeting mine as he scrubbed his hand over the back of his neck.

"At some point in your life, you're going to have to let Emaline go. Her death has haunted you since the day you discovered her body, and here we are, ten years later, and it's still following you around as a thick shadow."

I couldn't argue with him, yet I didn't know how to separate my past from my present. For years, I'd thought I'd escaped the pain of losing my sister, but one summer spent near Sheldon had brought all of it back to the surface, revealing to me that I hadn't escaped anything...I'd merely tucked it away to allow it to fester and grow.

Dizzy's gaze softened. "Tell me the truth, Lennon, and don't give me any bullshit because you're too afraid to reveal your heart: How do you feel about Amelia?"

Shaking my head, I almost told him I didn't know. But then, that would be a lie, wouldn't it? In truth, I felt more for Amelia than I'd felt for any person in my life...any person, that is, except for my sister.

"I can't be the reason she gives up on Hastings-"

"That's not what I asked you," Dizzy said, cutting me off. "I asked how you feel about her."

My lips tilted into a grin because I should have known he wouldn't let me redirect the question so easily. "I-"

Fuck! Why was this so hard to say out loud?

Taking a breath, I spit it out. "I think I could love her."

Dizzy laughed. "You think you could? Or you know that you already do? Don't lie to me, Lennon. I'll know."

He slapped my shoulder. "Hell, I already know the answer. It's about damn time you admit it to yourself."

Behind us the guitar strummed. Dizzy nodded his head at whoever had walked through, his eyes returning to me. "Tell you what, I have a lesson I need to teach, but if you want to hang around, we can continue this in an hour."

Glancing at a clock on the wall, I realized it was getting late. By now, Amelia would have finished her performance, would have learned whether she was moving forward or if she'd been cut. Despite the argument we had this morning, I wanted to know what happened.

That, and I needed to apologize to her for how critical I'd been with her over the past few weeks.

Emaline's death had nothing to do with Amelia, yet I'd unloaded all that weight on her shoulders so I didn't have to bear it alone. Until this morning, she didn't know even know she'd been carrying it.

"Actually, I should get going. Amelia will be back at the house and she'll either need a shoulder to cry on or someone to celebrate with her."

Reaching out to slap my hand and knock his knuckles against mine, Dizzy smiled. "I hope she made it. And if she did, tell her congratulations from me."

I left after promising him we'd hang out again before the summer ended and I left town. The drive home was quick because I had been too lost in my thoughts to pay attention. Pulling into the driveway, I was happy to see Amelia's car there, but worried about what I would find when I walked inside.

Taking a deep breath, I turned off the SUV and climbed out, my steps unhurried as I wound my way up the path that led to the side door.

The house was silent when I stepped inside. Worried what that could mean, I searched the downstairs rooms for Amelia. Not finding her, I ran upstairs to find her curled into a ball, asleep on the bed.

Concern flooded me instantly. Running over to sit beside her, I touched her shoulder, fear tracing a path up my spine when her eyes flicked open, the rims swollen and stained red from crying.

Damn. I should have known better that to leave her the way I did this morning. There was no doubt in my mind that our argument played a part in her losing the scholarship – that my exhausting her for weeks on end had taken away the spark of the music inside her and replaced it with the same robotic bullshit I hated to hear in other players.

Watching her without saying a word, I waited while she pushed up into a seated position, her teal eyes meeting mine with so much heartache behind them that it strangled a part inside me as well.

Brushing the hair away from her face, I searched her face, anger tightening the muscles in my shoulders to think that a bitch like Jillian would move forward in the competition.

"What happened?"

My voice was barely a whisper, the silence in the room so thick that I felt anything louder would crush the beautiful girl who was staring up at me like she didn't have a friend in the world.

Clearing her throat, Amelia darted her gaze away from me, the teal color glassing over with new tears now that she was awake. "I won," she admitted on a voice that was gritty with sleep and heartache. "I'll continue forward to the final competition in two weeks."

Surprise shot my brows up my face, my heart thumping harder to hear she would continue in the program. Pulling her to me, I rested my cheek against the top of her head, surprised to feel her body shaking with silent sobs.

"Is this about our fight, Amelia. Because if it is-"

She pulled away from me, her eyes meeting mine as her features twisted until it was a mess of sharp lines. "Lennon, there's something I have to tell you and you're not going to like it."

Pausing, she scooted away from my touch, a breath rattling her chest as she lifted her eyes to meet mine. "Actually, it's more something I need to show you."

Confused by the pain I clearly saw in her expression, I reached out to touch her. She pulled away, her head shaking just a touch as she moved and placed more distance between us.

I felt like a complete ass for what I'd done to her this morning. "Amelia, I'm sorry if I upset you. I didn't mean to compare you to Emaline. I'm just so fucked up by being near Sheldon that it's hard to separate what happened in my past with what's happening with you."

Her eyes lifted to mine, her arms crossing over her chest as if she couldn't stand to be this close to me.

Clearing her throat, she admitted, "It's not that. Well, it is that, but-"

Her voice trailed off, more tears slipping down her cheeks. "I need you to follow me, Lennon. I learned something today that," sobs broke her words apart, her hand reaching to slap away the tears. "You just need to see this, okay? You'll understand in a few minutes, but I can't keep secrets from you. I promised you no secrets."

Not understanding where this was going, I didn't move until she'd crawled off the bed to walk to the bedroom door. Stopping before she'd passed through, Amelia turned to me with apology written into her face.

She had nothing to be sorry for. Still, worry swept in to mingle with my anger with myself. "What is this about?"

Exhaling a heavy breath, she answered, "Ben came to my school today-"

Son of a bitch. I should have killed him when I had the fucking chance.

"Lennon, he found out what happened to Emaline."

Every muscle in my body was tense, pain shooting down my jaw for how hard I clenched my teeth. My voice came out on a low growl, "What do you mean?"

Rubbing her hands over her arms, Amelia begged, "Just come with me, please? You need to see this to understand."

"Just tell me."

I couldn't move, my body rooted to where I sat because I wasn't in a state of mind to deal with this. How the fuck had Ben been able to figure out what

352

happened to my sister so quickly when I'd spent years trying to do the same with no fucking answers?

Keeping my eyes locked on Amelia, I didn't miss how her body shook on unsteady legs. She was terrified of whatever it was her brother had discovered.

"Please, Lennon."

It was obvious she wouldn't tell me unless I followed her. Pushing up onto my feet I followed her down to the entertainment room on the first floor, silently leaning a shoulder against the doorframe as she moved to the DVD player and slipped a disc inside it.

Holding the remote in her hand, she walked back and gave it to me, her eyes lifting to meet mine.

"I'm sorry," she whispered, confusing me even more because she hadn't done anything that would have caused Emaline to kill herself.

Terrified to see whatever it was on that disc, I could barely speak above a whisper. "Just tell me what it is."

Her upper body shook with another tremulous breath, her hands reaching for my body before she reconsidered and pulled them away. The space between us was too heavy, a million unspoken thoughts colliding against each other until she made a decision and admitted what she was too afraid to tell me.

"Something in the note you showed Ben triggered a suspicion in his head. Over the past three weeks, he's been digging through our storage shed, going over years of recordings my parents kept of their students."

A memory came back to me at the mention of those recordings. Often Emaline would bring them home to watch in order to critique her performance and perfect it. I'd often sat with her to watch the tapes, Lila's voice speaking off camera to point out all the areas in the music where Emaline could improve.

I'd completely forgotten about them after my sister died, and whatever tapes that had been left behind were destroyed in the fire that eventually claimed my parents house. The same fire that left it condemned, a gutted skeleton of what had been my childhood home.

Wringing her hands, Amelia couldn't look at me when she said, "When my father first started experiencing problems, he hid it from us. I don't know why. He was probably scared to admit it to himself that he even had a problem. We think he continued teaching for at least a year before his condition became so severe that there was no denying it existed. During that year, he had slips..."

Her eyes met mine again. "And during those slips his past bled into his present. He didn't know, Lennon. He was ill and he didn't-"

I didn't need to see the tapes to know where she was going with this. I wasn't sure I wanted to see them, but if it would answer a question I'd had for ten long ass years, I would endure whatever it was on that disc.

Whispering, Amelia said, "Just watch the tape. Ben compiled what he found and transferred enough onto the disc to clue us in to what happened."

With that, she brushed past me to leave the room, my legs weak as I stood at the doorway with remote in hand. Stepping deeper into the room, I sank down onto a seat on one of the leather couches, my thumb hovering over the play button while my mind raced to make sense of what Amelia had confessed.

I didn't want to believe, couldn't figure out how to process it, refused to accept that for the past ten years I'd known the name of the man that had pushed my sister into taking her life.

My hand was shaking when I finally found the courage to hit play, my eyes unblinking as an image of my sister appeared on the screen, her back to the camera as James Dillon paced behind her. She was playing her favorite song, the same one I'd played to James to calm him down at Amelia's house. The same song Amelia had admitted to me had been her mother's favorite as well.

While Emaline played, James stopped his movement behind her, the music still playing, her fingers fumbling over a measure I knew she knew by heart when James reached to brush his hand down her long brown hair.

The tape cut off, a new image coming into view of Emaline playing yet again, the camera set to the side of her this time as her lips pulled into a smile I believed I would never see again for as long as I lived. When she spoke, I shuddered, the memory of her voice forcing its way through me with such violence I couldn't stop my body from reacting.

"I love you, James. I hope you know that..."

A deeper voice answered from off camera, *"Keep playing..."*

Again, the frame changed, another day, another song, but this time, Emaline pushed up to her feet when her fingers left the keys, a man's body tugging her closer, their heads coming together for a long kiss.

I was going to be sick, the rage inside me mixing with such horrible sorrow that I couldn't swallow

355

down the fetid taste of bile crawling up my throat, couldn't hold back the tears that stung my eyes as an answer to all my questions played out in front of me.

The scene kept changing, bits and pieces coming together like puzzle pieces of a nightmare I would never escape and by the time I reached the end, the truth of what happened was set free.

In the last clip, my sister sat on the edge of the piano, her skirt pushed up to her hips, James Dillon's body wedged between her knees and when she told him she loved him again as his hand fisted in her hair, he kissed her softly before calling her Lila.

I expected my sister to act surprised to learn he didn't know who she was, but what I didn't expect was for her to smile, despite the pain that was so clearly visible in her eyes, before nodding and pretending she wasn't a student in love with her teacher, but instead that she was the wife of a man who was too confused and ill to remember that his wife had died.

Emaline had known he thought she was someone else, and yet her love for him was so strong that she'd destroyed her own soul just for a few moments where she could pretend to be everything he loved and needed.

This is what Amelia had meant when she said her father didn't know. It all clicked together that while my sister had believed her teacher was falling in love with her, he was a victim to his condition, believing that his dead wife was still alive and well.

James Dillon had been the reason my sister heart was torn apart. A man who, through his condition had made Amelia's life hell. A man I now supported by paying for the nursing home where he lived.

I wanted to hate him for the role he'd played in my sister's death, but what was worse was that I couldn't stop hating Emaline for what she had done.

This is what she'd meant by saying she'd taken advantage.

This is why she'd died believing she was too horrible to continue living her life.

But yet, I still couldn't stop blaming James.

He had destroyed a part of me. And through a cruel twist of fate, I had fallen in love with his only daughter, so much so that I'd taken him off her hands and put him in a place where he could live as comfortably as possible for the rest of his life.

The television screen cracked after I threw the remote at it, my mouth opening on a scream of pure rage.

And as all the anger and heartache that I'd barely contained over the ten years since my sister had died came pouring out, I destroyed the room around me, the couches ripped apart, the walls taking the brunt of my fury and pain as my fists punched holes into the plaster.

Everything around me was destroyed just as thoroughly as I felt destroyed inside. I could no longer contain the monster that had existed within me for too long.

I don't know how long I raged inside that room, but when I finally stopped, when my chest heaved and blood was left dripping from my knuckles, I looked up to see Amelia standing in the doorway, tears streaming from her eyes as she watched me lose control and shatter apart.

CHAPTER TWENTY-EIGHT

Our hands are the outlet of our deepest desires. What we do with them is the truth of what we carry in our soul...

Amelia

Where are we?

Will we ever come back from this?

Is it even possible?

Three questions that had gripped onto my mind through the last weeks I'd spent with Lennon, one harrowing uncertainty that only existed because fate was a cruel and twisted bastard.

How was it even possible that two people who'd never known each other could have family secrets and painful shames that were so inextricably linked.

At the beginning of this summer, I never would have believed that I'd meet a man I could fall in love with.

Had a person told me he would meet me in a dirty back alley, I would have laughed my ass off.

Had someone explained he would be my teacher, I would have punched them in the throat for lying.

Had someone pulled me aside and warned me that he would have been the only man who could shatter my heart as thoroughly as Lennon was breaking it now, I would have listened and run the opposite direction.

Yet, there I was, my eyes blinking away another round of wet, hot tears, my fingers punishing the keys of a piano while I poured out my soul to a man who was walking away from me.

I knew this would happen, knew when Ben showed me the truth of what Emaline and my father had done that there was no other option but for Lennon and I to walk away from each other. Not because we didn't fit together perfectly. Not because the heart-wrenching music inside him didn't harmonize with the dissonant melody inside me. But because we were two people who had become images of the hurt we tried to hide. We couldn't look at each other without being reminded of how painful a person's life could be.

Still, I played for him.

Still, he hovered behind me making sure I hit every note.

Still, we couldn't keep our hands off each other when the moon held court in the sky, our bodies entangling because it hurt too badly to know that one day we would be forced to let go.

"That's good," Lennon said after clearing his throat, his deep voice filling the room to blend with the last echo of music that vibrated from the piano's strings. "I think you're ready for this tomorrow."

My body sagged, my head far too heavy, my soul puddling over the stone floor beneath my feet because I was too much of a coward to ask the questions screaming in my head.

"I don't feel ready."

His hands touched my shoulders and electricity sparked down my spine. He always had that effect on me, since the minute he ran me down when we first met.

"It's like I told you the first day in class. Music isn't only about the technical skill, it's about how it can make a person feel."

And how does it make you feel? I didn't ask. *How will it make me feel if you were to give up on us and walk away?*

Spinning around on the bench, I lifted my eyes to a man that had deep shadows darkening his gaze. Beyond those, I knew there was heat, but since the day he learned the role my father had played in Emaline's death, I couldn't shake the feeling that, when he looked at me, all he could see was a person to blame.

No, it wasn't my fault, but I was the daughter of a man who'd played a part. Not that my father had known what he was doing.

I wasn't only the daughter of James Dillon any longer, I was the woman who had opened Lennon's eyes and given him a reason to hate his sister for what she had done.

Do you know what it's like to love and hate a person at the same time? Do you know how much it hurts when they're dead and gone, giving you no hope of healing the pain they caused in your life?

Lennon knew...because I had shown him.

And I knew he couldn't look at my face without being reminded of why he should never have come back to Sheldon in the first place.

Even with pain swirling behind his blue eyes, he was still the most beautiful man I had ever seen.

Lennon's voice was a whisper, his dark gaze locked to mine. "You're ready for this, Amelia. I wouldn't lie to you about that. And one day, I'll be proud to listen to the music you'll make in your life while knowing I was one of the people who trained you."

My heart clenched at his words, the tone of them so final that it scared me to ask if he would still be by my side when that day finally came.

Upstairs, boxes were stacked against walls, his belongings packed, his boxes labeled, mine packed and ready as well. Even while preparing for the day we'd leave this house, I hadn't yet found the bravery to ask what he planned to do once we learned if I would be leaving for Hastings.

It was ridiculous, really, that fear - but every time I tried to ask the question, it always swelled and became stuck in my throat, tears threatening my eyes at what I somehow knew would be his answer.

In truth, I was a coward and a fool. I knew that, by not asking the question, I wouldn't have to face the truth that he would be leaving me at the end of the summer.

"Thank you," I said around a lump in my throat.

Humor danced in his eyes. "For what?"

There really was only one answer. "For disciplining me."

The reference was sexual, yes, but it covered so much more than he realized. Lennon hadn't just taken me under his wing to push me toward a future in the only area I cared about, he'd also stepped in to strip me away from a life that was running me down a path of destruction.

Before him, I hadn't feared making a living by committing crimes. Before him, I hadn't valued myself enough as a person to stick up for myself against my brother. Before Lennon, I'd never realized that there was music inside so breathtaking and beautiful that I never wanted to fall asleep again without it singing me to sleep each night.

His skilled hands had created that song, and even though what would occur between us was dark and uncertain, I knew I would never stop singing it as long as he walked this Earth.

Lennon's lips tugged up into the arrogant smirk I'd grown to love, his hands reaching to grasp mine and pull me to my feet. Letting one of my hands go, he reached up to wrap his fingers within my hair, a war going on inside him that was so obvious it brought tears to my eyes.

Tugging me toward him, he leaned down to press his mouth to mine, my lips parting as his tongue swept in my mouth to slide over mine. Shivering at the intensity of his kiss, I tried to memorize every detail: his scent, his heat, his taste.

My fingers twisted into the fabric of his shirt and my heart pounded against my chest as he picked me up from the floor, one strong arm bracing me around my lower back as my legs wrapped around his waist.

How he safely navigated the halls and climbed upstairs while still kissing me was anybody's guess. Dropped backwards into the bed, I stared up at him beneath heavy lidded eyes, my body coming to life to see in his hard expression all the dirty things he wanted to do to me.

However, beneath the desire ran a cold line of fear. I worried that this would be the last time I saw him this way. Call it paranoia...or maybe even precognizance...but I couldn't shake the feeling that if I won the scholarship tomorrow, Lennon would say goodbye and I would never know what is was like to touch him again.

His voice was a deep croon. "Take off your clothes for me. Slowly, so I can enjoy this sight."

Why did it feel like he was memorizing this moment as well? Taking that one last look before turning his back on all we had.

I did as he said while his gaze held me in its grasp...dark, penetrating, so damn erotic that it consumed me.

His lips parted as I slid the panties off my legs. Moving forward, he locked his hand over my shoulders to shove me down against the mattress, his other hand grabbing my knee to spread my legs wide open.

"Stay like that," he demanded his eyes sweeping down my body, studying me with such lazy fascination that I could feel his gaze as if it were fingers exploring me.

"Fuck, Amelia, just like that."

The muscles of my inner thighs burned in the position he'd directed me, but I wouldn't dare move, wouldn't take the chance of disappointing him.

Lennon ran his fingertip down my slit so gently that my body trembled, my chest arching up to silently beg for more.

"I wish you knew how addicted I am to this tight, wet hole."

His mouth was so hot against my swollen, needy flesh when he dipped his tongue inside me that I cried out in surprise and pleasure, my fingers gripping the sheets beneath me.

Licking up to suck my clit between his lips, he slid three fingers inside me, pumping them before pulling his mouth away just enough to growl against my skin, "Come on my face, beautiful. Show me how much you want this."

It was impossible not to obey, my thighs shaking against his hand as he lapped at my clit, pumping his fingers inside me with one hand while holding my leg open with the other. My climax roared through me like a ravaging storm, my back arching off the bed as my head rolled over the mattress.

He chuckled against my skin when I'd finally relaxed again, an arrogant man that knew he owned my body.

"Eyes on me, Amelia."

Flicking my eyes open I almost came again to see the shimmer of my arousal wet on his lips, his hands moving slowly to open his belt, unbutton his black slacks and push them down his legs. He'd stripped off his shirt before demanding I look at him, and I couldn't stop tracing every hard ridge of muscle with my eyes.

A work of art, he was a man that had been carved by the Devil, steel temptation wrapped in velvet sin, a tease like nothing I'd ever known before. My eyes lifted to his face and locked with his, our stare unwavering as he crawled over me to grip my cheeks and open my lips, his tongue invading my mouth as his cock was driven into my body.

I moaned and he latched onto my bottom lip with his teeth, his hips dancing between my legs slowly at first, a pounding rhythm that increased in speed.

It wasn't long before he forced me to come again, my inner muscles gripping him with the desire to never let go.

Even when tender, Lennon was rough, but I'd learned that he knew every dark need of my body, an instrument he'd mastered from the moment we first touched.

After an hour of taking from each other all that our bodies could give, I found myself wrapped in his arms, my hands gripped over his wrists, my eyes closing as my tears slipped down my cheek to soak into my pillow.

. . .

"You look perfect, but if you don't hurry, you're going to lose that scholarship simply for not showing up."

Although his tone was filled with bemused humor, something about Lennon's voice sent a spike of panic down my spine.

Glancing at him through the reflection of the mirror, I fixed my lip gloss, dabbing at the corners of my mouth with a tissue. This was my third attempt at applying my makeup. Unfortunately my arms were shaking with nervousness, making it practically impossible to apply everything just right.

"Sorry, but it's hard to paint all this crap on my face with my hands trembling."

"You don't need all the crap on your face. Natural beauty shouldn't be covered up."

I turned and smiled to see that, even for this performance, he couldn't be bothered to dress in anything another person would consider appropriate. But then, that was Lennon, as usual. The only time he'd ever followed dress code was for his symphony performance.

"Penguins," I said, my shoulders shaking with quiet laughter.

His eyes glimmered, a tiny flicker of sadness rolling behind them when he shrugged his shoulder. "This jacket is good luck."

Tilting my head, I forced a grin, my eyes searching his for answers. "Oh yeah? And why's that?"

"I was wearing it the first night you let me spank your ass."

We stared at each other for several silent seconds, his body finally pushing away from the wall as he extended a hand for me to take. "Let's go. I've invested way too much time in you for you to piss it all away because you couldn't get your makeup just right."

Allowing him to lead me downstairs, outside, and to his SUV, I buckled myself in as he rounded the back, my eyes sliding his direction as he climbed behind the wheel.

"Aren't they going to wonder why we're showing up together?"

He grinned while starting the engine. "I'm not sure it matters anymore. It's not like I'm your teacher."

No. He wasn't, not in profession at least. But in other ways, this man had taught me everything I knew. "Julia

367

is going to be pissed to see she was wrong about which student you were fucking."

Lennon watched the backup camera as we pulled out of the driveway, the corners of his lips curling as he purred, "I'm almost eager to see her so scandalized. Should we tell her how I was sure to fill every hole in your body?"

My mouth fell open and he glanced at me before reaching to tip a finger beneath my chin and push it closed. "Careful, Miss Dillon. Keep looking at me like that and you might be late for far different reasons."

The drive to the performing arts center took half an hour, my hands wringing in my lap as we tore down the highway. Every so often, Lennon would reach over to lay his hand over mine, his eyes darting my direction for just a second.

"You're ready, Amelia. Stop letting your nerves get to you. I've never heard any person play the piece you picked as perfectly as you do."

Not that my choice was hard to make. Stravinsky's Firebird...a piece that perfectly described my life. Dark. Chaotic. Discordant and atonal. A piece that was intended for an entire orchestra to play, and yet I was playing it alone.

It was a confusing mesh of sound that assaulted the ears, but in parts, the melody came together making a person understand just how beautiful the music really was.

I thought of Lennon in those parts, and I worried that while I played this afternoon, I wouldn't be able to hold back my tears.

"I didn't realize we'd be performing in such a large place. It's a bit ridiculous if you ask me."

He laughed, grumbling under his breath, "I knew you never read the program materials. I'm surprised you were able to find your way to attend the first class."

Slapping at him, I told him to shut up, but my voice went silent when we pulled into the large parking lot to find it full of cars.

"Why so many people?"

Lennon paid the parking attendant and drove forward. "Music teachers and directors from high schools and youth symphonies attend this event every year. They like to know what's expected of a finalist for a Hastings scholarship. I'm sure there will be alumni here as well. The rest of the audience are music lovers from the area who come to hear what the future of talent has to offer. This is a big deal, Amelia."

Pulling into a spot around back that was reserved for performers, he killed the engine.

"I wish you wouldn't have told me that," I answered, my stomach rolling over in my stomach.

My head spun his direction when he gripped my chin and tugged. Expression serious, he held my stare.

"You have this. I've never doubted you. Be excited, beautiful, because today is the day you achieve everything you've ever wanted." He paused, his hand reaching so he could trace his thumb along the line of my jaw.

"You are an amazing woman, Amelia. Which is surprising considering how I met you."

I laughed, my nerves easing just a little at the joke.

His gaze caught mine, expression serious again. "You make me proud for how far you've come along. This summer has been..."

Sighing he didn't finish the thought, but he didn't need to. His eyes told me all I needed to know.

Heart hammering in my chest, I hoped he would be part of that *everything* he told me I'd achieve. A life in music, and a life by his side, would be a dream I'd never believed I could have.

A sigh blew over his lips, his expression softening. "We should get inside." Lennon almost sounded sad to say it.

After exiting the car, he ran around the front to open my door and help me step down. The champagne colored silk of the gown he'd bought me swirled around my ankles as I wrapped my arm in his and followed him inside.

Entering through a back entrance, we rushed backstage, Julia's eyes widening immediately when she saw me with Lennon. I smiled at her, trying not to hold a grudge at the part she'd played in getting him fired.

Before letting me go to take my place, Lennon lowered his mouth to my ear and whispered, "I'll be watching you from the audience. Just pretend it's me you're playing for."

The only thing about that was that it was true. When it came to who heard my music, he was the only person that mattered.

Lennon's blue eyes met mine and held my stare for a few silent seconds, his lips brushing my mouth when he leaned in to kiss me before letting me walk away.

Leaving me standing in place, Lennon walked toward a side door that I assumed led out to the main auditorium, his steps pausing as his hand fell on the knob, his head turning so that he could look at me one more time. Flashing me a sad smile, he pushed the door open and disappeared into the hallway outside, just in time for Mrs. Crux to step up behind me.

"You look stunning, Amelia. Are you nervous?"

Stripping my eyes from the door through which Lennon had left me, I spun in place to meet Mrs. Crux's kind stare. "Yes."

She touched my shoulder, her gaze glimmering. "I snuck a peek at what Julia's chosen student is going to play. Trust me, Amelia, if you pull off The Firebird like you did in class, you'll run circles around your competitor. Most professionals can't play that piece. But the competition is beginning, so you need to take your place."

I followed Mrs. Crux to a side area, my hands smoothing down my skirt as the lights over the stage brightened and Julia walked out with her student to introduce him to the audience.

Nerves have a funny way of speeding up time, because by the time I felt like I could catch my breath, it was my turn to play, my legs unsteady as Mrs. Crux led me onstage. I did my best not to look out over the audience before taking my seat at the piano, my hands hovering over the keys as my name was stated over the loudspeaker, Mrs. Crux's eyes meeting mine to tell me it was time to begin.

It was instantaneous, the transformation, the audience disappearing the moment my fingers pounded the first chords. Retreating to a place inside my head, I let the music pour through me, all my heartache, my frustration, my victories and losses bleeding into a song that represented my soul.

I saw my mother dying as my fingers ran across the keys. I heard my father screaming for his wife as my wrists snapped and my hands came down to violently pound out the chaos and discord. I heard Lennon whispering to me in the moments he rode my body, his voice as dark and beautiful as the slowest measures, his face as captivating as the melody.

Sweat trickled down my temples as tears welled in my eyes, my body moving in time with the frenetic music as I lost all sense of my surroundings until the last notes hovered through the auditorium, an echo of exhaustive sound.

Pure silence met me when I stood from the bench to face the audience, a few stunned claps transitioning into a loud crash of applause, the entire audience pushing to their feet on a standing ovation.

Despite my best efforts, I couldn't see a single face in the audience, only the outlines of their bodies, the occasional flash of light glimmering off a woman's gown.

All I wanted was to see Lennon staring up at me, but the stage lights were too bright.

Once the applause had died down, I exited the stage to stand next to the student Julia has chosen.

Silence was awkward between us, but eventually he blew out a breath and turned to offer a handshake. His brown eyes met mine, a smile pulling at his lips. "Uh, yeah. If they don't choose you after that performance, the judges are all idiots."

I laughed, thankful for the comic relief that helped ease my nerves.

Prior to the official announcement on stage, Julia and Mrs. Crux approached us twenty minutes later.

"As a courtesy," Julia explained, "we like to let both of you know who won before it is announced."

She turned to me, her eyes beaming with pride. "Amelia Dillon. Congratulations, sweetheart, you've won a scholarship to Hastings."

Her student shook my hand one more time before walking off backstage while Julia and Mrs. Crux walked onstage to make the announcement. At the sound of my name, the audience broke out into another round of lively applause, a crescendo of sound meeting me when I walked out to face the audience and take my final bow.

My lips hurt from smiling, my eyes frantic to find one familiar face in the crowd. After searching for what felt like forever, I finally met a pair of proud blue eyes, Lennon's hands coming together to applaud me where he stood among the audience.

To say my heart exploded with love would be an understatement. I was practically drowning beneath the unrelenting waves of how much I felt for that man.

He was the only person I wanted to run to, my body stilling in place for only a few seconds before Julia directed me offstage, back where the audience could no longer see us.

"So," she said, a smirk pulling at her lips. "You were the inappropriate student after all? I had my suspicions, but then saw Jillian in the room with him."

Although I wanted to continue the conversation, I was too excited to see Lennon to stand still. "Thank you for everything, Julia, but I need to go find him. If it wasn't for him this summer, I wouldn't be standing here right now."

She laughed, her hand fluttering over the bodice of her gown. "Young love. Run along, Amelia. We'll talk again before you leave to start school."

Flashing her a huge smile, I walked as fast as I could in my three inch heels, my hand gripping the skirt of my dress to hold it up and keep from tripping.

As soon as I burst through the doors of the hallway leading between backstage and the auditorium, I pushed myself even faster until I turned a corner to see the crush of bodies moving toward the exit doors.

I'd thought for sure Lennon would have been waiting for me here, but maybe he'd been caught in the crush. Not wanting to get lost, I stood in place for at least fifteen minutes, my heart jumping into my throat when a hand landed on my shoulder.

Spinning to look at Lennon, I couldn't hide the surprise on my face to see Ben's grey eyes staring at me instead.

"Congratulations, Sis. I always knew you had it in you."

I had no idea my brother would be here. "Ben? Oh my God..."

Wrapping my arms around him, I let him pull me in tighter for a hug, his cheek resting against my head for just a few seconds before he pushed me away to hold me at arm's length.

There were actual tears in his eyes, pride radiating in his gaze as he stared at me.

"You look. Ah hell, Amelia, you're all grown up."

Laughter floated over my lips. "Um, thanks?"

Shaking his head, Ben wrapped an arm over my shoulder and began leading me to an exit. Pulling back, I glanced out toward the main auditorium to see that it was almost empty.

"No, Ben. I need to wait for Lennon."

Frantically, I searched the room, looking for any sign of the man I couldn't live without.

"Amelia," Ben said, his hand cupping my cheek to turn my eyes back to him. "Just come with me, okay?"

"But-"

"Everybody's outside," he said, cutting me off. "Come on."

Shaking my head, I smiled. "You're right." More than likely, Lennon had already headed out to meet me by the car.

Allowing Ben to lead me through the exit doors and into the back parking lot, I headed in the direction of where Lennon had parked, only to have Ben pull me back.

"Hey, stop for a second, Amelia."

His voice was careful, soft...as soft as the afternoon I'd come home from school and he'd grabbed me before I could walk down the long hall of our house to find out mom had died while I'd been gone.

375

Ben had been the one to break the news to me that day, and the expression on his face now was just as conflicted, just as careful as the day he'd told me about mom.

"What's going on?"

A tick of his jaw and Ben cursed beneath his breath, his gaze flicking over the parking lot before meeting mine again. "He's a coward, okay? A fucking bastard, but he cares about you, Sis. He sought me out for you. I mean, me, you know? A guy he last saw as we were pounding our fists into each other's faces."

Heart sinking into my feet, my bottom lip trembled.

No...this couldn't be-

Lennon wouldn't -

Would he?

Barely a whisper, Ben explained, "He said it would be easier this way. That if it wasn't a clean break, neither of you could have walked away. He said you have a future to focus on and no man should threaten that."

Tears sprang from my eyes, Ben's expression twisting with anger and pain to see them. "Amelia, don't cry..."

"He left me?"

How the fuck could he do this?

"That's it? He's just gone?"

No. I refused to believed it. Refused-

My body collapsed against Ben, the sobs erupting from my chest so violent that a keening noise echoed across the parking lot that I didn't recognize as coming from me.

Brushing his hand down my hair, Ben kept whispering, kept trying to make me understand.

"I'm sorry, Amelia. But he's right. You need to go to Hastings and show the world how amazing you are. Your lives are going in two different directions and-" Another growled curse word, his arms tightening around me to hold me up.

"He loved you, which is why he had to go."

It didn't matter what Ben said to me, didn't matter that Lennon had sought him out to be here and make sure I was okay. As he kept talking and telling me about how he'd grabbed my boxes from the house after Lennon and I left, I only partially understood his words.

It's hard to listen when you're shattering apart, hard to accept that just when life has handed you your dreams, it would take another part of you that was necessary to survive.

They say when one door closes another one opens...I just never knew it would destroy me to walk through that new door and lose all that mattered behind the other.

"Come on. I'll drive you home."

Shaking my head, I nearly fell down onto the ground, my body too weak to move, my brain too scattered to believe Lennon was really gone.

Eventually, Ben picked me up and cradled me against him, his lips brushing my forehead with a soft kiss, his arms tightening around me as he whispered once again.

"I'm so sorry, Amelia. But you have to move forward, you have to understand that he's doing this for your own good."

My own good...

I almost laughed to hear the phrase.

If Lennon wanted what was good for me, he wouldn't have walked away without a word to leave me broken.

If he'd wanted what was in my best interests, he wouldn't have allowed me to fall in love with him, only so he could rip my soul from my body and leave me in a state where I couldn't breathe.

CHAPTER TWENTY-NINE

Always look to a person's hands, Amelia...and if they warm your soul when they hold yours, never let them go...

Amelia

Five months.

That's how long it took for me to gather the pieces back together of my shattered heart.

That's how long it took for me to only vaguely understand why Lennon left the way he did.

Five months.

And in that time my life had changed drastically. I'd left Florida to attend Hastings. I'd moved into the conservatory dorms to meet a new friend who became my second half. I'd learned that while Lennon had walked away without so much as saying goodbye, he continued paying for my father to stay in a nursing home without one word to either Ben or me about it.

Every day, I wanted to hunt him down and demand he remove himself from my life entirely, yet every day I realized how stupid I would be for making the demand.

I could go to school without worry because of him. I could show the world that I deserved the scholarship I'd been given.

In those five months, I'd not only proven myself as an accomplished and disciplined pianist in a school meant for the elite, I'd somehow managed to secure a spot as first in my class, a virtuoso that the other students looked up to.

They said the pieces I played sounded different when elicited by my hands.

Soulful.

Brilliant.

Perfection.

They saw the stories I told them when my hands touched the piano, but despite their praise I couldn't tell them I was bleeding on the inside, hemorrhaging my pain onto the keys.

Why is art and music always better when the person who creates it is broken?

Not that it mattered. The one person whose opinion I wanted would never be around again to hear it.

"You dressed? We need to leave if we want good seats. I'm sure the auditorium will be packed."

Tying my shoe, I lifted my head to watch Constance step out of the bathroom, her long blond hair knotted at the name of her neck, a simple flower patterned sundress showing off a body I would kill for.

Her green eyes met mine, a wicked grin pulling across her lips. "Maybe if we hurry, we can sit next to Thomas and Jon. Those two are so damn fine, I can barely keep my eyes off them in class."

She leaned a shoulder against the doorframe. "I think Jon has the hots for you, by the way. I keep catching at him staring at you whenever we walk by."

Laughing, I straightened my body on the side of the bed. "You can have him. I'm not interested."

I pushed to my feet and she wrapped her arm with mine as we left the room. "One of these days, you're going to tell me why you're so turned off by men. If you're not careful, I'm going to start thinking you bat for the other team and you're secretly in love with me."

Shaking my head, I kept my eyes trained down the hall. "I don't bat for any team. I'm just focused on my future. If I can graduate Hastings with honors, I can secure a seat with a symphony and make something of my life."

Just like Lennon wanted.

Just like he'd intended when he left me without saying goodbye.

Did I understand his reasoning? Of course. But that didn't mean I had to like it.

"Woman, you need to live a little while marching ahead. Have fun. Be young and stupid every once in a while." She hit the button to call the elevator. "And for the love of all that's holy, get a little dick before you're too busy to enjoy it."

"I'm busy now."

"Yeah, but not as busy as you'll be later on in life when you're traveling and playing in front of massive audiences."

Dropping the conversation, we made our way to the auditorium. The stage curtains were closed and students milled about finding seats next to their friends. Constance and I took a programme from the girl handing them out at the door.

Early enough to grab a spot near the front, we dropped our weight into our seats, my eyes scanning the list of alumni who would be performing.

Constance whistled softly. "Damn, these are some heavy hitters. I didn't know all of them graduated from here."

Today's performance was a myriad of different instruments and talents, the musicians well known within the industry. Scanning the list of names, I was surprised to see Julia's name listed as a pianist. She hadn't emailed me to let me know she'd be here.

Time passed quickly, the auditorium growing quiet as the lights above our heads dimmed and the stage curtains opened.

Jeffrey Deitz, the program coordinator for Hastings stepped on stage dressed in a tailored black suit. An older man, he had silver peppering his black hair, the look giving him an air of dignity and refinement.

Explaining that today was a selection of notable Hastings graduates, he didn't talk for long before introducing the first performer, a cellist who landed first chair in the New York Symphony.

The piece was somber, something I didn't recognize but pulled at my heart regardless. No matter how often I tried to get past everything that had occurred over the summer, I couldn't seem to stop going back to those nights Lennon and I spent alone.

I wasn't sure any man would ever compare to him in my life. Wasn't sure there would ever be another person who perfectly harmonized with the music I carried inside me.

Lost to my thoughts, I wasn't paying attention as the performances continued forward, the music a mix of styles, the musicians all insanely talented.

As we were nearing the end of the show, the stage lights went dark, the auditorium bathed in pure darkness. Around us, students whispered and murmured, all of us believing something had happened and the power had gone out.

But then the first few notes from a piano echoed through the dark room. Quiet and tranquil, the piece one I recognized from the scholarship program over the summer.

Debussy's Clair De Lune - the first song I had played for Lennon in class, a melody that transported me back to a day I would never forget.

As the piano kept playing a piece that hushed the whispers among the students, a single spotlight grew brighter over a piano at center stage, my eyes drifting to the musician whose head was bowed over the keys.

"Who the fuck is that guy?" Constance whispered against my ear. "Holy shit, he is hot as fuck."

I couldn't answer.

Couldn't think.

Couldn't move.

Not with my heart splitting to pieces again. Not with my pulse pounding a soulful beat in my throat.

I would recognize the style of his clothes anywhere. The dark length of his hair. The hands that could master any instrument he was given as expertly as he'd mastered my body.

Lips parting as Lennon continued playing a piece I now knew by heart, I couldn't stop the tears from welling in my eyes.

"Hey," Constance nudged my shoulder, "You okay?"

I shook my head, still not able to find my voice.

The bastard.

How fucking dare he agree to this while knowing I would be in the audience?

The song came to an end and Lennon stood from the piano. Dressed in a white jacket, a bow tie and those damn suspenders he'd used to tie me up and drive me insane, he bowed when the students applauded his performance, his eyes scanning the audience until locking with mine.

I saw pain flash across his expression, his gaze unmoving, blue eyes that had taught me how to feel something in life.

It was all too much, and before I knew what I was doing, I pushed up from my seat and shoved past the students to get to the aisle, Constance calling out my name as I practically ran from the auditorium.

Before pushing through the side doors, I glanced back to see that Lennon was watching me leave. Not caring that the entire auditorium was staring my direction, I shove through those doors and began making my way through the halls.

By the time I turned left and was nearing the exit doors, I heard a familiar deep voice call out to me, the heavy beat of boots pounding the floor in chase.

No. He couldn't do this to me. He wasn't allowed to show up and remind me of everything I'd lost just so he could walk out of my life again.

I kept running, but my feet weren't fast enough, my body wasn't strong enough to outmaneuver the man that ran after me.

"Damn it, Amelia, stop."

Lennon's hand locked around my arm. Before I could break away from him to keep running to my dorm, he pulled me back and spun me to push me up against a wall.

His scent washed over me as he caged me with his arms, blue eyes meeting mine with so many emotions rolling behind them that I couldn't focus on just one.

"Why do you always make me chase you?"

He was breathless from running, his lips tipping up at the corners to form a smirk he had no right using against me anymore.

Glaring up at him, I shivered to be this close, pain and anguish gripping my heart to feel his heat brush over my body.

"I'm sorry, it's just that I thought you enjoyed running considering how fast you bolted out of my life when the summer ended."

Wincing at the anger in my tone, Lennon closed his eyes and opened them again, his chest moving with heavy breath, his eyes searching mine.

"I have no excuse for that."

"No, Lennon, you don't. And if you've come here to fuck with my head, then you can let me go because I will not let you ruin school for me."

Sorrow bled behind his gaze as his mouth tipped into a grin. "Although I'm happy to hear you say those words, I'm not here to ruin anything."

"Then why are you here?" I practically yelled, my heart beating a chaotic rhythm beneath my chest.

His voice was so soft compared to the vehemence in mine. "To ask you to forgive me," he answered, his eyes refusing to release mine. "To beg you to take me back."

My body stilled in place, a thousand competing thoughts crashing into one another until it was impossible to think or breathe.

Eventually, I found the strength to speak again, my heart bleeding out inside of me. "How could you just walk away like that? Without even saying goodbye. How could you fucking do that?"

My fists slammed against his chest, but he just stood there and took it, his gaze pinning me in place, his eyes darkening to see the pain rolling out of me as my body shook against the wall.

When I'd settled down enough, he opened his mouth to say, "Because I was scared, Amelia. Fucking terrified. I knew that I could never look at you and walk away. I had to run, had to hide from all the bullshit that has happened in our lives."

"So why didn't you just keep running?"

A breath blew over his lips, true remorse obvious in his expression. "Because no matter how fast I tried to run in the opposite direction, no matter how much distance I put between us or how much time passed, I couldn't escape loving you with everything I have inside me."

A bark of laughter burst from my throat. "Don't use that word unless you mean it, Lennon. Don't you dare say that if you plan on running away again because you can't look at me without thinking about your sister."

He flinched at the truth I'd tossed at him, his jaw ticking as his eyes searched mine.

"What happened with her wasn't your fault. It wasn't either of our fault. It just took me some time to understand it."

Silence crept between us, my body warring with itself. I wanted to shove him away and pull him close to me at the same time. Wanted to tell him to leave while begging him to never let me go.

I wanted all those things while I stood there shattering apart while being pieced back together by a man I knew I could never live without.

My eyes lifted to his as a tremulous breath rattled my chest. "You left me because you thought you would ruin my life, didn't you?"

He nodded, his gaze falling to my lips, making me feel things I hadn't felt in the five months we'd been apart.

"I needed to fix the broken parts inside me before I could trust myself not to break you," he confessed. "But after doing what I thought was right, I understood that I was even more broken without having you by my side."

Curling my fingers against my palm to keep from reaching out to touch him, I asked, "Don't you know you ruined me the moment you walked away?"

Lennon's gaze met mine, sorrow mixing within the blue color.

"Please, Amelia, will you give me another chance?"

Tears streamed down my cheeks as I nodded my head. There was no question about whether I would love him again...because in truth, I'd never stopped.

On a whisper, I said, "You have no idea what that word does to me, Mr. Carter. I like it when you say please."

He grinned, fire dancing behind his eyes to destroy the anguish that had been there previously.

Gripping my chin between his thumb and his finger, he leaned down until his mouth was hovering an inch from my lips.

On a whisper of sound, he asked, "Who are you, Amelia Dillon?"

Confused by the question, my thoughts went back to the first time he'd asked it in class.

"I'm a musician?" I answered, my feet pushing up on the toes to close the distance between our mouths.

Speaking against my lips, he said, "Yes, beautiful, you're definitely that," he paused his teeth nipping at my bottom lip before he added, "but you're also mine."

There was nothing left to say after that.

Our mouths pressed together and his tongue slipped in my mouth to slide against mine. And when I reached out to pull him close, I somehow knew I would never have to let him go.

CHAPTER THIRTY

I love you more than anything and I promise that you'll be able to forgive me someday. I promise that the music inside you will harmonize with another and you will be whole again...

Lennon

The guitar strummed over Dizzy's door as I walked inside Jennison's to catch up with one of my oldest friends. As usual Dizzy came bounding over, his lips stretched into a grin as he reached out to slap his palm against mine, knocking our knuckles together before he pulled away and ran his hand over the top of his head.

"Well, I'll be damned. Lennon Carter has returned home to Sheldon again. I never thought I'd see the day."

Laughing, I followed him deeper inside the store, the musty smell of old sheet music blending with the oils used on the instruments taking me back to a childhood I'd believed I'd never wanted to face.

"Whatever, asshole, you knew I was coming back here. It just took some time to get a new place and for Amelia to finish up and graduate."

Shaking his head, he took a seat on a stool while I dropped my weight on a piano bench opposite him. Staring at me, Dizzy asked, "Are you going to be able to handle it? Living here again?"

After blowing out a breath, I scrubbed my palm over the back of my neck. "This is where she wanted to be. Despite offers in ten different states, Amelia wanted to come back here to be close to her dad."

Dizzy chuckled, his grin stretching wider. "Man, I knew you loved that girl. After watching you chase after her that night at Majori's, I was damn sure she'd already sunken her claws inside your chest without you even knowing what was happening."

"Yeah, thanks for that. You could have warned me."

"Nope. Amelia brought my best friend back to me. If anything, I should be thanking her."

Leaning back, I rested my elbows on the keys of the piano, a few jarring chords ringing out from the strings. "I'll be here as much as I can be. I still have obligations to the bands I assist."

"A little time is better than no time at all, brother. Where's Amelia now?"

"Down the street visiting her brother at his house. She'll walk over when they're done."

Behind us, the guitar strummed again, Dizzy's star student, Kyle, walking inside to begin his lesson.

The kid walked with an added bounce to his step, excitement brightening all his features as he rounded the bookshelves.

"Dizzy! I got in!"

Turning my head to hide my smirk, I listened as Kyle practically screamed with excitement. "Holy shit, man! I got into the Hastings program. I'll be leaving for Orlando as soon as I graduate next week."

Standing up to pull Kyle into a hug, Dizzy glanced my direction. He knew I'd played a part in getting Kyle a seat in the scholarship program.

We spent the next hour playing around on the instruments, the guitar strumming again when Amelia walked through the doors. Stepping over to us, she hugged Dizzy and Kyle before turning her attention to me.

"You ready to go?"

"Where are you lovebirds off to?" Dizzy asked.

"To go see my dad in the nursing home. They have a music room where Lennon and I can play for him. Ben told me his condition hasn't improved, but he's doing a lot better there than he was at our house."

She was ecstatic, her face beaming now that she'd landed a seat with the Florida Symphony and could be close enough to her family to see them regularly.

Grabbing my hat from the top of the piano, I wrapped my arm over her shoulder. "Let's go."

After saying our goodbyes, Amelia and I headed outside, the Florida sun baking both of us as we walked beneath it.

We were almost to my car when a memory came to me, a moment in time that had changed my life in ways I could never imagine.

As Amelia reached for her door, I slammed my palm against the side to keep her from opening it. She looked up at me in question, her brows pulling together when I looked at her and grinned.

"You know, we have a couple minutes before we have to leave." My gaze darted to the alley and back at her, realization as to what I was saying settling into her expression.

"You can't be serious, Mr. Carter," she laughed.

"Do I ever joke about these things?"

Casting a quick glance at the alley, Amelia's eyes met mine again as a smile crept over her face.

I leaned down to her, brushed my lips against hers and whispered, "I'll give you a head start."

She shook her head and laughed, but then took off toward the alley at a dead run.

I counted to five in my head before chasing after her.

It didn't matter that I was back near my hometown, didn't matter that fate had returned me to a place I never wanted to see again.

Not with her by my side.

Rounding the corner, I caught Amelia turn to look back at me, a cry of surprise bursting from her lips as she pumped her legs attempting to get away.

I caught her before she could reach the next corner, and I caged her against the wall, my hand brushing up the side of her body.

"Well well, Miss Dillon, it looks like I've caught you."

Her breasts brushed my chest, breath pouring over her lips, and she stared up at me with desire rolling behind her eyes.

Kissing her before spinning her in place, I lifted her skirt and ran my hand over the palm of her ass, my cock hard and ready to take all she had to give.

It was in that moment that I knew my story had come full circle, that the ending to my song had been the beginning of the music we played together.

And I just like always, I dreamed of that music in the way that most people dreamed of love...except this time the dream had teal eyes that crinkled at the corners as Amelia's mouth pulled into a smile.

This time, the dream had a voice that called into the shadows, a voice that would always harmonize with mine while it was welcoming me home.

THE END

Coming Next
Treachery (Antihero Inferno Series, Book#1)
Keep reading for the first chapter

treach·er·y

noun

A betrayal of trust; deceptive action or
nature

CHAPTER ONE

Never listen to the people who tell you evil doesn't exist in this world. Never smile and nod, never pander, never walk off with the belief that you're guarded against everything that can go wrong. I can give you that advice because I've been the stupid woman not to follow it. I can promise you that evil does exist only because I am the woman who has stared it in the moss green eyes, the same woman who dared it to do its worst and stood dumbfounded when it delivered.

Tanner Caine is just one of the deceptive and tantalizing demons waiting to be summoned at the crossroads. He is an underground giant forged in fire and stamped with the Devil's personal seal of approval. He is a man barely challenged and a barrier never crossed. He is also a specimen of the male form that is a siren song to the unlucky women who run across him.

I've seen better woman ruined because they dared to play a game with him they had no business playing. I've seen smarter women on their knees before a man who managed to remain one step ahead while laughing to watch them fall.

You see, that's what happens when you make a deal with evil. Everything goes fine until the day comes when he calls in his debt. Tanner doesn't mess around with interest rates or repayable loans. No. If he does something for you, you can bet he'll extract his pound of flesh in the most creative of endeavors.

We are all pawns to be played in Tanner's world. Man or woman, it doesn't matter.

I didn't know what would happen when he waltzed back into my life after running from him in college. But what I did know is that, where Tanner is involved, yours is a story that can never end well.

. . .

Luca
(past)

"Go with the white booty shorts, Luca. You have the ass for them. Mine's a little too flat."

A sigh burst over my lips as I dug through my roommate, Everly's, closet. Standing in here was like searching through a fashionable slut's dream, everything way too short, dangerously tight, and designed specifically to highlight a woman's curves.

Her style was opposite to mine. Never one to cater to what men wanted, I preferred casual clothes, my comfort taking precedent over what most would consider sexy.

The deep bass of some popular rap song pounded behind me, Everly's shoulders bouncing in my peripheral vision as she sat at a makeup table to apply what had to have been a third layer of foundation.

"I don't know about this, Evy. Maybe you should go alone tonight. I have some homework to catch up. It's probably best I spend the next few hours in the library."

"Shut your hole, Luca. You're coming with me. This party is all everybody has been talking about on campus and there's no way in hell I'm letting you miss out all because you're scared of being social."

Grabbing the white shorts she'd suggested, I pulled them from the hanger and held them up to my hips. These were more suited to be a bathing suit for how tight and short they were.

My head spun to look at her just as she turned to glance at me. "Plus, Clayton will be there. And I know you have the hots for him."

She had me there.

Clayton Hughes was a big man on campus. Not as big as the Inferno boys, but he ran with them all the same.

Normally, just his association with the Inferno would have put me off and sent me running the opposite direction, but we worked together on a mock trial and had gotten to know each other better.

He was the son of a Senator and had money coming out his ears. Not to mention he was hot as fuck... and intelligent, which was a bonus in my book.

After working together, we'd hit it off and had been texting back and forth for the past week.

But that didn't mean I had to go to this party just to see him.

"I'm sure he wouldn't mind if I didn't go. I'll see him in class on Monday."

"Shut. It." Everly spoke in time with the music's beat.

"I have a hot night planned with Jase, and you, my bookworm friend, are going to be my wing-woman."

Rolling my eyes, I sat in a chair just outside her closet to tug off my jeans. "If you already have a hot night planned, then you don't need a wing-woman."

Shaking my head, I couldn't believe she was stupid enough to get involved with any of the nine men who lived in the Inferno house.

All of them were bad news, each one a known manwhore that couldn't keep it in their pants long enough to carry on a week long relationship with one woman.

Evy had been sleeping with Jase for longer than a week, however, and it made me wonder how in the hell she'd pulled it off. I suspected she wasn't the only ass he was getting.

As if reading my thoughts, she answered, "He might have some stupid bitch all up on him when we get there. You know how he is."

"I'm surprised you put up with that," I commented under my breath. She heard it regardless, her lips kicking up into a grin.

"He's Jase Fucking Kesson. Are you kidding me right now?" Laughter poured over her lips. "I'm determined to tame that man, even when everybody else assumes he can't be."

Yeah, except Jase Kesson, also known as *Lust* in the Inferno circuit, was just one of the nine guys who practically ran the school.

Each one was someone I wanted nothing to do with and had, until now, been able to avoid. I'd never actually met any of them, which was surprising, but after tonight, I'd finally know what they looked like.

It was akin to meeting a celebrity...or a character from a fable. You know they exist, but actually meeting them in person makes them more *real*.

Shrugging a shoulder, I leaned back in the chair. "I'm not comfortable being around them. I've heard horrible things-"

"Rumors," Everly laughed. "Don't let it get to you. They're actual pretty cool guys once you get to know them. Gorgeous, too. All except..."

My eyes snapped her direction. "All except what?"

Her hair fell over her shoulder when she shook her head and dropped the tube of deep red lipstick on the desk. Turning off the lights of the makeup mirror, she spun in her chair to look at me.

"It's like I said: every one of them is sex on a damn stick, but Tanner gives me the creeps. There's something about him. Like his chest is empty of a beating heart and instead of being warm to the touch, his skin would be ice cold. I have no idea how any girl climbs into bed with him, but he's never without, you know? Those idiots line up to be with him and I don't understand it. Thankfully, he hasn't said so much as two words to me, and I'm fine with that."

Pausing, Everly checked her makeup in the mirror one last time before pushing to her feet. "Just avoid him and you'll be fine. It's time to go."

She flashed me a wicked grin and I groaned.

Grabbed by the arm and pulled from my seat, Everly walked me out of our dorm room. We were halfway down the hall when I asked, "How the hell am I supposed to avoid this guy if you're forcing me to go to his house?"

Laughing, she tugged on my arm, leading me down a back stairwell past a group of girls climbing up to our floor.

"That's easy. You suck face with Clayton the entire time and then you won't have to worry about coming face to face with Tanner."

"And how will I know which one is Tanner?"

Another laugh, "Oh, trust me. You'll know him when you see him."

She wasn't wrong.

There was no mistaking Tanner Caine when we walked into a large room in the Inferno House. And just as she'd described him, the man had a way of sending an ice cold chill down your spine the second you laid eyes on him.

After paying the driver of the Uber we'd taken to get to their off campus house - a sprawling three story monstrosity of a mansion, complete with winding driveway and manicured lawns- Everly had led me inside the front door and dragged me through a rowdy crowd that was packed wall to wall through the rooms of the first floor.

Reaching the stairs, she continued leading me without saying a word until we reached the third floor, swung a left and walked down a hall to a large room at the end.

People lingered outside the doors of the room, talking and drinking, laughter rising up their throats as Everly shoved between them to drag me along behind her.

As soon as we passed the doors, her eyes scanned the men seated on chairs and couches, my eyes immediately taking in the half-dressed women dancing and sitting on their laps.

The scent of pot smoke filled the room, loud music pounding the walls with a steady bass beat.

"There's Jase," Everly whisper-yelled against my ear. "And of course, some bitch is all up on him. It's time to teach these sluts who the Queen Slut is around here."

Leaning into her, I answered, "I'm not sure you should brag about that."

She laughed and tossed her hair back. Rounding her shoulders, she set her eyes on Jase, her lips pulling into a grin that meant trouble.

"Clayton should be here soon. Stick around and I'm sure you'll find him."

Off she went, leaving me awkwardly hovering by the doorway, my eyes scanning the room before turning to watch her approach Jase.

It wasn't hard to see why she was practically tripping over herself to get with the guy. Relaxing on a leather sofa with legs spread and his arms stretched out over the backrest, Jase was any girl's wet dream.

Rugged and sculpted in ways that would have made the Greeks jealous, he had disheveled brown hair that framed his face. I couldn't see the color of his eyes, but his nose was straight, leading down to a set of lips that tipped up at the corners as if he knew a secret.

Wearing a tight black T-shirt that struggled to contain broad shoulders and a strong chest, he lifted his eyes to Everly as she crossed the room toward him, a hint of his trim waist and perfect abs peeking out from beneath his shirt when the girl straddling him ran her hand up his abdomen.

How Everly put up with that shit, I didn't know, but it was entertaining for me to watch what she would do about it.

I stared at the scene curiously, noting how Everly approached with a clipped stride, her gaze meeting Jase's when she was within reach. Leaning down, she whispered something in the other girl's ear before straightening and curling her lips into a devilish smile.

The girl quickly crawled off Jase's lap, red burning her cheeks as she turned to leave immediately. The girl brushed past me on her way out the door, tears glimmering in her eyes, barely visible beneath the low lighting.

Across the room, Jase just shook his head, crooked a finger and grinned as Everly took the former girl's place, her hands running up his chest as soon as she was settled over his lap.

To each their own, I guessed, making a mental note to ask her what she'd said to the other girl that had her running from this room like it was on fire.

Pulling my eyes away from them as soon as she leaned forward to press her mouth to his and his hand moved to cup her ass, I scanned my gaze over the rest of the room, noticing the four other guys that sat around, all of them with drinks in hand while women giggled and danced beside them, one set of cold dark eyes catching my attention in particular because they were focused directly on me.

It's common courtesy among strangers to look away during moments of unwanted eye contact, but the one staring at me now didn't seem to give a damn about courtesy. The hard lines of his face tightened as soon as our eyes met, his glare boring into mine with a ferocious intensity.

He had a devil may care curl to his full lips, shadows dipping down beneath high cheekbones that gave him an aristocratic air.

In front of him, a pretty girl danced in only a short skirt and bra, her body on display as dark red hair fell down her back in a waterfall of waves.

Even with the eye candy he had bouncing around in front of him, those dark eyes locked to mine, a glimmer of some unspoken thought flashing behind them.

I knew instantly that I was staring at Tanner Caine, a man known as Treachery among his friends.

Giving in to the wordless exchange between us, I was the first to look away, my arms coming up to wrap around my stomach as if to chase away the chill he conjured inside me.

Despite not looking at him, I could feel his eyes on my face, somehow knew he hadn't let me out of his sight while I stood waiting, my legs shaking beneath me because I was suddenly terrified.

Cursing Everly beneath my breath for dragging me here, I considered leaving the room, but then worried I wouldn't find Clayton and would end up spending the night wandering among drunk students grinding against each other.

As for this room, I felt like I'd walked into a damn orgy, all the woman slowly losing their clothes while the five men who sat around like Kings in their damn harem smoked joints and sipped from glasses of different liquors and alcohol.

No, the rest of the men sat like Kings in their thrones, but not Tanner. He sat in the center of the room against a far wall, his demeanor that of a dark god.

I needed to get out of here, but as the seconds ticked by, a poisonous glare pulled me back to him, my head turning just enough to see that Tanner was still staring me down, the half dressed girl no longer dancing now that she'd crawled to straddle his lap.

Running her fingers through his hair, she leaned over to kiss the pulse point in his neck, but his attention was focused on me despite the promise of sex grinding against his crotch.

And fuck me, that man was beautiful, unlike anybody I'd seen before.

With dark hair and cold eyes, he had the face of a cover model. His cheekbones were blades that ran beneath his focused stare, his cheeks sinking in just enough to darken with a day's worth of black stubble that peppered his jaw. His lips parted just enough that I could see the bottom was full, and he had soot black hair that was shaved on the sides while longer on top.

It looked like silk running through the woman's fingers, his arms casually relaxed on either side of her body. When our eyes met again, his narrowed just a touch from where he was watching me from over her shoulder.

Knowing better than to stare, I couldn't seem to pull my gaze away from him a second time. It was like being stared down by a predator, cornered and shaking while he licked his chops with every intention of taking a slow leisurely bite of me to make it as painful as possible.

Where his eyes were tiny slits with a cunning soul staring out from behind them, mine were wide and anxious, my arms tightening around my center as if they could protect me from whatever it was he was thinking.

It was stupid to keep staring, but I couldn't ignore my morbid fascination, and before I could snap out of it to do what any intelligent person would do, like turn around and haul ass, Tanner broke our locked stare to glance across the room, his chin nudging in someone's direction just before the music suddenly stopped and the room was bathed in jarring silence.

I turned to see what happened, my gaze slowly drifting back his direction to see he was once again staring at me.

If that wasn't bad enough, his beautiful lips parted, a deep tenor voice floating across the space that stilled me in place.

"Either join in or leave."

Everybody in the room turned to look at whoever Tanner was talking to, my neck twisting left and then right to realize that person was me.

Swallowing down the knot of apprehension that was clogging my throat, I looked back at him, his eyes now blazing with menace, the girl straddling him still rolling her hips as she ground against his lap.

It was then that I noticed she'd abandoned her bra to the floor at Tanner's feet, her full breasts shamelessly displayed to the entire room.

She was oblivious to the fact he had his eyes on another woman...that his dead stare was locked directly on me.

Opening my mouth, my voice came out as a weak croak. "What?"

The corners of his lips curled, a feline smile from a cat that couldn't wait to pluck the feathers from the bird it had trapped.

"Are we entertaining you? Getting you off while you stand there deciding whether to touch yourself just to pretend you're on one of our laps? Why be shy? I have enough cock to go around. Strip off your clothes and climb up."

He shoved the girl away, a cry of surprise falling from her lips when her ass hit the floor.

Shaking my head, I couldn't find my voice to respond, not that I would have known what to say even if I had.

Desperate for help, I turned to where Everly was watching me from across the room, her expression worried. Leaning down, she whispered in Jase's ear and he laughed softly.

Jase took a hit off the joint he held pinched between two fingers, rolled his head over the back of the couch and said, "Leave her alone, Tanner. She's Everly's friend."

"I don't give a fuck who she is," Tanner barked in response. "She wasn't invited here and now she's watching everybody like we're fucking Pornhub or some shit."

His eyes snapped back to me. "So, what do you say, *Everly's friend*? Are you going to join in or get the fuck out? There's space on my lap if you're feeling neglected."

Laughter filled the room, all eyes on me while I stood dumbfounded. Terror rolled down my spine, anger chasing after it that I couldn't seem to grasp onto enough to defend myself against the asshole.

He smirked, his voice a dark croon. "That's what I thought."

Tilting his chin toward me, he demanded, "Walk your ass out of this room if you're not willing to take part."

Mortified, I looked to Everly again, but she shook her head, a silent plea that I do as he said without arguing.

He didn't have to say another word for me to get the hint that I wasn't wanted.

On unsteady legs, I fled the room, ran through the hall and downstairs, people chuckling and whispering as I passed them.

Bursting through the front door, I ran down the large circle steps. Reaching the bottom, I sucked in air to cool my burning lungs - fear, anger and embarrassment rolling through my veins to mix into a toxic poison.

Face flushed, I leaned against the half wall that lined the steps, a faint yellow glow beaming from an exterior gas lamp by the side of my body.

Tears pricked my eyes and I smacked them away while music filtered out from the windows of the house.

Hugging my body with trembling arms, I finally calmed down enough after several minutes to breathe evenly again.

There was no chance of me going in that party to look for Clayton. Choosing to wait outside for him instead, I glanced up at a window to see a familiar set of cold, dark eyes staring down at me.

TO STAY INFORMED REGARDING THE UPCOMING ANTIHERO INFERNO SERIES, SUBSCRIBE TO LILY'S NEWSLETTER HERE:

http://eepurl.com/Onoeb

If you are interested in reading additional books by Lily White or would like to know when new books are being released, Lily White can be found on:

Facebook, Instagram and Twitter

Join the Mailing List!

If you are interested in receiving email updates regarding additional books by Lily White or would like to know when new books are announced or being released, join the mailing list via this link.

http://eepurl.com/Onoeb

Join the Facebook Fan Group!

If you are interested in receiving exclusive previews for upcoming novels, or to participate in giveaways, join the fan group for Lily White Books.

FAN GROUP LINK

Follow Lily on BookBub!

https://www.bookbub.com/profile/lily-white